THE REAL MOTHER

THE

REAL

MOTHER

JUDITH MICHAEL

Doubleday Large Print Home Library Edition

wm WILLIAM MORROW *An Imprint of* HarperCollins*Publishers*

**This Large Print Book carries the
Seal of Approval of N.A.V.H.**

"As long as we feel like a family," Sara said,
"that's all that matters."

The Real Mother is dedicated to all families
who weather stress and turmoil
and constantly reinvent themselves
to create love, joy, support, and friendship.

THE REAL MOTHER

ONE

Sara arrived at the airline terminal as the Corcorans walked out, trailed by a young man pushing a cart piled with luggage. She wedged her car between taxis and stepped out to open the trunk and the two passenger doors before extending her hand to Lew Corcoran. "Sara Elliott," she said. "Welcome to Chicago."

"Right." His handshake was perfunctory. Squinting in the bright sun, he pulled a five-dollar bill from his wallet, considered it, replaced it with two singles, and shoved them into the young man's hand. He slid into the front seat, turning to Sara.

"I don't have a lot of time, I'm a busy man."

"We'll move quickly, then," Sara said with a smile, and when Pussy Corcoran, fur-clad and rosy-cheeked, had anchored herself in the center of the backseat, she drove toward the city.

"Never used one of you people before," Corcoran said, staring moodily through the window. "Taking a chance. Could be a waste of time."

"We'll try to make sure it isn't," Sara said pleasantly.

Everyone asked her how she managed to deal with her clients, spending her days with strangers who did nothing but make demands on her. "It's like a grab bag, your job," they said. "You never know who'll pop out when you answer your phone. It could be anybody. Anybody. The oddest people."

Her office telephone number was posted at airports, train stations, and rest stops on highways leading into the city. "Welcome to Chicago," the signs said above the mayor's signature. "For an official Welcome, and assistance with your visit or becoming a Chicago resident, our City Greeter is ready to serve you." Beneath, in bold type, were

Sara's name and City Hall telephone number and e-mail.

Officially, her title was City Greeter; unofficially, she was General Factotum, Global Secretary, Walking Encyclopedia, Personal Telephone Directory, Everybody's Schlepper. Officially and unofficially, she was always supposed to be smiling.

"We'll be looking at three apartments," she said when they were on the highway. "And I have the names—"

"You a broker?" Corcoran asked. "Otherwise, why bother, if we have to find a real estate broker when we're done with you?"

"I'm a real estate broker," Sara said, smiling. "I've lined up three apartments for you to look at. And, as Mrs. Corcoran requested, I have the names of four personal shoppers for her to interview."

"You're the one supposed to do the interviews," Corcoran said. "Weed them out."

Sara smiled. "You telephoned yesterday; that gave me very little time."

He rubbed the large ring on the fourth finger of his right hand as if ordering a genie to spring forth. The ring looked vaguely military, Sara thought. He filled his seat, a large man, ruddy-skinned, jowly, with a spreading nose and strangely small eyes, his sleek suit tailored to minimize his bulk. In back, Pussy Corcoran was small and round, perspiring gently inside her furs, her sprayed hair shining metallically in the April sunlight.

"All the apartments are available immediately," Sara said, "so if you decide on one, you would be in a hotel only until your furniture arrives."

"Don't bother with anything that doesn't have a view," Corcoran said. "I require a view."

"And a garage?" said Pussy. "So I don't go out in the rain?"

"Attended," said Corcoran. "Twenty-four hours. Same for the doorman. Twenty-four hours. *Numero uno* on my list, top-notch service twenty-four/seven."

"Maid service?" Pussy said. "And big bathrooms? Room to move around in, and one for each of us . . . that keeps a marriage together? Stays together?" Her chirping laughter trickled down the back of Sara's neck.

"Stupid." Corcoran snorted. He lit a cigarette.

"Smoking is not allowed in our cars," Sara said. She smiled. "If you'd like, I can stop at a hotel; you can smoke in the lobby, and I'll wait for you."

"Fucking son of a bitch," he exploded. "I'm a *client,* you don't tell a *client* what to do; you make clients *happy,* for Christ's sake. I'm *paying* you; it's *my* money, and if it's *my* fucking money I can fucking smoke in your fucking car."

Sara pulled into a turnout on the highway, and turned off the car engine. "I'm sorry, but I did not invent the policy."

"Lew," said Pussy, "it's only a few more minutes. Is that right?" she asked Sara.

"About fifteen minutes," Sara said.

"Lew, it's only fifteen minutes," said Pussy. "Couldn't you—"

"Shut up." He scowled at the cars speeding past, then opened the window and flung the cigarette away. "Satisfied?" he asked Sara. "Never been treated like this," he muttered. "Been all over the world—"

Pussy interrupted. "They wouldn't let you smoke in that limousine in—"

"Goddamn it, I said shut up!" There was a silence. "Well, what the fuck," he said to Sara. "We going or not?"

"Of course." She started the car and rejoined the flow of traffic.

"And closets?" Pussy said brightly. "Big ones? And a cedar one for our furs? Big enough for the coats to breathe? You know how they need to breathe. Well . . ." In the rearview mirror, her appraising eyes met Sara's. "Well, probably you don't; but they do, you know. Breathe? They need more room than a bunch of fatties at a convention!" Her laughter chirped again.

"Shut up," Corcoran said absently. They turned onto Lake Shore Drive, and he gazed heavily at Lake Michigan, its choppy steel blue waves and tossing whitecaps stretching to a horizon that cut across their view like a knife edge between dark lake and pale blue sky. "Not like the ocean," he muttered.

Sara hated both of them. But her hands were steady as she drove, and there was a smile on her face.

"And maids?" Pussy said. "These apartments come with maids?"

Sara shook her head. "I'm afraid not. I could show you condominiums in hotels that do provide—"

"No hotels!" barked Corcoran. "Can't stand hotels. Everybody out to cheat you."

"I can arrange for a maid," Sara said evenly. "As many as you wish, as often as you wish. Or I can give you a list of the cleaning services we've found reliable and efficient."

"They cook, too," he said.

Again Sara shook her head. "I can recommend two private chefs who are available right now, if you wish to interview them."

"Don't push me," he said. "Nothing I hate more than being pushed. First we get an apartment, then we talk about cooks and maids."

Sara kept the smile on her face, and drove in silence to a sleek high-rise overlooking the city and the lake and south to Indiana, and pulled into the garage.

"Golly," Carrie said that night as Sara banged pots and pans in the kitchen. "You must have had a doozer of a client."

"Right," Sara said shortly.

"What was their name?"

"Corcoran."

"Did they—?"

"Hey, Carrie," Abby said quickly, "come see what I got at school today. Back in a minute," she said to Sara, and led Carrie from the room.

In the midst of her black mood, Sara smiled, grateful for Abby's sensitivity in giving her time to calm down. Between juggling a job and a house and raising two younger sisters and a brother, it was a relief to see Abby, at fifteen, growing into an adult who could step in now and then, almost another adult in the house.

And Abby kept it up at dinner, taking charge of the conversation so that Sara could relax, listening or letting her thoughts float free. Mostly she let them float, to her work, dinner invitations she hoped to accept if Abby would stay with the younger ones, the college catalogs on Abby's desk that meant site visits all over the country. Too much to do, not enough time, and, if they weren't careful, not enough money. And then she heard Doug say, "I hate it; it sucks."

"Not for me," Carrie said. "I love school. I love eighth grade. What else would you do all day, anyway?"

"Everything. A million things."

"Such as?" Sara asked.

"Oh, you know." He turned cagey as he realized Sara was listening, and pushed lettuce and tomatoes around his salad bowl. "Do my carving and clay stuff—you're always saying how good I am, Sara—and, you know, read . . ."

"Bullshit," Abby said contemptuously. "You never read unless you have to. Ten years old and you hardly ever pick up a book. *Read,* he says!"

"I do read! I read a lot! Sara knows . . . don't I, Sara?"

"He does," Sara said to Abby. "At night, when he's looking for reasons not to go to sleep. Doug, you might try eating some of the salad; it's part of dinner. And why does school suck?"

"Well, there's this power structure—"

"This *what*?" Abby exclaimed. "How the fuck would you know anything about power structures?"

Sara put down her fork. "Abby, your vocabulary is so boring. Couldn't you think of some interesting words that don't sound like everybody else?"

Abby stared at her.

Sara shrugged. "I know that most people your age are too ignorant to have a creative vocabulary, but I never thought you were just like them."

Carrie looked up from cutting her meat loaf into squares and triangles. "It's important at Abby's age to be like everybody else," she said wisely. "When you're fifteen you need mostly to be accepted; otherwise you'd feel rejected and left out in the cold."

"So, will you be like that when you're fifteen?" Doug asked.

"Probably." Carrie sighed loudly. "It's really depressing to think about. I'm quite interesting now, but I'll be so *boring* then."

"Stop it!" Abby cried. "What's wrong with all of you? I'm not boring! I'm not ignorant! You're awful! Why is my own family making fun of me like this? I don't make fun of *you*!"

"We don't talk the way you do," Carrie said reasonably.

"What's so awful about it? *Everybody* talks like—" She stopped abruptly.

"Don't say it," Sara warned, looking at Carrie, whose mouth had been open to say that that was exactly what they all meant. "Abby gets the point. Doug, if you're not going to eat your salad, stop playing with it. And why does a power structure mean school sucks?"

"Because I'm *powerless*," he said. "I mean, it's bad enough at home, with Mack gone so I haven't even got a man to talk to, but school is the worst. I mean, you're my big sister and you take care of me and you tell me what to do, but you're good—you don't run my *whole life,* every *minute* of every *day,* like they do at school, *everybody* at school has more power than me, even the janitors; it is hugely disgusting. I mean, some people might think it's cool, like if they don't have a clue about what to do and they need somebody to tell them, but that's not me, I don't need anybody telling me what to do, I can make my own decisions, I *hate* it when people put my whole day together and then they say, 'Here it is, every minute, and if you don't like it, that's too bad, you're going to sit there all day, in that chair at that desk, and DO WHAT WE SAY BECAUSE WE SAY IT.' Boy, if that doesn't suck, I don't know what does."

There was a brief, stunned silence at the table, then Carrie said, "He's a rebel. They're always quite difficult."

"I'm just *me,*" Doug shot back. "And I'm *not* difficult. I'm lovable."

Sara laughed. "You certainly are. And you're absolutely right about school; it's awful, and you definitely should quit."

"Sara!" Carrie exclaimed.

Doug's mouth was open. "What?"

"She doesn't mean it," Abby said.

Doug began to mangle the slice of bread he was holding. "Sara, *what?*"

"Well, no one else has those problems," Sara said, "so why should you? I'm sure no-body tells Carrie and Abby what to do in school; I'm sure they do whatever they want all day until it's time to go home. And of course I can do anything I want at work; no one ever makes me do one single thing I don't feel like doing. So I think you should quit school and then you'll be perfectly free, like the rest of us."

There was another silence. "You're making fun of me," Doug said at last.

"She is, she is!" Carrie said gleefully. "You deserved it; you were really dumb."

"I was *not*! You all *do* have it easier than me! If you were ten, you'd understand; you wouldn't make fun of me. When you're ten, you're under everybody's thumb, but when you're older you're more like a grown-up; you get to pick your courses, and go to different classes and choose your teachers, and go out at night—"

"I can't," Carrie said, but Doug rode over her voice.

"—and drive and—"

"I can't," Carrie said again, but Doug was in full flight.

"—*do your own thing*. And you *do* do your

own thing, most of the time," he said to Sara. "You don't have to sit at a desk all day like I do, or stay in one room; you're all over Chicago, and you're with jillions of people, and I'm stuck with one teacher all day, and *I'm oppressed*!" He glared at Sara. "You *can* do what you want. If you decide you don't like your job, you can leave and nobody will stop you—"

"And nobody will pay me, either!" Sara snapped. She tried to hold on to her self-control as she felt it slip away, but she was tired, and tired of being reasonable. She glanced at the empty chair at the other end of the table. Coward, she raged silently. To leave just because things were getting tough.

And then, even as she told herself to calm down, she let go. "You don't know what you're talking about," she said to Doug, "and it's about time you took some responsibility for what you're saying. If being ten is such a big deal, you're old enough to hear yourself and stop before you say things that are ridiculous and hurtful."

"Hurtful?" Doug asked in a small voice.

"I can't walk away from my job; what would we live on? Who else is earning any money in this house? You're all in school, where you belong, and I'm at work *because I don't have any choice.* I'll tell you what: you *will* leave school . . . I'll call tomorrow and tell them you're not coming back because you have to get a job so that we can buy groceries and clothes and all the other things you take for granted. And when you're earning enough for all that, then I *can* walk away when I have an awful day and I never want to see that place or any of those people again, but until then *I have no choice.* If you were a little less self-absorbed, you'd be able to fathom this, but then, of course, you're ten, as you keep reminding us, and all you think about is what *you* want and what *you* don't like—"

"Sara's mad!" Doug shouted. "I don't like it when Sara's mad at me!" He began to tear chunks off the thick slice of bread he was mangling, and stuff them in his ears. "Can't hear," he said in a cheerful singsong, "can't hear, can't hear. Sorry, can't hear a thing."

"Oh, gross," Carrie exclaimed, and shoved her chair back. "Excuse me, I may throw up."

"We're out of here," Abby said, and they left the dining room.

Sara gazed at Doug, then burst out laughing. "Okay, sweetheart, it's okay, take that stuff out of there."

"Can't hear," he sang. "Sorry, Sara. Sorry Sary. Can't—"

"You can hear me perfectly well. Clean out your ears; I don't want bread clogging up the drains when you take your shower tonight."

Doug peered at her. "You're not mad anymore?"

"I'm annoyed. That's different. Have you done your homework?"

"No."

"Well, clean out your ears and then go upstairs and do it."

"I don't have to do the dishes? I mean, isn't it my turn?"

"I'll do them tonight; the next two nights are yours. Go on; do your homework. Do you need any help?"

"Could you quiz me on my spelling words?"

"Later. I'll come up as soon as I've finished here. Go on now, get everything else done."

"What about dessert?"

"There isn't any. You can take an apple up to your room."

"An apple isn't dessert."

"An apple is dessert tonight in this house. Do you want it or not?"

"Sure."

Left alone, Sara stared at the gummy wads of bread Doug had pulled from his ears, the cold mashed potatoes and scattered bits of meat loaf on the plates to the left and right of her, the peas that had fallen to the floor, the two empty glasses of milk, and Abby's water glass, decorated with a neat red lip imprint. She refilled her wineglass and drank slowly, letting silence settle around her. Her day had begun at five that morning; it would not end until the others were settled in their rooms. Reflexively, she glanced again at Mack's empty chair, then away. What good did anger do? Nothing would fill that chair. And so she sat, too tired even to change her position.

The dining room could soothe or oppress her, depending on her mood, but tonight it was soothing, with its dark, solid eighteenth-century English dining table, ten velvet-cushioned chairs, and a pair of matching, heavily carved sideboards. Her mother had furnished the house the year Sara was born, when there had been plenty of money and no hints of what lay ahead. Fringed Oriental rugs overlapped at angles on dark wood floors, the walls were papered in faded vines and florals, and brass and cut-glass chandeliers cast a warm yellow wash over oil paintings of still lifes, pastoral scenes and portraits, and tall, paned windows with weighty antique gold draperies held back by tasseled ties.

Sara often wondered if her mother and father had created that feeling of sanctuary because of some nameless fear, something that led them to buy the hundred-year-old house and fill its square, high-ceilinged rooms with everything that proclaimed haven. Had they spent money easily and behaved as if the future were certain, yet still had a sense that everything would fall apart? She could not ask them. Her father was long dead, and her mother could not tell her.

Abby peeked into the room, Carrie just behind her. "Is everything okay?"

Sara sighed, wanting only to be alone. "Yes, thanks, Abby. Fine. You don't have to—"

"He didn't mean it, you know. I mean, Doug sounds so grown up—he knows all these big words—but he's really just a kid."

"I know."

"And you had a rough day. People are such shits a lot of the time."

"That is enough!" Sara pushed back her

chair. She told herself to stop—Abby was a *help* to her, she had been thinking not so long before—stop, keep quiet, don't do this—but, as before, she could not even slow down. "I've tried to be patient, but I'm sick and tired of hearing you talk like an ignoramus with a few choice words you plug in because you're too lazy to think of good ones. I hear that kind of talk from ignorant, crude people in my work and I don't have to hear it at home, too. You are to stop it right now. If you can't think of a good word, keep your mouth shut."

"But I didn't—"

"I know what you did and I've had enough of it! Do you know what *shit* means? Do you?"

"Yes, but—"

"There is no *but*. When you're talking about excrement, you can talk about shit. When you're talking about people you don't like, you have a few choices: ill-natured, brutal, uncouth, gross, unfeeling, mean, malignant, heartless, virulent, cold, callous, inconsiderate, malicious, malevolent, hateful, cruel, vitriolic, crude, coarse, brutish, barbarous. Shakespeare wrote about 'sharp-toothed unkindness.' That describes my clients today better than all your *shits* put together. From now on, if that's all you can think of, we'd appreciate silence."

In a small voice, Carrie said, "I don't think Abby could be a Shakespeare."

"Probably not," Sara snapped. "But how about something between Shakespeare and cretin?"

There was a long silence. Sara sighed and went to them, putting her arms around them. "I'm behaving very badly tonight and I apologize. Go on upstairs. I'll be there in a few minutes." Abby and Carrie looked at each other. "I promise. I'll be upstairs soon. I told Doug I'd quiz him on his spelling, and I'll come talk to you, too. Okay?"

"Okay," said Abby, and they left. Scuttled out in fear and trembling, Sara thought, hating herself. She began to pile dishes on the table.

Why do I do that? I start out with such good intentions, and then—

I didn't mean to jump all over them—how awful, the way I practically buried Abby under a whole thesaurus—and Doug, before that— twice in one evening—more than usual. It was just that I had such a miserable day—

But maybe they did, too. I didn't even ask them.

I'll ask them when I go upstairs.

She sat down again. She had wanted so desperately to be alone that her hands had been clenched as she tried to get the girls out of the room. Now she sat without moving, without thinking, her thoughts once again floating free, soaring like birds until they grew heavy and dipped down into one memory or other.

She had been young and excited about a limitless future.

Her father died, and her mother remarried.

Abby and Carrie and Doug were born.

(And Mack. But she never thought about Mack.)

And then Abby and Carrie and Doug were left alone, and Sara was the only one to keep the family whole.

What is a family? she wondered, sitting motionless in the dining room. Any group of people who love each other? Well, we do. But nothing else about us fits anybody's definition.

I can't think about that now. I can't ever think about it. It does no good.

The minutes stretched out. She heard music from Abby's room, and pictured her doing her homework while rocking to her music and dreaming of . . . what? Boys? Drugs? Clothes? Probably all of the above. Sara could only guess, and rely on hints and behavior. She was pretty sure there was not too much to worry about . . . so far. But she had no idea how strong Abby's resistance was to the pressures of her friends, her group, the movies they saw every weekend, television, the very air she breathed.

Too much to think about. So I won't. It's all unproductive anyway.

And I won't move. I won't clean the kitchen; I won't even go upstairs. I'll stay here until it's time to go to work tomorrow.

But I promised.

"Sara!" Doug shouted from upstairs. "Are you coming?"

"In a minute."

What the hell, she thought, and stood up and resumed clearing the table.

Doug heard the clatter of dishes and knew it would be more than a minute before Sara came upstairs. "She always says that," he muttered. "'In a minute, in a minute.' How many zillion minutes does she think I have to wait around?" He kicked a pile of socks to the corner of his room. Sara had told him to do the laundry . . . when was that? A couple of days ago? No, yesterday morning, when he was getting dressed. *Put a load of wash in before you go to school.* Well, he'd meant to, but he had a lot on his mind yesterday and laundry just got . . . He looked at the pile of socks, and grinned. Kicked into the corner.

Anyway, he had three sisters . . . why couldn't one of them do laundry? They pulled rank, that was the problem, they were older, they talked faster. Three against one; it wasn't fair. It wasn't natural, either. What it was, was a pain in the butt, being the only man in a house full of women. Mack shouldn't have left. *That* was the thing that really wasn't fair. *Mack* wasn't fair, walking out, leaving his only brother in the lurch, trampled on by women.

Of course Mack got famous, at least for about fifteen minutes. His picture in the *De-Paul Neighborhood Voice,* with a whole story about him. A little one, but still, nobody'd ever written *anything* about Doug, and they gave Mack lots of attention.

Mack Hayden, seventeen years old, a freshman at Roosevelt University—

Well, that wasn't exactly true; he'd

dropped out once and been kicked out once and told he couldn't come back.

—has been reported missing by his sister Sara Elliott. Abby, Carrie, and Douglas Hayden say they do not know where their brother is. When asked, Douglas replied, "If he was going on a trip, he didn't tell me anything about it." Mack Hayden occasionally had filed sports-related stories to the DePaul Neighborhood Voice; *the management of the newspaper is unaware of other jobs he might have had. He seems to have disappeared on November 3, and has not been seen by friends, family, or co-workers at the paper. His parents, Tess and Will Hayden, are dead.*

Not true, not true, not true. Doug hated that part. His mother was in a nursing home, in her very own room that Sara had decorated, and she loved them, she loved them passionately, she just couldn't tell them in *words* that she did. He didn't know where people got that idea, that she was dead; Sara had called the newspaper to tell them to take it back—*run a correction,* she'd said—but they never did. You couldn't trust anybody to do anything right.

But Mack was gone, that part was true, he took off on November 3—three years and six months ago—and he'd actually said good-bye, in an e-mail he sent to Doug. And some guys at school, Doug found out later. "The time has come," he wrote in red capital letters. "This is for everybody, all you little bitty blobs of chicken fat in school and college la-la land. You can keep oozing on your own little plates until you get old and wrinkled and congealed, but I broke the plate, broke the mold, and I'm standing up and moving out. You know what happens to old, moldy chicken fat; it ends up in the garbage, ground up and buried. That'll be all you guys. But I'll be on my feet, on my way, nobody grinds *me* up. Have a greasy time, guys and gals; I'm out of here."

By the time Doug read that, Mack was gone.

And he left me stuck here. A little bitty blob of chicken fat. While he's having adventures.

Doug kicked the socks out of the corner and they slid across the floor and came to a stop at Sara's feet in the doorway. "For me?" she asked.

"Sorry," he muttered. "I forgot to do the laundry."

"I noticed. I did it."

"But—" He looked at his socks.

"When you run out, you'll wear dirty ones or you'll do a load of laundry. There's really no rush."

Doug glowered at her. "There's three women in this house to do laundry."

"And they do."

"Not all of it!" he yelled.

Sara sat on the edge of his unmade bed, pushing aside the bunched sheet and blanket. "I know it's not fun, it's not what you want to do, it's not your line of work. We all feel exactly the same way. If we could afford a maid, we'd have one. I'm sorry we can't. I'm sorry I have to ask you to help out. I'm sorry you're not happy. I'm sorry you don't have a man in the house. Is there anything else you'd like me to apologize for?"

Doug bit his lip. "You always make me feel *little*."

"I do?" She stared at him, her eyes filling with tears. "Do I really? I don't mean to. Oh, Doug, I *am* sorry. I love you and I think you're wonderful and I never want you to feel little or bad or—"

"Don't! Don't cry! I didn't mean it! I didn't mean anything! I'm sorry!"

They looked at each other and began to laugh. "We're the most sorry people in the world," Doug said happily, and Sara held out her arms and he leaped into them, hugging her with tough, wiry arms. And in a few minutes, as if nothing had happened, Sara began to quiz him on the next day's spelling test.

Everything was okay, Doug thought later. He hated spelling tests—he hated thinking about spelling at all—but this time he got all the words right, Sara loved him, she'd hugged him again when she said good night and went to her room, his sisters were in their own rooms not calling him dumb or anything, and nobody would bother him if he stayed up for a long time, doing IM with his friends, and reading his new mystery in bed, all night if he wanted; everybody else would be asleep.

It was a slow night for instant messaging; most of his friends said they were still doing their homework, and after a while he gave up trying. But before he shut down his computer for the night, he opened the e-mail from Mack. He read it every night before he went to bed.

I'm standing up and moving out.
. . . nobody grinds me up.

Doug looked across the chaos of his room and he could see Mack, as clear as if he were really there, sprawled in the armchair the way he always did, in the work shirt and khakis he always wore, legs crossed at the ankles, hands folded behind his head, grinning, the way he always did. "You have to know all the rules, little bro, so you can know which ones to break. Well, actually, eventually you break all of them, that's the goal, anyway. Rules are like that bunch of nerds down the street—the Nevinses?" Doug nodded, feeling uncomfortable; he liked Oliver Nevins; he liked the whole odd family. "Losers. The kind that stop at red lights, eat vegetables, make the bed every day . . . you name it. Too scared to step out of the box. We're different, aren't we?" Doug always nodded, though he was never sure exactly what he was agreeing with.

I wish you were here, Doug said silently. I could ask you what you meant, exactly. Like, what does that mean—to get out of the box? Which box? And where am I when I'm out of it? And which rules should I break? I mean, Sara gets mad at the way Abby talks, and she got mad at me tonight for something I said, I'm not even sure what I said, well, I mean, I know what I said but I don't know why it made her mad, but I don't want to make her mad again, and if I don't know why she was mad tonight, how do I know which rules I can break that won't make her really mad some other time? It isn't worth the chance. You know?

But there was no answer. There never was an answer from Mack. Except—

I'm moving out.

A sudden yawn stretched Doug's face so that it hurt. He put on his pajamas, dropping his clothes on yesterday's clothes on top of a forgotten sundial kit he'd gotten for his birthday a month ago that was on top of the unicorn he'd carved last week and then discarded because he had an idea for an elephant like the one he'd read about in a book on India, and crawled into bed, opening the new mystery Sara had bought him on her lunch hour. After a minute, he groaned and slid out of bed, and went to the bathroom to brush his teeth and wash his face.

"Doug, why are you still awake?" Sara asked from her room down the hall. Her light was on and Doug knew she was reading on the chaise next to the window, the glass shade on her lamp spreading peacock colors all around the room.

"On my way to bed," Doug shouted briskly. He closed his bedroom door firmly behind him, crawled under the sheet, and picked up his book.

To bed, but not to sleep, Sara thought, smiling. She imagined him propped against his pillow, knees up to hold his book, intent on the story even as his eyes began to droop, sprang open, then drooped again, and, finally, stayed closed. In about half an hour she would go in to put the book on the night table and turn off his lamp and kiss him on the forehead, closing the door behind her as she left. The next morning, when she would knock on his door to awaken him for school, he would be sprawled under the twisted sheet, hair standing almost straight up, and neither of them would say a word about his late-night reading.

Never would I stop anyone from reading, Sara mused the next morning as she drove to work. There are so many times parents say no to children, why would we ever do it for wanting to read?

Anyway, she thought lightly, I'm not a parent, I'm an older sister, and I can do sisterly things.

Except that she had to do everything a parent had to do, and she had to go to work, and she could only hope this day would be better than the one before. And, in fact, it was, from the beginning. The client was waiting in his hotel suite when Sara met him; he knew he wanted to buy a house, and he had faxed a list of preferred neighborhoods a week before, a vast improvement, Sara thought, over other days and other clients.

"Reuben Lister," he said, his handshake firm and cool. He was tall and lanky, slightly stoop-shouldered, his face long and narrow, his dark hair and neat dark beard streaked with gray. His brown eyes were almost overpowered by horn-rimmed glasses. They should be wire-rims, Sara thought, but, watching his firm mouth curve into a smile as cool as his handshake, she thought he looked so formidable that probably no one gave him advice about his glasses, or perhaps anything else. *Maybe he's a lawyer, or a corporate raider, or a spy.*

"I've been reading about Chicago," he said as they sat at a conference table in the living room of his suite, "so I'm pretty confident about the neighborhoods I chose. But you may have other suggestions."

"No, your choices are good; you've done your homework." Sara took the fax from her briefcase. "You want a house, not an apartment; you want to be in the city, and you want to be close to your office in the Hancock Building. I have four houses in mind, but perhaps we can narrow that down. How soon do you need to move in?"

"By the end of the month. Someone in the mayor's office named Donna Soldana said I should talk to you instead of a Realtor and decorator. Do you really take care of everything?"

"Within reason." Sara smiled, liking him because he had remembered Donna's name, which meant working people were real people to him.

"But you have a staff."

"I have people I can call on. Are you afraid everything won't get done on time?"

He contemplated her and smiled. "I'm sure you can handle any job you accept, or you wouldn't have accepted it. What can I do to make it easier for you?"

"Tell me what you like."

"Easily done." He opened a folder. "A large

house, not modern, with large rooms, high ceilings, one or more fireplaces, at least four bedrooms, an office or a room that can be converted to one, a library, a large kitchen, not necessarily new—I don't mind renovating, in fact, I enjoy it." He spread out pages torn from magazines, photographs, and computer printouts. "I like fine antiques: rugs, furniture, lamps. These caught my eye in Europe; I don't expect to find the same things here, but this is the idea."

"And the printouts?"

"Appliances, kitchenware, linens, the things I'm used to and like. I'm keeping my apartment in New York, so I'm starting from scratch here."

"For yourself and your wife? And children?"

"For myself," he said shortly.

There was a brief silence. "You mentioned a large house," Sara said. "Are you thinking of houseguests, or entertaining?"

"Both."

"And you would want maids' living quarters?"

"No, I have no need of live-in help. A housekeeper during the day, and names of caterers when I need them. Can I call on you for those, too?"

"Yes. And plumber, electrical, furnace . . . whatever you need." Sara glanced at her notebook. "How much land do you require? A yard? A garden? A terrace?"

"They aren't at the top of my list, but a terrace and a garden would be pleasant. I'm not looking for an estate."

Sara nodded. "Two of the houses on my list are in a neighborhood a few blocks north of the Hancock Building; I think either of them would meet your needs."

"The Gold Coast. Colorful if not completely accurate. Yes, I'd like to see them."

That night, Sara was humming as she stirred the veal stew she had made the night before. On her way home that afternoon, she had stopped to see her mother, and the two of them had had tea as she talked about her day. "So much better than yesterday, and in fact better than most days. I don't know why that surprises me. I'm always expecting patterns: today was unpleasant so there will be a bunch of unpleasant days until the pendulum swings back, and then the pattern will be reversed." She laughed slightly. "We're so desperate, all of us, to believe there's order in everything. I'll bet Lew Corcoran is sure there are patterns and he controls them, so he does what he wants and treats people any way he likes, including his wife . . . and you'd feel sorry for her, except that she doesn't seem a lot kinder than he is. But I'll bet sometimes he wakes up at three or four in the morning feeling uneasy and worried and wondering if he really understands anything. At least I hope he does. In fact, I hope he can't sleep at all; I hope he lies there, in the dark, with no one to impress, and knows exactly how unpleasant he is, how arrogant, uncouth, mean, solipsistic—goodness, I sound like I'm still talking to Abby. Poor Abby, I really jumped on her . . ."

Her mother smiled with one side of her mouth, a smile always touched by sadness, no matter how much humor or pleasure might be in it. Once she had been lovely, lithe and vibrant, now she was faded, shrunken, her chestnut hair streaked gray and white, her face drawn, her once silken complexion lined with sorrow and helpless rage. Her children resembled her, but Abby was the one with her remarkable beauty: in her, Tess saw herself as she was before her stroke, and the pain and joy of looking into that illusive mirror made her feel uniquely bound to Abby, her daughter and her past. She loved all her children, she ached to be a mother and companion to them again, but it was with Abby that Tess was a dancing girl again, whirling toward a horizon that had no inkling of tragedy.

She smiled her half smile at Sara, and held out her good hand, palm up: a question about Abby.

"Okay, I'll tell you what happened." Sara pulled her chair closer and refilled their cups, feeling herself relax into the slow pace and stillness of her mother's room. She had furnished it herself when she acknowledged, finally, that she could not take care of everyone; that the nursing home was their only choice. A week after her mother was moved in, Sara had transformed the large room, filling it with beauty instead of cold anonymity. She covered the bed with a log-cabin quilt, her mother's favorite pattern, and at the foot folded a cashmere afghan in bright red, her mother's favorite color. She set a reading lamp with a stained-glass shade on the bed table and a matching floor lamp beside the elegant, brocade armchair in which her mother spent her days. Three vivid paintings of the Italian countryside brightened the pale yellow walls, and a branching fig tree in a wide brass planter stood beside the window that took almost the whole wall. She found a small Oriental rug on which her mother's feet rested when she sat in the brocade chair, and a carpenter built a stand that pivoted across the chair so that her mother could read or work with her good hand on needlepoints of scenes from her favorite books. At first her stitches were wildly erratic, but little by little she had learned to control the simple up and down movements of pushing the needle from above or below, and she took pride and delight in her work. As if to remind herself of how much she had improved, she kept on the table beside her bed her first finished piece, framed and signed in stitches, TESS HAYDEN.

Now the needlework stand held Tess's teacup and a porcelain teapot Sara had found in an antique shop in Wisconsin, and the two women sat quietly, watching a soft April rain film the window with a silvery sheen. "It rained last Wednesday, too," Sara said. "I had to work late, and Abby was furious because she wanted to do homework with a group of friends at Sue's house—you remember Sue Poston: the tall one with a braid to her waist and a kind of loping walk; once you said it reminded you of a giraffe; I loved that; it was so perfect—"

She stopped, staring at the rain, forcing back the pain that clutched her even now, more than three long years after a stroke paralyzed her mother on her right side and left her unable to speak in anything but grunts and incomprehensible mumbles that left her in tears as she struggled to form words. "You always had the right word, the right image . . ."

She turned, and saw despair in her mother's eyes. "Anyway," she said briskly, "Abby was not happy when she had to wait for me, but of course she got over it; she always does, because she understands that I can't always control what time I . . . oh, and speaking of that, let me tell you about dinner last night. Your creative son Doug invented a new kind of earplug. And then I'll tell you about Abby. Confession time," she added ruefully.

She told the story in vivid detail, scrunching up her eyes as Doug had done—"as if he couldn't see *or* hear me"—and mimicking his

"Sorry, sorry, sorry Sary," adding, "Which was pretty clever, I thought," and laughing so that her mother's eyes could laugh with her.

"But I did yell at him," she said after a minute. "I never mean to; I tell myself to keep my mouth shut and wait until I calm down, but then my mouth opens, almost by itself, and out come all the words I'd just been telling myself not to say. I did the same with Abby when she started sprinkling everything she said with four-letter words. I know she does it for effect—all her friends think it's cool, but it gets to me, and I let her have it, and then I hear my voice and I hate what I sound like. I know I shouldn't yell at them, I should be reasonable so that they can understand why I'm upset, but I'm too upset to do that, so what comes out is—" She shrugged. "I suppose all parents go through that."

But I'm not a parent, she thought again. And I probably never will be. I'm twenty-seven, and this is my only family, and no prospects for my own.

But this is my own family. Of course it is. I just meant . . .

She saw Tess's frown, and said lightly, "It's really nothing, you know; mainly, I was in a bad mood, and when that happens the others get the brunt of it. It's not fair to them. So I apologized." She smiled. "They'll all be happy tonight, because I'm in such a fine mood."

Again her mother held out her hand, palm up.

"Oh, because of my first client of the day, a man named Reuben Lister, from New York. Polite, civilized, pleasant, and he'd done his homework; he knew what he wanted, he had pictures and printouts, he'd studied Chicago. He made my job so easy; he was everyone's dream of the perfect client. He even likes people; he remembered Donna Soldana's name."

Her mother's hand rose, palm up.

"You've never met her, but I've told you about her; my secretary who left home because her father—" She hesitated. She had never told her mother the whole story. "Because she didn't get along with her father. She rented a room near her house, to be near her mother, but her father found her and was making threats, so one day after work we found her a place in a building a little farther from home, but close enough. She's fine there, and she and her mother

see each other in her sister's house in Forest Park. She told me she still wakes up with
nightmares, though; how terrible to live in
constant fear."

Her mother's head drooped to the side.

"I know," Sara said quickly. "Constant sadness is just as bad." She stood and bent to
kiss her mother. "You're tired, and I have to
get dinner; veal stew that I made last night
just before I went to bed. I'll see you in a couple of days. I love you."

Her mother's finger jabbed at her.

"What? What haven't I told you?"

Her mother pointed at her briefcase.

"My work? But I've told you about yesterday and today . . . Oh." She smiled. "Reuben.
Yes, I liked him." Her mother pointed at her
hand and Sara sighed. "I'm not about to
marry him, Mother." She smiled again. "But I
am going to lunch with him next week. He
said he wanted help in getting to know
Chicago."

Her mother's hand returned to its place in
her lap, restlessly fingering the afghan's
soft yarn.

Sara kissed her again. "I'm going. And I
love you, even if you assume every time I
like someone, I'm ready to marry him."

Her mother touched her cheek.

"I know, you want me to be taken care of. But there are three people in our house who need to be taken care of right now, and I'm thinking of them, not me. I'll think about me when Doug goes to college. It's only another seven years; I'll still be young. Anyway, that's the way it is, and it's fine." She kissed her mother and walked to the door. "I love you, I'll see you this weekend."

Veal stew, she thought as she stood at the stove, stirring with a long-handled wooden spoon that had belonged to her grandmother. My mother and grandmother and great-grandmother made veal stew; theirs tasted about the same as mine. Something else my mother lost: years and years of holding her place in that continuous line, sharing the lives of her children and grandchildren, watching them become part of the world, until she died in old age, knowing the next generation was firmly in place, and the line intact. Now all she can do is hear about it, from me, from Doug and Carrie and Abby. A shadow play of the life she expected to live.

"You look serious but happy," Carrie said from the doorway. "I'm glad you're happy. I'm going to set the table."

"That makes me even happier."

"Why are you happy?"

"Because I had a good day, because I stopped to see Mother on the way home and she was glad to see me, and because I have a cheerful, loving family overflowing with goodwill and the desire to be helpful."

"Oh, my," said Abby, walking into the kitchen. "You're preparing to ask us for something."

"I am always prepared to ask you for something." Sara tossed her an apron. "Salad and dressing. And please slice the bread. Where is Doug?"

"Watching a video and making something out of clay."

"That is exactly the answer you gave yesterday."

"He's doing exactly what he was doing yesterday. And the day before, and the day before that, and every evening at this time."

"Well, let's get him in here; he can help Carrie set the table. And then I want to hear what you've all done today. And after that, I'll tell you about a man I saw in a hotel lobby today."

"What kind of a man?"

"He was selling something."

"What was he selling?"

"I can't tell you; that's part of the surprise. Go on now, get your brother."

Dinner was lively and relaxed—so much depended on her moods, Sara thought, and felt guilty because she did not do a better job of controlling herself so that all their times could be happy ones—and when Abby brought in a chiffon cake she had made after school, Doug shouted, "I want to know what the guy was selling."

"Don't shout," said Carrie.

"I like to shout. What was he selling, Sara?"

Sara paused dramatically. "Noses."

"WHAT?"

"He was selling noses. You could look through a book of pictures, and choose the one you want, and he'd put you in a trance and wave a wand, and when you woke up, there you'd be with a new nose."

"That isn't true," said Carrie. "I wouldn't even write that in a story; nobody would believe it."

"If Sara says it, maybe it *is* true," Doug said with a frown.

"Oh, dear." Sara leaned over and kissed him. "Even Sara exaggerates now and then, little one."

"So is *any* of it true?" Abby asked.

"Yes, oddly enough. A small man, wrinkled and bald, but with a big bushy mustache, and wearing a dark green suit—"

"Is this true?" asked Abby suspiciously.

"Absolutely. I saw him."

"Well, he sounds like an elf, not a real man. It sounds like you made him up."

"You're right, he did look like an elf, but I didn't make him up. Maybe he was an elf, or a gnome, or a sprite, but I thought he was a real man. Anyway, he had a big book of photographs of noses—just noses, not whole faces—and people who were interested (you'd be amazed how many actually were interested) could pick out a nose and he would very swiftly draw a portrait of them with the new nose. So they could see instantly how they would look if they decided to switch noses. Then he'd hand over a business card of a plastic surgeon—maybe it was his brother; who knows?—and turn to the next person in line."

"Then he wasn't really selling them," said Carrie.

"He was a shill for his brother," Abby said.

"Because his brother is probably even smaller and uglier than he is," said Carrie, flying off on the idea for a new story, "and can't get his own patients, and besides he's too shy because he was in love with a tall girl once and she made him feel little and insignificant, so now he hides in his operating room doing noses."

Sara laughed. "If he really has a brother, I'm sure you're right."

"I want a Rudolph the Red-Nosed Reindeer nose!" Doug shouted.

"Don't shout," said Carrie.

"I like to shout."

"I actually like my nose," said Abby, "but I'd like a Julia Roberts mouth."

Doug said, "I want a—"

"You've already said," shouted Carrie. "It's my turn!"

"Don't shout," said Doug.

They laughed, their laughter filling the dining room, so that it was a moment before they heard the doorbell.

"I'll get it!" Doug shouted, and dashed through the living room to the foyer. The others waited in silence, hearing nothing. But then Doug was in the doorway, beaming with

excitement, a tall figure in the shadows behind him, with a hand on his shoulder. "Sara,
look! Look who's here!"

"Hi, sis," said Mack.

TWO

He sat at the head of the table, hands folded behind his head, legs stretched out and crossed at the ankles, telling stories. He had torn through a plate of food, and two re-fills, and drained a full bottle of wine. Then, sitting back, he had begun to talk, the words spilling out in a torrent, as if no one had paid any attention to him for weeks.

And maybe no one has, Sara thought. Does anyone in the world care about him?

Carrie and Abby cared; they could not take their eyes off him. And Doug sat on the arm of Mack's chair, leaning into him, mes-merized.

"So finally we said, 'Well, fuck it, let's try it, what have we got to lose?' And guess what—?"

Abby and Carrie looked at Sara, waiting for sharp words about Mack's language, but Sara was silent.

"What?" Doug breathed. "What happened next?"

"We snuck up on the tiger, had our rifles ready, but, shit, this asshole tourist from Florida shouted something like 'Watch it, he's waking up,' and the fucking tiger—"

Sara shoved back her chair. "Let's clear the table." Furiously, she stacked plates. "Abby. Carrie. *Now.*"

"But couldn't we . . . I mean—" Carrie was stopped by the grim line of Sara's mouth. "It's Doug's turn," she said loudly.

"Not tonight," Doug cried. "Tonight's special."

"It's special for all of us," Carrie retorted.

"Then let's all do the dishes." Mack stood up, smiling broadly at Sara. "It's only fair: we ate, we clean up. Why should Sara worry about the dishes, when she already has so much on her mind? Come on, I'll race you to the kitchen." He grabbed five water glasses, plunging his fingers inside to grip them firmly—Doug watching with his mouth open in amazement—and with his other hand hefted the casserole of veal stew. "Great stew, sis; didn't Mom and Grandma used to make something like it? Not as good, though, couldn't have been. This is the best. I guess I ate enough to show it."

He was already halfway to the kitchen. The others snatched up plates and knives and forks and dashed after him. Sara heard water running, and loud laughter.

Slowly, she sat down again and reached for the wine bottle before remembering that Mack had emptied it. She felt angry and resentful, then guilty. What was wrong with her? Her brother had come home after three and a half years, pale, gaunt, hungry, and lonely, needing a family. And he had a family, and some of them had welcomed him with love and joy. But she could not.

He promised to stay and help me take care of them; he said he'd go to college part-time and I'd be in medical school part-time, and we'd both work and take turns at home. He promised.

But he was only seventeen years old. He wanted to be free.

I was only twenty-four. So did I.

But, suddenly, she realized that was why he had come home. Of course it was; what else could it be? He'd had his fling; now he wanted a family. He'd known that Tess had had a stroke soon after he left—"I heard it from a friend," he'd said vaguely—and he wanted to make amends for that, too. He was ready to come back to them, to get a job and help support them while she went back to school.

It's not too late, she thought; I can do it. Even if I have to repeat some courses to get back to where I was . . . I can do that. I can do anything.

That was why he'd come back: to reclaim his family. He'd had over three years—three and a half, really—of freedom, or whatever he'd call it, and he was lonely and maybe guilty over walking out and leaving Sara to take care of everything, and now he wanted to make it up to her, to all of them.

Her excitement was building. This was April; she could take courses in the summer and begin a regular school year in the fall. And she could start studying right away; all of her textbooks were here, stored in the attic.

I'm sorry I wasn't very nice at dinner, she

said silently to Mack. I was confused, and you didn't seem—

He had not seemed warm. Or loving. Or brotherly.

Or guilty.

But we were all so surprised. And he was probably as confused as we were, so many adjustments to make, all at once. Tomorrow will be better. We'll all get a good night's sleep, and then, it's the weekend, I'll be home; we'll get to know each other, and make plans.

But Mack was asleep when Sara awoke the next morning, and he still had not come downstairs when the four of them had finished breakfast. "I have rehearsal," Abby said. "The play opens in two weeks and I absolutely have to be there. Could you call me if something happens? I'll keep my phone on."

"I don't think anything will happen," said Sara, "but of course I'll call if anything does. When will you be home?"

"Four o'clock? Five? Something like that. Thanks, Sara," she called, already on her way out. "Love you."

"Can't we wake him up?" asked Doug. "Oliver's mom said she'd drive us to a movie if you said it was okay, but—"

"We *have* to wake him up," Carrie said. "I'm supposed to go to a movie with Fran and Debbie, lunch and everything, but I have to at least say hello, it's his *first day*. So *please* wake him up."

"He was exhausted last night," said Sara. "Let him sleep. There's plenty of time for us to get acquainted, and today Mack and I need to talk. You go on, both of you. We'll all be together at dinner."

Torn between attractions, they perched on the edge of their chairs. Carrie sighed. "Life is so hard, figuring out what's best to do."

"Isn't it," Sara said drily. Then she laughed. "I've made the decision for you. Let's clean up the kitchen, then you'll go. Are your beds made?"

Carrie nodded. Doug's shoulders slumped. "I meant to; I forgot. I'll do it later. Mack used to say only nerds make—" He shot a glance at Sara. "I mean, it's sort of stupid, you know; I'm only going to mess it up again tonight."

"Neatness is a virtue," said Carrie.

"So is not wasting your energy on dumb things."

"Neatness wins," Sara said. She kissed them both, and kissed them again as they were leaving, thinking how much fun they were, wishing they were enough to fill her life, and then wishing she could stop thinking that way. Right now, today, they were her life. Tomorrow, with Mack here, she would have more. But for now, it was enough that they were wonderful, and that she loved them.

Upstairs, before she went into her office, she walked the length of the hallway, and climbed the narrow back stairway to the third floor, where Mack had reclaimed his old room. The door was open, and on the wide bed Mack had kicked off the blanket and sheet and lay sprawled sideways, face buried in his pillow, wearing only his shorts. His arms were spread-eagled, fists clenched. The window was wide open and a breeze lifted the burlap curtains he had hung when he was ten ("It's his back-to-earth stage," Sara's mother had said), but still a faint sweetish smell that Sara recognized hovered in the room.

Oh, yes, we do need to talk, she thought, and went back downstairs to her office. This was her space. She had made her mother's large corner bedroom her own when Tess had been settled in the nursing home, but she had kept the furnishings her mother had collected with such care: nineteenth-century

French bureaus, dressing table, chaise, and a huge four-poster bed so high from the floor it came with its own step stool. She had changed only the colors, replacing her mother's pale pastels with vivid shades of blue and ivory, and hanging three portraits by Vanessa Bell, their bold colors and slashing strokes giving her special pleasure on those days when she felt most sharply the constrictions of her new life.

Her mother's adjoining dressing room had become her office. A large window centered in one wall overlooked their backyard with its towering oak tree, tulips and hyacinths struggling for sunshine beneath the canopy of leaves, and a row of lilac bushes along the back fence and the side of the garage that jutted into the yard. Beyond, the view was of the backs of houses that faced the next street over, all three stories high, some of painted wood, most of red brick or Gothic stone blocks like her own. All the houses had garages opening onto the alley, as hers did, and backyards enclosed by fences like her own, shaded by bushes and trees that blended in with her own, and back porches like her own. Whenever she was at her desk Sara caught glimpses of other lives on those porches: moments of laughter and tension, affection and conflict, now and then a family moving in on the heels of the one moving out. A drama in every house, she thought, making her own story seem dull and plodding.

Isolated from it all, the office was her retreat, furnished with a couch she had retrieved from the attic and reupholstered in cranberry-red suede, an armchair striped in red and brown, a Turkish rug of startling reds, browns, and golds, and an eighteenth-century table found in an antique-filled barn in Iowa. Her computer and printer sat on the table like a joke, amusing anachronisms, but Sara liked that: it was comforting to be reminded that things that didn't seem to belong were really necessary. People, too, she thought. We never really know what, or whom, we can't do without . . . until we can't do without them.

She had finished her notes on her meetings with the Corcorans and Reuben Lister, and was answering e-mail when Mack appeared in the doorway, two mugs in one hand, a thermos in the other. "I made coffee," he said. "I hope it's okay."

"Of course it is." Sara was unnerved by the

thought that he had risen and gone down-stairs, passing the open door of her bedroom, brewed coffee and walked upstairs again, and she had not heard him. Sneaking around, she thought, and then was ashamed. "Come in and sit down. I see you found your old bathrobe."

He grinned. "Feels fine. Coffee?"

"Thank you."

He put the mugs on the desk and filled them. "A fine robe finely made that feels fine. A little big, though."

"It wasn't always."

"I know. I've lost weight."

There was a silence. Sara watched him as he looked around the room. His lips were full and oddly sensuous in his gaunt face; his blond hair fell limply to his shoulders; but everything else about him seemed tense and watchful, from the sharp lines of his cheekbones to the taut muscles in his neck. Watching for what? she wondered. Waiting for what?

"This is terrific," he said, turning back from his scrutiny of the room. "You'd never know it was Ma's."

"It isn't," Sara said shortly. "She's been gone almost as long as you have."

"Which is three years and six months, as Doug pointedly pointed out, pointing his finger." He took a long drink. "Good coffee; you buy the best. You're good at everything, you know? Dinner last night was terrific. The veal stew was—"

"The best. Thank you. Mack—"

"And you're as beautiful as ever, Sara. More. The kids have changed a lot—God, have they grown up—but you are just the same. I kept seeing you, all of you—well, but you know, it was funny, I couldn't really *see* you; every time I tried to focus on your faces they were all sort of foggy—blurs of blurriness—it kept reminding me how far away you were, far, farther, farthest. I could picture every room in the house, even the way the light looked mornings and afternoons. But I couldn't see you. It made me sad. I missed you."

"We missed you," Sara said.

"But, fuck it, Sara, you are really the most beautiful—"

"Mack, I don't want you talking like that in this house."

"Saying you're beautiful?"

"You know what I'm talking about."

"Yeah, but what's the problem? It's the way

I talk, sis; it's the way everybody talks. It's no big deal, you know. Anyway, it's how I *like* to talk; those are some of my favorite words."

"I'm sure of that," Sara said lightly. "Mack, I know a lot of people talk like that as casually as they button their shirts; I even know that the world has a lot more serious problems than this one. But I've been trying to convince the children, especially Abby, that it's not a lovely way to talk, in fact, that it's crude and offensive, and that it mostly reveals ignorance. So you'll have to understand that I won't have it in this house."

"Well, but, look— Oh, what the hell, this is getting too fucking heavy." He sprang from his chair, and, encircling Sara's waist, lifted her off the floor. "Lighten up, little Sara. Life can be *fun*."

Furious, she pushed against his chest with a strength that took him by surprise, and he almost dropped her. She backed away, shaking as she sat down again, her hands gripping the edge of the desk. "You are never to touch me again."

"God, where did you get that cold voice? No, I know where. I recognize it. That was Ma when she didn't like my friends, or what I was doing, which after a while was most of the time. But, Sara, sweet Sara, I'm your *bro*! Bros hug sisters all the time. Sisters *like* to be hugged."

"If I want you to touch me, I'll tell you."

There was a pause. "Right. Okay. I'm sorry I upset you. God, I really am sorry. I didn't do it to hurt you. I'm just so happy to be home. I *love* you."

Sara took deep breaths, amazed by her fury. Of course she had been surprised, but it was far more than that. She had felt violated. Because, she thought abruptly, she didn't trust him. After all the excitement she had allowed herself to feel last night, in the cool gray light of a cloudy April morning, watching the changing expressions on Mack's face, she did not trust him.

"Mack," she said, "we have a lot to talk about."

"Right. Right, I know, but . . . this minute? Don't you think it's nice just being . . . easy? Just *being* here. I mean, it's like I walked in and nothing had changed, you know, I could reach into my closet without looking, or around the kitchen when I was making coffee, and everything was just where it was supposed to be, my hand just got to it, like it was waiting for me. It's like walking into a photograph, a sepia photograph—"

"Meaning old-fashioned."

"Well. Could be. Yeah, right—good for you—that *is* the way I see it. All this old furniture, kind of *musty* and *past,* not part of *now.* And the house—shit, sis, when I walked up the front walk last night I couldn't believe it, all that gray stone piled up into a dark castle some giant made, like he scooped out a front porch and windows and put on a tile roof, stacking the tiles like a kid with blocks, and I thought—"

"Did you make that up?"

"What?"

"The giant. The scooping out. The kid with blocks."

Mack hesitated, then grinned widely. "Actually, no. Last night, Carrie was telling me about a story she's writing about this house, and a girl who makes friends with elves, and they have a party in the backyard . . . she said it gets pretty complicated, but she didn't go into that part. She's good, you know."

"I know."

"She says she writes lots of stories."

"She does, about everything, wonderful,

fanciful stories, sometimes about people she knows but most often about people and places she makes up. She loves it, and the more she experiments with different ideas the better she gets."

"You're proud of her. You should be. They're all terrific, Sara, you've done a hell of a job. Big sister Sara . . . who would have believed it? You were so fierce about going off and being a famous doctor doctoring the world, saving everybody, and here you are, right where you started: the most amazing mother. *I'm* proud of *you*."

Sara felt her anger rise, and waited until she could push it down. Finally, she said evenly, "And now that you're back we'll pick up the pieces. We'll each go to school part-time and work part-time, just as we planned. We'll finally be able to do all the things we've wanted to do."

"Of course we will." He refilled his mug. "More?"

"No, thank you."

He sipped the hot coffee, blew on it, sipped some more. "Tell me about your job."

"Mack, I want to go back to school."

He nodded again. "I know you do." He rolled the mug slowly between his palms. "I know you do. We'll figure it out. Believe me. But tell me about your job."

"*Not now.* We have more important things to talk about."

"No, we don't. Sara, the most important thing in the world to me right now is learning about my family. The kids told me a lot last night, but I have so much catching up to do. That's what I want to do for the next few weeks: get to know my family, my neighborhood, look up a few people, play tourist in Chicago. I've never done that. Time I got to know my own city."

"Weeks?"

"A few weeks. Not a lifetime, just a few weeks. Sara, Sara, what's more important than family? Who knows that better than you?" Mack's face began to twist; tears were in his eyes. "You've been walking through all these rooms, being part of them, and I've been walking down strange streets, a stranger strangely strange, not part of anything. I need to feel part of these rooms, part of this house. And part of you. We'll take long walks, you and I, talk long talks about the world, get to know each other. And I'll go places with the kids, museums, whatever." He leaned toward her, his body a long angle tensed with anguish. "What could be more important than that? *Getting acquainted. Belonging.*"

Instinctively Sara leaned back. She watched him roll the mug back and forth as if he were washing his hands, watched the first tear roll down his unshaven cheek. He brushed it away. "Shit, I forgot to shave. Sorry; hell of a way to greet my big sister my first morning home."

Confused, Sara was silent, trying to understand him. She pitied his aloneness and his anguish; she wanted to ease the pain that was etched in his face and respond to the pleading in the angle of his body. And wasn't he right? Wasn't family more important than anything?

But for three and a half years he didn't care about family at all.

"Why did you leave?" she asked abruptly.

"What?" He frowned. "I wanted to."

"What happened that made you want to?"

"Nothing happened. I was seventeen years old and itching to see the world. I didn't like our little patch of it—too small, too comfortable, too organized—so I took off. Happens all the time in nice middle-class families."

"All the time? I doubt it. But something did happen here. Your father disappeared."

"That was four months earlier. I never thought about him. Never thought about a thoughtless man. Never heard from him, never looked for him, never cared."

"Really? Never cared?"

"No, why should I? The son of a bitch walked out on us. He threw us away. I threw him away. We were even."

Sara waited while the vehemence of the words stirred the air, then faded. "You left on your seventeenth birthday," she said then. "You told us your friends were giving you a party, so we put off our own celebration until the next day. But of course there was no party. So what was it? Your father? Your birthday?"

"It wasn't anything. Damn it, sis, I just wanted out. How many seventeen-year-old guys want out?"

"Maybe a lot of them. But how many actually leave?"

"Hey, if other guys are scared, is that my fault? Sis, I was seventeen. I itched. I left. What difference does it make now? I'm home, where I belong. And I intend to take a few weeks to settle down here. It's my home, too, you know. It's not just yours, it's mine, too."

Sara's eyes narrowed. "Who do you think you are, telling me this is your home, and what you *intend* to do in it? What have you done to take care of it for the past three and a half years? Or help the people whose home it really is? People make a home by living in it; they don't wander in and out like an *itching* hotel guest and then whine, 'It's mine, it's mine, it's mine.'"

Mack had both hands spread in front of his face; he peered at Sara through his fingers. "What did I do? All I said was, I want to live here; I feel like I'm home. God, Sara, you make me feel criminally criminal. I left; I'm home. What's so awful? Am I the only one who ever did it? Maybe it was a mistake, leaving, and I'm sorry Ma fell apart after that, but are you sure that was my fault? Maybe it was the old man taking off, leaving her in an empty bed. What the fuck, Sara, it's all the *past.* I can't undo it now. I *could* call this home, though, if you'd let me."

Sara told herself it was better to remain silent when she was angry.

"I'll tell you what *is* awful"—Mack lowered his hands and smiled tremulously—"is that I do feel like a stranger here, in my own house. I need time to settle in, to feel that I truly belong. That I'm welcome. There's nothing worse, you know, than feeling like a stranger in your own house."

"A stranger," Sara echoed. "You said you were a stranger on all those strange streets, but here you reach into your closet or around the kitchen without looking, and everything is just where it's supposed to be."

There was a pause. Mack gave a small, chagrined laugh. "I exaggerated. God, I forgot you have this fantastic memory; I always envied you for it, did you know that? Anyway, I'm sorry; I exaggerated. I've forgotten more than what a great memory you have, and it's sad and embarrassing, and I wanted you to think I remembered everything. I wanted to impress you with how much I belonged. The sad truth is that I really do feel strangely like a stranger in a strange house, and I was afraid if you knew it, you'd think I hadn't missed you and you wouldn't want me here, and, damn it, Sara, *I want to be here.*"

The tears were back and he stood up abruptly. "I hate to cry in front of people. I'm going to shower and shave or you really won't want me around. I'll see you later. How about I take you out to lunch?"

He bent down and kissed the top of her head and then left, swiftly and silently on his bare feet.

Sara sat still, listening to sounds from the third floor of drawers opening and closing, of the toilet and then the shower, so clearly that she knew he had not closed either his bedroom or his bathroom door. Strange, she thought, but maybe he's used to living alone.

His words hung in the room. *I want to be here.* Said with a kind of desperation. As if he had fled here. From what? Strange streets, loneliness . . . and what else?

Or, as if he had to be here, had to have a place to stay, a family, respectability, while he . . . what?

She had no way of knowing. No clues, no obvious connections between the gaunt man who had sat here, crying, and the boy who had vanished.

She wanted to believe him. She wanted to believe *in* him, to like him, even to love him. She wanted to welcome him as her brother.

Well, I will, she thought. I guess I owe him that. And it's good for Abby and Carrie and Doug to have a solution to the mystery of what happened to Mack; it may even be good for them to have an older brother. And he did agree when I said we'd go to school and work. I said we'd do all the things we wanted to do, and he said we would. He said we'd work it out. It will just take some time, I guess, but I've waited this long—

I don't want to wait any longer.

She shrugged. How often had she told the three children that wanting something did not automatically and magically make it happen?

Her telephone rang and she answered it absently. "Sara," Donna Soldana said, "Pussy Corcoran—is that really her name? Anyway, she called, she wants you to call her back. And Reuben Lister called, left his cell-phone number. And a few others—" She read them and Sara jotted them down.

"Why are you in the office on Saturday?" she asked.

"I had a lot to do; I'm just working another hour or two. I thought I might as well give you these. Do you mind?"

Sara gazed at the list. "No, it's fine. Do you have someone to take you home?"

"Sara, it's the middle of the day. He won't try anything. Even if he does, there are people all over the place. I'll be okay."

"If you're worried, I'll come down and drive you home."

"I'm not worried. Really. What happened last week was crazy; he's never done that before. I mean, coming after me in a shopping mall . . . it was just crazy. And he left when I said I'd call the security guard; it wasn't a big deal."

"I'd feel better if you were with someone."

"Thanks, but you shouldn't worry. Anyway, I can't have a keeper every minute of every day. I'll deal with it, Sara, I have to."

"I know." And she does, Sara thought. We all have to deal with whatever comes our way, because in the end we can't count on anyone being next to us, as Donna says, every minute of every day. "Will you call me when you get home?"

"Yes, Mama."

Sara laughed. "You probably don't need another mother. I apologize."

"It's okay. I like it, actually. And I'll try to call."

"One more thing," Sara said. "Reuben Lister's cell-phone number."

When she hung up, she read down the list of calls. Pussy Corcoran could wait until Monday; the others could wait until Monday.

All but one. She reached for the telephone and called Reuben Lister.

"Good morning," he said. "I was expecting to return to New York today, but it will be tomorrow instead. Would you have dinner with me tonight?"

Sara smiled to herself. *A man of few words and direct action.*

"I'd like that," she said.

"If you'll give me your address, I'll take a cab—"

"No, there's no need. I'll pick you up at your hotel and we can drive from there."

"Thank you, but I can walk. On the chance that you'd be free, I made a reservation at Spiaggia. They only had six-thirty; earlier than I wanted, but Saturday night is difficult. Is it all right with you?"

"Yes. I'll meet you there."

"And can you tell me where the Museum of Contemporary Art is? At the moment, I'm coming up to the Water Tower."

"One block east, on Chicago Avenue."

"How satisfactorily close everything is. Until tonight, then."

More like a business discussion than making a date for dinner. Sara began to laugh. A strange conversation, but somehow comforting. Two people who didn't play games, but got right to the point.

Except that of course they would play games, she reflected as she turned back to her work. People always did, at least until they began to know each other.

And maybe it never ends, she added, thinking of Mack.

Showered, shaved, dressed, and cheerful, Mack stood in her office door. "Time for lunch. A date with my sis."

They walked to the restaurant, a long walk with Sara setting the pace and Mack, breathing hard, half a step behind, all the way to Rush Street. "Do you always walk like that?" he gasped as they were shown to an outside table. "Or was that for my benefit?"

"I always walk like that. I don't have much time for exercise."

Seated, no longer breathless, Mack began to talk, and Sara relaxed. They talked of changes in Chicago and the university neighborhood around their house, friends Mack remembered, and Sara's job. "I'm pretty sure they'll let me work part-time when I go back to school," she said once, but then the talk turned to something else, and from there to another topic, and on to a dozen more. It was all light, pleasant, and inconsequential, Sara thought as they left the restaurant. But she had enjoyed herself, and enjoyed Mack's company.

On the way home, she said, "I'll be out tonight; Abby will stay with Carrie and Doug."

"Golly, another date, sis? Two in one day; not bad!"

She looked at him and did not reply.

"Ouch," he said. He put his arm around her. "Hey, it's fine with me if you have a hot date; better than lunch with your bro any day, and what good is getting up in the morning if you don't have something hot to look forward to later on?" Sara walked faster, and he struggled to catch up. "In fact," he said between short breaths, "a hot date might warm you up. What's with you, sis? Are you always such a fucking icicle—sorry, you don't like that awful word—are you always an icicle, or is it just me?"

Sara walked faster, leaving him behind. *Let him find his own way home.* He made her feel prim and rigid. An icicle. And mean. No one else made her feel that way.

Except the Corcorans, she thought, and then she smiled. What a social evening that would be: Mack and the Corcorans. I'll have to get them together.

By the time she got home, she had lost her anger and was exhilarated by the fast walk, by her strong, steady heartbeat and sense of well-being. She loved Chicago's cloudy days when the light lay like a pale mist on the new leaves and bursts of daffodils and tulips that brought the earth to life each spring; she loved breathing deeply the fresh moist air hinting of rain; she loved the scent of damp earth and new-mown grass and the perfume of lilacs blooming in bouquets of bushes in the front yards of houses solid and protective, like her own. There was so much love inside Sara Elliott that often she did not know how to contain it.

Not prim, she thought. Not rigid or icy. Not mean.

Just waiting.

"I have plans to go out tonight," she said later, when they all were in the sunroom. She and Abby were watering the plants, Doug was carving a bar of soap into a horse, and Carrie was deep in her book. "Abby, if you want to have a friend over, it's fine."

"But—" Abby stared at her in dismay. "I

can't be home tonight. There's a party for the cast and crew, and I *have* to *be* there!"

"You never mentioned it," said Sara. "You told me you'd be home all weekend."

"I know, but then we all decided, this morning, it's sort of impromptu? Everybody wanted a party—it's for everybody, the cast and the crew, *everybody*—at Mr. Barker's? The director? The head of the drama club? You met him at conferences in February. I mean, it's at his *house,* it's not like we're going out *carousing.* Sara, *everybody's* going to be there. And I'm the *star;* I *have* to be there."

Sara nodded. Of course she had to be there. And Carrie had an early babysitting job next door. And on a Saturday night, there was no way to find anyone else. "What time will you be home tonight?" Sara asked Carrie, who had looked up from her book to listen.

"They said six-thirty to nine-thirty. Maybe earlier, but they weren't sure. But the kids will be fed, so I'll have dinner here first."

"Okay," said Sara, giving up. "You can go to your party, Abby; I'll stay home."

Mack, coming in, said, "You told me you had a date."

"A date?" Abby cried.

"A dinner engagement," Sara said.

"Abby's going out," Doug said to Mack, "and Carrie's babysitting and Sara doesn't trust me to be alone so she's staying home. Of course I *could* be by myself, all night, even, but everybody thinks I'm a baby."

"What the hell, Sara," Mack said. "You are fucking not going to—" He looked at Doug and Carrie, then at Abby. "Shit, I keep forgetting—" He struck his forehead with the side of his fist. "Christ, there's no way I—" He groaned. "Sorry, sis. Christ, I might have to stop talking. Shit," he muttered. "Listen, sis, you are not going to stay home . . . what the hell, *I'm* here! I'll stay with the gang . . . well, gang minus Abby and Carrie . . . and we'll have a terrific time. I can even cook, you know? Not anything like my big sister, but I can throw together a bunch of goodies and call it dinner. We'll have a great time . . . right, gang?"

Doug threw his arms around Sara. "Please let Mack take care of me, Sara. That's what big brothers are for. Please, please, please! I'll be very good!"

Sara smiled. "You are very good."

"And I'll be home by nine-thirty," Carrie

said gravely, "so I could help Mack. Please say yes, Sara. Please."

Sara wondered why she was reluctant. *Because I don't know what to think about him, and when I don't know, how can I decide anything?*

"I won't hurt them," Mack said quietly, and Sara suddenly felt ashamed.

"Fine," she said. "I'll be at Spiaggia—"

"Hurray, hurray!" Doug shouted, and threw his arms around Sara again.

Over the top of Doug's head, she met Mack's eyes, and for a moment it seemed as if, finally, there were indeed two adults in the house. "—and I'll have my cell phone if you need me. Carrie and Doug can tell you where everything is; there's enough veal stew left, and Carrie makes an excellent salad. Bread in the freezer, and—"

"Hey, we're cool," Mack said with a grin. "Cool and cooled off and coorious to see how well we coo together. Shouldn't you be getting ready?"

Carrie and Doug were giggling. Sara nodded, feeling stingy because they were excited and she was doubtful. "I'll be down in a little while," she said.

When she reappeared, they had heated

everything in the microwave and were sitting down to a perfectly set table in the breakfast room. Carrie had even lit candles, Sara noted. It looked very festive. Mack looked up and said, "Wow," and Carrie and Doug said, "Wow," in a disquieting echo. Then, in unison, and well rehearsed, they all sang, "Bye, Sara; have a good time."

She smiled. "A chorus in our house. Thank you. I won't be late." She heard the words come out almost as a warning, but it was too late to take them back. She hesitated, but there really was nothing more to say. She blew a kiss, and saw them sit down as she turned toward the back door. "Okay, let's all hold hands," Mack said.

"What for?" Doug asked. "How do we eat if we're holding hands?"

"Have to thank God for our food." Sara froze in the doorway to the backyard. *Thank God for our food?* Since when—?

"Thank you, God, for this good food," said Mack, "which was cooked by big sister Sara and will soon be devoured devotedly by three devoted people who thank her very much. Okay, now we eat."

Stunned, Sara walked through the backyard to the garage, and sat in the car for a moment before backing out. And all the way down Lake Shore Drive and into another garage in a skyscraper of offices and apartments, she tried to put together the pieces she knew of Mack Hayden, tried so intently that Reuben Lister, seeing her emerge from the elevator on the second floor, was struck by her absorption in her thoughts. "Is everything all right?" he asked.

"Yes." She smiled. "I must have looked as if I were trying to solve all the problems of the city."

"Of America. Maybe the world." He returned her smile, appreciating how attractive she was. Not beautiful, he thought, but her eyes were wonderful, dark blue flecked with hazel, widely spaced beneath level brows and slightly upturned at the corners, which gave her a mischievous look when she smiled. Her hair was a dark tawny gold, cut short to frame her face, and her cheekbones and the line of her jaw were decisive. She wore black, a simple dress that fit her closely (well built, he noted with a judgmental eye; slender but not exercised to scrawniness), with a V-neck, long sleeves, and a long slit skirt. Gold earrings and a gold necklace with some kind of ancient coin were her only adornments. No wedding ring; no rings of any kind. She looked about thirty or thirty-one, and carried herself with the poise of a woman who knew that everything attractive about her was enhanced by simplicity. Reuben knew almost nothing about her, but her gaze was direct, she seemed strong and confident, and he liked what he saw. "Can the problems be put aside long enough to eat?"

Sara laughed. "They won't even lurk in the background. Have you been waiting long?"

"Two minutes." They walked through the corridor to the restaurant and were led down a few steps to a table beside the wall of windows overlooking Michigan Avenue and the lake.

Sara raised her eyebrows. "How did you get this table with such short notice?"

"A lucky cancellation. I have good success with restaurants, maybe because my father owned a bakery. Though I fear that sounds like a non sequitur."

"It does." They smiled. "Where was the bakery?"

"Brooklyn. It still is. Actually, there are three: Brooklyn, Queens, and Manhattan, in the Village, all called Lister and Sons, based on my father's firm conviction that my brothers and I would take over when he retired. All of us worked there for years, my mother as well, but only my youngest brother stayed to run it. My father still pops in unannounced to make sure everything tastes the way it should, and to take dessert home to my mother."

"Your mother doesn't go with him for the tastings?"

"She doesn't go out. She had a stroke some years ago, and stays home and plays Scrabble with her friends and writes outraged letters to various people in the government, beginning with the president."

"How wonderful for her to be able to do that."

He heard the wistful note in her voice. "Your mother can't, or won't—?"

"She also had a stroke, but she's paralyzed on one side and can't speak. She's in a nursing home and friends do visit, but they're uncomfortable, trying to fill the silence, and when they do talk she isn't really interested in their monologues about lives she can't share."

"And your father?"

"He died when I was three."

"So you're alone now?"

She laughed. "Hardly. I have a brother and two sisters." She paused, and he saw her consider how much detail to provide. To give her privacy, he conferred with the sommelier on wine, then turned to contemplate Michigan Avenue below them, its hazy streetlights softened by the mist that lingered after the early-evening rain. The sidewalks and streets, still wet, reflected the lights and the bright mannequined windows with crowds streaming past, some still hidden beneath umbrellas, others lifting their faces to the newly washed air, strolling, talking animatedly on cell phones, window-shopping, signaling for taxis, or rushing to catch an oncoming bus. Far off, in the gathering darkness of Lake Michigan, the lights of a city cruise ship shone like a beacon.

Reuben turned back as Sara said, with a small smile, "We've got a peculiar history. I'm sure it isn't unique—a writer once said that every happy family is alike but every unhappy family—"

"—is unhappy in its own way," Reuben finished. "Tolstoy."

"Yes, but it doesn't really apply, because we're not unhappy. A few years after my father died, my mother remarried, and my brothers and sisters were born—"

"Brothers?"

She hesitated. "I did say I had one brother. In fact, I have two brothers and two sisters."

As she paused again, Reuben said, "And your stepfather?"

"He was an engineer, director of quality control for an electronics company for ten years, but when it was sold, he was let go. He looked for work for a while, about a year, I think, and then, one day, just . . . left. We never heard from him again."

"Your mother had no idea where he went?"

"He'd said he would write when he found a job. When he didn't, my mother hired a detective, who found nothing. Four months later, my brother Mack left. It was his seventeenth birthday, and one morning he . . . was gone." She laughed slightly. "I worry about Doug. He's ten. He doesn't have the best role models."

"You didn't find Mack, either?"

"We didn't have a chance to look for him; my mother had a stroke shortly after he left. I was in my second year of medical school; I came home, to take care of Doug and my sisters."

"How long ago was that?"

"Three and a half years."

"So Doug was six."

"Yes, almost seven. Carrie and Abby were ten and twelve."

"And you've brought them up. And taken a job."

"Yes."

"That takes courage."

She smiled ruefully. "Mostly being able to get by on very little sleep."

"I'd call it courage." He paused as the waiter displayed the wine bottle, then said, "Tell me about Doug and Carrie and Abby."

Sara described them, with anecdotes, snatches of conversation, bits of dialogue. "But you can't possibly be interested in all this."

"I'm interested in children. I'm a trustee of two community centers with after-school programs in New York. What do they think about their brother? Do they think he abandoned them? You never even heard from him?"

"Mack appeared on our doorstep."

The waiter poured their wine, deep ruby

against the white tablecloth and the black of Sara's dress. They touched their glasses. "To new friends."

Sara opened her menu. Reuben thought briefly about asking more questions about Mack, but rejected it. She would tell him what she wanted; he wasn't about to turn their dinner into an interrogation.

His thoughts stayed on her as they scanned their menus. She was so quiet some might call her diffident, but in fact, when she decided to talk—even about herself, which she probably seldom did (he was pretty sure of this)—she was open and honest. There was nothing fake about her, nothing evasive or stingy (he was certain of this), yet, clearly, she had built up defenses, keeping feelings and reactions under control. He wondered if she ever let herself get angry, and, if so, how long she would cling to it.

"Well, Ms. Elliott!"

Reuben and Sara looked up at the bright voice, too cheerful, too loud.

"Mrs. Corcoran," Sara said flatly.

"Isn't this amazing, that you're here? I mean, you gave us such a long list of restaurants, isn't it amazing we chose this very one on this very night? We don't have a window," she added peevishly, and Reuben could see her calculate the chances of success if she asked them to trade tables with her and her husband, and then drop the idea. At least she has some discretion, he thought. "Isn't it the darndest thing, though? Lew offered the maître d' a healthy little bonus to get a table right here by the window, instead of up there"—she waved vaguely toward the upper level of the restaurant—"and can you believe it? He turned it down! That was a shocker to Lew, let me tell you." She laughed gaily. "I teased him and teased him about it. 'Not everybody jumps,' I said. 'You're going to have to learn the local customs, now that we're living here.'" She looked pointedly at Reuben until Sara introduced them. There was a silence. "I did call you today," she said to Sara. "You must have a rotten secretary, not to give you your messages."

"I got your message. I'll be calling you Monday morning."

"But I needed you today! I called because *I needed you*!"

"I'm sorry. I don't work on weekends unless there's an emergency."

"This was an emergency! I lost the list of hair salons you gave me. What am I supposed to do to get a haircut? Pull a name out of the Yellow Pages?"

Reuben looked interested. "What did you do?"

Puzzled, she stared at him. After a moment, with relief, she said, "Reuben. That's right, isn't it? I was thinking maybe I forgot, and Lew gets so mad, he practically throws things—well, he does throw things—I forget so many names . . ." Her voice trailed off. "Asked the concierge in our hotel," she said. "She gave me a list of places."

"And you did get a haircut?"

Her hand went to her hair, patting softly in several places, as if to make sure it was all there. She nodded. "He was good. I forget his name. But"—she wheeled on Sara—"when I call somebody, I expect to be called back. I do not expect to be told I'm *being called on Monday.*"

"Mrs. Corcoran, I do not work on weekends." Sara's voice was pleasant, but Reuben noted the clenched line of her jaw, the slightly narrowed eyes, the white-knuckled fist she lowered to her lap, thus answering his question about her ability to get angry. "The mayor's office does not ask or expect me to do so. In fact, only two clients have ever called me on a weekend, and both had medical emergencies. My agreement with you is not open-ended."

"Listen, miss, *you work for me.* You *work for me!* You're a flunky for the city, my taxes pay your salary—"

"*My* taxes," Lew Corcoran growled, coming up behind her. "Shut your face, Pussy, you're making a fucking idiot of yourself." A swift flash of terror lit Pussy's eyes, so briefly that Reuben would have doubted seeing it, except for the tremor of her lower lip, caught now between her teeth, and at that moment he understood her attempts to dominate Sara, and, he assumed, all others who worked for a living. Those who live in fear, he thought—those who are dominated by others—are always the harshest to those they think weaker than they. Self-confident people are kind to others because they have no need to convince themselves, over and over, of their own worth. But poor Pussy Corcoran had to try to make others feel weak, at least weaker than she felt herself.

Now, her husband's hand resting heavily on her shoulder, she forced a wide smile and gazed with determined gaiety at the other diners as Corcoran nodded to Sara. "Sorry you had your dinner interrupted." He turned to Reuben. "We've met."

Reuben stood, putting himself between Sara and the Corcorans. "If you'll excuse us, we are trying to have dinner."

"New York? Something to do with money. Investments? Banking? What was it? I never forget a face."

Reuben shook his head slightly. (Like a grown-up, Sara thought, weary of the antics of a three-year-old.) "You're probably thinking of a meeting in Newark a few months ago on Carrano Village."

"Goddamn, you're right. You're the developer."

"Project developer."

"Right, right." He scowled, calculating possible opportunities he might be missing. "What're you doing in Chicago?"

Reuben moved forward, forcing the Corcorans a step backward, and then another. "I hope you both have a pleasant dinner. I would very much like to enjoy my own. Good night."

He stood still, a few inches taller than Corcoran, waiting. Corcoran's face was flushed, his eyebrows drawn together in a dark slash. "I'll call you," he said. "Always open to new projects." He put his hand beneath Pussy's elbow and turned her with him.

"Well, it *is* time to eat, isn't it?" she chirped. "You must be starving, Lew, I know I'm so hungry I could—"

He dragged her away. Sara watched her stumble on the steps.

"I'm sorry," she said to Reuben as he took his chair.

"I should apologize to you. I was rude to your client."

"And he won't call me again, and neither will she, for which I am deeply grateful."

They laughed. "You have a beautiful smile," Reuben said.

The waiter came to their table from the discreet distance at which he had waited for the unpleasantness to pass, and refilled their wineglasses. Sara's hand, relaxed now, came up from her lap. "It *is* time to eat, isn't it?" she mimicked mischievously, and Reuben laughed again, admiring her because indeed she did not cling to anger.

He sat back, more at ease, it seemed to him, than he'd been in months. Perhaps years. This pleasant, softly lit room, the intriguing woman opposite him, were an immeasurable distance from Ardis and her distorted world, the mockery she made of marriage, the greater mockery of all attempts to reach a civilized ending to theirs.

When they had ordered, Sara said curiously, "Do you work with him?"

"No, good Lord, no. His company invests in real estate and insurance, but the rumors are that most of his dealings aren't written about in the business pages until someone is indicted. He may be an investor in Carrano; I doubt it. I think he was just sniffing it out."

"What is Carrano?"

"A planned village in New Jersey, near Princeton. Fifteen hundred houses around a commercial core, an elementary school— the high school is in Princeton—public library, recreation center, small theater."

"And Carrano—?"

"Isaiah Carrano. A most wonderful man, a dreamer who's determined to provide clean, safe, beautiful towns all over the country for low-income families. He has no children of his own, no relatives left, he's wealthy and optimistic, and he wants to do good for children. His rule for Carrano Village is that only families with children, or about to have children, can buy there."

"Isn't that discrimination? Age, if nothing else?"

"We've discussed it. Isaiah is considering opening it up, with a quota for childless couples. Also probably illegal."

Sara smiled and asked about the library and recreation center. The waiter brought soup spoons and poured another inch of wine into their glasses. Around them, the hum of conversation was punctuated with the light clink of silver and crystal; waiters glided from table to table along the gentle curve of the room beneath chandeliers that seemed to sway slightly as diners left and others arrived; occasionally laughter rose, and drifted past. Sara and Reuben's dinners arrived, the first course and then the second and third, and another bottle of wine, and the hours passed, and their talk flowed from one topic to another, one idea to the next, a word or phrase changing the directions they explored without flagging, without a break.

They talked about their work; about books, theater, and music; about New York and Chicago. Sara did not ask what Reuben had left behind in New York, and he did not bring it up. He did not ask if she was involved with anyone, and she did not volunteer it. But they did not run out of talk, and when they left the table, Sara asked, "May I drive you to your hotel?"

They smiled together at the absurdity of it: his hotel was three blocks away. But three miles wouldn't be enough, Reuben thought. Three hundred. More. "I'd like that; thank you."

Sara glanced at her watch as they rode the elevator down to the garage. "One o'clock," she exclaimed in dismay. "I had no idea. I told them I wouldn't be late."

"But isn't your brother with them?"

She nodded slowly.

"But you still wanted to be home early."

"I thought . . . I wasn't sure I should leave them for a long time."

"You said he was good with the younger ones."

"Yes, they're excited about him, happy to be with him. I don't want to be the Wicked Witch of the West, spoiling the reunion they're all having, such a happy one . . ."

"But you yourself aren't happy?"

"Not . . . yet. I don't know him or understand him. I'd like to, but I really don't know anything about him. He was a spoiled kid when he ran away, always angry and ready to strike out—at me, because I was older, at the others because they were there, crowding his turf. I'm sure he could have changed in these years—he's told us very little of where he's been, what he's been doing, and I don't even know how much to believe of what he does say—but do people ever really change, fundamentally?" She stopped. "This is not right. I apologize. You don't know Mack"—*and you barely know me*—"I shouldn't force you to listen to anything about him."

"He seems to be taking up a large part of your thoughts."

She felt a swift moment of resentment. Her thoughts were her own; where she focused them, and for how long, was her business. Why did he probe so much? Most men were only interested in themselves.

"And who takes up a large part of your thoughts?" she asked abruptly.

He was surprised. He watched the cashier tear the charge slip from the printer, and they were silent as Sara signed it and they walked from the vestibule to the garage. The attendant drove up with her car, she tipped him, and it was not until she drove out of the garage onto Oak Street that Reuben said, "Turmoil and complications—probably not unique, but new to me—which I'll tell you about sometime, if you'd like me to. They don't involve a family; only one other person, and shameful behavior on my part that I don't like to dwell on, and a situation from which I'm trying to extricate myself with the least possible damage, which is why I don't talk about the whole thing very much. It does take up a large chunk of my thoughts. The rest of the time I focus on Carrano Village, and, lately, the possibility of a similar village west of Chicago."

Sara turned the corner. "And you," he added. "Thank you for sharing dinner on such short notice; I've enjoyed it. Would you have dinner with me tomorrow night?"

"Didn't you say you're returning to New York tomorrow?"

"Sunday," he said, realizing it. "Yes. But I could put it off until Monday morning."

She smiled. "I should be with my family tomorrow night." She brought the car to a stop at his hotel. "Thank you for tonight; I've had a wonderful time."

The doorman was holding the car door. Reuben did not move. "As did I. Everything about it."

Sara's smile turned mischievous again. "Even the Corcorans?"

"Even the Corcorans. They provided a minor villain we could dislike together. I'll call you from New York, if I may."

"I'd like that."

"Tomorrow night. Unless you're busy with your family."

"I can manage a telephone call."

It was a short drive from the hotel to Fremont Street, and Sara would have liked to drive slowly, to extend it, to give her thoughts a chance to settle down. But she also was anxious to get home. At least they'll all be asleep, she thought, turning the corner. The house will be quiet.

But the downstairs windows were blazing, and before she could take out her key, Mack had opened the front door for her.

"Welcome, welcome to my modest home," he said with a grin. "Come in and rest your weary feet."

After a tiny pause, Sara laughed. "Thank you, sir, I'll do just that." She heard him lock the front door as she went into the library. It was perfectly neat. Whatever games and books had been taken out had been put away, whatever snacks had littered the coffee table had been cleaned up. The fire was expertly set and burning softly, a bottle of cognac and two glasses were set out on the small bar Sara's father had built in the corner of the paneled room.

"Lovely," Sara murmured. Mack went to pour the cognac. "Not for me, thanks. I've had quite enough to drink for one evening." He hesitated. "But don't let that stop you from pouring your own."

"Thanks." He joined her on the couch. "I didn't want to drink with the kids around, so I waited."

Sara's eyebrows rose. "You drank most of a bottle of wine at dinner last night."

"Ah, well, caught out. So I did. And I must confess I did tonight, too. The whole bottle, in fact. You have an admirable wine cellar, sis. I congratulate you; a woman of many talents."

"You drank a whole bottle of wine?"

"Well, Abby had a couple of glasses."

Sara sat straighter. "She's fifteen, Mack. She doesn't drink."

"She does but she doesn't tell you about it. What the hell, sis, it was only two little glasses, and it was *wine,* not gin or vodka or something really and truly sinister like marijuana. Merry meritorious marijuana," he hummed. "Anyway, where better to learn to

handle alcohol than at home with an innocent glass of wine *when you're fifteen and all
your friends are doing it*? Hmmm? Also"—he
pointed a playfully accusing finger—"you do
give her wine."

"I do. Half a glass. Because of course her
friends drink, and I assumed she's tried
most everything they do. She knows half a
glass, *from me,* is what she can drink at this
age. I don't want you giving her wine, or anything else."

"Why not? Why ever not, he asks plain-
tively, knowing the answer, which is that his
sis does not trust him. His very own sis does
not trust him! I ask you, gentle audience, is
that fair? I'm her loving bro and she does not
cut me one teeny little bit of slack. Slack off,
sis. Trust me. I promise you I want only the
best for these kids. For me, of course, I don't
deny that, but also for the kids. Listen, I'm
very happy because we had a great time together, and we were all happy, and that's
what I want. For you, too. Did you have a
good time tonight?"

Sara contemplated him, his bright shining
grin and tousled blond hair, the thin face and
hollowed cheeks that made him look like a
youthful refugee, the intense gaze that

made him look like a supplicant. She remembered Doug saying she made him feel
little. Mack made her feel dull. Slow, unresponsive, unexciting. And stingy. *The Wicked
Witch of the West.*

But Reuben hadn't thought she was dull
or unresponsive. It depends on the context,
she thought, and the context with Mack just
isn't—

"But obviously you had a great time," he
declared, "because you're more gorgeous
than when you left and that means somebody's made you very happy. Right? I'm always right about things like that. Things like
happiness and good times and, oh yes, love."

"Are you?" Sara moved to the wing chair
in the corner, and adjusted the reading lamp
so it did not fall on her face. "What do you
know about love?"

"Well, you know."

"No, I don't. I don't see a smiling bride in
the picture; I assume you didn't get married
in the time you were gone."

"Christ, no. Why would I do that? Somebody clinging, hanging on, *needing.* Need-
fully, needlingly, needing. Can't see me there
at all. Well, maybe someday," he amended.
"Right now, I'm too young." He refilled his co-

gnac. "See, sis, I have a lot to do. Big stuff. My destiny is big. So I'm getting ready for it. First of all, I settle in here, get my directions straight, establish a base. You know? You can't go anywhere until you have a place to come back to, where the door is open and people are waiting . . . with smiles. I learned that." His wistful voice and the childish grandeur of his inchoate dreams made him seem vulnerable, and Sara warmed to him.

"We'll help you," she said. "We're glad you're here. But you need to go to school, Mack; you don't have an education or a profession; you don't really know anything—"

"I *don't know anything*? What the hell do you think I've been doing for three-plus years?" He drained his glass, his face as tight as it had been open. "I've been fucking *earning my living,* that's what, and I could fucking well do it tomorrow if I didn't have to—" He stopped abruptly and took a long breath. The muscles in his neck relaxed, his shoulders dropped. He gave a wide smile. "Too much time on the road, too much time alone; I need some civilizing, is what I need." He crossed the room and kissed Sara on the top of her head. "The thing is, you sure know how to push my buttons. I really—"

"If you didn't have to . . . what?"

"—really didn't mean to yell at you. *Mea culpa. Mea* very *culpa. Mea* exceedingly abjectly *culpa.* Here I am, all I want to do is make a good impression and I keep saying stupid things." He drained his glass. "Hey, you must be totally exhausted. I know I am. Your kids wear a guy out. Let's talk some more tomorrow."

"My kids?"

"Oh, shit, you know what I meant. *The* kids. The offspring. The siblings. Those little people who live here with us. Jesus, sis, lighten up. I'm trying to be nice."

"If you didn't have to . . . what?"

"Get settled before I can get started. I thought I said that. Hey, I am really and truly zonked; can't keep my eyes open. I don't know how you stay up so late." He put down his glass. "I'm for bed. Don't forget to turn out the lights when you come up."

"What?"

"It was a *joke.* Christ, can't say anything around here. *Mea* even more than last time *culpa.* Am I in the doghouse?"

"You're not at the right hand of God." She stood up. "Listen carefully, Mack. I'll tell you where you are. You are in my house, with my family, and you're here as long as I tolerate you. I don't know what you're after, other than free meals and a bed and a place to keep dry, but you're not going to tell me how to run this house, or how to take care of my brother and sisters, or how to think about you. No one tells me those things: I am in charge around here, and I'm not about to let an outsider elbow his way in and take over. I'm here because I have to be. I had a life, a plan for a life, that got cut off in the middle and I have to live with that, but I don't have to live with you. If you think you can move in and talk as you want, and smoke pot in your room, and contradict the ways I'm trying to bring up these three children, you'd better leave now. I am indeed going to bed and if you're still here in the morning it will be because you've decided to live by my rules and my decisions, not your self-centered whims. Good night."

He was watching her, mouth tight. And then, as she turned to go, his bright smile switched on and he leaped toward her. "Thank you, thank you! God, I needed that. You're wonderful, sis, not only gorgeous but smart. And wise! You are truly a wise woman! I get fucking carried away, I admit it,

I go too far, it's always been a problem with me and I hate myself for it—hate, hate, hate—and I always swear I'll behave better next time, but then I just lose it, lose control and let go and say things that offend people or hurt them . . . God, I can't tell you how I hate it when I do that—and to you of all people!—but you are so right, there's no way I could tell you how to run this house—what do I know about running a house?—or bring up the kids—shit, you've done such a great job with them, how could I even come close? But I'll try, sis, I promise. Just don't call me an outsider again, please don't do that. I'll help, I'll be good, I'll do whatever you say, let me stay, please don't make me leave, let me stay, I promise I'll be the best damned brother . . . well, not better than Doug, who could be better than Doug? But as good as Doug, and I can help you in ways he can't, drive, you know, and—"

"Earn a living?"

"Yes! Absolutely! Let me get on my feet and I swear I will ease your burden, do what I can, *all* I can, Sara, please please let me stay, I need you, all of you. And I love you!"

"You can stay as long as you follow the rules," Sara said shortly. She turned again to leave the library. Behind her, she heard, "Are you going out again tomorrow night?"

"No," she said over her shoulder. "Please bank the fire. And don't forget to turn out the lights." She walked toward the stairs and paused there. She heard the glass fireplace doors opening, and Mack striking a log with the poker. He was humming, too softly for her to make out the tune. The poker struck another log; then repeatedly struck the coals to break them up and push them to the sides. The glass doors were pushed into place and latched, the reading lamp above the wing-backed chair was clicked off.

Sara climbed the stairs. *Are you going out again tomorrow night?*

What an odd question, she thought.

THREE

We practically never see him," Doug complained. He pushed his spoon around his cereal bowl. "He's asleep when we leave in the morning, and he's gone right after dinner. Where does he go all the time? It's like he doesn't like us anymore."

"Of course he likes us," Carrie said. "He said he did. He said he loved us. He has people to see, that's all. He's only been here three weeks; maybe he's looking for a job."

"Like Dad?" Doug said, suddenly anxious. "But then he'd be gone forever, and he isn't; he sleeps here and eats dinner—"

"Gobbles it."

"Right, and then he's outta here. So he isn't really *gone,* like Dad, or . . . like he was, too, before he came back. He could do that again, you know. Just go away. Anyway, what difference does it make if we never see him?"

Carrie put her arm around him. "He was with us all day Sunday, and he brought a movie home for all of us to watch, and that was fun, wasn't it? We had a good time. He really does like us, Doug. Don't worry about it."

"Worry about what?" Sara asked, coming from her office upstairs.

"Mack," Doug said mournfully. "It's like he hardly lives here anymore."

"I told Doug he's probably looking for a job," said Carrie.

"Wouldn't that be a fine thing." Sara pulled on her suit jacket. "I have to go. You have everything for school?"

"We're fine," Carrie said. "I'm taking my story—the one about the happiest dog in the world? That I'm going to read in class?—and I fixed cereal for Abby."

"She'll be right down; she's finishing some elaborate bit of makeup. And I loved that story; your friends will, too. Good-bye, my loves, I'll see you tonight. Have a good day in school." She kissed them and went out, through the backyard to the garage.

"I don't think she likes Mack so much," said Doug when they were alone.

"Sure she does. She'd just like him better if he got a job."

They heard the front doorbell, and then impatient knocking.

"I'll get it!" Abby called, running down the stairs. "Yes?" she said to the woman standing there. She was short and round, and wore a fur coat. Standing nearby, Carrie whispered to Doug, "She must be hot; it's almost summer."

"I have to see Sara," the woman said. "Sara Elliott?"

"She's not here, I'm sorry, but—"

"Where is she? I have to see her. Why is she always so hard to find?"

"She's not hard to find," Abby said coldly. "She's on her way to work. If you want, I can give you—"

"This early? I don't believe it. She's hiding in there; she doesn't want to see me. She never wants to see me. She doesn't return my calls, either. I demand to see her! I'm a client. Tell her Pussy Corcoran has an emergency."

"She's not here," Abby snapped. "She doesn't hide from people, what are you talking about? Corcoran? Oh."

"What?"

"I think Sara mentioned your name the other day. I can give you her cell-phone number, if you'd like."

"Well, obviously. What have you been waiting for? God, all these incompetent people I have to deal with."

Doug and Carrie watched Abby debate slamming the door in Pussy Corcoran's face. Instead, in a level voice, she recited the number.

"Honey, can you write it down?" Pussy asked wheedlingly. "I guess I shouted, didn't I? If Lew heard me, he'd get so mad he'd throw things. At me," she added with a high trill of laughter. "Right at me." She squeezed her eyes briefly. "Write it down?"

Abby took a pad of paper from the hall table and wrote the number. "She won't be home all day." There was a small note of warning in her voice. *Don't come back.* She closed the door. "Never in a million years could I do Sara's job," she said to Carrie and Doug. "She has to be a saint. She ought to be a doctor, the way she wanted."

"Then she could get Pussy Corcoran when she's sick and even meaner," Carrie said wisely.

"Pussy Corcoran?" asked Mack, coming downstairs. "She was here? I mean, was that her screaming? Shit, she woke me up. Probably woke up the whole neighborhood."

"The neighborhood is awake," Abby said. "You're the only one who sleeps late around here."

"Hey!" Mack put his hands up in self-defense. "What did I do?"

"You're never here anymore," said Doug.

"Sorry, guys, I've busily been busy at busyness. Did you think I was ignoring you?"

"Yes," Doug said boldly.

"Oh, fuck it, Doug, you know I wouldn't do that. I'd much rather stay home with you, but I've had business. Let's have breakfast, now that that bitch woke me up."

"You shouldn't talk that way," Abby said uncomfortably. "Sara doesn't like it, and it's not really nice."

"Nice?" Mack demanded. "*Nice?* What the fuck does that mean?"

Abby shrank into herself. "The way nice people talk. People who aren't . . . ignorant and crude."

"Is that what our sweet sis says?"

"Yes," Carrie said loudly. "She made us feel awful, but it sounded right. She's usually right," she added mournfully.

"There's lots of other words," Doug said. "Like, jillions."

"As good as *shit*?" Mack asked. "Really and truly as good?" He grinned at them as the noise of the coffee grinder filled the kitchen, then, as he emptied the grounds into the coffeemaker and poured in water, he said, "Well, so what are they?" The others frowned, thinking. "Jillions," Mack snorted.

"Uncouth," Abby said. "And *gross* . . . and . . . uh . . . *mean,* and . . . uh . . . *coarse*—" She stopped. "I can't remember!" she wailed. "There were so many, a whole string of them, and they sounded really good—oh, *hateful,* that's another one—but I can't remember all of them, if Sara was here she'd rattle them off, they're all in her head."

"*Shit* is a perfectly good word," said Mack firmly. "A wordy, wordworth wordwonderful word, colorful and vocabulary expanding. And it *communicates.* Right? What else do we want from words? *Shit* communicates. Right?"

Abby nodded. "Right, I know, but—"

"And I'll bet everybody uses it at your school, right?"

"Yes, but Sara says that just shows that they don't have creative vocabularies."

"*Shit* is *part* of their vocabulary. They've *enriched* their vocabulary. I think our sis, sweet as she is, is a bit of a prig when it comes to language. Slightly over-the-top rigid. Right?"

Abby frowned in confusion. "That's not a nice thing to say."

Mack put bread in the toaster. "Another not-nice thing? It isn't a criticism, sweetheart, just a statement of fact. She's as nice as can be, nobody knows that better than me, it's just the saddest thing that she's so uptight. She can't let go and enjoy life with all its diversity and variety and highs and lows, the way the four of us can. She's not like us, right?"

Doug was watching Mack with fascination. "Sara runs the house," he said. "We don't . . . I mean—" He stopped, unable to express an idea as huge as challenging a king.

"I think she's a lot like me," Abby said. "Or I'm like her."

"We *love* her," Carrie cried.

Mack struck his forehead. "Stuck my foot

in it again. Shit, guys, I never meant we don't love her. She can be totally absolutely different from us and we can still love her. We do love her. She's terrific. The very best—"

"And it's not nice to talk about her when she isn't here," Abby said.

"And can't defend herself," said Carrie.

"Hey, hey, hey, stop ganging up on your poor defenseless bro! I'll shut up, not a peep will you get from me. Sara's great. She's gorgeous and she's smart, a lot smarter than me—more gorgeous, too, I must admit—" Carrie giggled and he grinned at her. "She's the very best sis anybody could ask for, and I daringly dare any daredevil to say anything different."

"And she's not different from us," said Abby.

"Well, she seems different to me, sweetie; the four of us seem a lot more together, more—but, hey, listen, that's enough of that; you want to hear about the African wedding geese I ate?"

Doug looked up. "What?"

"Well, the thing is, some people buy African wedding geese for watchdogs— they're huge, you know, waist-high, about forty pounds, fast on their webbed feet, pure white—and they honk loud enough to wake a whole fucking army, and, even better, they eat grass. Acres of it. No lawn mower needed. They're terrific; you'd love 'em."

"But . . . you *ate* one?" Doug asked.

"Well, part of one. A bunch of us were really hungry, no money, no place to sleep, you know, one of those bad weeks, or maybe months, I don't remember, so we got together with the neighbors who were sick of the honking and poached a couple for Christmas dinner. A tasty taste of tastefully carved almost-turkey."

"I don't believe it," Abby said flatly. "If they're that fast, you couldn't catch them."

"I don't believe it, either," Carrie declared.

Mack covered his face with his hands. "You're mad at me for criticizing Sara. I wasn't, you know, I was just explaining that everybody in the world is different—good thing, too, or we'd be bored to death—and that Sara—" He peered out between two fingers, and sighed. "Can't even say her name. Okay, my sweets, not another word. I deeply, humbly, abjectly, and groveling grovelingly apologize." Holding out his hands, he grinned at Abby. "Forgiven? What I really want is to hear about your play. Tell me all about it. I can't wait to see it."

"I'm going to see it before everybody else," said Doug, his face brightening with the change in subject. "They invited the fifth grade to come tonight to the dress rehearsal."

"Well, then, I'm coming, too," Mack declared. "I like to get in on things early."

"You can't," Abby said. "Only the fifth grade. We open on Saturday night, and you can come then. That's when Sara and Carrie are coming."

"Shit, I'm busy Saturday night." He saw Carrie and Abby scowl at him. "Christ, you're as uptight as your sis. Oops, sorry. But, no shit, you guys really ought to loosen up; there's room for everything if you make space for it and welcome it welcomingly with welcomeness and not have a narrow mind like . . . some people."

"We have to go," Abby said to Carrie and Doug. "Oliver's mother will be here in a minute."

"Oliver's mother?" Mack asked.

"Mrs. Nevins. They live down the street."

"Oliver Nevins. He's still your friend?" Mack asked Doug.

"Right," Doug said defensively. "We're friends."

"Well, that's terrific. Good for you; it's great the two of you are friends. Abby, can't I come tonight? I really am busy Saturday night."

She shook her head. "Nobody but the fifth grade."

Doug was staring at Mack. "You didn't used to like him. You made fun of him."

"Oliver? I always liked him."

"No, you used to say they were all losers, his whole family."

"Did I? Well, I must have been crazy. After all, if you like him, he must be terrific, 'cause *you're* terrific."

Doug's face brightened. "Really? Thanks. I mean . . . thanks a lot."

The telephone rang and Abby picked it up. "Abby," Sara said, "something's come up and I have to work late tonight; I tried to change it, but I can't. Will you take Carrie and Doug with you to rehearsal? I can't think of any- thing else; you can all go together, and I'll be back in time to pick you up."

"I can't, Sara! You can't work tonight! I have to be there an hour early, and what will they do all that time . . . and Carrie can't go, eighth grade wasn't invited."

"I'll call your teacher; he'll arrange it.

They'll take books and read for an hour, or Doug will make a carving, or both or neither . . . They'll figure it out, they're not babies. Please, Abby, I don't want them coming home this afternoon to an empty house and Doug has to get to the play somehow, and then Carrie would be alone until ten o'clock or whenever I can get home."

"Mack will be here."

There was a silence. "Abby, please do this for me."

"But Mack—"

"We don't know where Mack will be. Please, Abby."

"Problems, problems," said Mack. "Let me talk to her." He took the telephone. "Sis, listen, whatever it is, I'll take care of it. What do you want me to do?"

"Nothing. It's under control."

"Doesn't sound like it. Come on, you need help and I can give it. I'll take Carrie and Doug to the play if you make it legit with whatever muckety-muck is in charge. It's not a big deal, you know. In fact, I was just telling Abby I really want to go tonight." He waited, and when Sara was silent, he said, "Okay, it's all set. I'll make dinner for us, and then we're off. A perfect solution; you don't have to worry about a thing."

"Dinner's made," Sara said after a moment. "Baked chicken and wild rice in a casserole in the refrigerator, and roasted vegetables in the dish next to it. Abby can finish baking them."

"We'll figure it out. Have a good—"

Abby grabbed the phone. "Sara, Mrs. Nevins is here, we'll see you later. Love you."

Sara hung up the telephone and stared through the window at the gray street. Far above the solid row of office buildings, the sun shone brilliantly in a clear blue sky streaked with silver where planes caught the light. But in an office on the second floor of City Hall on LaSalle Street, it was almost always gray. A great way to start a day, she grumbled silently, in a bad mood before her work had really begun.

"Pussy Corcoran called," Donna Soldana said, coming in with a sheaf of papers. "She said she tried your cell phone."

"I forgot to turn it on. Please call and tell her I'm out for the day. And the evening, too, as it happens. And forever, but I don't suppose telling her that would stop her from calling." She stared at Donna. "Is that a new bruise?"

"No, it's . . . well, it is. I banged my head on the kitchen counter."

"And bruised your neck?"

Donna was silent.

"How did he find where you're living?"

"Mother told him," Donna said after a long hesitation. "I might have to find another place."

"Yes, you will. Here—" She scribbled a number and handed it to Donna. "This is Nancy's cell phone; call her now, before she gets to the office. She has a lot of small apartment rental listings; she'll find you a place faster than anyone I know. And I'll help you move."

"No, Sara, you won't. I have friends who can help me. Thank you for this; you're wonderful. I don't know what I'd do without—" She choked back tears. "Is there anything else you need me for right now?"

"No, go ahead; call Nancy. Tell her I said it's an emergency."

So now she had to worry about Donna, on top of everything else. The longest, heaviest days were the ones that began with a bad mood. Even here, in her own office, the one place where she knew she was in control, she could feel too much was crowding in. But not that much, she thought. She still was in charge of her day, of the way the hours unfolded, of how she spent her time.

Everything was entirely manageable. A client needed a conference room that night, set up for fifty people, with PowerPoint, caterer and staff, and Sara there to supervise. She had done it dozens of times; she could handle it. The city of Chicago had no budget for a full-time assistant for her; she could handle that, too. Abby was starring in a play, and Doug and Carrie were really too young to be alone for long chunks of time (or she was unwilling to let them be alone for long chunks of time, though she knew other parents did . . . and she wasn't a parent, but what difference did that make at a time like this?), and she could handle that, too; she always did, somehow.

And Mack? Could she handle him? She had no idea what that meant. But if things went badly, it would be his fault. Blame Mack, she thought, for anything I can't handle.

Especially for making me feel uneasy in a dozen different ways.

When he could have been a lifesaver.

Her private line rang. Someone's sick, she thought, and snatched it up.

"Good morning," Reuben Lister said. "How are you?"

"Fine," said Sara. She made her voice lighter. "Fine, thank you."

She turned her chair and sat back, facing the windows. LaSalle Street suddenly had brightened considerably. He called two or three times a week, and each time they talked generally and casually, as if they had decided together that a telephone call is a poor way for two people to share or bare confidences. Once he had asked her to describe her office—"so I can picture you when I talk to you"—and she had asked him to do the same. Now she asked him, "Where are you? Which office?"

"At home, looking at clouds and rain, and if I look straight down on Sheridan Square I can see a river of black umbrellas. Wouldn't you think people would buy the brightest colors to fight back on dreary days?"

Sara pictured him at his steel desk, gazing through the broad windows of the corner office, pushing up his horn-rimmed glasses as they slid down his nose, his lean body absolutely still in his desk chair, while his thin, restless fingers betrayed the fact that, though for the moment quiet and thoughtful, in a moment he would leap into action. She smiled as he asked, "What color did you choose for your umbrella?"

"Red, to match my raincoat. And yours?"

"Brown. Not colorful enough. I'll buy another one today. I might need it in Chicago."

Sara felt her heart lurch. "Are you coming to Chicago?"

"On Sunday, for a month or more."

A month, she thought. A month or more. But what she said was, "Your furniture isn't being delivered until the end of next week."

"I'll be at the Whitehall until then. Will you have dinner with me Sunday night?"

"Yes."

"My plane should get in at five-thirty. Would you choose a restaurant? Just let me know where to meet you. Some place interesting. Elegance is not a requirement."

Smiling, Sara jotted down the names of a few restaurants. "Japanese? Korean? Filipino? Mexican? Thai? Vietnamese?"

He laughed. "All of the above. Sequentially. This is going to be a long process."

They discussed restaurants and menus with the serious attention of people who understand good food. "Jin Ju, then," Sara said at last, when they had settled on Korean food. "It's some distance from your hotel; I can pick you up."

"Thank you. Seven-thirty, if that's all right, in case my plane is late."

Reuben put down the telephone, then remembered that he had meant to ask about leasing a car. He reached for the redial button, then stopped. What he really wanted was to hear her voice again. He shook his head. Like a teenager, he thought, and instead called his regular leasing company, to have them arrange a car in Chicago on Monday morning.

"Hi," said Ardis, emerging from the upstairs bedroom, rubbing her eyes. "Thanks for letting me sleep; I was really wiped."

She was small and thin: her hair hung limply in pale blond curls, her eyes were pale blue, her face was pale and drawn, deeply scored in lines of dissatisfaction from the sides of her nose to the corners of her mouth. When they had met, twenty-two years earlier, her face had been bright with promise and high color and a smile that Reuben saw as mysterious and enticing, even as his friends called it cunning. She was seventeen, Reuben a year older; she was doll-like and fragile, with a porcelain beauty that caused others to stare when she entered a room. Reuben had stared, and fallen in love.

"What time did I get to bed?" she asked, dropping into a leather chair near his desk. "Must have been the crack of dawn; I still hardly feel like I got enough sleep. What time is it?"

"You passed out at nine-thirty. It's now eight-thirty in the morning."

"Nine-thirty? Not two or three in the morning? God, I really was wiped. Passed out? You mean nodded off. Wiped out."

Reuben opened a folder and began to read.

"I'm talking to you."

"More to yourself, I think."

"To you! To you! I haven't seen you in six months and I'm talking to you! I love talking to you, Ben, you never lie to me. Well, you did once; you told me you loved me."

He looked up, and after a moment said, almost in wonder, "I did love you. I couldn't think of anything but you. That was why I married you."

"You married me because I got knocked up."

"I married you because I loved you and wanted to take care of you. There was a vulnerability about you . . ." He made a gesture of despair. "You couldn't take the chance of waiting, to find out, but I would have married you if you weren't pregnant. You could have saved yourself the trouble of an abortion."

"That's a lie." Her voice rose thinly. "I got pregnant because you started talking *all the time* about that girl you did blueprints with in that architecture class."

"I was trying to tell you about my work. I was trying to believe that you could be interested in what I cared about. I was trying to make you part of my life."

She was not listening. "And when a man starts saying this girl's name every other word it always means the same thing: she was getting her claws in you and I'd be out on my ass and nobody to give a damn about me." She tucked her legs beneath her and hunched over, fetuslike. "No mama, no papa," she crooned. "No brothers, no sisters, no cousins, no friends. Nobody but my Ben, my Benny, my Reubenny who was going to

be famous and rich—everybody said so—
and I was damned if anybody else was going to get her hands on that. Or on you."

Reuben's mouth tightened in disgust, and
he picked up the folder, trying to concentrate
on it while wondering yet again, still and always, why he wasted time responding to
her. And, as always, he came up with the
same reasons: at one time he had pitied her,
he'd been flattered by the fierceness of her
desire for him, he'd ached for her vulnerability in a world she found terrifying, and he
had loved her so overwhelmingly that none
of his friends' caustic comments and warn-
ings could pierce the armor of his determination.

No one had coerced him; he had been the
responsible adult. What he had not realized
in the miasma of his besottedness was that
he had taken on Ardis Fitch not as a wife,
but as a project, saving her from the streets
of New York and the slums of New Haven,
where she had virtually raised herself in the
two-room apartment of an alcoholic mother
and three brothers dealing drugs and fighting rearguard actions against a larger,
better-armed gang. Her father was in prison
for knifing a friend forty times in a street

brawl ("What's left to do to your enemies?" the prosecutor had sneered in court).

They had been married for twenty-two years. For twenty-one years, Reuben had known that, like her mother, she was an alcoholic. She had aborted their first child as soon as they were married, and two more in the five years after that. When he was twenty-eight years old, he moved out, the same day they quarreled over her drinking and she flung at him the story of the third abortion. He gave her the town house on Tenth Street and a monthly income, and moved into a loft apartment half a mile away, close enough to respond when her calls became desperate.

But the harshness in him that he usually managed to keep submerged had come to the surface. Inexorably, it seemed, he had moved from being her protective savior—endlessly sympathetic, encouraging, ritually armored against diatribes and tantrums—to annoyance and frustration, then to disgust and an anger deep enough to match hers, and finally to cruel indifference.

Yet, somehow, he still felt responsible. He still, though far less than before, pitied her. She had lost control of her life and, largely, of herself. Reuben, confident of his own steely control, watched Ardis flail about, saw the fear in her eyes, and could not refuse to try to rescue her, before she drowned. "You should have some breakfast," he said, closing the folder. "There are scones in the warming oven and coffee in the thermos. I'll make eggs if you'd like."

"God, no." She fingered the sash of his robe, wrapped almost twice around her emaciated form. "I suppose you'll make me go home today."

"You can stay for a couple of days."

"I could stay for good."

"No."

"I could, Ben. I'm fine now; I'd be fine for you. You need a wife—God, this place echoes when you walk through it—couldn't you get some carpets? If I lived here I'd put thick carpeting all over the place, fuzzy and soft on your bare feet."

"What a shame you'll never get to do that."

She winced. Restless, she looked about her, at the space he had created, as different as possible from the town house where she still lived. There he had chosen antiques and rare Oriental rugs; here he had white walls, bare wood floors with a few brightly colored

Indian and Turkish rugs, bare windows, couches and armchairs that were deep and comfortable but unadorned, belonging to no period or place but here and now. A long gallery was hung with contemporary paintings and lithographs; at the far end he had hung a dartboard.

"But I really could," Ardis said at last, having decided, Reuben thought, that he had to be unhappy in such stark surroundings. "I'm already your wife, so it would be easy. We'd be *happy,* Ben. Six months in that weird place drying out . . . I'm fine, there's nothing to worry about, I'm fine."

"You were drinking before you got here last night. You drank in the bathroom instead of eating dinner. Where was the bottle? In your purse, your coat pocket, your makeup kit . . . maybe all of them. I should have searched you before letting you in."

"This isn't an airport," she snapped, "and I'm not walking through any fucking security gate to get in. Unless"—she giggled—"you want to pat me down." In the silence, she took a long shuddering breath. "I didn't mean that. I mean, it was a joke. All of it. Ben, please, if I promise not to drink anymore, can I stay awhile? Not forever, just . . . for a while."

"Two days, then you go home. I'll hire someone—"

"This *is* home!"

"—to come to your house every day and cook and clean and do your shopping; you should have let me do that long ago."

"I don't want 'someone'! I want my husband! I want somebody in my bed when I wake up in the morning! I want to go places at night and have a good time!"

"You go out every night."

"I want to go with you! You're good-looking, Ben; people envy me for being with you. And I'm not as—" She stopped.

"Not as beautiful as you once were," he said bluntly. "Not beautiful at all. Not even close." He picked up his briefcase, slipped the folder inside, and crossed the library, passing her on his way to the door. "I'm going to work. If you want to stay, you'll do it on my terms. Two days, and you will not drink. The minute I catch you drinking, or paying the doorman to buy you liquor, as you did last time, you're on your own. And you will not be allowed in again."

He left without waiting for a response, her haggard image, mouth open in dismay or rage or fear—he was not sure which, and he did not care—staying with him as he walked to the subway. But as he rode uptown, to Carrano Tower, he shoved it aside. He had carried the image of that face with him for too many years for it to intrude now on the life he had created alone.

. . . shameful behavior on my part that I don't like to dwell on.

He had told Sara that much, at dinner, and it was true, though evidently he was not sufficiently ashamed to contain himself with Ardis when he reached a certain point of anger and disgust.

. . . a situation from which I'm trying to extricate myself with the least possible damage.

Also true. That much he had told Sara; how much more he would tell her, he did not know. Oddly, he wanted her to know the whole story, but at the same time, and just as strongly, he wanted to keep it from her. (And why did he think she even wanted to hear it?) He might never tell her. Probably he should not. He had never been good at revealing himself to anyone, much less a woman he liked and wanted to know much better.

Everyone is a moon and has a dark side

which he never shows to anybody. Wise fellow, Mark Twain, thought Reuben; captured the whole of humanity in one sentence.

He wondered what was Sara's dark side. He liked everything about her, and could not imagine one. Perhaps she's the exception, he thought. (He did not believe in exceptions to what seemed incontrovertibly true, but he could be wrong.)

In his office, he pushed to one side the work his secretary had laid out for the day, and called Sara again. She was not at her desk, so he called her cell phone. "Is this a bad time?" he asked when she answered.

"No, I'm in my car, between clients. Is something wrong? You sound distracted."

Because Ardis's voice was still in his head, he thought, and Sara's voice, low and pleasant, could not wipe it out, at least not right away.

"Just a lot to get through before I leave." He cast about for some reason he could give for his phone call. "I forgot to ask you earlier if you'd heard anything more about delivery of the two tables for my office."

"Wasn't that in my last e-mail? I'm sorry if I left it out; the repairs on the conference table are finished; the larger one will be ready Wednesday. I've checked on everything, Reuben; the only pieces we won't have—" She began to list the pieces that needed more extensive repair, then stopped. "I did write you all this. You didn't get it?"

"I did get it. I'm sorry." He wanted to say more, to apologize for giving in to his desire to hear her in the middle of a workday, but in the instant between thought and expression, he backed away from honesty. And then thought, as he had earlier, *Like a teenager,* angry at himself for his failings. "I shouldn't have interrupted your day," was all he said. "Until Sunday."

"Yes," she replied neutrally, wondering at the strangeness of the conversation—*as if he couldn't think of anything to talk about*— until she arrived at her destination and saw her clients emerging from their hotel. She handed them two pages stapled together. "Cleaning service, caterer, florist, automobile leasing company. The second page has numbers for a law firm, an accountant, a physicians' referral service at Northwestern Memorial Hospital, a dental referral service, specialty shopping consultants at several stores. As I told you on the telephone, these are all firms and individuals we have found reliable, efficient, and well priced. If you decide later to buy a house, I've added two brokers who are excellent. For today, as we agreed, I'll take you to the cleaning service and the caterer and help you get set with them; all the others you can easily handle at your leisure, and those on the second page involve matters you'll want to manage in private. I'll have to leave you by noon, to meet another client."

And there goes my day, she thought as they drove to the first company on her list. And evening, she added, filled up with PowerPoint (a point has more power than I have right now, she thought wryly) and a conference that does not touch on anything in my life.

Her moods were always volatile, and this morning everything seemed exaggerated. One minute she felt trapped and angry and depressed, and the next she would think of Abby saying "Love you," even as she was running off to the many excitements of her young life, and her mood would swing upward. And a moment later she would see her day dissolving in meetings with people she didn't care about and her annoyance would return, until she would think of the story Carrie had just written, and Doug's carvings, and know that they were well and happy and loving, largely because of the home she created, keeping them all together and safe, and her mood would tilt up, and up. Until she would remember that she would spend her evening supervising an event for people she would never see again and would not even remember tomorrow, or want to, and the oppression of being trapped and helpless would return. But then she would think of Reuben's two telephone calls, and as soon as she guessed that his second call had no purpose other than to continue their conversation, however lamely, in an instant she would feel lighter, everything would seem manageable, and she would smile.

She went through gyrations like these a dozen times a day. It was exhausting and fruitless, but she seemed unable to stop the lows from dragging her down, nor could she extend the highs that buoyed her up. And by the time she returned to her desk, just after five, what she wanted most in the world was a hot bath and a deep chair, with a book, a glass of red wine, and a quiet dinner.

Instead, what she got when she walked into her cubicle was Pussy Corcoran standing beside her desk, fur coat buttoned to her throat, though the day was still exceptionally warm for May, her hands out, pleading. "I need you, Sara! I don't have anybody to talk to, anybody to help me, and I keep calling you and calling you and your secretary says you're busy and the girl at your house said—"

"My house? What are you talking about?"

"I went to your house! What else could I do? She was very nice, a very nice young lady, she actually said you'd talked about me, she recognized my name, can you imagine that? I couldn't believe you cared that much about me; it made me feel good, but then she kept saying you weren't home and wouldn't be home all day and she gave me your cell-phone number and even wrote it down for me, she must have thought I didn't have a good memory; anyway, I called you but I got a *recording,* what good is a cell phone if you don't keep it on?"

"Mrs. Corcoran, listen to me. You are not to go to my house again. Do you understand that?"

"Wait a minute, miss, you don't talk to me like—"

"How did you get the address, anyway?

I'm not listed in the telephone book, and my office never gives out that information."

"Your secretary did, a very nice young lady—"

"Donna would not do that."

"Well, I confess I told her you'd given it to me and I'd lost it, that you promised we'd have some private time together, you know, away from Lew . . . and that's why I'm here, Lew is why, listen, Sara, I need your help—"

"You will leave this office at once. I can't believe this: you lied to my secretary and you forced your way into my house—"

"I didn't! I didn't force anything! I didn't even *get* inside, the little girl, your daughter, right? You look too young to have a daughter that age, but things are different now than they were in my time, but Sara, listen, I never forced—"

"I don't want to talk about it. I don't want anything to do with you. Just go. I have another client in an hour and I haven't had a chance—"

"But *I'm* a client, too, and I *need*—"

"Not anymore. Can't you understand that? You are not a client anymore, and I am telling you to leave. If you don't, I will. If you insist on staying here after I've asked you to leave, told you to leave, you may stay here as long as you want, but the office will be empty. The office is closed."

Pussy Corcoran's face crumpled. She shoved her small hands into her coat pockets and stood still, looking at the floor. "I guess you won't help me," she whispered.

"No." Sara sat down, too tired to continue standing.

"Well, then." She turned and took a few steps.

"Your purse."

"Oh." She came back and took one hand from her pocket to pick up the bag. Sara noted abstractly that it seemed strangely heavy for a small woman's handbag, but if she gave it any more thought, it was to surmise that Pussy Corcoran was trying to demonstrate how weak and needy she was, or simply that she had filled it with purchases in a day of shopping. She could barely make out Pussy's whispered "Thank you" as she left.

For what? Sara thought. I wasn't nice to her. I should have been nicer; she seems so . . . helpless. And that was the problem, she thought as she pulled her chair to her desk and began leafing through the day's phone messages. I don't have much sympathy for people who can't make it on their own. Not one of my nicer traits.

Eight calls from Pussy Corcoran, she found, stacking those slips beside the phone. And she had seen Pussy's phone number pop up on her cell phone half a dozen times that day, and had ignored it. Fourteen calls in one day, she mused. It sounded like a lot more than helplessness; more even than willfulness, an insistence on getting her own way in a world where people usually jumped to do the bidding of those with money. This sounded like worry. Or panic. Or fear.

Not just an annoying woman, she thought; something more serious. She reached for the phone to call Pussy, but it rang beneath her hand. "How you doing, sis?" Mack sang out. "Just reporting in, nothing to worry about, in fact, everything's great. I just had to tell you how great these kids are, sis; you've done one hell of a job with them. I have to hand it to you, you did it alone, nobody to help you, I really let you down. You are truly a great lady." There was a pause. "You still there, sis?"

"Yes. I'm catching my breath. Are you smoking something?"

He laughed. "Not a fucking . . . sorry, not a single thing. I'm having a good time with your wonderful kids, that's all. We're having a cozy family dinner at Mexico Lindo, and we're about to drive over to Parker and be enthralled by Abby's performance. It's a fun evening, sis; I wish you were with us."

"So do I. Did Carrie and Doug bring books to read?"

"Three books each—how fast do they read, anyway?—and Carrie brought a notebook to work on her latest story, and Doug has a piece of balsa he's carving into something too secret to reveal. They'll be fine, no kidding, sis, everything's under control at this end."

"Yes," Sara said, and heard the note of wistfulness in her voice, a note of feeling left out for the first time since she had taken over the family. "What did *you* bring?"

"I found a couple books in your library. Hey, by the way, what's with this guy Corcoran?"

"What?"

"Corcoran. His little woman was here this morning practically banging the door down, looking for you. I knew Corcoran—Lew, right?—in New York . . . fact is, I mentioned you to him, told him to contact you when he got to Chicago, you'd steer him to the best places—but I didn't know his wife was some kind of nut. Pussy? Crazy name."

"You told Lew Corcoran to call me?"

"Right, I figured you'd—"

"How did you know what I was doing?"

"You mean your job? Sis, I kept up with you, never lost track of you. I told you, I *missed* you. It made me feel closer to you, knowing what you were doing. I figured I'd be coming back and helping out, and I wish now I'd done it a lot sooner, it's so good, sis, it's really *great* to be with all of you, with these terrific kids, and next time we have to do all this together. Okay? Dinner and a movie or whatever you want. It's so special to do things like a family. Better than I thought. Better than I ever *knew.* Let's do it a lot. And if you ever need me again, like tonight, just sing out. I'm always available, and happy to help."

After a moment, deciding there was too much to absorb all at once, Sara let her questions about Lew Corcoran go—she would bring them up again tomorrow, she thought—and said, simply, "Thank you, Mack. I appreciate that." She hesitated again. "I do plan to be out on Sunday night; it would be nice to know you'll be there."

"No problem. Wonderful, in fact. I'll write it down. I've gotta get Abby to school; thespians can't be late, you know. See you later."

Sara gazed through the window at the darkened street, seeing in her mind the contrast between the shadows of LaSalle Street and the soft violet and blue haze of the May evening far above. But this time she did not find it depressing.

"I brought you some dinner," Donna said, coming in with a plate of salad and bread, and a covered container of coffee. "Not much, but it was all I could find. I figured you wouldn't have time for anything else."

"Donna, you're wonderful." Sara cleared a space on her desk. "But I thought we'd talked about not giving my address to anyone. Didn't I make that clear?"

"Oh, damn, Sara, did she tell you that? She begged and begged, you know, and I could tell she wasn't a dangerous character, I figured she wouldn't attack you or your family, and she was so damn *clingy,* I mean, you know, I just wanted to get rid of her. *You* know, I'll bet there are people who make you feel—"

"Just don't do it again," Sara said shortly. "Ever. It's not up to you to decide who's dangerous or not; we have a rule about giving addresses to anyone." She looked at the food Donna had brought, and sighed. "Go home now, it's late. Oh, wait. Were you able to find another place to live?"

"Not yet. Nancy had a studio in Lincoln Park, but it was all women, so I said no."

"Why? You don't have a lot of choice now, Donna, and wouldn't that be the safest place of all?"

"Oh, I don't know. It's just so . . . I don't know. I just didn't want it."

"But if your father is coming after you—"

"I'll be okay tonight, and tomorrow I'll find a place. I'll work it out, Sara, I promise. See you in the morning."

Something odd there, Sara reflected as Donna left with a cheerful wave. All of a sudden, she's not worried. Or at least not worried enough to live in a place that doesn't allow men.

But there was only so much she could focus on at once, and Donna, and Pussy Corcoran, and her husband as well, would have to wait until tomorrow. Right now she had less than an hour to get her notes together for the evening ahead and eat her dinner.

But first she took a moment to let the

moods of the day settle into another mood, steady happiness as peaceful as the sky she could only imagine: a wash of evening pastels arching all the way from Mack, loving and helpful, to Reuben in New York, planning to be with her on Sunday, and to stay in the city for a month. Or more.

FOUR

See, this is what I mean," said Doug, handing his mother a carved dancing bear about six inches high. "It oughta be soapstone, that's what the Eskimos use, but I only had wood. Anyway, it's for you."

Tess ran her thumb back and forth over the bear's silky, grained surface. She smiled her crooked half smile at Doug. "You like it, right?" he asked. "Sara said you would. So did—" He stopped, hearing Abby's warning in his head, that none of them would mention Mack when they visited their mother. "So did Abby and Carrie; they liked it, too. But, see, that's what I mean, *this* is what I want to do. All the time, you know? I mean, I hate all that boring stuff at school, and what do I need it for when I'm going to be a famous artist? I mean, I'm wasting all this time, and nobody cares, nobody listens to me, I'm this *little kid* who doesn't know what's good for him. You know?"

Tess made a sound that Doug took for agreement. "Well, but so what? I mean, nobody's about to help me. Like, I could go to school at the Art Institute, but Sara says I'm too young. So would they, I guess," he added dolefully. "Boy, ten is the worst age in the world, I wish it would go away and I could be fifteen, or sixteen . . . or, you know, *older.*"

"He's always complaining," Abby said, coming in and kissing her mother on the forehead. "I'm sorry I'm late; did Doug tell you how long we waited for the bus? And then Carrie and I stopped in the drugstore; she's still there; she'll be here in a few minutes. You look so pretty; is that a new sweater? Oh, it is, isn't it? I saw it when Sara wrapped it up. I brought you something, too; I thought maybe if you get cold sometime, like there isn't enough heat late at night . . . I know you wake up a lot at night . . ." She opened a box and held up an angora shawl in variegated silver and red. "Do you like it? I love it; it's so dramatic, like something Carmen would wear when she dances."

Embarrassed, she fell silent, remembering Tess dancing with their father, swooping and twirling about their living room on a laughing New Year's Eve, and, another time, dancing with Mack when he was thirteen, teaching him to waltz and tango and do a funny kind of jitterbug she had seen on television. But Tess took a corner of the shawl in her good hand and rubbed it, as she had rubbed Doug's carved bear, and smiled her crooked smile at Abby. She pointed to her shoulder, and Abby, grateful because Tess never made her feel guilty, let the shawl settle gently across her mother's back and brought it forward, around her shoulders. "It looks wonderful on you. Your colors." She sat in the chair next to Doug. "What shall I tell you about?"

"She's got a boyfriend," said Doug helpfully. "She can talk about him all day."

Carrie was in the doorway and saw Abby's scowl. "Maybe she doesn't want to talk about Sean. At least not in front of *you*." She ran across the room and kissed her mother on the cheek. "Sorry I'm late, I had to buy some shampoo and Abby told me what kind she uses, but I couldn't find it and everybody was too busy to help me . . . nobody likes to wait on teenagers, did you ever notice that?" She kissed her mother again. "You look so pretty. I miss you, we all do, did Abby and Doug already tell you that? Sara told us a silly story the other night about an elf selling noses, and we wished you were there 'cause you were always telling funny stories like that."

Tess pointed at Abby. "What?" Abby asked. "Sara always knows what you mean, but I don't—"

"She wants you to tell about Sean," said Doug.

"Really? Oh. Well . . . He's really handsome," she said to Tess. "And nice. He's Irish, but he's lived in London for the last five years. He's seen practically the whole world, and he said he'd take me to all the places he likes best that I haven't seen. I haven't seen *anything.*"

"How's his English?" Doug asked.

"They speak English in Ireland, and anyway he's lived in *London,*" Carrie said impatiently.

"Then what's Gaelic?"

"Irish, but just about everybody knows English. Anyway, he's lived in *London.* You know: *England.* You've heard of England?"

"So why is he here?" Doug asked Abby.

"Because," Abby said.

"Why?" Doug insisted.

"His family just wanted to come here."

"But you were telling—" Carrie stopped short. "Telling Sara—weren't you telling Sara?—that the police in London said his friends set a bomb outside Harrods—that's a department store," she said to Doug, "and a lot of people were hurt, so they had to—"

"A bomb?" Doug shouted. "He's a terrorist?"

"Of course not, dummy," Abby snapped. "*He* wasn't accused of anything, but he was friends with this bunch of guys and the police kept dragging them all in and asking lots of questions, and it got—difficult—so Sean's parents decided they had to leave, and his father owns a business that's in London and Chicago, so they came here. That's all; it's not a big deal."

"*Did* one of his friends do it?" Carrie asked. "The bomb?"

"I don't know."

"You mean your boyfriend didn't tell you?" Doug asked.

"I didn't ask him."

"Did he want to talk to you about it?" Carrie asked. "Like, for sympathy? I mean, he might have been afraid they'd come after him, you know, if it was a gang."

A terrorist cell, Doug mouthed.

"It wasn't a terrorist cell," Abby exclaimed. "God, Doug, you're a real pain in the ass."

"I'm not—!"

"Doug's too young to understand sex," Carrie said to her mother, "so he makes fun of people who are in the throes of it, like Abby."

"What?" Doug yelped.

"In the throes?" Abby demanded.

"Well, you know, all caught up, *consumed—*"

"Would you like to hear about the play I'm in?" Abby asked her mother loudly.

"I could tell about it," Doug said, instantly deflected. "I saw it. It was terrific. It's about—"

"I saw it, too," Carrie cut in, "but Abby should tell about it. It's her play, after all."

"Yeah, but she can't say how good she was; then she'd be bragging. She was dynamite," he said to Tess. "She was so good, one time she made everybody cry. Everybody except Mack; he said he never cr—oh. I mean . . . I mean . . ."

There was a terrible silence. Tess Hayden's hand rose up, trembling. Her mouth worked; her good eye began to flutter.

"Oh, God," Abby breathed.

Tess stabbed a finger toward Doug, again and again.

"Well, yeah, see, he came back, like, a few weeks ago, something like that, and he's really great, but, you know, Mom, we couldn't tell you, I mean, Sara thought, I mean, we didn't know—"

Tess's thumb began to twitch; her hand fell to her lap and she slumped forward. A low moan came from deep in her throat.

"I'm sorry!" Doug yelled desperately. "I didn't mean it!"

"Call somebody!" Carrie screamed, but Abby had already run to the door and was calling for a nurse.

"Call Sara!" Carrie wailed. "She'll know what to do."

"She's not home," Doug shouted. "She said she was going out with what's-his-name, the guy with the funny name."

"Reuben," Abby said. She was dialing her cell phone. "Sara!" she cried a minute later. "Where are you? We need you! Mom's fainted or something, she just fell forward, she—yes, the nurse is here, but *please,* Sara, please come! Oh, okay." She held out the phone to the nurse. "She wants to talk to you."

The doctor came in, and Abby and Carrie and Doug retreated to a corner, no one paying attention to them. They held hands, Doug buried his face in Abby's sweater, and none of them spoke. The bright room Sara had filled with reds and purples and golds had darkened . . . like a cave, Carrie thought, her imagination lifting her above the scene she could not bear to face; *a cave with ghosts and dragons and a brave bird, a huge bird, with a red crest and gold wings, injured but still able to fly above them all and find a way out.*

By the time Sara arrived, half an hour later, Tess was in bed. The doctor had left. "She's sleeping," the nurse said, "and she'll probably sleep through the night. It was an ischemic stroke, actually not uncommon in people who have had strokes before, and not as serious as it might have been. She'll probably be fine when she wakes up, well, that is, she'll be about the same as before. This wasn't life threatening, you know, really, it wasn't."

When the nurse had left, Sara looked at the three in the corner. "What happened?"

"I did it," Doug said. He looked at his feet and began to cry. "I was telling about Abby's play and how she made people cry and I said . . . I said that . . . Mack didn't. Didn't cry." He was sobbing in loud gulps. "I didn't mean to, Sara! I was being really careful, but then . . . it just came out, sort of, you know, slid out, and Mom was pointing at me and I didn't know what to do, so I said he was here. You know, he came back. And then she . . . she . . . *fell over* . . . Sara, I'm sorry, I didn't mean to! Do you think I killed her?"

Sara put her arm around him. "Of course you didn't. You heard what the nurse said."

"Yeah, but she could be wrong. Or Mom could be worse than ever. And she'll hate me for making her worse, and everything is all my fault, and I didn't mean to!"

Sara held him close. "You didn't kill her, sweetheart, and I'm sure you didn't make her worse, and she would never hate you. You made a mistake, but—"

"It wasn't Doug's fault," Carrie said loudly. "He was doing all the right things; he brought Mom his bear that he just made and we were all talking and laughing and she was really happy, and she was wearing the new shawl Abby brought, and everything was *fine.*"

"I know," said Sara. "And it was bound to happen, it was silly to think we could keep it a secret forever. As long as we tell Mom about all the things we do, all the things she wants to know, it's impossible to keep somebody who lives in our house a secret."

"It was so awful," Carrie said. "I hated it, her head fell down and her thumb was twitching and it was scary and *awful,* and you weren't here . . . Where were you, anyway? I mean . . . where *were* you?"

"She was *out,*" Abby said. "She has a right to do that."

"Not when we need her," Carrie shot back. "She should be close, in case we need her."

Right, Sara thought ruefully. And if "close" isn't good enough, perhaps I should stay home all the time, in case someone decides I'm needed. That definitely would be best, as far as my family is concerned: stay put, where I'm always available.

She turned to her mother's bed, angry and guilty and hungry: she and Reuben had been planning to have dinner after visiting the River North art galleries. Leaning down, she listened to Tess's breathing and kissed her on the forehead, then moved away from the bed and picked up her shoulder bag. "Let's go home," she said abruptly.

"Shouldn't we stay here?" Carrie asked. "I mean, if Mom wakes up she'll wonder where we are."

"The nurse said she'd probably sleep all night, and even then they don't think she'll remember much of what happened. Come on, Doug, stop sniffling; it happened and it's over, and it would have happened eventually, so let's try to figure out how we're going to deal with this from now on."

"We don't have to, if she forgets about Mack," said Doug hopefully.

"I'm not sure she'd forget that. Anyway, it's bound to slip out again, and we have to be prepared to deal with it. Come on, I'm hungry, and I left dinner at home for you, so now we'll all share it."

They sat at the round table in the breakfast room, their voices subdued. "We have to be honest," Sara said. "We can't lie; she'd hate that worse than anything."

"But Doug said Mack was *great*." Carrie groaned. "How do we get around that?"

"He *is* great," protested Doug. "Mom would like that, wouldn't she? I mean, he's her *son*."

"But he treated us like shit," Abby said despondently. She shot a look at Sara. "I'm sorry, I mean, he treated us abominably. He *walked out* just when we needed a man around here!"

"I was here," Doug said.

"You were six years old. What could you do?"

"Nothing. I can't do anything now, either. I'm no good for anything."

"You're good as part of this family," Sara said. "You're important to us, and we love you."

"And stop feeling sorry for yourself," said Abby. "Just because you messed up with Mother—"

"Abby," said Sara firmly.

"Sorry."

"But Abby's right," Carrie said reasonably. "I mean, he turned his back and walked out and so now he's walked *in* and it's okay, I mean, you know, it's okay that he's here, but it's kind of hard to tell Mom that everything's fine when all she remembers is that it wasn't fine and she had her stroke because of him."

"We're not sure exactly what caused her stroke," said Sara.

"We have to just . . . talk about him," Abby

said. "Like he's just another thing we do. I mean, we talk about school and my play and Carrie's stories and everything and . . . Mack."

"Like it's *normal*?" Carrie asked.

They all looked at Sara. She nodded. "That's really the only way. And I guess it is normal, at least as long as he's here. But let me talk to her first, okay?"

"Yes," Abby breathed in relief. "Thank you, Sara."

The telephone rang and she ran to answer it. "It's Sean," she said to Sara. "Can I go out with him for a while? He wants to walk to Webster Place for dessert."

"It's been quite a day—" Sara began, but then, as Abby's bright eyes began to cloud, she said, "Have you finished all your homework?"

"Yes! Can I go?"

"Fine. Not too late, though."

"Ten o'clock?"

"Fine, but he has to walk you all the way home."

Carrie said to Sara, "When can I go on a date?"

"Has someone asked you?"

"No, but I just want to have some idea of the parameters."

Sara laughed. "Fifteen, almost sixteen seems a good time to start."

"Like Abby."

"Like Abby."

"Back in a minute," Abby said, running upstairs.

When she came back, Doug said, "That was *fifteen* minutes."

The doorbell rang, and Abby made a face at Doug. "No time to argue with somebody who can't tell time. Bye, everybody. Love you."

They seemed to have forgotten their awful afternoon, Sara thought. How wonderful to have that kind of memory.

The house was quiet, Sara reading in the library, Doug and Carrie in their rooms, when Mack came in. He went straight upstairs and was heading for the stairway to the third floor when he stopped at Doug's open door. "Hey, you're getting ready for bed? Is it that late? Sorry, bro, I meant to have a quiet evening at home, but things got busy." He sat on the edge of Doug's bed. "What were you up to today? You get in any trouble I'd enjoy hearing about?"

"I got into trouble," Doug said uncomfortably, "but I don't know if I should tell you about it."

"Oh, come on, you think I'm not old enough to hear it? I'm old enough. Tough enough, too. Whatever it is, if you could handle it, I can, so, come on, spit it out."

"Well, it was just . . . I mean, you know, I didn't mean to . . . I just . . . sort of accidentally told Mom that you're back. And we weren't supposed to tell her."

After a moment, Mack said, "Ever?"

"Uh, I don't know," Doug said. "I mean . . . I don't know."

"Well, sure you'd tell her. After all, she's my mom, too, and she'd want to know. She'd be mad if you didn't tell her. So you did the best thing, you oughta congratulate yourself." There was a pause. "She want to see me?"

Doug looked wildly at his door, willing someone, anyone, to come to his rescue. When no one appeared, he mumbled something.

"What?" Mack asked. "Didn't catch that."

"She got sick," Doug said loudly. "Really sick. So I don't know if she wants to or not."

"Sick, how?"

"Uh, she fainted, sort of."

"Passed out?"

"I don't know. I guess so. They said it was

some kind of stroke, I forget what kind. The doctor and the nurse put her to bed and said she'd sleep all night, so we came home."

"She passed out when she heard I'd come back."

Doug said nothing.

"Shit," Mack muttered.

Doug heard the telephone ring, and Carrie answer it in the hallway just outside her door, and then her voice, calling down the stairs to Sara.

"The boyfriend," Mack said, perking up and grinning at Doug. "Romance is in the air. Sounds like the four of us are about to have some time together again. That'll give me a chance to tell you about the time I was on a ferry that sank."

"It *sank*?"

"Right out from under us. Three hundred people, two hundred and ninety drowned. Real dramatic stuff."

"Were you in a lifeboat?"

"Nope; I swam."

"How far?"

"A long long way, but it's too late to tell a story with great dramatic twists and turns tonight. Next time big sister goes out."

"You could tell it to all of us."

"I sometimes think sweet Sara doesn't always believe my stories. You ever think that?"

"Oh. Well, I guess, but, you know, she just doesn't have all the facts."

"You don't, either, and you believe me."

"I guess I want to more," said Doug shrewdly.

"Well, fuck it, you do amaze me, little brother; you are one sharp guy." He raised his hand, palm out, and they gave a high five. "See you tomorrow, bro." He waved over his shoulder as he walked out. "Sleep tight."

In the hallway, he hesitated, then went to the top of the stairs. No sound came from below. He walked halfway down, listened again, then walked the rest of the way, and moved quietly toward the library. He heard Sara's voice, low and level. "There isn't much I can do, Mrs. Corcoran. You need friends; you're too isolated. The quickest way for you to meet people is to get involved in some organizations. I'll be glad to introduce you to the presidents of some boards of directors; you'll be surrounded by people . . . No, I can't do that. I have a family; I can't spend my evenings with you . . . No, certainly not; do you know what time it is?"

There was a long silence. Mack frowned,

wondering what the Pussy bitch was going on about this time. And why had she come to the house this morning? Weird thing to do.

"I'm sorry," Sara said at last, "that's the best I can do. I'll call the board presidents tomorrow, and if you come to my office at about ten, I'll give you a list of those who want to talk to you about joining them. And, please, listen to me: do something on your own. Go out and explore the city, get to know it. You'll feel better; you might even begin to enjoy yourself. It's destructive to close yourself off and brood about everything you don't like and can't control. Good night, Mrs. Corcoran, I'll see you tomorrow, about ten."

"How do you know that?" Mack asked from the door of the library.

Startled, Sara stared at him.

"Sorry, didn't mean to scare you," he said. "I was on my way to the kitchen to make some coffee. Can I make you some coffee?"

"You can stop sneaking around this house," Sara snapped. "Haven't you anything better to do than spy on me?"

"Hey, sis, not fair! Why would I spy on you? I was just walking by, and I heard you say it's destructive to close yourself off and brood about things you don't like. True, absolutely true, I know from personal experience, and I thought maybe, if you still feel that way, I could help."

"I've already told you what you can do. More than once."

"And I'm doing it. I've got a job. I was going to surprise you when it was a done deal, but this is almost as good. Are you proud of me?"

Sara walked around the couch to the bookshelves that lined the wall, putting the couch between them. "Should I be?"

"Sis, it's a *job*. I might make a lot of money, you'd be glad, then, wouldn't you? And proud of me?"

"You 'might' make money. Which means, if you do get this job, whatever it is, you won't have a salary."

"Well, no, not if you mean the every-other-week paycheck most people are slaves to. But this will be big, sis, I promise. I worked for this guy in New York and he's big, his ideas are big, his company is big. He likes me and I like him, and this is going to be fine. I promise, sis. After all, I owe you big-time, I know it, and I'm so glad to be here, you know, part of a family, *my* family, I'll do anything I can to make life easier for all of you."

Sara contemplated him. "Who is it? The big man you're going to work for."

"I can't tell you. Not yet, anyway. Not till it's a done deal. But if you're worried about his being real, you know, having a real company, all that, you can stop worrying; he's everything he says he is. More."

Sara studied the shelves and stepped on a small ladder to reach a book on the top shelf. "I'm going upstairs. I'll see you tomorrow."

"Sis, wait. Please. I'm asking you. Don't go yet. Can't I make you a cup of coffee? I like late-night coffee; it never keeps me awake; it's relaxing after a hard day. Let me do this for you; I want to talk to you for a while; we've been so busy we haven't talked much lately. Please, Sara, coffee?"

Her shoulders sagged, but she nodded. "For a few minutes. I'm tired and I have a long day tomorrow."

"Right. I know." He walked into the kitchen ahead of her, to the brick fireplace on the far wall, and lit paper and kindling while Sara sat in one of the two armchairs flanking it. She watched him as he moved about the kitchen with only the firelight to guide him, taking the jar of coffee beans from the cabinet beside the sink, going from task to task with casual familiarity, as if he had always lived there. As he worked, he chatted about Abby's play and Doug's latest carving and Carrie's short story that she was submitting to the school magazine. He talked proudly, and intimately. *My family.*

Sara watched him, the warmth of the fire curling about her, its half-light turning the kitchen's sage green and ivory to a dreamy wash, like a desert at dusk, close, warm, silent, the only sounds domestic ones. Languid from fatigue, she let herself sink into the depths of the armchair and the spell of the late hour, for the first time soothed by Mack's familiarity with the room, the house, Abby and Carrie and Doug: their life, the life he said he wanted to share.

"Now," he said. He set the pot and two espresso cups on the low table between them, and took the other armchair. Fleetingly, Sara thought how strange it was that they were there, exactly as her parents had been, and later, after her father died, her mother and Mack's father, sitting here every morning, drinking coffee, reading newspapers. We're running the house, she thought, as our parents used to. It was a pleasant thought: sharing the burdens of the family.

Mack filled the cups. "Not the Italian machine I'd rather use," he said, "but that's at the top of my list of things to buy as soon as I can."

They sat in companionable silence, drinking coffee and nibbling almond biscotti Mack had found in the pantry. "Nice," Mack murmured. "I like nighttime silence. Better than daytime. Deeper."

He was wearing dress pants and a crisply ironed shirt open at the neck. His socks matched his pants; his shoes were polished. His face had lost its gaunt pallor, his hair was combed.

"You look very handsome," Sara said.

He grinned. "High praise from a sister; thanks. I try to keep up with the general atmosphere of the house and the Elliott/Hayden family. You're really gorgeous, Sara, and you're terrific, the way you dress. Abby ought to take a few lessons."

"Abby is fifteen and has to dress the way her friends dress; it's not an age when young people want to stand out from the crowd. I'm not gorgeous, Mack, and you know it. Why do you keep saying it?"

"Do I 'keep saying it'? I guess I must mean it. You gonna argue with how I feel about my sister? I'll tell you: I think my sister is gorgeous. Beautiful. Stunning. All of the above. And also too tired. My sister works too hard." He paused, but Sara was silent. "And I plan to make her life easier. Take some of the burdens off her shapely shoulders. Pull my weight around the house. Look, Sara"—he leaned forward and refilled her cup—"I know you don't want the kids running around, coming home to an empty house, all that stuff— they think they're old enough, but you don't feel comfortable with that, and I can't say I blame you—but you've got this new guy and your own life to live, so why not let me help? I can be here most evenings and weekends, so you can make plans without worrying. That would lighten the burdens, right?"

"All of a sudden you're going to be here evenings and weekends?"

"That's the plan. I told you: I'm a working guy now; I don't have to see people at night to get things settled. Things *are* settled; everything's in its proper place. A place for everything and everything in its—"

"And Mother?" Sara asked bluntly.

Mack stopped midsentence. "Shit." He put a hand over his eyes. "I don't know what to say about her. Doug told me what happened—sort of. Told me enough, anyway, that I got the picture. Christ, aren't mothers supposed to be good at forgiving people? I thought—" He shook his head and took away his hand, looking at Sara beseechingly. "I thought she'd understand me. Love me. You know? Like mothers do. I love *her*. I missed her, I even missed her calling me names, telling me how selfish I was . . . you know, the whole bit. I thought, if I was missing her, she had to be missing me. Then I heard she had a stroke, and I thought it was because Dad was gone and she'd lost two husbands and that was more than she— well." He shrugged. "I thought a lot of things, thought thoughtfully about a lot of things. Anyway, don't worry, Sara, I'll take care of it. I'll find a way to explain everything to her, and we'll be fine again, she'll love me the way she used to, and she'll forget what happened. Mothers do forget, you know; it's like they make a specialty of it."

He reached for the coffeepot, then looked up sharply. "Hey! Maybe we could bring her home! If we all take care of her together, I'll bet we could manage it. Who knows what we could do, all of us, together? Sara, listen, it's what I was telling you: I'm *settled*. I'm home, where I belong, where I love everybody and everything, and I hope everybody loves me. So here I am, ready to work." He sat straight and gave a smart military salute. "Marching orders, please, ma'am; I'm prepared to tighten my buckle and buckle down."

In the warm, shadowed room, in the close silence with the faint hum of the refrigerator and freezer like a gentle current buoying them up, Sara could not recall why she had been so suspicious of Mack, so unpleasant to him, snapping at him almost every time they talked. Looking at him through half-closed eyes, she saw her mother in his full lips and blond curls, and in the gaiety of his smile that brought back the mother they had lost years before. She was ashamed of herself for her stinginess in welcoming him back, and for thinking only of medical school and a life for herself when he first appeared, instead of helping him rejoin the family and rebuild his own life. He's one of us, she thought for the first time, and held out her hand to her brother.

"Thank you," she said. "It's wonderful to have you here."

FIVE

With a flourish, Mack placed the tiny, silver-wrapped package in the center of the breakfast-room table, and stood back.

"There's no card," Doug said.

"Maybe it's for all of us," said Carrie.

Doug shook his head. "Too small."

Mack looked at Abby.

"For me?" she asked. "It's not my birthday."

Mack grinned. "I don't remember when your birthday is. Or Doug's or Carrie's. So it's a good thing I didn't wait for it."

"That doesn't make sense," Carrie said reprovingly.

"Open it!" Doug shouted. "Open it, open it!"

Abby pulled the silver bow off the package, and carefully peeled back the tape, preserving the paper. Peeking inside, she said to Mack, "What is it? A pin?"

"You figure it out," he said.

She took out the key and held it up. "It's not a pin, it's a real key."

"It's a car key," said Carrie.

Abby stared at Mack, her eyes widening. "A *car*?"

"Try outside." He grinned.

They ran through the dining room and living room, and flung wide the front door. "Up the street," Mack said, pointing. "It was the only place I could find to—" They dashed down the steps and up the street to the small red car gleaming and beckoning, its front window almost hidden by an enormous red bow.

"That's *Abby's*?" Doug breathed, for once subdued.

Mack had followed from the house. "All hers. Maybe she'll take you for a ride."

"But I can't." Abby was staring at the car, tears in her eyes.

"Sara didn't mean it," Carrie said. She put her arm around Abby; they were the same height and Carrie felt a sudden rush of happiness at being, for a minute, the comforting sister. "She only said you couldn't have a car because we couldn't afford it right now. But it's okay, you'll see, she'll be *happy* to know Mack gave you one." When Abby said nothing, she added, "You can help her with shopping and, you know, errands. She'll be really happy about that."

Abby turned to Mack. "How can *you* afford it?"

"Got a job," he said easily. "Happens to the best of us, you know, and then we buy nice presents. Go on, Abby, take the kids for a spin."

She shook her head. "I can't."

"Come on, damn it, it's your car! You do know how, right? They still teach it in junior year?"

She nodded. "But I don't have a license. Or a permit. And, anyway, Sara said—"

"Forget Sara," Mack said impatiently. "She won't be home for a couple of hours, and the time has come to take action and act actively. The car is here; we are here; the night is young, and we're going to try out the new toy. Come on, we'll take her for a test drive, and if Abby doesn't want to drive, I'll do it.

Come on, come on, before this shiny new car gets old and dull!"

"But my play opens tonight—" Abby began, but Mack had shoved past her, past all of them, grabbing the key from Abby's hand.

"I'm going if nobody else is," he said over his shoulder. "There's *hours* before you're supposed to be at school, we'll be back before that, before anything." He waited. "Am I the only one who isn't afraid of Sara?"

In a rush, Doug and Carrie followed him. "Come on, Abby," said Doug. "It's okay, Mack says it's okay."

"And it's your car," Mack said. "You've got to sit in front for the first ride, or it's not official. Come on, try it out behind the wheel, just sit there if you don't want to drive."

And Abby slipped into the front seat as Mack removed the huge bow from the window. Now she could see the world, and how different it looked from her own car! Her hands rested lightly on the steering wheel, her right foot settled gently on the accelerator; she breathed in deeply the scent of new leather and fabric and shiny plastic.

"Looking good," Mack said happily. He gave Doug and Carrie a light push into the backseat, then walked around the car and sat beside Abby. "Go ahead. Drive a few blocks."

"I don't have a—"

"What the fuck, Abby. I'm with you. Until you get your permit, I'm the designated driver, but I'm giving you this chance to try her out. Nobody'll notice; why should they? Come on, she's yours; you have to give her the first spin so she knows who's boss."

"Go on, Abby," urged Doug, behind her. "I've never seen you drive."

So Abby drove her new car. Frowning in concentration, she drove around the block, then around two blocks, and then three. Behind her, Doug and Carrie were laughing delightedly, beside her, Mack hummed a little tune, but she barely noticed. She focused on the width of the streets, the corners where her turns soon became tighter and more controlled, the stop signs that loomed in stern authority, ordering her to come to a full stop, to look both ways, and then to cross the intersection with care, in case a reckless driver should come from nowhere to try to beat her across. In a few minutes, her shoulders relaxed, her clench on the steering wheel eased, and she smiled. She was very happy.

"Pull up there and park," Mack directed. "I have a deep, hungry, hungering hunger for a chocolate sundae. Anybody else?"

It was like a dream, Carrie thought, watching Abby's serious frown as, with Mack putting in words of advice, she parked without hitting either the car in front or the one in back. And after they all had ice-cream sundaes ("Sara will say we spoiled our dinner," said Doug, happily spooning fudge), Abby drove home with growing confidence, feeling she had sped through several birthdays in a few hours and was now totally grown up. When she found a parking place half a block from their house, and neatly backed into it, she leaned over and kissed Mack on the cheek. "Thank you, thank you, you're wonderful, I love you."

"You were *good*," said Doug proudly.

"That was excellent," said Carrie. "I can't wait to tell Sara what an excellent driver you are."

Abby's elation faded. She sat in the car, her hands in her lap. "She'll be furious."

"Worry not," Mack said gaily. "I'll take care of Sara. She'll be fine. We'll all be fine. Come on, my little brood, let's get you inside." He replaced the enormous bow on the front window, and stood back to admire it. "Okay, come on, come on . . . in we go."

He was full of energy, shooing them inside and sending them all upstairs while he went downstairs, chose a bottle of wine, and brought it to the kitchen. He set it on the low table between the two armchairs, opened it, and arranged two glasses and a dish of pistachios beside it, then stretched out in one of the chairs, crossing his ankles, feeling deeply satisfied. And that was where Sara saw him when she came in, earlier than usual, because of Abby's play.

"Have a good day?" he asked, pouring wine for them both.

"It was fine. Is everyone upstairs?"

"Well, *I'm* not, but, yes, everyone else is."

"Have you been home long?"

"Long enough to have a great time with the kids. Here, sis: sit, drink, chat. I'm glad to see you."

Sara heard a rustling nearby, and then Doug and Carrie dashed in, followed more slowly by Abby. "Did you see it?" Doug shouted. "The car with the big bow?"

Sara smiled. "I was going to ask if you'd seen it. Someone's present, obviously; it's parked in front of the Bennetts'."

Doug looked at Mack. "You said you'd tell her."

"Tell me?" Sara asked.

"About the *car.*"

"Doug," Abby whispered.

Sara turned to Mack, whose hands were high in surrender. "*Mea culpa* yet again. I did something rash. Happy, but rash. It seems I bought Abby a car. Abby was afraid you'd be angry, but I told her of course you wouldn't be, you'd be happy for her, but to prevent any misunderstanding, I'd be the one to tell you about it."

There was a silence.

"Sara, it's spectacular!" Doug cried, running into the kitchen, unable to remain on the outskirts of the action. "It's red and it smells great, well, sort of peculiar, but Mack says it's a new-car smell, and everybody wants it, you can even buy it in a spray can, but we have our very own, well, Abby has it, and she *drove it* and she didn't hit one single thing, it was spectacularly cool!"

"Abby drove," Sara said. It was not a question.

"She was terrific," said Mack easily. "I was right next to her, but she was fine, a real pro.

Good practice, you know; it's the best way to learn."

"Sara?" Abby asked, coming into the kitchen. "Can I keep it? It's really beautiful, and I won't drive it unless you say I can, but can I please keep it?"

"I don't know," Sara said slowly. "Let me think about it."

Once again Carrie put her arm around her sister. "It isn't Abby's fault," she said to Sara. "She didn't ask for it. Mack bought it without telling her. Or anybody. It was a surprise. And she really likes it, and she *is* a good driver and she could help you with shopping and errands and driving us places and things, and it would be awful to make her give it back."

"You wouldn't make her give it back!" Doug cried.

Sara looked at the four of them.

. . . *the Wicked Witch of the West spoiling the reunion.*

"I'll think about it," she repeated.

"Sara, I really want this," Abby said, a sudden edge in her voice. "I'm old enough and I'll be careful and . . . it's *my* present."

A swift stab of alarm made Sara hesitate. "I know that, Abby," she said after a moment, "and I'm not in the habit of denying you things you really care about. This is just very sudden, and I want to think about it. Right now I have to get dinner on; aren't we eating early so you can get ready for your play?"

"Yes, but *Sara,* I need to *know.*"

Sara nodded. *She's nervous about the play; she's nervous about what I'll say; she's swept with a dozen emotions a day that all seem overwhelming at her age, and on top of it all she has a conflict between two adults, one of whom offers her treats while the other offers . . . discipline. And how can I fight such a wonderful gift? What reason could I have? Which means there isn't much I can say but—*

"All right. You can keep it. But we'll have to—"

"Sara, thank you!" Abby was hugging her and kissing her cheek over and over. "Thank you, thank you, you are so wonderful, I love you, oh, thank you! I'll do anything, just tell me what to do and I'll do it. Oh, you are so wonderful, isn't she wonderful?" she demanded of Mack. "See, she's not different from us at all!"

"Different?" Sara asked from the circle of Abby's arms.

"I said you were like me," Abby said happily, taking a few dancing steps. "Or I'm like you. You know, we're the same. And I was right!" She ran to the doorway. "I have to get ready; can you drive me . . . oh." Confusion swept briefly over her face, then she took a breath. "Can you drive me there about six-thirty? That's when we're all getting there."

Sara let out a silent sigh of relief, and went to Abby and kissed her. "Of course I will. And tomorrow you'll show me how you drive. We'll work it out." She turned to Mack. "You're still going out tonight? Your plans haven't changed?"

"Plans haven't changed, sis. Leaving in a few minutes."

Sara nodded, and said to Abby, "I'm going to pick up Mom for dinner and the play—"

"While Mack is gone," said Carrie shrewdly.

"Right," Mack said evenly.

"—so you can set the table while I'm gone." She turned on the burner beneath a casserole and adjusted the flame. "Why don't you all run upstairs now and get your homework done before dinner, since we're going to the play later?"

But not even the undercurrents could diminish the excitement of the moment, and Carrie was giggling from the release of tension, Doug was whooping like an Indian as he took the stairs two at a time, and Abby followed slowly, silent and dazed, still trying to absorb it all.

"Got to leave in a few minutes," Mack said, "so this is for good luck." He kissed Abby on her forehead. "I won't say break a leg, because who knows? Just kill 'em dead. You will, too, my thaumaturgic thespian."

"Thaumaturgic?" Abby asked suspiciously.

"Magical," he said easily, and kissed her cheeks, one and then the other. Abby flushed, and Sara noted the brief sexual flare in her eyes as Mack's lips touched her cheeks, as his hand lay on her shoulder. Something else to watch out for, she thought, but then wondered if the sexual awareness had been there for some time, though she had not seen it. Not because of Mack, she thought, or not only because of Mack. There is, after all, a boyfriend. Sean. And how much do I know about him? Or where they go, or what they do?

Practically nothing. Though I can guess what they do. Even at fifteen, which seems to be a lot different from fifteen when I was fifteen.

When Abby had gone upstairs, Sara turned to Mack. "You should not have bought it for her. And you know it."

"Right. You're right; I shouldn't have. I'm sorry, sis, I got carried away." He poured more wine, raising an eyebrow at Sara, who shook her head as she took a casserole from the refrigerator and put it on a burner. "I wanted to do something special," he went on to Sara's back, "and this seemed right, you know, timing and all. I mean, all the other kids in that fancy school of hers will have cars by the time they're seniors, and this way she'll keep up with them. Means a lot at that age, to keep up; shit, I remember too well. And she's happy. Happily happy and happiest with happiness. A great way for a kid to be. You saw that."

Of course I saw it. Excited; ecstatic. Still a child, almost an adult, ready to take on the world, unaware of, or maybe just indifferent to, subtleties and subtexts. Whatever they might be.

There was no choice, and she knew it. "It's a wonderful gift, Mack, extravagant but wonderfully generous, and I'm as grateful as Abby. But you must have gone into debt, and I'm sorry you did that."

"I'm on top of things, sis, don't worry about me. Everything's okay. In fact, I wanted to talk to you about my paying rent."

"You don't have to do that. This is your home. I've never asked—"

"Nope, you're too nice. You're the generous one. But some things are right and proper. So from now on, you get a check every month; just tell me how much."

"I have no idea."

"Sure you do. Half your expenses. Two actual grown-ups in the house, two people paying bills. And as soon as I'm sure everything's nailed down, we'll talk about you going back to school. That's what you wanted, isn't it?"

Sara sat on the arm of an armchair. "Nailed down? You're not sure about your job?"

"I'm sure."

"Then what does—?" She paused. "Tell me about it."

"About what?"

"Your job."

He shrugged. "You'd be bored. It's not glamorous or exciting, you know, just working for a guy in real estate." There was a brief pause. "Actually, you know him. Lew Corcoran. The guy I told to call you? He's a little crude, well, more than a little; the guy has no class—classically classified as quite class-less—but what the fuck . . . sorry . . . he's my meal ticket: a big operator with lots of opportunities for a go-getter. That's me. So I'm learning the business. You are frowning fiercely and fearsomely. Bad for your beautiful forehead, sis. Did I say something wrong?"

"Did you work for him in New York?"

"No. Well, now and then, you know, something special'd come up. Not exactly full-time. But when he told me he was coming to Chicago and I told him I had family here, he, you know, offered me this job."

"So you knew when you came here that you already had a job?"

"Nope. I'd been offered one, but I didn't know I'd take it. I told you, remember? I wanted to look around, get to feel at home again, sort of settle in."

"And you decided—?"

"That real estate was as good as anything. Why not? Maybe I've got a great future. Uncertain world, uncertain times, people looking for security, something solid they can hold on to that makes them feel they have some control of the future, even if they don't know what's going to happen that afternoon. Sounds good to me."

There was a pause. "And you're already making enough to buy a car for Abby?"

"Lew gave me an advance. Don't worry about it, sis; he's solid and so's his company and I can move up fast, even go international. It's all up to me, how hard I work. There's big money in real estate, sis; I never knew it, never knew anything about it, but, you know, like I said, it's the wave of the future. Which yours truly is going to ride."

And why did she still have doubts? What could she see wrong with his open smile, his bright, warm eyes, his easygoing voice telling her that he was willing to work hard to move up in a real estate company? There's something wrong with me, Sara thought. I've turned sour and suspicious.

But . . . the car. The odd hours. The evasiveness. The way Lew Corcoran keeps popping up, first a name on a fax, then a client, now my brother's employer.

"What's the name of the company?"

"Corcoran Enterprises. Not exactly original, but nobody asked me. We have a Web site if you want to check it out."

She nodded. In the silence, Mack refilled

his glass. "You haven't touched yours. Have some. One, anyway, for luck. For Abby's luck tonight. I'm sorry I won't be there, but she's really good, you know. You'll like it. I mean, I thought it was so trite, shit, another performance of *Our Town,* which everybody and his uncle and aunt and all his cousins . . . well, you know. But they make it seem almost new. Good cast. And Abby is fabulous as Emily."

"Doug said you didn't cry."

"I never cry." He held up the bottle, raising his eyebrows.

"No, thank you." She struggled not to ask the next question, but it came out anyway. "I thought we talked about your drinking a bottle of wine before dinner."

"Oh, sis." He put his arm around her, then quickly, remembering another time, pulled it away. "Not a full bottle, just a few drinks. Just the right amount. I told you before I can handle it; I always stop one drink away from having too many. By the way, the plumber called; said he'd be here tomorrow with the new showerhead. Which bathroom?"

"Yours."

"Mine? Have I complained?"

"You used to, and I remembered that and

checked it, and it really doesn't work properly."

"You checked it. You went into my room?"

At his tone, her eyebrows rose. "I went into the bathroom and then out again. Is that a problem?"

"I don't like people in my room. An old phobia. One of my many peculiar peculiarities, which I ask you to honor."

"Of course," Sara said easily. "Would you like me to call a carpenter to install a lock on your door?"

"Sure, if you want to. Why not?"

They talked about the plumber, the planting of summer flowers, preparing the vegetable garden, having the chimneys cleaned out. By the time Sara put dinner on the table, she felt a new comfort, sharing the maintenance of the house. And yet, she thought after he left, as she drove to the nursing home to pick up Tess, it was not a solid comfort: rippling beneath it was an uneasiness she was beginning to recognize as an accompaniment to every conversation with Mack: a sense of being somehow negligent, leaving much unasked, unsaid, still unsettled between them.

Whatever that meant.

They all kept up a steady stream of talk to Tess through dinner while she picked at her food. In most ways, Tess seemed to have returned to the place she had been before her last stroke. Once again she sat all day in her brocade chair, embroidering, reading, watching old movies, greeting the few friends who still came, and welcoming all of her family. All but Mack. Sara had told him not to come, that Tess knew he was there, ensconced in his old room on the third floor, but she made it vehemently clear that she would not see him. The beloved son she had tried to excuse through his teenage years when she never knew whether he would come home drunk or presenting her with bouquets of flowers, when he switched back and forth from cursing her for interfering in his life to thanking her floridly for helping him resolve conflicts with teachers or parents of his friends, when he swung from rage to meekness when asked to do tasks around the house . . . that son, she had finally acknowledged, was gone, as irrefutably as if he had died. Tess had almost no control over her life, but she made this clear: she would not see him.

And so whenever Tess came home, Sara made sure Mack was gone before she arrived. There were not many such occasions: Sara knew her mother was uncomfortable there, that as much as she loved her children and longed to be part of their lives, she did not like to leave the nursing home. Away from its familiar corridors, the faces she had come to connect with different times of day, her own room where warm colors enfolded her, she felt more helpless than ever, more adrift. Even worse, when she sat, immobilized, in the house she had furnished and decorated, where she had danced on New Year's Eve with her husband, surrounded by her laughing, applauding children, she felt more than ever that Tess Hayden had vanished as surely as had her husband; that the woman who had lived in that house existed no more, and would never return.

Nothing and no one returned, her eyes said: not Fred Hayden who had run off, or his son Mack after him; or Rob Elliott, Sara's father, who had died so long ago; not the fortune that had grown steadily smaller as Fred Hayden looked for work and kept spending and spending, to prove to himself that their lives really had not changed; nor Tess Hayden herself, whose frozen face and shrunken body bore no resemblance to the glowing beauty and graceful form of the proud mistress of this proud house. Those men, that woman, that fortune, that world had vanished into nothingness.

"Can Abby drive me places?" Doug asked. The conversation had been mostly about the new car—"A present from Mack, and it wasn't even my birthday," Abby said—but that was the only time his name was mentioned. Tess wanted details about the car, but not about Mack. Nothing about Mack.

"When she has a license," Sara said.

"When I'm sixteen," said Abby. She pushed back her chair, too excited to eat. "Can we go, Sara?"

"The rest of us are still eating," Carrie pointed out.

"You and Doug and Mother take your time," Sara said. "I'll drive Abby, and be back in a few minutes. There are brownies in the oven, Carrie, please take them out when the timer goes off, and serve everyone."

It was easy to pretend they were a real family, she thought as she drove Abby to school, picturing Doug and Carrie at the table talking animatedly to their mother. And of course they were a real family. *If a family is any group of people who love each other, that's us. I just wish we were more . . . symmetrical.*

But she even could pretend symmetry when they sat together in the school auditorium, Tess beside her, in her wheelchair at the end of the row, Doug and Carrie on her other side, reading their programs, pointing out Abby's name—"in *big* letters," Doug whispered—and watching the Stage Manager place chairs and tables on each side of the stage as the auditorium lights dimmed and the lights onstage grew bright.

"So weird," Doug whispered to Carrie. "No scenery. I mean—"

"Shhhh!" Carrie said. "He's talking."

The Stage Manager was Abby's friend Harlan Drakovich, and he was alone on the stage. Leaning against the right pillar, he said, "This play is called *Our Town.* It was written by Thornton Wilder and in it you will see Abby Hayden playing Emily—"

Doug poked Carrie in the ribs with his elbow. "He said her name out loud, like she's famous!"

Someone behind them said, "Shush, young man!" and Doug said, "But she's my sister!" and Sara murmured, "Doug, hold it down until later," and Doug shrugged impatiently and subsided.

"Every child born into the world," said the Stage Manager, "is nature's attempt to make a perfect human being."

Sara and Tess looked at each other and smiled. *We do keep trying.*

"People were meant to live two by two," said the Stage Manager.

And when that doesn't happen? We do the best we can, one by one.

And then came the third act, when Emily dies in childbirth and appears in the cemetery with the dead of her own family and of the town, seeing herself as a young girl, her family absorbed in the tasks of each day, serenely taking their togetherness for granted. "Mama," Abby-as-Emily pleaded as her mother concentrated on stirring a pot on the stove, "just look at me one minute as though you really saw me . . . Mama, *let's look at one another.*"

Sara leaned forward. How had Abby learned that painful urgency? Did she really understand how quickly life slips away in little moments of busyness? Or did she feel that no one at home truly listened to her, truly paid attention to her uniqueness and the turmoil of being fifteen-almost-sixteen in a complicated world where it was hard to feel in control of things?

"It goes so fast," said Abby-as-Emily, and there was a sob in her voice. "We don't have time to look at one another. I didn't realize . . ." Slowly, she sat down in her straight chair, one of many in neat rows representing tombstones in the cemetery. Her low voice trembled. "Goodbye, Mama and Papa. Good-bye to clocks ticking . . . and Mama's sunflowers. And food and coffee. And new-ironed dresses and hot baths . . . and sleeping and waking up. Oh, earth, you're too wonderful for anybody to realize you . . . Do any human beings ever realize life while they live it?—every, every minute?"

Sara blinked away tears. Around her, people were sniffling and rummaging in purses and pockets for tissues.

"See?" Doug said. He wiped his eyes. "She makes people cry. All except Mack."

We don't realize it, Sara thought. We don't realize all of life's wonders; we're too busy getting through each day, worrying about the little slights we think we've suffered, agonizing over not getting whatever we want that very minute, fighting for our own small space in the sun.

She leaned over and kissed Doug and, past him, Carrie. "I love you," she said.

The Stage Manager was pulling the curtain across the stage. "Goodnight," he said softly, and slowly, very slowly, closed the curtain while the audience sat in absolute stillness. The auditorium was dark and silent. And then came an explosion of applause. Everyone stood and cheered; the actors' classmates pumped their arms above their heads.

Doug cheered, too; freed from orders to be quiet, he scrambled up to stand on his seat, shouting Abby's name over and over and pounding his hands together high in the air. Once again Sara's eyes met her mother's, and both women smiled through their tears in a moment of simple understanding. "Yes," Sara said quietly, beneath the applause, "she's wonderful, and the play is timeless. Do you think she'll remember what it's really about?"

Tess made a gesture. "You're right," Sara said. "She'll put it aside as soon as she's back in her own world. I just hope it surfaces now and then. I hope we all remember what it's about." She took her mother's hand. "I'm so glad you're here."

Abby stood onstage with the rest of the cast, and when they pushed her forward, she stood alone, and bowed deeply, accepting the applause and the cheers, trying not to cry because everything was so wonderful. Everyone loved her. Life was perfect. She saw Doug, standing and waving above all the others, and Sara, smiling at her, and her mother, trying to smile. Everyone was smiling at her. Perfect, she thought again. This is the perfect moment of my life. Nothing ever again will be so perfect.

But on Monday, after *Our Town* had finished its three performances, and the cast had celebrated on Sunday night after the final closing curtain (laughing but crying, too, because where was the excitement in life if there were no rehearsals to go to, and no play to look forward to, and no stage fright to make one feel like dying but also more alive than ever?), on Monday morning, at school, everything was still wonderful. It seemed that everyone had seen the play, and everyone, even the teachers, said it was wonderful, that Abby was a real star.

And when the talk about the play began to

flag, Abby added to the glory of the morning by dropping the bombshell of her new car and describing it in envy-creating detail to clusters of friends and onlookers. Mack had been right about her classmates knowing they would have cars in their senior year, but Abby was the first, and for that one shining day, she reigned over the junior class.

And then, on top of all those wonders, Sean was impressed. He held her hand as they walked from the computer lab to their history class, and he pulled her into an empty room to kiss her quickly. "You are one special lady," he murmured into her ear. "In all respects, I find you quite irrefutably irresistible."

Abby smiled—mysteriously, she hoped—because, whenever Sean turned excessively wordy and gallant, she could not tell how serious he was, and so it was easiest to smile and say nothing. But then his hand went to her breast, and his mouth was on hers again, and she moaned, low in her throat, where only he could hear it. He lifted his head, and made a little scrabbling motion on her buttocks in a playful, proprietary way that she hated. "Please—" she started to say, but at that moment the bell rang, and so it was in dizzying confusion that she ran across the hall, behind Sean, and ducked into their classroom. They were the last to take their seats, and everyone turned to look, some—most of them, it seemed to Abby—suddenly smirking instead of praising her.

Her underpants were wet and she shifted uncomfortably, in turmoil from the aching urgings of her body and the embarrassment she always felt when Sean fingered her in unpleasant ways. The history lesson buzzed behind her, like bees in Sara's garden, rising and falling and now and then coming close enough to be noticed. This week they were studying the Irish War of Independence, and usually Abby paid close attention, because it was Sean's country and he talked about it a lot (once he'd said that her name was the same as the name of the most famous the-ater in Ireland—"spelled differently, but close enough to make you especially special," he said; *special* being his favorite word), claim-ing in his carelessly contemptuous way that American teachers didn't understand zip about Ireland; that they always sided with the British even though where would America be today if *they* hadn't beat the British . . . which is exactly what the Irish were trying to do?

But today she could not pay attention; she could not even focus on enough of the lecture to be able to talk to Sean about it later. Which meant he would do the talking until he'd said all he wanted to say (or listened to himself long enough, Abby would think when she was feeling particularly sharp and objective), and then he would begin to caress her and kiss her and try to get his hands inside her sweater and up her skirt, and Abby's body would lean into his, strain against his, even as *shouldn't* and *don't* and *never* tumbled through her thoughts, mixed up with images of the ideal romance she and Sara sometimes talked about: two people sharing ideas and hopes and fears, and then, at some point, turning to sex because it was the natural next step, sort of *flowing* from the closeness they'd already built . . . which, Abby had to admit, she and Sean had not built, were not even close to building.

"Stupid," Sean said when Abby pulled back once and told him, haltingly, what she hoped for. "A stupid waste of time. We're young and full of sexual energy, it's a special time, and we have to take advantage of it before it drains away. We can always talk. Old people talk; you get to be forty and that's all you've got: talk talk talk and dried-up bodies. But look at us! Young and full of juices . . . and you'd throw that away! Not for me, my little lady."

"But—" Abby tried to force out the words *I won't go to bed with you,* but her throat closed up in fear: Sean would laugh the mocking laugh he used with others, never with her (so far, she thought honestly, and he could; I'm probably not that special . . . maybe nobody is), and he would leave her and she couldn't stand that, she'd die.

I'm not sophisticated enough to handle Sean, she realized, but even though she recognized the shrewdness and accuracy of that assessment, and knew, in moments of such clarity, that she should walk away from him, she could not do it. She could not walk away when she was alone and saw him clearly, and certainly not when his hand was on her breast, or his mouth was opening hers, or his light blue eyes were focused on her as if she were the only person in the world and he adored her and only her, forever. She could not leave him then. She could not leave him at any time. She would die.

Trying to shut out the buzz of the history lesson, Abby shifted disconsolately in her seat. She could not understand how everything had collapsed so quickly, from the triumph of her curtain calls in *Our Town* to the misery of uncertainty Sean could create with a flick of his fingers or a twist of his mouth.

"It's awful," Abby said to her mother in the nursing home the next day, a miserable afternoon after Sean had ignored her at lunch, sitting with gorgeous Marjorie Bassett and laughing a lot, and then disappearing right after school, instead of walking Abby home, as he usually did. At times like this, her mother was the only one she could talk to, because (and she admitted this was really terrible, but it was true) her mother couldn't criticize her. She couldn't even look really surprised or disgusted; the paralysis on one side of her face made her expressions so ambiguous you could sort of decide for yourself what they were, and however you interpreted them they were always on your side.

Sometimes her mother wrote a word or two on the pad of paper on the table that swung across her lap, but it was hard for her to control her hand to write, and she hated it, so most of the time she gestured with her hand or pointed until someone got the idea of what she meant. But whether she tried to write or not, her mother always listened to Abby with unwavering attention; she loved her and thought whatever she did was right. Abby could always tell that.

"So, the thing is," Abby concluded unhappily after describing much, though not all, of that crazy day that started out absolutely perfect and then crashed, "if I'm going to die if I don't see Sean, and if I feel terrible a lot of the time when I do see him, I mean, if those are my only options, life is really the pits. Being *fifteen* is the pits. I mean, Carrie doesn't have any problems and neither does Doug and neither does Sara, so it's me being fifteen, and I always thought it would be so great and I couldn't wait because it was almost grown up and, you know, everything good would happen. Now I'd rather be seventeen, or twenty-seven, like Sara. I really envy her, you know? She's so totally put together. But seventeen would be good, seventeen would be great, because then you're in college, and then you can handle anything, all the things you can't manage at fifteen, which is a really awful age—"

(An endless year from September till I get there, she thought mournfully, and wondered how she would be able to live until then.)

"—and I hate it." She saw her mother frown—a real frown that couldn't be called anything else—and she said hastily, "Well, I don't really mean that, I don't really *hate* it, at least not all of it—" She paused. "Maybe not even most of it. I mean, I totally loved being in the play and I'm going to try out for senior-class play next year—everybody says I should, that I'm really good—that sounds like bragging, but you heard the applause, they really *liked* it—and you know, Mom, when I was up there I really *was* Emily, wanting my mother to tell me whether I was pretty or not, and falling in love with George and getting married . . . it was totally amazing. Did that ever happen to you, that you could be somebody else? You know, just for a little while really *be* somebody else? I mean, you could go back to your real self whenever you wanted, but, you know, for a while your problems would just disappear. Well, I guess you'd have the problems of this person you are now, but they're not real because it's only a play. Except then," she added sadly, "you've got your own again.

"Anyway," she said hastily, rattling off a list at random instead of whining, "everything's great, the play and my friends and my family and my new car—" She stopped abruptly. Why couldn't she remember they weren't supposed to talk about Mack? *Talk about other things,* Sara had said. But it was hard, because he seemed to be wound up in just about everything that went on these days. "—toon, cartoon that somebody made me"— this was true, so she did not have to lie to her mother, which she didn't do well, anyway— "showing me in the middle of the stage, like I'm a real actress on Broadway, and Sean isn't even that important . . . What?"

Her mother was gesturing with her hand and Abby wished Sara were there to translate . . . except that if Sara were there Abby wouldn't be talking like this about Sean, because she'd rather die than have Sara know about her problems with him because then she might not let her go out with him, and Abby would die if she couldn't go out with . . . "What?" she said again. "I don't understand . . ."

Her mother was struggling to write, and
Abby stood up to read it. *Pride yousel.*

"Pride myself," she said aloud. She repeated it slowly. "You mean you want me to
take pride in myself. But I do, don't I?
Doesn't everybody?"

Her mother made a small movement with
her head. *No.*

In the silence, Abby thought about it. Sara
had talked about pride when she talked
about the Corcorans, about how Pussy Corcoran had been beaten down by her husband, not physically (though who knew that
for a fact?), but by his denigrating her again
and again until she had no pride in herself;
she never stood tall, believing in herself.

"There are a lot of insecure people in the
world," Sara had said, "who puff themselves
up by denigrating others. They find people
who are vulnerable, and they tear them
down, making them feel little and worthless,
less than human. It's probably the cruelest
thing people can do to each other: to rob
others of belief in themselves, pride in themselves."

"So what can you do?" Abby asked, thinking of Sean (later she wondered if Sara had

raised the subject because she knew more about Sean than Abby thought).

"Protect yourself," Sara said. "If you have confidence that you are valuable, that you have control over who and what you are and what you'll become, you can guard your own worth so that no one can take it away from you. People can still cause you pain, but they can't make you feel worthless."

Remembering that, Abby stared at her mother, who was trying to tell her exactly the same thing. In the fading light of early evening, her mother looked firm and decisive, not the vibrant beauty Abby remembered, but still a woman with definite ideas and a will to nudge what she could no longer control. "But you can't just make it happen, pride," she said. "I mean, if somebody makes you feel bad, what do you do? Sara says you should protect yourself, but she didn't say how. I don't *want* anybody to tear me down, but sometimes I feel really . . . slow. Like I might think of the right thing to say when I'm in bed at night, but when I need it, I can't think of it. I'm not sharp and sophisticated, and Sean knows everything, he's been all over the world; he's been . . . he hints about being with lots of women, older women, too, and I haven't been with anybody. I'm still a virgin, and that's okay . . . I think . . . I mean, I *want* to be, but sometimes I'm not sure if . . ."

Tess shrugged one shoulder, as if to say, *That will come; there's time.*

Or she might have meant, *So lose it; it's not such a big deal.*

Or, perhaps, *It's up to you; it doesn't make much difference either way; whatever makes you happy.*

"Oh," Abby cried in frustration. "I wish you could just tell me what to do so I could do it, and I wouldn't have to worry whether it was right or not. I wish *Sara* would tell me, or *somebody.* But nobody does. Well, you know, Sara thinks I'd probably be happier in the long run if I stayed a virgin, but she doesn't say I have to stay one or she'll kick me out of the house or make me do hard labor or anything like that. Not that I want her to say that . . . I don't want her to. That would be a dictatorship and I wouldn't like that either." She looked at the clock on the wall. "I have to go; Sara will have dinner, and I have homework and . . . Sean may call." She put her strong young arms around her mother's thin, bowed shoulders and hugged as hard as she dared. "I love you. I'll be back Saturday, so we can talk some more then. I love to talk to you. I love you."

On the bus home, she thought of driving her own car, in just a month, when she finished her high school course and took the test and passed it with a gold star (did they give gold stars when they gave you a driver's permit?), and then, in September, when she was sixteen, she'd get her license and drive without anybody else in the car (if Sara said it was okay), and the more she thought about those things, the more cheerful she became, until she walked into her house humming and smiling and loving everybody.

"Well, that must have been a wonderful visit," said Sara, stirring risotto at the stove. She kissed Abby, thinking of Emily begging her mother to *look at me.*

"Oh." Abby realized she had not thought about her mother once, not while she was with her and talking about herself, not on the bus coming home. She took the wooden spoon from Sara. "I'll do this; I like to. She seemed happy," she improvised, about Tess. "I told her about school and—"

"And about *Sean*?" Doug said, leering around the doorjamb.

"And about the usual stuff," Abby said, making a face at him. She ladled simmering stock into the risotto, and kept stirring. "She said she was proud of me."

"For what?" Carrie asked. She was slicing mushrooms at the center island, her tongue caught between her teeth as she concentrated on making them the same size.

"Just . . . for being me."

"I'm writing a story about a girl who doesn't know who she is; she forgets her name and her address until—"

"Amnesia," said Doug, swinging around the doorjamb, staying away from the action so he would not be given a job.

"Doug, it would be so helpful if you would set the table," said Sara, and smiled at him as he gave a deep sigh.

"I know it's amnesia," Carrie said loftily. "I wasn't sure you'd know, so I was careful not to use it."

"I know every word you know," Doug retorted.

"How can you? You haven't lived as long or read as much or thought as much or talked as much."

"Well, nobody *talks* as much as you, that's for sure. You could talk a guy's head off."

"How was your day, Sara?" asked Abby, making up for not paying much attention to her mother that afternoon. "Any more miserable Corcorans?"

"Do I set a place for Mack?" Doug asked.

"Of course," Sara said. "He lives here."

"But he doesn't eat here a lot, unless you're going out."

"We'll set a place for him anyway."

"He's so *erratic,*" Doug said gloomily, shooting a glance at Carrie as he emphasized the word.

"Like *unpredictable, irregular,* and *inconsistent* plus just plain annoying?" Carrie shot back, and they both burst out laughing.

And Sara was laughing as she described it to Reuben on Sunday morning. "They have such a good time; words are their favorite toys." They were walking from her house to the lakefront, the first time they had been together in the morning, the first time Abby and Doug and Carrie had made sufficiently extensive arrangements with friends that Sara and Reuben could plan an entire day and evening together. "We all grew up with Mother creating word games at the dinner table, and in the car, even when we worked in the garden . . . whenever two or more of us did anything together, at least part of the time was spent playing with words."

"Lucky," said Reuben. "What I learned was the vocabulary of bagels and *schnecken,* the varieties of rye flour, the ingredients in challah and knishes—"

Sara was laughing. "Not true."

"Only partly," he admitted. He grinned. "However, I did absorb an astonishing education in baking, none of which I've forgotten: not one of my parents' lessons in front of a mixer or oven. One of these days I'll make you apple strudel according to my mother's recipe, and I promise you'll say it's the best you've ever eaten." They crossed the street into the park, and turned toward the lagoon. "In fact, will you let me make you dinner one night? All your restaurant suggestions have been excellent, but I'd very much like to cook for you."

"I'd like that," Sara said. "But then it will be my turn. It's time you met my family."

"It is," he agreed, as casually as she, and they crossed the path crowded with bicyclists, skateboarders wearing their caps backward as they sailed off curbings and benches, and a steady stream of joggers, and took to the grass. It was almost as crowded there: lovers sprawling under the spreading trees; young families picnicking, playing volleyball, gliding dreamily in swan boats on the lagoon or holding one-sided conversations with animals in the zoo and its miniature farm; nannies gossiping within fenced playgrounds where small children swarmed like chattering monkeys on jungle gyms and pumped their legs to swing ever higher, their delighted and somewhat scared laughter rising in the sun-gold air; and groups of tourists disembarking from buses to stroll through the gardens and the conservatory, photographing each other in front of the spraying fountain or the city's skyscrapers barely glimpsed through the trees.

"Lovely," Reuben said. "What a wonderful job this city has done with its open space. Parks and the lakefront stretching from one end to the other. This seems to be the friendliest; it may become the model for the one at Carrano West."

"It's hard to think of building a whole village. Have you planned where it will be?"

"We have; we've bought the land, but we still need one more approval before we can start building. The county insists that the neighboring town, River Bend, annex our development, and that's fine with us. We thought everyone agreed, and the River Bend City Council was ready to vote to approve, but in the past couple of weeks the townspeople and some neighboring farmers have made a few statements—one of them wrote a letter to a neighborhood newspaper—objecting to what we're doing, or what they think we're doing. It's not serious, probably a few malcontents; we'll talk to them, and as soon as the annexation is approved, we'll begin."

"Why wouldn't they like it?"

"We don't know. We don't even know how many are complaining. There was the one letter to the paper—we don't worry about isolated letters—but yesterday an editor at the *Tribune* called for a comment about two letters that will appear in tomorrow's paper. Two letters in a citywide paper. It begins to sound as if someone is organizing it."

"Why? To stop you from building? Who would benefit from that?"

"We don't know. And it may not be true. Would you like to see it? Where it will be?"

"Yes, I'd like that."

"Then we'll drive there. It's about an hour away. Shall we find a place for lunch first?"

"Why don't we buy something to take with us? We'll be the first people to eat in Carrano Village West."

He smiled. "I find it quite wonderful that you come up with the right answer to every question."

"Oh, not every one," she said lightly (thinking, Reuben assumed, of her family or her job—or another man?—but the sun was shining, the day was warm and fragrant, and the hours stretched ahead of them; it was not a time to probe).

They turned to walk back to Sara's house, past the apartment buildings near the lake, to the houses of Sara's neighborhood, most of them more than a century old, survivors of the great Chicago fire, the Depression, two world wars, and how many family traumas, tragedies, and triumphs played out in each one? They all stood exactly the same distance from the street, three stories high, their massive oak front doors bearing brass handles in the shape of monsters—dubious choices, Reuben thought, for welcoming guests—myriad chimneys sprouting from steeply slanting slate roofs that shaded the

front doors like the straw hats of Asian farmers, and small front yards surrounded by low
wrought-iron fences. Each yard was a carefully tended garden of ground cover dotted
with sculptures, or flowers that changed with
the seasons, or rose and peony trees rising
amid evergreens pruned in the shapes of
deer and owls.

The air was fragrant with damp earth and
new-mown grass, honeysuckle, magnolias,
and early roses, even some late, lingering
lilacs. Tunnels of oaks and maples shaded
the streets, sunlight filtering through their
leafy branches and spilling to the sidewalk
like gold coins.

As Sara and Reuben walked, they heard
through open windows the sounds of Sun-
days at home: scales practiced on a piano, a
radio broadcasting the news, a father calling
children in from their backyards to wash their
hands for lunch, the clatter of dishes, a dog
barking as a ball thumped against the wall.
Reuben breathed deeply, feeling wonderful.
He took Sara's hand. For this moment, when
the world seemed serene and ordered, it
seemed quite believable that there were no
problems of the past, only possibilities for

the future. He glanced at Sara's profile, admiring it, happy that she could be as absorbed in her thoughts as he was in his, that often she was content to be silent, not desperate to fill every moment with chatter as so many people seemed to be, as if any space in a conversation meant failure, and had to be glossed over with sound.

But that sound most likely would contain personal information, many might say, especially when two people are still getting to know each other, with much to explore. And that was true of him and Sara: they had much still to explore. But there was no reason to hurry.

"I love it here," Sara murmured. "I love being part of the city, part of the beating heart of other lives."

Reuben nodded. "A nice way to put it. I think that, or something close to it, whenever I walk anywhere in New York."

And was she giving him an opening for their first truly revelatory conversation? If she was, he let it go by. He was not ready to open many of the closed doors in his life. How many of us are comfortable revealing personal disasters we might have prevented had we been more analytical, less fervid, firmly in the driver's seat rather than a passenger driven by our gonads and insecurities?

Had we been, he thought wryly, grown up.

But by the time we're grown up enough to see what we did wrong, we would much prefer to keep it to ourselves, so that others—especially those we want to impress—might not wonder if there could be residue of those weaknesses still in us.

And, in fact, might there be?

He reflected on the fragments of information he and Sara had shared so far: there were quite a few of them. And there could be more, if they came to trust themselves to reveal what could be painful or embarrassing or even shameful; if each came to trust the other to receive it without ridicule or censure.

Or they would never get to that point. In which case, he thought, we won't talk about the past at all. Today and tomorrow can fill hours of conversation if we work at it, and the door to the past kept firmly locked.

And Sara, too, he reflected, seemed quite satisfied to talk about subjects other than herself and her family, that large bunch of people who filled so much of her life with their needs and demands, and their delights. And yet, he reminded himself, she had invited him to dinner. *It's time you met my family.* Yes, but there had been no mention of a date. No necessity for whipping out calendars to inscribe dinner and introductions. A simple, vague *It's time.*

And so be it, he said to himself with finality. (And knew, beneath all the bravado, that it was not true: that, this far along, he knew he wanted Sara to understand who he was and how he had come to this point in his life, and that he wanted to understand what had made her the person she was today. It was just that it had been so long since he had truly opened up to someone that he did not know how to begin. Or whether she would want him to, if he did figure it out.)

So they talked about the architecture and history of the houses in the neighborhood; about Chicago and the people who built it from the ruins of the Great Fire; its commerce and culture and evolution into a city of sophistication, influence, and wealth, while the rest of the country, entranced by the drama of both coasts, missed entirely what was happening in the center. They talked about theater and music and the politics of Chicago, until they came to Sara's house, where Reuben had left his car.

With Sara giving directions, they drove to Fox & Obel and made up a picnic basket, then drove west on the expressway, past commerce and industry and clusters of frame houses giving way to low buildings with shops on the ground floor and apartments above, gasoline stations and auto shops, storefront restaurants, and then more industrial parks.

"It seems to go forever," Reuben said.

"Its easy to spread out when there's nothing but prairie," Sara said. "New Yorkers live on an island; Chicago never had even a hill to slow it down."

"You have a lake."

"But open prairie on the other three sides. I like thinking about those people who decided every once in a while to leave everything and move farther out, and create a new life for themselves and their families."

"Or," Reuben said thoughtfully, "they discovered that it didn't really happen that way: that they'd brought so much baggage from their other life, all they'd really done was change landscapes."

"I hope it was more than that," said Sara, wondering what circumstances in New York led him to say that. "I do believe people can change their lives. Unless they're so locked in . . ." She gazed at the changing scene as Reuben turned onto another expressway. Now fields of wheat and corn stretched between the towns where vignettes flashed by: neighbors chatting, planting gardens, mowing lawns, children on swing sets or splashing in backyard pools. Sara gave a quiet laugh. "Chicago has always believed lives could be changed, as the landscape could, because there always were places for new beginnings, new ways of doing things, new dreams. Did you know engineers reversed the flow of the Chicago River? It's wonderful to think about how to control the flow of rivers . . ."

On either side, the prairie spun out to the horizon, dotted with white farmhouses, red barns, the bizarre sight of a huge auto dump of rusting cars tossed as if by a careless giant onto precarious piles. And then they were on roads slicing through small communities of small frame houses, run-down, sorrowful looking, crouched beneath huge trees in yards overrun with weeds. Beyond, they glimpsed a river glinting in the sunlight. Riverfront property, Sara thought. In most parts of the country, that's where the largest homes would be. She was going to ask Reuben about it, when he pulled off the road onto a dirt track beside a chain-link fence, and in a few minutes stopped the car to unlock a gate.

"Carrano Village West," he said, almost formally, and she heard anticipation and pride in his voice. He relocked the gate behind them, then bumped along the track until stopping at what seemed a randomly chosen spot in the middle of a prairie exactly like the ones through which they had been driving for over half an hour. "The Fox River is our western boundary." They walked toward the other side of the expanse, carrying the picnic basket between them. "A creek flows through the property, deep enough for rowboats and kayaks. And there's pretty good fishing in the Fox." They walked toward a long line of trees. "Lunch by the creek?"

They spread a checked cloth beneath ash and hawthorn trees, and set out duck pâté, smoked salmon and a long loaf of French bread, Manzanilla olives, and almond biscotti. Reuben opened a Rhône wine. "My favorite kind of lunch. Do we have glasses?"

Sara handed him two glasses from the picnic basket. "Is this Carrano village limited to young families, like the other one?"

"Isaiah refused to consider anything else. If we're sued for discrimination in New Jersey, and lose, or if we open that one to all buyers to avoid a trial and a nightmare of publicity, this one will open up, too. I hope it does."

"What happens if you do restrict it to young families, and they get older?"

"They're not forced to move. But if they move, they have to sell to a young family. It's crazy, you know, and it can't work, but Isaiah is a stubborn old man with a vision, and so much money he most often gets his way."

"We'd all like some of that," Sara said with a smile.

"A vision? So much money? Getting your way?"

She laughed. "All three, wouldn't you say?"

She began to fill their plates, and Reuben poured the wine. He watched her, admiring the way she looked, in jeans and a blue shirt open at the neck, her sleeves rolled partway up. (In fact, they both wore jeans and a blue shirt, which, foolishly, pleased him, as if it were an omen.) She wore walking shoes and looked perfectly at home sitting on a tarpaulin on prairie grass, with flies buzzing above her, and a few bees, which she ignored. Much more than simply a city person, he thought.

Once again, he was aware that they both were comfortable when silences stretched between them, and for the first time he understood that silence created an intimacy that conversation often cannot.

They contemplated the creek, narrow and languid in this flat stretch of land, gleaming pewter in the sun, leafy shadows stretching across it like lace curtains lifted by a breeze, small birds hopping along the shallow banks in intense pursuit of the insects that skipped over the water's surface, leaving a trail of concentric ripples. Sara's gaze circled the land that would become Carrano Village West, from the river to the distant chain-link fencing, from the prairie grass rippling around them to groves of trees, and back to the river. Wildflowers and tall wild grass in greens and browns reached as far as she could see; a green snake, thin as a pencil, rustled nearby and disappeared around a boulder at the river's edge; far above, a hawk rode a current, its motionless silhouette black against the piercing blue sky. Nowhere was there a hint of the strident commerce of a great city an hour away.

What a shame to bulldoze this, she thought. To destroy one of the few places left where people can sit beside a river and be part of a prairie that was here from the beginning.

"Someone will build here," Reuben said quietly. "If not Isaiah, another developer, who could make a real mess of it."

She was dismayed that her thoughts were so obvious.

"I'm not reading your mind," he said, reading her mind again. "Many people have the same reaction when they come to these wonderful untouched places that seem almost prehistoric. And of course you're right; it would be better to leave them alone, for their own sake, and for us to touch earth's history. But those people you talked about who kept moving farther and farther out didn't think of that; they just wanted land, a new place. And that's still happening, so we don't even have the option of leaving it alone. The land is owned, owners have a right to sell, buyers have a right to build and to make a profit. And some of them maximize their profit by building the maximum they're allowed, until nothing is left, not a blade of wild grass or a single wildflower."

He picked something from the ground and held it out to Sara: a tiny snail shell, grayish white with black discolorations of age. "Once, this was all a sea; when it receded, snails were left behind and evolved into these land snails. They're all over the world; you can even find them in the mountains."

Sara contemplated the shell in the palm of her hand. Snails on the Midwestern prairie. She had lived here all her life, and had never known about them. *How much we don't know about the things around us, maybe about our own lives.* Unnerving, she thought, and exciting.

"It isn't a sea anymore," Reuben said, "and it won't be prairie anymore, but what we're trying to do here, what good developers try to do everywhere, is have the best of all possible worlds. We build houses that blend with the landscape, we make a profit on them, and we leave as much open space as possible. Not golf courses masquerading as open space, though we'll have those, too, but as many acres as we can of the real thing, the prairie that's been here for thousands of years. The prairie belongs to all of us, I do believe that, and I'd like to see more of it open and free, not anyone's property, but that's not the way the world works."

He refilled their wineglasses and spread duck pâté on slices of French bread. "This is my favorite spot; I'm hoping it stays exactly as it is."

"Hoping?"

"I don't have control over everything."

"But over some things?"

"Some. Mostly we negotiate. When anyone builds a whole new town, there are so many specialists and interest groups and experts and neighbors, every one with absolute ideas of what to do and how to do it, that it's like a dance: we spend a lot of time trying not to step too hard on anyone's toes."

"So it's all compromising?"

"Most of it. When we can't do that, we're in gridlock, and someone has to break it with a decision one group or another will vociferously hate."

"Are you that someone?"

"Often. Just as often, it's Isaiah. But we don't decree anything unless it truly is gridlock. It's a question of learning when and where to draw a line. Knowing when to fight, what is really worth fighting for. If you're sure of that, you can do almost anything."

"Except keep out people who don't have young children."

Reuben laughed. "Probably. You could do it in a dictatorship, but even Isaiah wouldn't want that. Would you like to see how we're going to develop the land? We can walk the property, if you'd like, and I can show you where the buildings and the open space will be."

"Yes, I would like that."

"It's several miles."

"Even better, after all this food."

Later, Sara thought that that Sunday was the real beginning of her love affair with Reuben Lister. They walked the warm, grass-scented land, the only people there on a quiet Sunday afternoon, and it was as if they were the first people in the world, the first to discover flowers hidden beneath spreading leaves of burdock, wild fennel, Solomon's seal, and wild ginger; Rugosa rose bushes covered with pale pink flowers, their single layer of petals open flat to the sun; dry leaves from the previous fall rustling beneath the scurrying feet of unseen animals; the harmonic rippling of the grass beneath a sudden breeze; blue jays darting among groves of trees and bushes, bright blue flaring amid the shadowy leaves.

Reuben took Sara's hand and they walked for hours, stopping as he pointed out the four staked sites, widely separated, where houses would be built along curving roads, each house backed by a yard flowing into untouched prairie that stretched to the perimeter of the land; the area in the middle where the recreation center would be built, surrounded by a softball diamond, a playground for young children, tennis courts, a climbing wall—"and so forth," he said. "We haven't finished designing this part."

Along the main road at the edge of the property, a double row of stores would curve toward each other like two long parentheses with gardens and benches between them. "I want to put small apartments above the stores," Reuben said, "for employees, or anyone who's single."

"But Isaiah says no," Sara guessed.

"He has, so far. You know, sometimes I want to say, 'Save us from people with visions,' but, in fact, they're the ones who move the world. And I have my own visions, so I'm not one to talk."

"But you're not rigid."

"I hope not. We all get stuck in what we believe is best, and sometimes we get irrational, fighting for it."

"'It's a question of learning when and where to draw a line,'" Sara quoted mischievously. "'Knowing when to fight, what is really worth fighting for.'"

Reuben laughed. "You're right. I should listen to myself before I contradict myself. But in fact," he said, suddenly somber, "both are true. If we're irrational, we lose, and we know we will, but still we fall into it when we want something desperately, when there's a vision dancing before us, so real we can reach out and touch it. . ."

Sara waited for him to go on, and when he did not, she thought, Well, at some point he will. When he's comfortable enough, he won't stop in the middle of his sentences. And neither will I.

But the walk through that untouched prairie had changed both of them, as if they had indeed been the first people in the world and were open to all discoveries, especially the ones they would make together. And so that night, after a leisurely dinner at Tru, where widely spaced tables, low lighting, and a barely discernible hum of conversation created an intimacy even before wine and food were shared, it was quite natural, and inevitable, that Sara would return with Reuben to his house, and he would lock the door behind them, and they would climb the stairs to his bedroom, arms around each other, in warm and easy silence. They had not yet kissed; they had done no more than hold hands.

"A long wait," Reuben murmured, holding her. "But we both—"

"Yes." Sara kissed him. They had both wanted it to be right. Behind them, in their separate lives, lay sadnesses and disappointments, searchings, longings, lost chances. What they had found in each other, they both knew, was worth treating with care, and as they embraced and stood tightly together without words, their kiss was an affirmation of all they had built so far, and a prelude to all that lay ahead.

They had both been alone for a long time (though as yet they did not know that), and, in the soft light and silence of Reuben's bedroom, they undressed each other with increasing urgency, tumbling onto the bed like children allowed into a room that always had been locked, and discovering, through touch and sound and response, a rising passion that submerged thought and talk and surroundings. There were only the two of them, the one of them, enmeshed, enclosed, coming deeply together again and again, open, alive, illuminating each other, illuminated by each other.

They had known each other for six weeks, but tonight they met anew. And tonight, with both of them changed within themselves and with each other, they would begin.

SIX

My brother gave it to me," Carrie said proudly. She stood with her friends in the school courtyard at recess, watching as they passed from hand to hand the large leather-bound journal, dark maroon, embossed with Carrie's name in gold.

"Doug?" Will Farish asked incredulously. "This is, like, *expensive.*"

"No, my brother Mack."

"Mack? Who's he?"

"I *told* you. My *brother.*"

"You've got another brother? Since when?"

"He just came back from . . . a long trip, and now he lives with us."

"For good? Cool. How old—"

"It's like . . . sexy," said Martha Gold, smoothing the leather as if she were stroking a cat's soft fur.

Edie Stone threw Martha a scornful look. "It's for *work*. Carrie, you'll be a real writer with this."

"She's already a real writer," said Joanie Tavish. "She's a *great* writer."

"*He* must be great, your brother," said Brad Dorner, who often telephoned Carrie at night for help with his homework. "I mean, my brother never buys me anything like this. Actually, he never buys me anything at all."

"Your brother's too busy chasing girls," Joanie said.

"He doesn't; they chase him."

"Girls in high school don't chase boys. *I* won't when I'm in high school. My sister's a sophomore and she says there's no guys worth it; they're, you know, immature and whiny, and they sulk when they don't get their way." She gave an exaggerated shiver. "Ugh!"

"You don't know anything," said Brad weakly, unable, as always, to think of a cutting riposte until hours later, when it did no good.

"I'm going to use it for all my stories," said

Carrie loudly, dragging everyone's attention back to her and her shiny journal. "And Mack wants to read them all. He's really interested in me."

"I wish my bro—" Brad began, but Trent Felsen asked, "How old is he?"

"Twenty," Carrie said warily, because you never knew what Trent was going to say next; he didn't really fit in, and was always saying things that made people uncomfortable.

"*Twen*ty?" he repeated, stomping on the first syllable. "And he's *really interested* in you? In your mind or"—he leered—"*your virginal body?*"

"Oh, stuff it, Trent," someone said, while Brad searched in vain for a chilling comment, and Carrie, her face flaming, scurried away.

Joanie and the others caught up with her. "Don't pay any attention to him," Joanie said. "If my mother allowed me to use four-letter words, I'd say he's a shit."

Carrie gave a small laugh.

"Anyway, what *about* your brother?" Leonora Yates asked. "I mean, he sounds so cool; I'd really like to meet him."

"Don't tell Trent," said Joanie. "He'll think you want his body."

"Is he a virgin?" asked Barbie Vance, who always talked as if she were so experienced she was way ahead of all of them.

Carrie's face was flushed again. "How would I know?"

"But he *is* cool, right?" Leonora asked. "Could you introduce me?"

"I don't know," Carrie said miserably.

Susie rescued her. "Carrie's too nice to tell you that he wouldn't be interested in you. Why would he want to meet a thirteen-year-old?"

"I'm fourteen," Leonora said.

"Whatever. He only likes older women, I'll bet. Does he bring them home, Carrie?"

Carrie shook her head, wondering why she had gotten into this. "He's . . . he's just with us when he's home, you know, doing things together."

"Like what?"

"Oh, cooking dinner and going to movies and driving around and playing Monopoly . . . he's really mean when he plays Monopoly, but he says we have to learn that's the way the world works, that people are out to get you and you have to get them first, and if you start feeling sorry for them you slow down and lose your advantage and then they move in for the kill."

There was a pause as they absorbed this. Finally, Will said, "He sounds like Saddam Hussein."

"He does not!"

"He does to me. I mean, do you *like* him?"

"I *love* him. He's wonderful. That's a terrible thing to say: he's not anything like Saddam Hussein; he's really sweet, and fun to be with, and he tells the most wonderful stories, from his travels, you know, all around the world, and he bought Abby a car, and then he bought me this—"

"A car?" The group was suddenly silent, awed at the thought of a car. Abby wasn't even a senior! And it wasn't Christmas or— "Was it her birthday?"

"No. He just bought it."

"Wow."

"I wish he was my brother," said Brad at last.

"What's he like, Carrie?" asked Joanie.

"Oh, tall and handsome and he's got blond hair that he kind of musses up when he's thinking about something . . . he's like a prince, you know, who sort of just appears from nowhere and makes new things happen, and tells fantastic stories—"

"You told us about the stories," said Will, bored and disbelieving when it came to princes. "What else does he do?"

"Well, he works . . . somewhere; he didn't tell us where. But he must make a lot of money because he buys all these things and he takes us to movies and restaurants, and out for ice cream sometimes after we have dinner at home, and he buys CDs for himself and for us, too—"

"And you really *like* him?" pressed Will.

"YES! How many times do I have to tell you? I *love* him. We have fun all the time because we're so much alike. I mean, you know, he's really our brother. Sara's different, 'cause she's not really our sister—"

"What?" Joanie screamed. "She's not your sister? Since when?"

"Well, she *is,* but not really. Not *fully,* that's what Mack says. She's our half sister 'cause she has a different father from us. We all have the same mother, but, you know, her father, like, died, and then Mom got married again and she had Mack and Abby and me and Doug, so we're like a *full* family and Sara's kind of not part of it. Not *fully.*"

Brad looked worried. "That doesn't sound right, you know, I mean, she lives there and takes care of you, I mean, you always said she's in charge . . ."

"It sounds awful to me," Leonora declared. "Like you don't love her anymore."

"I *do* love her!" Carrie began to cry, tears running down her face. "She's wonderful, and I always love her!"

"Sure you do," Joanie said firmly, once again coming to her rescue. "You talk about her all the time, and you love her and *respect* her and . . . you know, like she's more your mother than your *mother* is."

"Mother *can't* be our mother!" Carrie cried wildly, feeling everything had gotten totally out of control. "She wants to, but she's *sick*!"

"Right, we know that," Joanie said soothingly. "It's okay."

"And I don't want to talk about Mack or Sara or Mother or . . . anybody!" Carrie wailed. "I'm going in."

"It's time, anyway," Brad said, looking at his watch. "Like, the bell is going to ring . . . right . . . now."

The bell rang. Triumphantly, Brad looked around to bask in admiring faces, but no one noticed; the whole group was walking along

the brick path that skirted the pond and led
to a large doorway in the wall of windows on
this side of the school. Carrie walked with
them, her head down, feeling helpless because she hadn't done anything right. How
could she say those things about Sara? Of
course Sara was their sister; the best sister
they could have, even, sort of, their mother,
and they loved her more than anyone. She
started crying again; she was a failure at
everything.

Doug was running through the corridor,
and he stopped short when he saw her.
"What happened?"

"Nothing."

"You're crying."

"I'm not!"

"You are!"

"I was sneezing."

"Sneezing?"

"Hay fever. Don't you have art class?
You're going to be late."

"Right, see you later," he said, and dashed
off, so happily focused on himself that it
never occurred to him to point out that Carrie
did not have hay fever, and even if she did,
the end of May was the wrong time of year
for it.

But half the time he couldn't understand Carrie anyway. They were really good friends most of the time, but then all of a sudden—*and you never had any warning*—she'd sort of disappear *inside herself.* She always said she was thinking of a new story, but it was weird and kind of scary the way she'd just all of a sudden be gone, like she couldn't even see him and he was right in front of her, waggling his fingers and dancing around and sort of singing, up and down the scale, *Hel-lo-o* and *I-see-you-do-you-see-me* and then shouting BOO!! but nothing worked, she'd be frowning and talking to herself, not him, and finally he'd give up and go somewhere and be by himself. So if she wanted to cry or sneeze or whatever, that was up to her; he couldn't figure it out anyway.

He was late, slipping into the classroom after everybody else was in place, taking out charcoal pencils. Oh, good, he loved charcoal almost as much as carving. He didn't like painting; no way could he make anything look the way it did in his head; the paints always seemed to do their own thing and it didn't matter what *he* wanted, but charcoal always did what he told it to. He was really good with charcoal, and that always made

things more fun; how could you like something you weren't good at?

"Sorry," he mumbled to Mr. Albert as he
sat down at the drawing table he shared with
his friend Jeff Vox. "My sister needed some
advice, so I had to stop and give it to her."

Mr. Albert raised his eyebrows. He always
raised his eyebrows when he didn't believe
you but wasn't going to make an issue of it
because it was what he called a trivial pre-
varication (one of Doug's favorite words ever
since he learned it from Mr. Albert) and rela-
tively harmless. "The subject is a person
who is afraid," he said mildly, and Doug set
to work, excited because he would rather
draw people's faces than anything else. Lots
of times he went to Oz Park, or Lincoln Park
near the statue of Hans Christian Andersen,
or the lakefront where people went to make
out, and sat on a bench or a rock filling his
sketchpad with quick drawings of people
who didn't know he was even interested in
them. Sometimes they'd look up and see
him, and then he'd turn around and begin
drawing a tree or something, or he'd move to
a new place and start again. He liked real
people doing real things. He carved people,
too, but so far he hadn't learned how to do it

right, and it was always a relief to go back to animals.

It wasn't always bad, being ten. Nobody expected you to be an expert at anything, so you could experiment a lot and make mistakes and people said you were great for trying. Well, Sara always said that. Mack sort of made fun of him when he did something wrong, like spilling things in the kitchen, or carving a man who was all lopsided, or losing his house key that day and Mack got really mad at that, *really* mad when Doug asked him to loan him his; he said he couldn't give up his key, how would he get in the house, and Doug said he could ring the doorbell and they'd let him in, and Mack said he had no intention of depending on anybody in that house, that's what he said, just those words, and Doug and Carrie were really scared because he looked so mad, Abby wasn't there, she was somewhere with Sean so she couldn't help, but then all of a sudden Mack laughed, just like that, and said he'd get Doug another key with a gold chain so he could wear it around his neck . . . and he did! And they joked around the rest of the evening and had a lot of fun.

Mack really was a lot of fun, and when he

made fun of Doug he wasn't really making *fun* of him, he was just sort of teasing, and everybody does that. Sometimes Doug thought Mack was the best friend he had because they could talk about things; Mack would sit in Doug's room, sprawled out, his feet crossed at the ankles, hands behind his head, and tell stories about his travels and he'd talk about women he'd known—he really made Doug feel grown up when he did that—and Doug could tell him about the kids at school he didn't like, the ones who made fun of him, calling him *pissy-ass* and other words they learned from their big brothers that he couldn't even understand (and a lot of the time he was pretty sure they didn't understand them, either) just because he liked to draw and make carvings and not get into wrestling matches at recess, and Mack would give him advice, like, *Tell 'em to fuck off; they're totally clueless assholes,* and *Tell 'em they think with their pricks because they haven't got any brains,* and even though Doug knew he'd never have the guts to say those things out loud, it was almost like he didn't have to, because talking about it to Mack made him feel better and that was all he needed.

Sara would never say he should tell somebody to fuck off; she was too straight.

At that disloyal thought, Doug's pencil skidded. Shit, he thought, just as Mack had taught him (because, Mack said, it makes you feel better, which it didn't, really; it made him feel bad, because he knew Sara would be unhappy, but he said it anyway, because Mack knew more about these things than just about anybody), and he carefully erased the errant line. It was true that Sara never said he should tell somebody to fuck off, but she did talk to him a lot about feeling good about himself, feeling proud of himself for the things he was good at; she always said that's what he should remember when anybody tried to make him feel bad. He couldn't always do it, but when he did remember, a lot of the time it worked.

Mr. Albert was at his shoulder, bending down and taking off his glasses to study his sketch. ("Why do you take your glasses *off* to read?" Doug had asked, and Mr. Albert had said something about elasticity of the aging eye muscles, and Doug thought it might be interesting if you were old, but it didn't seem to have anything to do with him, so he tuned out.)

"Excellent, Doug, quite, quite good," said Mr. Albert. "You can see he's frightened half out of his wits, but it isn't all in the mouth or the eyes, it's his entire face, even the angle . . . A very mature concept, I congratulate you."

"Mr. Albert," Doug said, following Mack's advice, "would you get me a show in a gallery?"

"A gallery. You mean an art gallery in town somewhere?"

"Right."

"Well, I can't do that, Doug. You're very good, *very* good, and you'll certainly be in shows we put on here at school, but you're quite young, you know, and still maturing—"

"You said this was a mature concept."

"And so it is. But you would not call yourself an accomplished artist, would you? You're still learning, you have a long way to go, years of studying the work of other artists, of wide reading and extensive observation to learn as much as you can about people, about life . . . My boy, you'll be a great artist someday, I predict it with confidence, and when it happens I will be proud to say I was your first teacher, but that time is not yet."

Doug scowled, and bent over his drawing. Mack thought he was good enough for a gallery show; he'd said so just last night. *Mack* didn't think ten was young and not mature. Mack thought he was grown up and a real artist.

But then, that night, Sara agreed with Mr. Albert. "Doug, sweetheart, there aren't many ten-year-olds who show their art in galleries; how many can you think of?"

"Maybe I'm better than all of them."

"You probably are, but are you at the same level as the twenty- and thirty- and forty-year-olds who finally have their own shows?"

Doug scowled, as he had done that morning in art class.

"It isn't that you're not good," Sara said, sitting beside him at the round table in the breakfast room. "You know you are, and so do we. But it takes time to find your own special style and point of view, to settle on what you want to express with your art—not just a pleasant picture, but something with depth that gives viewers new ways of seeing the world. That's why people love art; because it makes their worlds larger."

"I don't know what that means."

"One of these days you will. You're smart and talented, and the more you keep your eyes open and see everything around you, really see it and absorb it and think about it, the more you'll develop into an artist who helps us understand ourselves better, our emotions, and the things that make us behave the way we do."

"You, too?" Doug asked.

"Of course. I can learn about myself; we all can. And art is one way of—"

"So you'd figure out why you're not here all the time, why you spend so much time with what's-his-name?"

There was a pause. "His name is Reuben Lister," Sara said evenly. "I think I've told you that about forty times, every time you've pretended to be dense about it. And I already understand why I spend time with him; for the same reason you spend time with your friends: you like them and it makes you happy to share your life with them."

With his finger, Doug drew imaginary beasts on the pine table. He scowled again. Sara waited. "You won't get me a gallery show," he said at last.

"I can't, sweetheart; we'd be turned down

flat. When you're ready, we'll find the right place for you."

He drew another beast. He opened his mouth, then closed it. He wanted to tell Sara that Mack said he *deserved* a gallery show, but something stopped him. He was never sure how Sara would react when he repeated things Mack had said to them. It was confusing, because he'd always thought Sara was the smartest person in the whole world, but sometimes, as he was regaling her with Mack's ideas or suggestions, or his stories (well, sometimes they *were* a little wild), her face would tighten up and then he didn't know who was smarter, Mack or Sara. It was too confusing, so lately he just kept quiet a lot of the time.

Instead, he shrugged. "I guess," he muttered.

Sara looked at him closely, puzzled by his quick retreat—Doug, who usually fought tenaciously until the last argument had been exhausted—but just then the pot of pasta began to boil over, and with a quick kiss on Doug's cheek, she returned to the stove. "How about setting the table?" she suggested casually, thinking she would have to return to this subject at some time in the future; such an odd idea for a ten-year-old to have. Unless, she thought, it came from someone else.

"I love having you home," Carrie said, bouncing in with her new journal. "Look, look, look what Mack gave me. I got it last night, but you were out, and then you left so early this morning . . ."

Sara dried her hands and took the journal. "How beautiful, Carrie. It's wonderful. A very generous gift."

"Isn't he great? He saw me writing in those awful notebooks we get in the grocery store, and he said my stories deserved an elegant home. That's what he said, I really like that, *an elegant home.*"

"It certainly is that. A wonderful place to write your stories."

"And poems and just . . . thoughts. You know, something to write in whenever I feel like it."

"Too big to carry around," Doug observed.

"It's perfect," said Carrie defensively. "Anyway, I'm going to keep it on my desk, so when I have an idea I can write it down and then later write it into a story."

"What happens when you use up all the pages?" Doug asked.

"You buy refills. I'm keeping this forever and ever. Do you need help?" she asked Sara.

"Sure. We're ready to eat."

Carrie laid the journal gently on the desk in the breakfast room, and helped Sara carry the food to the table. "Where's Abby?"

"At a movie with Sean," Sara replied. "She'll be back by nine-thirty, and it seems Mack is out, too, so you two will be alone, but only for an hour and a half."

"Do you really have to go out?"

"I'm meeting a client who's only here for today. I'll make it short, I promise."

"I like it when you're home." Carrie watched Doug slurp strands of pasta so that the ends did a frantic dance in the air and flecks of sauce flew merrily about. "You are really gross."

"Tastes better this way." He mangled through a mouthful of pasta and puttanesca sauce. "And"—he swallowed, gulping for air—"I'll bet Sara's not really seeing a *client;* I'll bet she's going out with what's-his—" He saw Sara's sharp look. *"Reuben Lister,"* he said, exaggerating it. "Right? He's more fun than working, right?"

"He certainly is," Sara said, amused. "But unfortunately, tonight is really work. A very boring client, and I'd much rather be with you than with him."

"Would you rather be with Mack?"

"Of course. This client is truly boring, but I'm stuck. So—I'll say it again—I'll be home as early as possible. No later than ten. You can wait up for me if you want."

"On a *school night*?"

"Come on, Doug, you read in bed long after you're supposed to be asleep every night."

Doug grinned through another mouthful of pasta. "You're not supposed to know that."

"Reuben is an unusual name," Carrie said judiciously. "It means 'behold a son.'"

"What?" demanded Doug.

"It also means 'youthful, enthusiastic, ambitious. A born leader and organizer.' So, is he really like that, Sara?"

Sara smiled, but she felt a small chill of being behind the curve. *How do I keep up with them? How many thoughts do they have, and plans, and fears and even joys, that I know nothing about, and can't know unless they let me in on it?* "I'd say he is, from what I know. We haven't been friends very long, you know."

"It also means," Carrie proclaimed dramatically, "'rather wary of women unless he knows them well.' So is he like *that*?"

Sara laughed. "Where in the world did you find that?"

"On the Internet. Everything's on the Internet. So *is* he?"

"Not that I've noticed. He seems very comfortable with me, anyway."

"He's probably good at faking those things."

Sara contemplated her. "Carrie, have you considered the possibility that you will find something wrong with any man I seem to like?"

There was a small silence, then Carrie said brightly, "So when do we get to see this mysterious Mr. New York? We really want to, you know; we really *ought* to."

"And you will. Soon, I think. Maybe we'll all go hiking next weekend. By the way, he's not living in New York right now; he bought a house here, for a project he's building west of the city."

"What kind of a project?"

"A huge development. In fact, it's really a town."

"A *town?* A *whole town?*"

"It sounds like it. Houses, stores, a school,

playing fields, a library . . . Pretty much a real town."

"Wow," Doug breathed. "That is so cool. Can we see it?"

"Right now there's not much to see; it's still being planned. But the land is beautiful: wild grasses and flowers, lots of trees, and a stream running through—"

"Well, when they're *building* it, can we see it? When it's got cranes and bulldozers and earthmovers and stuff?"

"Yes."

"Promise?"

"Promise." She looked at her watch. "I have to leave. I wish I didn't, but I do. There are cookies and fruit for dessert, and then please clean up. And do your homework. Abby will be home—"

"—at nine-thirty," Carrie said. "Sara, we're *quite fine.* We're perfectly capable of taking care of ourselves; you let me babysit in the neighborhood all the time."

"You're not *baby*sitting," Doug said loudly. "'There's no baby in this house."

Sara laughed and kissed them. "I'll call to make sure Abby gets home."

Of course she'll get home, she thought as she drove toward Lake Shore Drive. She and

Sean had walked to the movie; they probably would be back well before nine-thirty.

"Nine-thirty," Abby told Sean as they left the theater and he wanted to drive to the lakefront and park. "Sara said I have to be home then, so I can't—"

"So you'll be a little bit late," he said impatiently. "What's the problem? Do you turn into a pumpkin or something?"

"Something," she said, trying to make it sound like a joke. Sean never seemed to worry about his family or anything that might interfere with whatever he wanted to do at that very moment. "I'm a free spirit," he had said soon after they met. "I do what's best for me and my cause."

"Your cause?"

"Having a good time. The contentment cause. The free-choice cause. The pagan pleasure principle. Whatever works." And then he had changed the subject. Sean was always changing the subject; it made Abby feel off balance a lot of the time.

"Come on, Abby," he wheedled outside the theater, his lips brushing her ear. "I haven't been alone with you for a week. I *long* for you when we're not close."

The blood rushed through Abby like the

wine Mack gave her when they had dinner without Sara; her legs felt shaky. She tried to draw a long breath, but what came out was a kind of hiccup, and all she could do was shake her head in a kind of desperation. When she found her voice, she said, "I can't, I just can't. I have to get the car back before Sara knows I've taken it."

"She doesn't know?"

Abby shook her head again.

"Well, what a girl. I'm proud of you. My independent free spirit. The pagan pleasure principle. You are my true love. So how will you get it back without her knowing? How did you *take* it without her knowing?"

"It was parked a block away; you know how crowded our street . . ." Her voice trailed away.

"So if you get back before her, everything's fine."

After a moment, Abby nodded. "Fine."

"And she gets home . . . when?"

"She's working till ten, but Carrie and Doug expect me by nine-thirty."

He looked at his watch. "Damnation. Well, you can be a little late, and still beat ten o'clock. Come on, my beauty, ten minutes to the lake, twenty minutes for lovemaking, ten minutes to get to your house. We can do it. Come on, come on, love's awaiting and time's a-wasting."

He hustled Abby to her car and watched impatiently as she fumbled with her keys. She knew Sean hated it that she would not let him drive her car, but she had promised Sara no one else would drive it, and she felt she had to keep at least one of her promises. In most other ways, it seemed she broke a lot of them in always giving in to Sean. Tonight what she wanted to say, but could not, was that she really didn't want to go to the lakefront; that the place she was happiest was not in the stuffy darkness of a car, but in the warm darkness of a movie theater, her shoulder touching Sean's, her breathing so light she felt she was floating, her hand held beneath his, pressed against his inner thigh. The truth was, she never liked the writhing and straining in a car, whether they were double-dating with Sean's older brother and one of his girl-friends, or they were alone when Sean took the car himself. She disliked it from the time they parked in a pitch-black corner of Lincoln Park to the wild moments when Sean's tongue twisted possessively around hers, one arm holding her in an iron grip, his hand pinching and rubbing her nipple, while his other hand thrust deep beneath her skirt, ruthlessly exploring, bringing her body to a pitch of desperate wanting and a fever that was so savage she would moan *please please please* and, then, shocked at the sound of her crazed voice, would jerk back, her eyes flying open, her frenzied hands pushing, pushing, trying to pry Sean's body from hers.

Of course that made him furious; she always knew it would. At first he would grip her more tightly, but when she kept pushing, becoming almost hysterical, he would spin around, his back to her, and stare out the window on his side while she tried to adjust her brassiere and sweater and skirt, and get control of her breathing and clear her mind, though it didn't really matter, because the evening was ruined, as if the contented hours in the movie theater (*her* contented hours) had never been. But whenever they were together in a car, the cycle repeated itself, as if Sean knew—from experience?— that eventually Abby would be worn down, more and more accustomed to his caresses, so that they began to seem a normal part of the evening, and then her arousal would finally be all that mattered.

Abby never talked about how she felt, and she was silent as they drove out of the parking garage. Sean turned on the radio—he had told her he hated silence—and accompanied by the mellow saxophone of a jazz group they both liked, they reached the park, and a corner they knew was seldom patrolled by roving police cars.

The park was quiet, almost drowsy: the joggers and volleyball teams were gone, the aging couples had turned home after their nightly strolls; the last dog walker, yanking on the leash, had dragged a reluctant animal into one of the apartment buildings across the street. The darkness deepened, the police cars made their sweep and were gone, and Abby and Sean had to themselves a small turnout behind a grove of trees near the lake.

The moment Abby stopped the engine, Sean pulled her to him, shoving down the V-neck of her sweater to clamp his moist mouth on her breast. Abby felt herself melting, opening, sinking into him until she had no sense of herself at all; she had disappeared into feelings. Indeed, by now it did seem the normal thing to do. Besides, it made Sean happy, and tonight she knew they had only a brief time, so she met him with a passion that seemed equal to his. "Oh, God," he moaned, and pulling his hand from between her legs, he unzipped his pants and forced her fingers around his stiff cock, hot and smooth, huge and menacing. It was the first time he had done this and Abby suddenly was dizzy, her insides churning, her mouth and throat choked by his insistent tongue. Sean's ruthless grip forced her hand up and down the rigid shaft, faster and faster, and Abby felt she was hurtling down an abyss where everything was unknown but terrifying, and a sob rose in her throat.

And then, suddenly, behind her closed eyes, came the vivid picture of her hand, beneath Sean's damp palm, vigorously pumping . . . Sara's wooden rolling pin. And with that, fear and desire shattered, and hysterically, Abby began to laugh.

Sean jerked away. "What the *fuck*!" He flung her from him, shoving her ribs and breasts into the steering wheel, and Abby gasped with pain. She met Sean's eyes, enraged, hateful, and saw the twist of his mouth and his outthrust jaw, and when his hand came up she cringed, expecting a blow. Instead he zipped himself back into his pants, grabbed his jacket from the backseat, and opened the car door. "You cunt," he spat, and Abby did not recognize his voice. "Cunt, bitch, who the fuck do you think you—" His face worked, then he slammed the door and with long running strides disappeared into the darkness.

Abby did not move. Her breathing came in harsh, desperate bursts, until the sob in her throat burst apart, and she stumbled frantically from the car and vomited onto the dirt road of that quiet corner of Lincoln Park.

When the retching stopped, she wandered from the car, dazed and without direction, until she came to the low wall of roughly squared limestone blocks that lined the lakeshore. She climbed up and walked along the top, glancing now and then at the rows of large blocks that stepped down to the restless water. She climbed down the first step, then the second, until her feet were wet from the waves slapping against the lowest tier. After a moment, she climbed back to the top and sat down, hugging her knees to her aching chest. To her right, the city's lights followed the curve of Lake Michigan, then shot upward in skyscrapers: spires of gold and black gleaming against an unearthly rusty pink sky, an urban sky reflecting the glow from streetlights and the headlights of thousands of cars.

"We never see the stars," Doug had complained just yesterday.

"We'll go far enough from the city lights to see them," Sara had replied.

"When?"

"Maybe this weekend, when we go hiking."

Abby gazed at the lights and the pink sky, thinking of absolutely nothing, until her head drooped, too heavy to hold up. Beside and below her, graffiti painted on the limestone blocks was barely discernible in the faint light: KEN LOVES AL. TO HELL WITH EVERYTHING. BETTY LOVES CATHY. BLACK POWER. I AM GOD. GAY LOVE. From the lowest tier of stone blocks, where waves and foam curled around mossy pilings, the dark expanse of the lake, broken by flecks of white, stretched to the horizon and met a sky of tumbled clouds.

I'm going to die, she thought.

One way or another, certainly she would.

Sean would kill her. (He could, she was sure of that; he often talked about killings in London as if they were just another part of the city, like double-decker buses and Big Ben.) Or her broken heart would kill her before he could.

I've had fifteen good years; maybe that's all I deserve.

I'm not a good person; I lied to Sara and I laughed at Sean.

I'd be better off dead.

Or I could disappear.

Like Dad. Like Mack.

Then I could live somewhere anonymously and sacrifice myself to helping the poor, and go hungry and be cold.

She began to shiver. It must be late. She could not see her watch and suddenly thought of Sara, worrying about her. *Oh, God, I just keep making things worse.*

She ran back to the car and turned the key in the ignition. The clock came to life: ten-fifteen. Abby rubbed her eyes. Was that all? It had felt like hours later; she felt as if she had aged a hundred years. She took her cell phone from her purse, and driving out of the park, she called home.

Carrie answered. "WHERE ARE YOU? WE'RE WORRIED!"

"Is Sara there?" Abby asked.

"No, she called and said she'd be here about ten-thirty. She asked about you and I told her you weren't home and she sounded mad. WHERE ARE YOU?"

"On my way home." She tried to think of a simple excuse that would put Carrie on her side, and remembered something Mack always said, with a wink: *Half-truths are better than total lies; easier to remember.* "I had a fight with Sean," she said. "And he . . . left, and I just stopped for a while to think about things."

"Was it a bad fight?"

"I guess . . . yes."

"So you're broken up?"

"I don't . . . well, probably."

"Is your heart broken?"

Abby started to cry.

"Oh, poor Abby," Carrie exclaimed. "We won't talk about it, I know how betrayals can crush the loving heart of a sensitive—"

"Stop it!" Abby cried. "Just shut up!" She threw the phone to the floor of the car and blinked away tears to drive the last few blocks to her street. Then she had to drive around the block until she found a parking place, and, finally, run back to the house.

Sara arrived ten minutes later. Carrie and Doug were watching television in the library. Exhausted from her long day, thinking longingly of bed, she determined to allow exactly five minutes for greetings and getting all of them upstairs. She kissed them and sat on the arm of the couch. "Is Abby upstairs?"

Carrie sighed mournfully. "With a broken heart. Sean betrayed her and she has given him up forever."

Sara's eyebrows rose. "They had a fight?"

"Well, that's what she *said,* but, you know, she puts up a brave front, as heroines always do."

Doug looked up from the bar of soap he was carving. "Carrie's making up a story. It doesn't sound as if it's going to have any blood or mayhem, though," he added sadly.

"Lights out, and upstairs," said Sara. "I'm as tired as you should be."

"I'm not," said Doug.

"It doesn't matter." Sara waited until they had turned off the television set and the lights, and followed them up the stairs. Why can't they have problems only on weekends? she thought, and knocked on the closed door of Abby's room.

"Go away," Abby said.

"Well, I'm not going to do that," Sara said mildly, "so why don't you save us a lot of time and let me in?"

There was a pause. "You can *come* in; it's not locked."

Sara opened the door. "I don't barge into rooms with closed doors; you know that. You have a right to privacy."

"So why are you here? All I want is to be alone. *Private.*"

Sara sat in the armchair beside the large window that Abby had hung with silk drapes striped in apricot and ivory. Three years earlier, Sara had given the three of them a budget for redecorating their rooms, to distract them from the frightening changes in their life: Mack gone, their mother in a nursing home, unable to speak to them, Sara no longer just their sister, but suddenly the only parent they had. They had grasped at the project as if she had flung them a lifeline, concentrating fiercely on small and large decisions alike: rugs or carpets, paint or wallpaper, colors for walls and window and door frames, pictures, lamps, furniture, bedding, the location of bookshelves and how they would organize their libraries. Carrie's and Abby's books were shelved by subject or author; Doug's by color.

The three of them had chosen furnishings and color schemes totally different from each other, and Sara, in her new role as sort-of parent (the term she wryly came up with each time she sought one), found she was discovering, through their decorating, their different personalities: Abby's striving for calm sophistication with subtle colors and country French furniture; Carrie's brightly assertive with red-and-blue plaid drapes, and a deep, oversize red armchair that swallowed her up when she tucked her legs under her to lose herself in writing or reading; Doug's searching for adulthood in a dark brown carpet, brown leather armchair, brown-and-black automobile-patterned quilt, and burlap curtains on his two windows . . . an exact copy of Mack's windows in his third-floor bedroom. Doug had stared at Sara, daring her to say something when she saw them, but she said only, "What an interesting touch," and helped him hang the sagging fabric before kissing him with a hug which he feverishly returned.

"Not a great evening?" Sara asked Abby, who sat on her bed, knees to her chest, as if—though Sara could not know this—she were still sitting on a limestone block beside the lake, still dazed, still in turmoil.

There was a long silence. "He got mad at me."

"For any special reason?"

The silence was even longer this time. "I laughed at him."

Sara nodded. "That's tough for boys to take. I guess it's tough for everybody. Though, sometimes, people just laugh back."

"He couldn't. He was—" Abby stopped, then sighed miserably. There was no way she could tell Sara about it. Mack said Sara was another generation and couldn't understand any of their feelings, and even though Abby knew perfectly well that wasn't true, at least not all the time, she could not bring herself to say aloud what had happened in her car that night. (Anyway, Sara didn't know she'd taken the car, so of course she couldn't talk about it; what was wrong with her that she did so many things wrong, so everything that followed seemed even worse?)

Sara assumed it had to do with sex.

Where were they? He didn't have a car, unless his father let him use his. Were they parked somewhere in his car, or did they have another place to go after the movie? But before she could frame a few careful questions, she heard the telephone ring, and then Carrie's voice, calling her. "It's your Mr. New York."

Sara hesitated, but Abby, relieved (but also disappointed, because in a way she had been hoping Sara would probe, forcing the story out, and then provide just the comfort Abby needed), said, "It's okay, Sara. I'm fine, really, it's okay; go ahead."

And though Sara knew she should stay, she went to her room to pick up the telephone, because Reuben had been in New York for the day, and they had not talked since last night, and what she most wanted at that moment was to hear his voice. Because, admit it, she told herself; it's a lot easier and more pleasant, especially at the end of the day, to talk to Reuben than to deal with a fifteen-year-old's romantic, probably sexual, angst.

(Much later, when she reflected on all the things she had not done in those days, or things she did but should not have done, she remembered this night, and could not recall a single word of her conversation with Reuben, though she remembered everything Abby had said, and still could hear the thread of pleading in her voice even as she said, *I'm fine, really* . . . It wasn't worth it, she thought then, but that was months later, when dwelling on past failures did no good, when all they could do was try to repair as much of the damage as possible, and go on from there.)

She did turn back to Abby's room after the telephone call, to continue their talk and to tell her that she and Reuben were planning to take the three of them to Galena (*so Doug can really see the stars*), but before she got there, the doorbell rang and Carrie and Doug dashed to answer it, and then ran back to the stairs.

"Sara," Carrie called, "there's a lady here and she wants you." She came partway up the stairs and whispered loudly, "The same one who was here before."

But Pussy Corcoran had followed her and stood at the foot of the stairway, looking up, fastening her too-bright smile on Sara. "I need you," she said.

SEVEN

I don't know what she expects me to do,"
Sara told Tess a few days later, at breakfast.
They were at a small table in the dining room
of the nursing home, Tess in her wheelchair.
Occasionally they glanced at the leafy
branches whipped against their window by
rain and wind, but mostly they were absorbed in each other with a closeness that
deepened each passing month as Sara became more firmly the mother Tess had been.
A waitress brought their omelets and muf-
fins, set a bowl of fruit in the center of the
table, refilled their coffee cups. "She appears
at my front door," Sara went on, "after I've

told her a dozen times she is not to do that, she stares at me as if I'm some kind of savior, and says she needs me."

Tess pointed to Sara's left hand, and Sara nodded. "She's obviously afraid of her husband, but there's someone else she's afraid of, someone who has some kind of connection with her husband, maybe works for him; she's so vague I have no idea what she's talking about. I don't know anything about him, really, but when she talks about him it's always in the context of knowing things she shouldn't know—she hears things and remembers them, and I got the feeling she goes through papers on a desk he uses in their apartment—and about Lew, her husband, mentioning this other person at odd times; as if, she says, he's some sort of secret weapon he could pull out whenever he feels like it. Last night she talked—"

Tess held up her coffee cup and looked a question, wanting the scene described, hungry for details. Sara nodded. "Yes, we were having coffee in the kitchen. I didn't want her standing on the stairs where the children could hear her, and she was so needy I took her to the kitchen and we sat in the armchairs and had coffee and cookies, and she talked. She talked for an hour, in fact, it was as if a faucet had been turned on, about hairdressers and shopping, and Lew forcing her to take back whatever he happens not to like, and how hard it is to keep maids and chefs when Lew makes demands and complains and springs last-minute dinner guests, including some man she doesn't like, in fact, may be afraid of—maybe the one who's the secret weapon. And evidently Lew accuses her of spying, listening to his telephone conversations, wandering into his study, and she says—though I don't believe this, and I guess Lew doesn't, either—she wouldn't have the faintest idea how to be a spy even if she wanted to, besides which she has zero interest in what he does all day, and even if she cared, he made it clear from the day they married—"

Tess made a gesture. "Four years ago," Sara said, "his fifth marriage, her first. She's in her late forties, maybe early fifties, but she says she's never even had a serious relationship before. She's not unattractive, but she's so needy . . . there's that word again; it really does describe her perfectly. Anyway, he made it clear that his business is his, not theirs, and all she needed to know was that her bills would be paid." Sara took a bite of her omelet, recalling Pussy's pleading eyes and fixed smile. "It sounds like an awful marriage, doesn't it?"

Tess turned her hand in a way Sara did not understand until Tess pointed again at the fourth finger of her left hand. "*Why* did he marry her? I have no idea. Unless he collects needy people he can manipulate and dominate, maybe terrify. I know there are people like that; it's just impossible for me to identify with them." She gazed at the branches flicking against the glass; the rain had almost stopped. A bird's descending song floated through a small opening at the bottom of the window.

"It's going to take a lot for Pussy Corcoran to begin to believe in herself, I think. The other day I introduced her to the directors of five nonprofit organizations. They all welcomed her and told her they'd be delighted to have her on their boards, maybe organizing benefit dinners, theater parties, concerts . . . things she'd probably enjoy. They gave her names of board members to call, to meet for lunch, to talk about the work they were doing, to make friends, for heaven's sake. You'd think she would have jumped at it. She did seem grateful, but she was distracted, too, and I have no idea how much really sank in. I gave her two days of my time, and I'm still not sure whether I helped her or not. She seems volitionless, almost frozen, as if she can't imagine herself empowered, no matter what she does, so why do anything?"

She shook her head slowly. "So many people feel helpless," she murmured, thinking of Pussy, and Donna Soldana, occasionally Doug and Carrie and Abby, as they navigated the uncertain years of growing up, even herself, when she first left school to come back here, and still, on the darkest days. "So many people feel vulnerable in a world that's too big and complicated to make sense of, or have some impact on, much less change. Then along comes a bully like Lew Corcoran, who is truly a mean man, who seems to get his kicks making weaker people feel small, even weaker than they felt before. Maybe he's as fearful as they are; maybe bullying is his way of feeling strong or grown up or both, but that's even worse: that he'd destroy people's confidence in order to feel better about himself. A lousy bargain, if you ask me. Contemptible."

She looked up, and saw Tess watching

her with tears in her eyes. "I'm sorry," she said quickly, furious with herself. "I know how helpless you feel, but truthfully, I wasn't thinking of you; I was thinking of Pussy. You have more pride and confidence in yourself than she does, you're more a whole person, even though you're stuck here, in a body that won't do what you want it to."

Tess held out her hand with her small half smile, and Sara took it between both of hers. "I never mean to hurt you; I admire you more than anyone I know. I can't imagine how I'd have the courage to face each day if I were in your place, but you do, and you're always here for all of us. We come to you with our problems and our triumphs, and we always feel welcome, not as if we're burdening you. You must know how incredibly wonderful that is; a lot of people who can walk and talk never take the trouble to listen when others come to them. And Doug and Carrie and Abby, especially, need so much attention, and they love you . . . Anyway, we all thank you."

Their hands clung for a moment and they smiled at each other, comfortably silent. They finished their omelets and raspberries and cream, and sat quietly, gazing at gray clouds thinning to filaments that drifted off, leaving the sky pale and washed clean, but already turning deep blue in the blazing sun that would make it a hot June day.

"I wish you could talk," Sara said at last. "I'd love to be told what to do. How do I know that anything I do with the three of them is right? How do parents decide what to do, what choices to make? How do they always know what will be best?"

She saw Tess's good eyebrow go up a fraction of an inch. "Well, okay, they don't always know. But my friends who are parents, and the parents I see at school meetings, look a lot more sure of themselves than I feel a lot of the time. I keep trying to figure out what you would do, but then something new comes up, and all the guideposts vanish. You were so fine; I'd just like to be close to what you were."

There was a silence. Finally, as if making a decision, Tess pointed to the pad of paper always nearby, and Sara slid it to her and held out the mechanical pencil attached to it by a thin chain. With difficulty, Tess wrote *Mack*.

It was the first time she had acknowledged him since Doug had revealed his presence, over a month before.

Sara stared at the wobbly letters. "You don't think you were fine with him? But he wasn't fine with you. He was . . . difficult, as far back as I can remember. He never thought of what you were going through, or any of us. He only cared about himself. And left when he felt like it, not caring what happened to us." She contemplated Mack's name on the pad of paper. "But I think he's changed," she said slowly. "He seems to have missed all the good things in our family, and now wants them. He has a job, and he's home all the . . . well, actually about half the time, but almost always when I have to be out, and he cooks and entertains, especially with Doug and Carrie, and he gave Carrie a wonderful gift, a journal for her stories. I have much more freedom now, and he's helping pay for groceries and managing the house—"

She stopped, hearing the forced tone of her voice. *Trying too hard to convince Mother and myself that Mack has changed, and everything is fine.*

And it probably is. Except that . . .

Tess was gazing at her with as much of a frown as her muscles could manage.

"He's quite different," Sara said, keeping

her voice light. "You might love him again. Would you like to see him?"

There was a long silence. Tess's eyes filled with tears again. She gave a small but definite nod.

Sara took a long breath. She had no idea if this was a good move or not, but she had begun it and now they would have to see it through. "Sometime soon," she said. "As soon as I know Mack's schedule, I'll let you know." She stood. "I have to go; we're driving to Galena with Reuben. Do you want to go back to your room?"

Her mother nodded, and Sara pushed the wheelchair into the gleaming corridor. "We're staying overnight in Galena. It's vacation until Abby's job starts." She saw Tess's hand go up, questioning. "I'm sorry; I thought Abby told you. She's a counselor this year at Lakeshore Day Camp. Doug will be there, as a camper, for one more year, and Carrie will be in summer school, so thank goodness they're all taken care of while I'm at work."

She pushed the wheelchair past small tables with vases of spring flowers, past paintings of seascapes and mountains, past open doorways giving glimpses of rooms ranging from starkly anonymous to a few that approached the sumptuousness Sara had created for Tess. "We'll be home early afternoon tomorrow."

Tess sighed as Sara helped her into her chair, and Sara did not ask whether she was fatigued from the disruption of being moved, or already regretting having agreed to seeing Mack. She embraced Tess and kissed her. "I love you."

She arrived at her house just as Reuben pulled up. "Good morning," he said, and kissed her. Sara smiled. "What?" he asked.

"I just kissed my mother good-bye; now I'm kissing you hello. This is an affectionate morning."

"I *saw* that," said Doug accusingly, coming out of the house.

Sara bent down and kissed him. "This is a day to kiss people. Where is your backpack?"

"Oh, I forgot. Back in a minute."

How strange, Reuben thought, when they were all in his car, driving west toward the highway, how strange to have three young people in the backseat. A dream—for how many years?—that he would have a family, that he and his wife, building their marriage, would watch their children grow: read to them, walk with them, drive together on a hundred, a thousand excursions, join their own exhilaration with life to their children's excitement as the world opened up before them, fresh, new, untested. Ardis had destroyed that, and he had all but given up finding it. What had never occurred to him was that he might find a family ready-made. And fatherless.

Would that satisfy him? At one time he would have rejected the idea out of hand, insisting, like most men, that his family be his, made by him, molded by him, imbued with him. Why would he have tolerated, much less welcomed, any family but one where he would see himself reflected, God-like, in his creations?

Put that way, it sounded ridiculous. But he could not be sure even of that; it was a subject he had never thought about. And now? He did not know. He glanced at Sara. She was absorbed in the road map, her profile to him, and as she made a mark with her pencil, he felt a sudden rush of well-being. He would not call it love, not yet, but, in that moment, the direction of his life until then, and his thoughts of the last few moments, seemed to settle into an extraordinary harmony.

There had been whispering in the back-seat, and now Carrie leaned forward as far as her seat belt would allow. "Reuben, will we be near the town you're building? Doug really wants to see it."

"You do, too!" said Doug indignantly. "We all do."

Abby was silent. She stared out the window on her side, generally miserable, convinced this was the worst time of her life and she would never recover, and Sara was making it worse by forcing her to go with them to *Galena.* Why should she? Why would anybody? It was this little tiny town on a river a long way from Chicago, with a lot of old buildings. Big deal. The fact that she had never been there did not make a bit of difference; it was a long drive, and she was stuck in the car with her family and this . . . stranger. (He wasn't even handsome, not nearly as handsome as Sean, but what difference did it make what Sean looked like? She'd never see him again, except at a distance, so why was she even thinking about him, and comparing him to this guy, who, she had to admit, was nice, probably nicer than Sean, though that wasn't saying much.)

"We'll take a detour, and drive past it," Reuben said. "There's nothing much there, except a fence, but you can see how much land we have."

"And we'll come back when all the construction stuff is there?"

"If he and Sara are still together," Abby muttered.

"What?" Carrie demanded.

Abby slumped deeper in her seat.

"You're really in a foul mood," Carrie scolded, "but you don't have to be obnoxious and take it out on innocent observers and act like *everybody* breaks up."

"Well, lots of people do," Reuben said mildly after exchanging an amused glance with Sara (which Carrie saw but decided to let pass without comment, a decision she considered incredibly mature, and wished she could tell everyone so they would admire her, but *that* wouldn't be mature, so she just had to admire herself by herself). "But," Reuben went on, "I'm not planning on going anywhere, which is a good thing, because if I decided to leave now, you'd be stranded a long way from home. Anyway, we're getting close now; we'll stay on this road and then turn onto a smaller one, and after that, watch for a chain-link fence and a dirt road, a track, really; that leads into Carrano Village West."

"How come you don't pave it?" Doug asked, thinking it sounded like a pretty lousy place.

"We debated that, but we decided just to widen it and hold off paving until later; construction equipment would tear it apart and we'd have to do it again. Expensive and a waste of time."

Doug beamed. Reuben hadn't made fun of his question; he'd taken it seriously. Why couldn't all grown-ups do that? "The fence!" he cried as the sun flashed off the steel. "There it is! Who are all those people?"

Reuben shook his head. "No idea. Bird-watchers, maybe?"

"But they're carrying things," said Carrie. "Wouldn't bird-watchers carry binoculars or something?"

The people were clustered beside the high chain-link fence, obstructing a construction sign; they dragged placards behind them or propped them on their shoulders. Sara saw old people and young, couples pushing strollers, children in little clusters of their own, one man in a wheelchair, a few teenagers on skateboards. Jostling and shuffling, they were forming a rough line that stretched more than a block along the dirt track outside the fence, and as the car came closer Doug read the placards aloud.

NO NO NO CARRANO!!!

DENSITY DESTROYS

DUMP CARRANO, NOT CONCRETE

BUILDERS + BULLDOZERS = BANDITS

GRASS NOT GRIDLOCK

Wow," Doug breathed. "They're talking about your town."

"They don't want you?" Carrie asked. "Why wouldn't they?"

"I don't know," Reuben said slowly, watching through narrowed eyes as a WGN Channel 9 truck spouting a satellite dish on its roof sped around them and pulled up beside the crowd. "But someone alerted the television—" Another truck topped by a satellite dish—NBC CHANNEL 4 CHICAGO—and then a third—WBBM-TV CHANNEL 2 EYE ON CHICAGO—passed them and parked behind the first truck.

"Son of a bitch," Reuben muttered savagely.

"Who?" Doug cried.

"I don't know yet. Generic," he added more

lightly, jolted into an awareness of the adjustments, small and large, that had to be made under the scrutiny of youngsters. Once again he met Sara's eyes, concerned now, steady on his face rather than the burgeoning demonstration at his site. "I'm sorry," he said to her, keeping his voice level. "I have to find out what's going on. If you don't mind putting off our trip for a few minutes . . ."

"For as long as you need. You had no warning of this? Usually there's publicity."

"Not this time." Anger tightened his throat, made his words flat, bitten off. "Whoever organized this—planned it, had placards painted and distributed, called the press— whoever did that knows the drill and can keep it quiet, which means discipline and direction. I'm going over there; what would you like to do?"

"Go with you!" Doug yelled. "I've never seen one of these in person. I mean, you know, on TV, but not *real*."

"I want to go, too," said Carrie. "I'll write a story about it. Like, somebody scared his neighbors with some kind of story, and got them to demonstrate, and then he disappeared and the neighbors took over the march and turned it into a picnic and met each other for the first time and made new friends, so everybody was happy."

"Why would he want to scare them?" Doug asked.

Carrie shrugged. "I haven't figured that out yet. Maybe he was some kind of criminal and he wanted to build his own building to . . . oh, you know, hide stolen treasure or make counterfeit money or maybe package marijuana in those teeny bags the kids have at school . . . something like that. Writers can't think of everything at once, you know."

"Abby?" Sara asked. "Do you want to come with us? We won't be long, so if you want to stay here, it's fine."

"I'll come," Abby said. She had been watching the crowd incuriously, until the television trucks appeared. There was no way she would sit in the car, invisible and ignored, when television cameras were around.

"Maybe he didn't scare them," Doug said as they walked up the road. "I mean, maybe he promised them money or something."

"That's not a bad idea," Carrie said generously. "I'll give it some thought."

"And who knows?" Reuben said to Sara as they walked ahead of the others, "maybe Carrie has the answer."

She smiled. "Do you happen to know any criminals who have stolen treasure to stash, and would build a new structure for it?"

"Not one. But they'd hardly keep me informed." He took her hand.

("They're holding hands," Doug hissed. "So?" Carrie asked, as if they saw a man hold Sara's hand every day. "They're friends," she said loftily. Abby said nothing, remembering when she had had someone to hold her hand.)

Reuben and Sara exchanged a swift glance of amusement. He had lightened up by now; whatever this was, he could deal with it. This wasn't the first time a large-scale development had aroused opposition, but at River Bend, he and Isaiah had found it easier than most, winning approval from the mayors, city councils, and police chiefs of nearby towns, presidents of clubs and organizations that had a voice in civic affairs, and from neighboring newspapers that had swung from tepid to enthusiastic. They had been expecting the final approval—a vote by the city council of the adjacent town of River

Bend to annex Carrano Village West—and then the county would sign off on it and they would begin.

But now there was something else. Reuben had told Sara about two letters to the *Chicago Tribune,* which might suggest someone organizing opposition behind the scenes. If the people here today, a ragtag semblance of a demonstration, had been convinced to show up, the entire picture would change.

Even as he thought that, the crowd was growing. Police appeared and spaced themselves out along the road, watching as people drove in from neighboring towns and took their places in the line, looking less ragtag and more organized by the minute. Laughing and chatting, dressed in shorts and jeans, jogging suits and gardening clothes, they carried banners and placards. One boy rested his on his shoulder, as if it were a rifle.

SAVE THE PRAIRIE

Another waved his as if swatting flies.

BUILD PARKS FOR THE PEOPLE

Reuben shook his head. "They should get together. Figure out how they're going to do both."

The straggly line now stretched around

the corner. The people at the front were making no move to start marching; the whole line stood comfortably in the warm June sun, talking animatedly as if they had just met at a shopping center, and had the whole leisurely day to socialize.

"What are they waiting for?" Sara wondered. She turned as cameramen and reporters piled out of the trucks. "Well, of course. What else could it be? These days nothing happens unless there's an audience. Reuben, this could be terrible publicity."

He nodded. "We'll counter it." They reached the front of the line, where Sara almost brushed against three women wearing aprons—*Aprons? As if they just dashed from the kitchen, foods merrily bubbling away while they take a quick break for a demonstration? How very spontaneous. Which could be exactly the appearance someone wanted*—and two young boys, each holding the end of a banner that flapped between them. Sara craned her neck to read it:

GOD MADE THE PRAIRIE

AND HE SAID IT WAS GOOD

The boys saw her, and one of them shrugged to show this wasn't his idea. They were about fourteen, handsome and supremely confident in rumpled T-shirts hanging out of baggy cargo pants dragging on unlaced running shoes. Meeting Sara's ruminative glance, they grinned conspiratorially and vigorously began to flap the banner like a sheet in the strong hands of a washerwoman, and suddenly they were in a slyly sexy tango, one wrapping himself around in the cloth as he whirled toward the other, then unwrapping as the cloth wrapped around his partner. *"Hola!"* one of them cried as they twirled, the center of a circle of watchers laughing and making suggestive comments, until the boys collapsed, out of breath, gasping with laughter.

"What the hell you kids doing?" A tall woman loomed over the boys on the ground. "This is a *march,* not a circus!"

"We ain't marching," one of them pointed out. "It's *boring,* Ma, you said it would be fun, but nothin's happening."

"You see the TV cameras? You want to be on the news tonight dancing like a couple a hookers? Idiots! Get yourselves up; we're starting in a minute."

Reuben stood behind her until she turned around. "Could I talk to you a minute?"

She appraised him. "You a reporter?"

"Yes," he lied easily. He pulled out his wallet and began to thumb through it. "My press card . . ."

She waved it away. "It's okay." She looked around. "You got a cameraman? You're gonna want my picture."

"He'll be here in a few minutes. He's somewhere along the line. It stretches a long way; how many people are here, would you say?"

"Oh"—she waved a hand again—"five thousand give or take."

Sara swiftly counted a dozen people near her and did a rough calculation of the line. Maybe three or four hundred. *But still large enough to get a lot of attention.*

Reuben was nodding seriously as he wrote on a pad of paper. "And you're the leader?"

She laughed. "I'm just that kid's mother. But I know everybody. You can ask me anything; you don't need to talk to anybody else."

Reuben nodded again. He saw Sara edging away. "You could stay."

"No, you do your . . . interview. I'd like to meet some of the people."

As she greeted one of the demonstrators,

Reuben turned back to the woman. "And your name?"

The woman whipped out a lipstick and slid it expertly over her lips. "Charlie Donavan. Short for Charlotte, but nobody but my parents, God rest 'em, ever called me that. They thought it sounded like a princess. I told them it sounded like the name of a city." Her laughter rang out again.

"Or a dessert," Reuben murmured, but she looked at him blankly, and he said, "Who organized this march? It's very impressive."

"Right." She looked with satisfaction at the line, beginning now to grow restive. Her glance lingered on Sara, taking in her brown-and-ivory checked shirt and narrow khaki pants, sleeker and probably a lot more expensive than any clothes worn by the marchers, then came back to Reuben. "Organized it? I don't know. I mean, I know, but I don't know. You know what I mean?"

Reuben shook his head.

"This guy, young kid, came to my neighbor, Ted his name is, and said he'd help get signs and banners, whatever, if we wanted to protest this village, what's its name, Carrano. He said we could force them to make it really small, or get rid of it period, if we had lots of demonstrations."

"And why would you want that?" Reuben asked, writing on his pad.

"Well, you know, all those people tramping in, more traffic, garbage pickup, fire protection, police . . . And they're only going to let in young families! Anybody tell you that? *Nothing but kids.* Not even a token grandparent! You know what'll happen to our taxes to pay for all those new schools? They'll go out of sight, and what could we do about it? Not a damn thing."

"But you'll have better fire and police protection than you have now," Reuben said, "and your schools will be better, because the larger and more diverse the area, the more attractive it is to the best teachers. And everything will be open to you, free of charge—gym, swimming pool, tennis courts, playing fields, meeting rooms—everything this area doesn't have."

Her eyes narrowed. "You the guy behind it?"

"Those are some of the arguments I've heard in favor of it."

She considered. "Maybe. Nobody told us any of those things. Swimming pool? Nobody said a word. But, *wait a minute.* You said diverse, right? I know what that means, it means people you don't want, that's what it always means. We'd be paying sky-high taxes and end up with *African-Americans*— now there's a hoot, they aren't from Africa any more than I am—and *Mexicans,* and they don't even speak English, so we'd end up paying for *English* classes in *American* schools. I mean, come *on.* And Jews, too, probably. This guy naming the town after himself, Carrano, his name's *Isaiah.* A dead giveaway. I'll tell you, it just *destroys* a decent town overnight, is what it does."

Reuben struggled to keep his face still. "Does that mean you'll be having more than one demonstration?"

"Right, right. This kid who helped Ted put it together? He said it has to be cumulative, you know, adding up to steady pressure, so they're already working on the next one. Ted says this kid says it's like a virus, if we let 'em build this town it'll spread like a, you know, virus, and pretty soon we'll be paying for all these outsiders pushing their way in every place you look. Where's your photographer? I gotta go; we're starting in a few minutes."

"Who says?" Reuben asked.

"What?"

"Who says you're starting in a few minutes?"

"Oh. I don't know; that's just the time."

"What is Ted's last name?"

"Ted Waszenski. But you don't need him. I've told you everything."

"And he agrees with you that you don't want diversity?"

"Listen, *nobody* wants that, you don't, either, I bet. You want to *know* your neighbors. You want *safety.* Diversity means everybody in the pool, right? It destructively destroys a decent town. That's catchy, isn't it? I really like it. I'm gonna put it on a banner for next time; really catchy for the cameras, you know?"

Reuben frowned. Twice she had broken out of her vocabulary. *She didn't get those phrases from Ted, I'll bet. The kid, whoever he is, the guy with the clever phrases, the catalyst.*

"I really gotta get going," Charlotte said. "Where the hell's your photographer?"

"I have no idea. But he'll be around. I'll tell him to look for you."

"Charlie Donavan."

"I remember."

"And there'll be a story about me."

"I'll do my best."

She stood uncertainly. "I mean, you know, we're a nice neighborhood here, we don't bother nobody. We take care of ourselves, we don't ask for any handouts, and it's not right for people to come shoving in here and expect us to pay for everything. Schools and all, you know. It's not right." She looked at him, as if waiting for approval, or at least understanding. "I mean, look, we just want to know what we've got, you know? What's ours. This isn't a fancy place, but it's what we've got and we like it. We like the way things are; we don't want them to change." She shook her head. "We don't want change, period." In a moment, when Reuben said nothing, she turned and drifted back to the line.

Reuben looked around and found Sara, closer to him than he had expected. "I don't usually lie," he said. "But if journalists can sometimes shade the truth, I assume so can developers."

She nodded. "Who seem to learn quickly."

There was a pause. If it was his turn to wait for approval, none was forthcoming. "Where are the children?" he asked at last.

"Wandering around, looking at people. I told them to meet us here in"—she looked at her watch—"now, in fact."

A television reporter and cameraman approached them. "Real ones," Reuben murmured.

"You're Reuben Lister," the reporter said. "Saw your picture when Carrano Village West was announced. Got a minute to talk?"

"I'll find the strays," said Sara, and left them, the reporter already asking his first question as some of the marchers looked on curiously.

Restiveness was making the line more ragged. Conversations flagged and people stepped to left and right, trying to see the head of the line, trying to identify a leader to tell them what to do. Reporters had talked to some of them, but as soon as they left, demonstrators began to drift away, bored and thinking now of other ways they could spend a sunny Saturday. Most remained, because cameramen were setting up tripods for the start of the march, and they did not want to miss the chance to see themselves on television that night.

Sara reached the end of the line as a helicopter swooped in, hovering above the demonstrators. *A helicopter for a small march that wasn't even publicized?* And then she recalled what Reuben had said. *Well planned, indeed.*

"Sara!" Doug shouted, and she saw him with some young people at the end of the line, Carrie a few steps away, talking to a girl about her age. Just then a cheer went up and the line began to move. Between the shuffling marchers, Sara saw Abby, talking to a young man with a crew cut who was smiling at her expectantly, as if hoping for her favors.

Abby saw Sara and bolted to her side. "See you!" she said over her shoulder, with a brief wave to the startled young man. "He is so boring," she hissed to Sara. "Thank heavens you came; I couldn't stand another minute."

"You couldn't just walk away?" Sara asked mildly.

"I could, but . . . he was so needy. You know?"

From the front of the line, a chant began, rolling toward them like the long swell of a wave. Sara and Abby found Doug and Carrie watching openmouthed as the demonstrators boisterously chanted, "No . . . no . . .

no . . . Carr*anno*! No . . . no . . . no . . . Car-
r*anno*!" Soon the rhythm and the words propelled the marchers: they pumped their
placards up and down, especially when
passing one of the cameras spaced along
the march. Sara saw several of them punch
their fists into the air, and wondered if they
knew that was an age-old gesture of revolu-
tion.

On impulse, she fell into step with a pretty
young woman pushing twins in a double
stroller. "What is this march all about?" she
asked.

"We're against the town," the young
woman said.

"Why?"

"Oh . . . lots of reasons. Somebody said
it'd be bad for us, too many people or cars,
maybe both. Tell you the truth, I don't really
care, you know? I don't know if I'd hate it or
not. But it's a gorgeous day and I wanted to
take the kids for a walk anyway, so I said,
why not? It's always nice to have a plan
when you're walking." She paused. "Actually,
you know, it might not be too bad, the town, I
mean. So many of the kids around here are
older; it'd be nice to have a whole town of lit-

tle ones my two's age. That's what they said, you know that? Only young families could buy in there. Tons of little kids. It sounds really nice. But," she added hastily, "don't tell anybody I said that; they're all against it."

"Maybe they agree with you and are afraid to say so," Sara said. "If you don't tell them how you feel, you'll never know what they really think. You could all have the same ideas and never know it."

The young woman frowned. "But if they're *really* against it . . ."

"Then you could change the subject."

After a moment, the young woman smiled. "That's a thought."

Reuben was at the corner where Sara had left him, standing with his back to the marchers, arms folded, his face dark with anger. "We're not staying for the speeches," he announced. "We're getting out of here."

"Why?" Doug asked.

"Because we've had enough!" he snapped. "*I've* had enough. Enough jabbering to last a lifetime from these—"

"Are you mad at us?" Doug asked in a small voice. "I mean, I know we didn't come back when Sara said to—"

"Reuben isn't—" Sara began.

"—small-minded, stupid, mean, petty, big-oted *cretins.*"

Carrie was watching Reuben admiringly as he reeled out the adjectives. "Sara likes that word, too."

"Us?" Doug asked in a frightened voice. "That's *us*?"

Sara put her arm around him. She was furious with Reuben. "Of course not. This is absurd. No one would talk about you that way."

"But . . . Carrie said you said Abby was a cretin."

"I did not!" Carrie cried.

"You did! You told me—"

"I said Sara said she could be something *between* Shakespeare and a—"

"Okay, you two, that's enough," Sara said sharply, too angry to be amused. "Come on, back to the car." They walked in silence, Sara's arm around Doug's shoulders. She could feel his tremors through the fabric of her shirtsleeve. "Doug, you're fine; don't exaggerate. It wasn't about you; Reuben wasn't talking about any of us."

"And I shouldn't have talked that way at all." Reuben turned to them as they reached the car, his eyes puzzled, as if he suddenly found himself in the middle of a play and had to find his place and pick up the right dialogue. His hands were still clenched, but as much with the effort to subdue anger as with anger itself. He told himself he had no right to dump his unfiltered visceral reactions on others who could not deal with them. And why should they have to try? What did they owe him that they should tolerate his explosions? Nothing; they had no debts (or affection, he acknowledged) that would lead to tolerance. If he could not handle opposition or intolerance unfamiliar to him because he did not choose intolerant people for friends, the least he could do was keep quiet. Especially with Sara and her children (not really hers, but, yes, hers) whom he wanted to impress, whom he wanted to like him, admire him, ask to see more of him. Especially, most importantly, with Sara, to whom he never wanted to show signs of weakness or failure, both of which he knew were demonstrated by giving free rein to fury.

And so: squelch the anger, wipe it from his face and voice. If he could not shed it, store it inside, deep enough to be ignored for today and set it loose only when he was alone, not facing the wide eyes of these kids. Or

Sara's anger, which he had not thought to see turned on him.

"I apologize," he said. "I was so angry I forgot everything else, and everybody else. Doug, I couldn't talk that way about you. About any of you. We don't know each other very well yet, but you all seem pretty smart and savvy, and I'll bet if you choose to dislike a fool, it's because he's a fool, not because he's black or white or prays on his knees or standing on his head."

Carrie giggled.

"It's the three of you I want to be with," Reuben said, "not that gaggle back there; you've got nothing in common with them." He held out his hand to Doug. "Am I forgiven?"

Without hesitation, Doug said, "Sure." They shook hands gravely.

"What's a gaggle?" asked Carrie.

"Literally, a flock of geese when not flying, but it also means an aggregation of people. Usually an uncomplimentary term."

She nodded, then cocked her head, thinking. "The gaggle giggled," she said happily. "I'm going to use that in a story about a bunch of people who were mad at somebody and then found out he was a hero in disguise and they all ended up happy and laughing." She looked at Reuben. "But didn't you mean 'the four of us'?"

"The four of— Oh. Well, I said 'the three of you' to make sure Doug got the point that you three weren't the target of all those adjectives. But Sara is always included. She's at the head of the list of people I want to be with. In fact, to be honest, I'd rather be with Sara than anyone in the world."

Abby burst into tears.

"Oh, Lord." Sara sighed. "Abby, please try to stop. I know you're unhappy, but we can have a wonderful day if you can stop thinking about—"

"Are we still going?" Carrie asked. "I mean, if Reuben is really upset, he may want to go home and drink."

Reuben burst out laughing. "Carrie, you are the best tonic for being upset; no drink could come close. Of course we're going." Amazed, he heard the lightness and affection in his voice. *Anger all squelched. When have I willingly put aside my own emotions to make others happy?* "I can be upset tomorrow," he said, "when I get back to the office and can do something about it."

In the car, Sara said, "Thank you."

They were on the highway again, driving northwest; there was little traffic and Reuben had set the cruise control, his hands resting lightly on the steering wheel. "For what?"

"For defusing the tension."

"That I caused."

"Yes, but you stopped it before it got out of hand. And also . . ." She paused. "Thank you for saying you enjoy being with me."

He smiled. "That was not exactly what I said."

"And saying it to the children instead of in private made it more like a . . ." She let the words float off.

"Declaration," he said quietly. "And it was."

Sara was silent. At last, Reuben said, "I owe you the greatest apology. I try not to lose my temper with people I care about (he thought of Ardis, with whom he was almost always out of temper these days, but it had been so long since he cared for her that he could not even remember what that had felt like) and I can't imagine a worse way to start out with these great kids, when I want them to approve of me and lobby for all of us to be together often. It's not the first time in my life that I've behaved badly, but I can't remember regretting it more than I do now."

"You know," Sara said mildly, "it's a little short of their discovering that you're a mass murderer."

There was a pause, then he chuckled. "I was overreacting."

"You were. And those people," she added after a moment, "the ones demonstrating, aren't really all the same." She told him about the young woman with the twins in the stroller. "I think a lot of them just don't know what to do with the information they're being fed by someone. Have you been doing any-thing in the past few months—neighborhood meetings for brunch, or dessert and cof-fee—to prepare them for such a massive project plunked down in their midst?"

"What does *plunked* mean?" Carrie asked interestedly.

Sara shook her head ruefully. She and Reuben had grown accustomed to being alone on walks, at dinner or lunch, at the-aters or concert halls. Now, suddenly, there were five of them and conversations were not private. She felt a brief flare of worry that Reuben would not welcome, might even walk away from, intrusions into their privacy. "I haven't found a man who's interested in a woman with three kids," she had said to

Tess, not so long ago. "I can't imagine any man being interested in me until Doug goes to college in seven years, and I'm alone."

(It was true that Reuben did not seem to mind, in fact seemed oddly content to have the children around. Still, she thought, better to space out the times she came to him encumbered with youngsters, or the novelty could quickly pall.)

"Plunked," she repeated thoughtfully. "Set down. Or, rather, dropped. At least, set down forcefully."

"Like, dumped?" Doug asked. "Are they mad because you're dumping a town on them, or because they don't know what it will be like?"

"They should know," Reuben mused. "We've had brochures and letters out to them for a long time. I'm more interested in who's behind this. Some kid, the estimable Charlotte said, who gave Ted all kinds of ideas. I'll pay a visit to Ted tomorrow night. Where are we, by the way?"

Sara laughed and gave him directions, using the map she had been marking earlier. "And what else did Charlotte say?"

"They're against higher taxes, too many kids, congestion, African-Americans, Jews,

Mexicans, anybody who's different from them. I'm with them on congestion; obviously we haven't made it clear how much open space we'll have, and how much the facilities will be available to them. But the most peculiar thing Charlotte said, two things, in fact, were phrases that sounded completely out of character. One, she said Carrano Village wouldn't have even a token grandparent. One of those clever phrases certain people use, but not like the rest of her speech. And there was a phrase she said she liked—meaning she'd heard it from someone else—about too many different kinds of people. She said they'd destructively destroy a decent town. Another odd phrase."

Sara frowned.

"Mack talks like that," said Carrie.

Reuben looked at Sara. "Your brother?"

"Yes."

"Pretty far-fetched, I'd think." There was a pause. "Wouldn't you?"

"Yes."

"Carrie!" Doug cried. "Look at the horses! They're *galloping.* With nobody on them!"

"Oh, fabulous," Carrie breathed. "Abby, *look.* They're so *beautiful.* Come on, *look.*

Right now you need lots of beauty in your life."

"How do you know what I need?"

"I have *empathy.* I'm a *writer.* Having beauty in your life helps when you're tragically suffering. Quick, look, they're almost gone!"

Sara and Reuben shared a smile. "A little more drama than I'd expected for today," he murmured.

"Heightened," Sara said, her voice low, "by three youngsters who create drama every time they walk across a room, or even sit in a car. They whip it up, like a huge froth of emotions they wallow in quite happily."

"They're great fun."

"A three-ring circus."

"And very attractive."

"And lovable. The dearest people I know. They've had a rough time, and they've handled it wonderfully."

"I would think that describes you."

"Well . . . I was older; it didn't shatter my life the way it did theirs."

Reuben, who thought her life had been, if not shattered, thoroughly dislocated, and who continually found additional reasons to admire her, admired her now, in silence, and they drove in silence across the state and into a lush valley and then to the town of Galena. As they approached the outskirts, Sara felt time slide away. The town looked as if it had been lifted from a picture book of early-nineteenth-century America, with re-stored houses, hotels, and businesses seem-ingly unchanged from those days. Some were brightly scrubbed and gleaming in yel-low, brown, or red Midwestern brick. Some were frame, painted deep magenta or yel-low, blue or blinding white, all of them with white, extravagantly carved trim. Their peaked roofs were like raised eyebrows above sym-metrical windows and doors; their front yards were small and manicured.

"Isn't it pretty?" Carrie exclaimed. "Come on, Abby, admit it; it's really a pretty town."

"Right," Abby grudgingly conceded. "Ex-cept that everybody in the world is here."

It was true; Main Street was traffic-clogged and nothing moved at more than a crawl. "Saturday," Sara said ruefully. "We should have known."

"A million people come here every year," said Carrie. "I looked it up on the Internet."

"Would you like to walk?" Sara asked. "We can meet you at the end of Main Street. You'll probably beat us there."

"Great idea!" Doug cried, and was out of the car before Sara could change her mind. Carrie followed—"Thanks, Sara," she said graciously—and waited for Abby, who did not move.

Sara sighed, but her voice was cheerful as she said, "Abby, would you check out a few antique stores? I thought we'd find a rocking chair for your room. You need another chair for when your friends come over."

Abby's face brightened. "Really? And can I get a cushion for it, too? One of those embroidered ones that look French?"

"What a good idea. Pick out some things and we'll look at them tomorrow morning."

Abby was gone; they all were gone. In the stalled traffic, she and Reuben leaned into each other, and kissed.

The tapping of a horn behind them, beneath the palm of an amused elderly man, pulled them apart. Reuben drove twenty feet until forced to stop again, and again they came together, smiling at the humor of it. "Drive a few feet," murmured Reuben against Sara's lips, "kiss, drive a few feet—"

"Kiss," said Sara, and they did.

And then drove another few feet as soon as the traffic moved. "All three of them are wonderful," Reuben said, "but I like having the two of us together."

"So do I." Sara struggled—that flash of worry back again—and finally settled on the simple truth, unmitigated. "I know they're an encumbrance, but the four of us are a package."

"You've always made that clear. And today was my idea, because I wanted to meet them, and I wanted them to know me. I would never ask you to choose between us, but I hope you and I can find time to be together."

"Of course we can. We will. I want that as much as you do. As long as we know that if something comes up—"

"They come first. There's no question about that. They're your family, in your care. You could no more walk away from them—"

"Goodness, is *that* what we're talking about? Or just getting away for an evening?"

He laughed and shook his head ruefully. "I tend to get carried away."

"It's all right when you're carried away with me," she said, smiling almost to herself, and he glanced at her in pleased surprise at her directness. "It's strange, being away from home," she said, in oblique response to his look. "Everything seems simpler."

"Then this will be the first of many trips."

They reached the end of the street. Doug was sitting on the curb, eating an ice-cream cone; Abby and Carrie stood beside him, sipping lemonade through straws. All three, even Abby, looked pleased with themselves, and, in the car, they chattered about the shops and people while Reuben finally was able to drive straight to their inn, drop their luggage, and drive on to the Pine Ridge trailhead.

"Reuben and I have lunch in our backpacks," said Sara as they all took packs and walking sticks from the trunk. "So if you think you might like food at some point, I suggest you don't wander off and lose us."

She shook her head in mock despair as Doug and Carrie ran on ahead, Abby close behind, and in a moment were swallowed up by the thick bushes and tall grasses that crowded in on the trail. "They'll find us as soon as they get hungry." She and Reuben kissed, and then they, too, entered the lush, hilly wilderness of towering cliffs, canyons, and rivers that was Apple River Canyon State Park.

Later, Sara was to look back on that afternoon as the beginning of a perfect moment in time: twenty-four hours of harmony and laughter and small delights that she would have treasured forever, but that were driven out of her thoughts soon after their return home the following afternoon. But until then, everything was bathed in a magical, golden light. The sun was at its highest point on this, the longest day of the summer; the air shimmered with heat waves and dancing reflections from the sunlit stream alongside the trail; leaves and tall plants quivered as insects darted from branch to twig to leaf; and the footsteps of Reuben and Sara and her family were silent on the soft earth as they glided through a green-and-gold world.

No one spoke. Amazing, Sara thought, that anything could keep Doug quiet. Sundappled, moving in and out of the shade of great trees, gazing up and up at canyon walls of variegated vermilion, buff and brown, with intrepid bushes growing horizontally from the tiniest of cracks where their roots could take hold, they all drank in the beauty in a silence that acknowledged it more meaningfully than any exclamations would have done.

"Guys, look!" Doug cried, and Sara laughed, because of course, with Doug, silence could not last. "Is than an *eagle*?"

It was an eagle. "Wow," Doug breathed as Carrie photographed it five or six times, and then kept her camera turned on as they spotted, in the next twenty minutes, two fawns, a squirrel that stopped halfway up the trunk of a tree, as if posing for its photograph, a ptarmigan and its two babies huddled under a bush, and a rabbit, frozen in fright, hunched on a rock close to the trail.

When they found a picnic spot, they paused in setting out their food to watch hawks soaring far above, and when their gaze returned to earth they saw, in a sweeping glance, dozens of varieties of ferns and unfamiliar flowers none of them could name.

"And," Sara said to Reuben that night, "no one complained that the hike was too long or the sun was too hot or the mosquitoes were annoying."

"They were having too good a time to complain."

The two of them were sitting on a broad porch overlooking the river, cognac and coffee on the table before them, a crescent moon suspended in the black sky with Jupiter below it, as if hanging by a thread. Abby sat on a swing at the other end of the porch, not brooding, it seemed to Sara, but dreaming, perhaps reflecting, with more calmness than she had shown since her disastrous night with Sean. Carrie and Doug had gone to their rooms with books and a game of Scrabble they found in the lobby.

The hotel was a converted mill, with a glassed-in restaurant overlooking the Mississippi River. Their five rooms took up the entire second floor, on both sides of a wide corridor. Abby's eyebrows had shot up when she discovered there were five rooms, instead of four. Standing in the doorway of her room, she had said incredulously, "You and Reuben aren't in one room? I mean, how old-fashioned. I mean, you didn't have to do that for us; we all know . . . I mean, even Doug knows . . . you know."

"That we're sleeping together?" Sara asked. "How do you know that?"

Abby flushed. "Well, because . . . everybody does. When they're in love, I mean. And you and Reuben look like . . . you know, like you're in love."

"Everybody?" Sara asked.

Abby's flush grew deeper, and she looked away. "I don't," she mumbled. "I mean, you know, most people. Anyway, people who are grown up, who can . . . *handle* it. I didn't mean *me.*"

Sara put her arm around Abby and held her close. "I'm glad you believe that. It's hard, when you're young, to understand how much more there is to sex than sex. So much to deal with."

"You taught me that."

"Yes, but we don't always know how much soaks in."

Abby clamped her lips shut, to keep from asking if Sara and Reuben *were* sleeping together. It wasn't really her business. Maybe, later, she'd hear Reuben's footsteps going to Sara's room when they thought she and Carrie and Doug would be asleep. No, he'd be barefoot. She could keep her door open a crack, and see if a shadow passed by when everything was quiet. Except that his room was right across the hall from Sara's, and he could get there without passing Abby's door. Maybe that was why Sara allocated their rooms that way. Probably it was.

Abby tried to picture Sara and Reuben

naked and in bed. When they'd been walking hand in hand that morning, they'd looked really good together: they were both slender, and Sara was almost as tall as Reuben and they moved with the same kind of rhythm, their steps the same length, their heads turning to each other at the same time. It was hard to imagine kissing a man with a beard and glasses—well, obviously he'd take off his glasses—but otherwise she could see the two of them stretching out in bed, their bodies long and warm pressed against each other, and his hand would be . . .

She couldn't stand it. She slammed shut the door of her room and threw herself on the bed, as aroused as if Sean were touching her all over, whimpering deep in her throat because she wanted him, and if only he'd suddenly be there, at her side, smiling at her, she'd never make fun of him again.

And give him what he wants?

Oh, I don't know!

By dinnertime, she was calm again, surprising herself by having a good time. Reuben was great at word games, they discovered, and he told stories about New York, funny stories and sad ones, and got them to tell him about their classes at Parker, and Carrie's latest story, and Abby's play ("I'm sorry I missed it," he said. "I'll make sure I don't miss the next one," which meant, obviously, that he intended to be with Sara for a long time, which, to be honest, Abby had mixed feelings about), and then Doug ran upstairs and brought down a balsa-wood carving he'd made just before dinner, and it was the rabbit they'd seen on their hike, hunched in terror on the rock, and it really looked afraid.

"So could you get me a gallery show?" Doug asked as Reuben turned the rabbit around in his fingers, admiring it.

"A gallery? I doubt it. Gallery owners are a cautious breed; they almost never take a new artist."

"Everybody's new in the beginning," said Carrie. "Even Picasso."

"Even Picasso," Reuben agreed. "But he studied for years in art schools and the Royal Academy in Spain, and was poor and unknown before people began to buy his works. And some of the world's most famous artists exhibited first in bars or shops or restaurants, wherever they could find an owner willing to display a painting or sculpture—often in exchange for meals—and if they couldn't find that, they held sidewalk shows. Then, when a few people started buying their works, and word got out that something special was happening, gallery owners 'discovered' them. Most gallery owners like to be the second or third on a bandwagon, not the first, in case they guess wrong."

"What happens if they guess wrong?"

"They feel foolish and they're out some money. If you call yourself an expert in art, both of those are unacceptable."

"I know somebody who can get me a gallery show," said Doug.

Reuben's eyebrows lifted. "A gallery owner?"

"No, but . . . he knows people."

"Then I think you should take him up on it. I'll be at your first show."

After a moment, Doug nodded, almost reluctantly.

"As if," said Sara that night on the porch with Reuben, "he doesn't want to put this miracle person to the test, for fear it won't work."

"Do you have any idea who the person is?"

"My guess is Mack. Filling Doug's head

with fantasies so that he can be the big daddy. Admired. Loved."

"And is he admired and loved?"

"Carrie and Doug love him, I think, or maybe it's just excitement; he's always churning things up. I have no idea what Abby thinks of him." She shook her head ruefully. "I'm doing this again; I'm sorry. You don't want to hear about Mack, or hear me agonizing about him, but somehow it always comes up. Let's change the subject."

Reuben put his arm around her. "Has it occurred to you that it always comes up because I make sure it does?"

"It has occurred to me, but even if it's true, I shouldn't let it happen. You have enough on your mind without taking on my family problems. What will you do about the demonstrations at your site?"

"Talk to the leaders. I'll meet with Ted, then Isaiah and I will meet with him and any others."

"Do you think perhaps the neighbors have a point?"

"You mean a legitimate gripe?"

"Legitimate concerns."

"Yes. I know they do. But we sent flyers to every mailing address, outlining our plans, and how we'd avoid some of the problems they're complaining about now. Everything was in the open; they've had months in which to respond, and no one's said a word."

"Are you sure they read the flyers?"

"I assume they did; it's their neighborhood, why wouldn't they? And what else could we do? Go up and down the streets holding their hands, making sure they read every word? That's not our responsibility; it's theirs, at least to pay attention to what's going on in their front yard." His anger was building, or he was allowing what had been simmering all day to come to the surface. "They're so wrapped up in their own lives they shut out the world: it's big and complicated and ambiguous, and they don't like that. They like small and simple. The rest they ignore because it might tax their little brains."

Sara moved away from his arm. "Then why are they out there in the fray, demonstrating and worrying about what's going to happen?"

"Someone stirred them up." He was so absorbed he barely noticed Sara's unmistakable distancing herself from him. "They're malleable, and someone used a lot of buzzwords, got them excited, and out of their easy chairs. More than once, evidently; Charlotte said they were already planning the next one. So we have to deal with them. Start from scratch, speak in short paragraphs, maybe use a sledgehammer, and somehow get through to them."

"I once thought," Sara said after a moment, "that you liked people."

Surprised, he turned to her. "I do like people."

"Always? Or just when they're not in your way?" There was a long silence. "Has your life been so easy you're not used to opposition?"

"No. Yes. In fact, for a long time it was easy, far easier than most people's. My family was strong and loving; it still is. We never went hungry; we never lacked clothing or books or toys. When we were kids our parents took us to the theater, concerts, museums, movies, the circus . . . every place that made the city our universe. Even after my mother couldn't go anymore, my father took us, and when we were grown, we took him, and my mother when she could manage it. I never thought about it when I was young, but I had everything I wanted, or could want."

"And then?"

"Oh, the usual struggles to get started, nothing surprising or unusual. We never really expect them because we're so sure we're ready to conquer the world and reach some kind of pinnacle . . . fame, I suppose, and admiration and, of course, money, though I never saw myself as a particularly wealthy man; that was never the goal."

"What was the goal?"

He leaned forward, hands clasped between his knees. "To build communities where people could live in harmony with the land and their neighbors. I wanted people to be able to experience the earth, whether it was a forest, a prairie, a lake, an ocean, or a mountain range. I wanted their lives to mesh with a living environment, not concrete rectangles filled edge to edge with brick and steel, and only photographs to show them what had been there before they arrived. And I wanted, as much as possible, to build houses far enough apart that each family had privacy but still was part of a community, so they could reach out to others, or retreat into the intimacy of their homes, whichever they needed at any given time."

He smiled at Sara. "I didn't mean to give a lecture. That actually is what I say when I talk to community groups, but tonight it sounds like a lecture."

"Did you say all those things to the Carrano Village neighbors?"

"Everything was in the flyers."

"Which I'll bet most of them never read."

"Why wouldn't they?"

"It may have looked like an advertisement, so they tossed it. It may have looked like a fund-raising pitch, so they tossed it. It may have resembled flyers they'd gotten during political campaigns, and people aren't too pleased with politicians these days, so they—"

"Tossed it." He nodded. "I'm sorry I came across as a Neanderthal. I don't dislike people, and I don't look down on them as if they've just crawled out of the sea." Sara raised her eyebrows. "It seems I'm exaggerating again."

She smiled. "I've heard far worse from those who truly dislike people. And there was no question of my disliking you."

"That would be the worst. But I don't want to disappoint you, either."

"No, don't say that. I'm not some superior being who passes judgment and has to be placated. I just want you to be you, and I'll

like some things and maybe dislike others,
but that's not unusual, is it? Or unexpected?"

"No." He put his arm around her again and
felt her move closer to him, and wondered at
how little he had been able to say to her. In
all his talk of his youth, and what he had
called the usual struggles to get started, he
had left out Ardis. Even now, after a magical
day, with a perfect opening for intimacy, for
revelation, he could not be honest with her.

And she had not asked anything that might
have opened other doors. Was it that she did
not care whether he was married or not?
Whether he ever had been married? Whether
he had children? Whether women, or just
one woman, shared any part of his life? If she
was truly indifferent to all that, how serious
could she be in her feelings for him? He
would have to ask her. But the minute he did,
those doors would fly open to all he had so
far kept to himself. *I will ask her. But not yet.*

They sat quietly, gazing at the river,
gleaming ripples of silver in the moonlight,
bordered by black, rustling trees. The night
was still. Abby had gone to her room, to read
or write in her diary or brood; Doug and Carrie had left their books and game of Scrabble to stand on the back balcony, identifying

constellations from a book Sara had given them the night before. "There's a jillion stars," Doug had breathed when full darkness had come. "A *billion.* A *gazillion.* And . . . look! The *Milky Way*! It's *real*!"

On the front porch, Sara and Reuben became part of the night, still and silent, so close each warmed the other as chill air drifted up from the river. "Abby says we're old-fashioned," Sara murmured.

"Not a bad way to be sometimes."

"No. I like it."

"As long as it's only for tonight."

She smiled drowsily, feeling his heartbeat pulsing with hers. "What I liked best was that we both knew this was the way it would be, without even discussing it."

"The manager was as surprised as Abby; did you notice?"

"I did. Does everyone expect every two adults to be sleeping together? What if we were brother and sister?"

"With three kids in tow?"

"No one would think that," she murmured, smiling. "Or that I'm their sister and not their mother."

He knew her well enough to understand— even, he fancied, to hear—the conflicted feelings that lay behind those words: the gains in love and family, the losses in an independent life and career. Now was the time to share gain and loss, to open the door on his past and present so that she could respond with her own secrets, and they truly would become a part of each other's life.

Because that was what he wanted. He knew it. He would kiss her now, and tell her he loved her, and then be as open with her as he was with no one else.

He kissed her. They clung for a moment, and then Sara murmured, "Is it very late?"

"Almost two."

"I hope the children are asleep." She sat up. "I think we should be, too. They'll make sure we're awake when their day starts, not when we think ours should." She leaned forward and kissed him lightly. "Good night."

Reuben stood with her, and took her hand. He started to say, *Wait, there are things I want to tell you—*

But he did not. Tomorrow was a better time, when they weren't so sleepy. Or the day after, when they were back home, and alone. Or the day after that, when . . .

"Good night," he said, and let her go.

EIGHT

Don't flutter," Lew Corcoran snapped at Pussy's reflection in the bedroom mirror. But, in fact, he was focused on himself, perfecting the knot in his tie, adjusting the triangle of his matching silk handkerchief, buttoning two buttons of his suit jacket. Inspecting his image, he released one button and stood sideways, contemplating his girth. "I might lose some weight," he said to Pussy, who, fluttering, did not answer. "What the hell is wrong with you?" he barked.

"My shoes . . . the black ones . . . I'm sure I put them . . ."

"You've got twenty fucking pairs of black shoes."

"The Escada ones, satin with the little button thing. Decoration."

"For Christ's sake, wear anything. Who the hell do you think is going to care what you look like? Or even notice?"

Pussy flinched. "I care," she whispered.

And you used to care, or pretended to, she thought bitterly, trying to remember which closets she had searched. How many closets did she have? She didn't know. She didn't even want to know. There were too many; she knew that much. And they were too big. Everything was too big. Lew liked big. Lew liked monstrous. Why had Sara shown them this apartment with huge cold rooms that, even with furniture, looked like hotel lobbies? Well, she had to. Lew insisted on big rooms and a big view, and Sara did her job and found it for him. For him, not for Pussy. All Pussy cared about were separate bathrooms so she didn't have to look at Lew first thing in the morning.

You used to care what I looked like, she thought again, rummaging on her hands and knees. Or said you did. Before we were married. You said I was a pretty little thing. And I was. Pretty.

Over the intercom, the chef said, "Mrs. Corcoran, you did not specify the serving dish for the crêpes."

Pussy turned around on her knees and looked at Lew.

"Go choose one," he said. "Probably copper."

"He knows more about those things than I do."

"Take care of it."

The dinner guests were all men, smooth-shaven with smooth hair and smooth suits. Greeting them, Pussy repeated each name as she was introduced, and promptly forgot it. (Thankfully, the young one wasn't there, the good-looking one who somehow scared her, she never knew why. She couldn't remember his name, either—Dick? Nick? Zack?—even though she'd seen him with Lew in New York, too. He was in and out all the time, getting orders; she couldn't hear much because they always shut the door of Lew's office, but she caught a few words when they were walking to the front door. The truth was, when she really came down to it, she didn't like either one of them, but she had to live with Lew, so she didn't let herself think that very often.)

She sat at the opposite end of the table from the confident bulk of her husband, sweating lightly in her black satin dress, a fixed smile on her lips as she watched the servers to make sure wineglasses were refilled and rolls replaced instantly on bread-and-butter dishes. She ate almost nothing (though it seemed to taste fine and she told herself to remember to thank the chef, who was intimidating but seemed to like praise) and drank steadily.

She hated being there. Lew Corcoran entertained frequently, but usually at his club, or in a restaurant's private dining room. He never told Pussy why some dinners were held at home; he simply announced the date and the number of guests, and then it was up to Pussy to consult with the chef, direct their two maids, and hire additional kitchen help or servers.

A long time ago she had dreamed of beautiful dinners, years ago, when she was thirteen, fourteen . . . up to the time she was seventeen and lived with Fred, who had talked so nice until she moved in, and then beat her and drank and was killed when he drove into a wall just before dawn on a blizzarding night when, even sober, a driver would have had trouble navigating the streets. Before Fred, though, she had spent hours posturing before the long mirror fastened to the inside of her closet door, narrowing her eyes at her fat, sweaty image, until she saw herself losing width, gaining height, and wearing black velvet sexily curving over her willowy form. Through hot summer afternoons she would stand there, in front of her full-power window fan, dreaming of dinner parties, of supervising a cheerfully obedient staff, charming her elegant guests with witty aphorisms and bons mots as bright as the chandeliers sparkling above, and basking in the smiling admiration of a husband (tall, dark, muscular, his face as yet a blur) at the other end of the table who glowed with love and gratitude for her beauty and skills, and barely could disguise his impatience for everyone to be gone so he could sweep her to their bed.

Beyond the mirror, what really happened was Augie and then Bob and then George, followed by two or three others she could not remember. None of them mentioned marriage, but they all promised to take care of her and then did not. Left alone each time, she flailed about for a plan of action. She knew she was not stupid, though she recognized that she was behaving stupidly, but, hating herself for her weight and the clumsiness that came with it (when she had dreamed of grace and elegance), and feeling she had no control over events that whipped her about, and men who manipulated her, she took whatever came along, almost as punishment for being Pussy. And then what came along was Lew Corcoran, who bullied her into a starvation diet and an exercise regimen all the more exhausting because she was weak with hunger, but she achieved plumpness, and obeyed Lew's dictates on hairstylists, clothing boutiques, and makeup experts and when not to speak (most of the time), and then he cuddled her and called her a pretty little thing and married her.

Four years ago. When she was forty. All her dreams had come true.

She gestured to a server that her wineglass was empty. When he hesitated, she knew Lew had told him not to give her any more. "Dominic," she cried gaily—she thought that was the server's name; if not, he could use it for a few minutes—"we're positively parched for wine at this end of the table."

And without hesitation, to avoid an emotional eddy disrupting the flow of his evening, Lew nodded at the server, who served her. And served her again when she gestured, ever so slightly, so that Lew would not notice. She sipped and smiled, and sipped and recalled the past, and in between caught fragments of the conversation around her.

". . . a thousand acres?"

"On a rise, about a quarter mile from the river." Lew's voice, explaining in that patient way he used with Pussy, when he was about to explode with rage because she wasn't understanding something. "There's a three-hundred-foot-wide swath cutting down to the river where we'll dock the boat. The town is a mile and a half upriver, River Bend—"

"Name of the town?"

"That's it: River Bend."

"Not exactly clever."

"They're not clever people out there. Small town, slow, don't even know Chicago exists."

Through the rumble of male voices, Pussy recalled Sara's voice telling her to get to know Chicago, to make friends, to join some boards of directors, to shape her days. And I tried, she thought. It's just that I need somebody to tell me what to do—I always have; every man I've known has told me how incompetent I am—and those people Sara introduced me to are so far ahead, they know so much, they *do* and they *go* and they *take charge.* Why would they be bothered helping me, when I can't do anything?

"You can do so many things," Sara had said on the phone on Sunday, "if you just settle on one project or one area and then concentrate on it. Take it one step at a time. Give yourself a chance, Pussy. If no one else will, you have to be the one to do it."

"Do what?"

"Give yourself a chance. Believe in yourself."

Suddenly, Pussy was desperate to call Sara. She had to talk to her, hear her voice, believe she was real, believe everything she said. Without thinking, she pushed back her chair.

"My dear," said Lew, the smoothness of it grating across Pussy's skin. "Is there something you need?"

They were all looking at her, the first time

since dinner had begun. "Just . . . to make a phone call," she said.

"But surely it can wait until later. We'll need you soon for the dessert."

She hovered between sitting and standing.

One of the men on her right said, "Well, if it's important . . ."

Lew drummed his fingers, lightly, almost delicately.

"No." She sank down. "It can wait."

A server pushed her chair back to the table. Without looking at Lew, she restored her fixed smile, gestured for wine, and drifted away.

Lew had been the nicest of all of them. His wife had died and he lived alone in a cavernous apartment overlooking the reservoir in Central Park; the first time Pussy saw it she felt blinded by the light. In those days she was alone, too, cleaning house and cooking for an elderly couple in exchange for a bedroom and her own bathroom in the basement of a house in Queens; two window wells filtered a sooty gray light that blinked on and off as people walked by. Lew's effulgent rooms, his masterful voice and bulk and sleek suits, and his broad hands, in bed, turning her compliant obesity this way and that, shoving her head between his legs, pushing her to crouch on all fours, her buttocks high, gave her subservience a new meaning. By the time he announced to her employers that she was leaving, she adored him and lumbered beside him to his apartment feeling ecstatically secure.

They were married two years later, when she could zip up a wedding dress, apply makeup with a skillful hand, and speak only when her husband addressed her. Four years ago. When Pussy Corcoran, humming her new name to herself, believed that all her dreams had come true, exactly as she had dreamed them.

She believed that from the moment Lew told her he would marry her to the first time (the only time) she had tried to show an interest in his work. She had turned her eager face to his and he had told her, not, then, unkindly, that she was to show interest in him only in bed and running his home. Anything to do with business was his. Only his. Not, he added, a difficult concept for her to grasp.

". . . the last parcel that size on the Fox River," Pussy heard Lew say, "with a town close by."

"But Carrano bought it."

"And doesn't have annexation approval from River Bend."

"So, they'll build the town without approval."

"The county won't allow it."

"You know that for a fact?"

"They don't want another independent municipality, like a Carrano Village West, with its own mayor and city council, and they want to upgrade River Bend without spending county money. They can do that by annexing a heavily subsidized village, or, even easier, they can watch jobs and taxes pour in from a casino. I've got three sure votes out of five against giving Carrano annexation approval, and in favor of our casino."

"Promises are easy to forget."

"These were paid for, with another payment due after the vote. They won't forget."

There was silence.

"But if Carrano can upgrade the town, why wouldn't they just vote to give him the annexation? Simplest thing, seems to me, without them starting to futz about Mafia or what all, people always do, with casinos. So they vote to annex, and you're out."

"They'll vote for the casino. They won't want the town built, period."

"Why the fuck not? Carrano's got every

approval but annexation, and you said the town needs help, and, like I said, villages are clean; nobody worries about Mafia and all. So who's gonna stop it?"

"The people." Corcoran smiled thinly. "This is a democracy, remember? The kid's out there convincing every hick Carrano's a danger to their way of life. He's good: honest face, big smile, nice way with words. Got a few hundred for a demonstration last Saturday—marchers, speakers, even had TV crews—and he'll be doing more of them, get a few hundred more each weekend. Keep things boiling; you think any politician's gonna vote against a local uprising?"

The kid, Pussy thought, the one whose eyes scared her. She had blessed some amorphous God (whom she could not believe in; she wanted to, but Lew always said the weak knelt and prayed, the strong stood up and *did*) when she saw that he was not among tonight's guests.

"So when do you figure to break ground?"

"Couple years. Soon as the legislature votes the license, we'll start the hotel and the dock for the boat."

"With the locals cheering you on? They're

gonna like a hotel and riverboat casino better than a new town?"

"They like money. You think there's any
other reason legalized gambling's popping
up all over the place? River towns are dying
right and left when their factories fold: old
run-down places on the Fox River, the Illinois, the Mississippi, all of 'em with blue-
collar people with nowhere to go, nothing to
do, their houses rotting away. They screamed
loud enough, they got riverboats. Casinos.
Jobs, tourists—busloads of optimists and
bored housewives—and tax money. The
towns get all spiffed up, and the states rake
in their share; they raise taxes every year on
the casinos and use the money for schools.
You tell me who's gonna vote against that."

"You're sure of all this."

"We've been doing a lot of legwork."

Carrano, Pussy thought. I've heard of that.
Somebody talked about it and Lew was interested. I can always tell; his right ear jerks,
like a dog that hears something. Her smile
widened. Like a dog.

But who said it? She tried to remember. It
was in some place with people and . . . waiters! A restaurant, and Sara was there. And

then she remembered: Sara with a man, older, stern looking, and he stood up and pushed forward so she and Lew had to step back. And when Lew asked who he was, or something like that, the man—Reuben! His name was Reuben! She remembered!— said he had something to do with Carrano Village. And Lew's ear jerked forward.

Maybe Sara was involved with Carrano Village. Close to Reuben, close to Carrano Village. And Lew was trying to stop her. I have to warn her, Pussy thought. I can't let Lew do anything to hurt her. She's my only friend.

Through the warm buzz of the wine she'd drunk, she tried to focus on what they were saying.

". . . twenty percent," Lew said. "The family's keeping a million shares; the rest we're offering at sixty."

"Can't buy into something that might be a pipe dream, shit, Lew, you know that. What if you never build it?"

"We'll build it. We're starting the day after we buy the land from Carrano. We figure he'll have to sell in the next six, eight months; he's got too much tied up to let it drag on much longer. Soon as he knows he can't annex, which means he can't build, he'll dump it, and we'll pick it up."

"So that's when we'll talk about buying in."

In his deadly patient voice, Lew said, "We're offering two hundred sixty thousand shares. You want options, now's the time. We're opening it up soon as we break ground. Let me know."

"How's the fishing out there?"

"Smallmouth, carp, some others. Not as good as it used to be, too polluted, but still good."

"Shoulda been with us last week, four days on the Roaring Fork, best trout you'll ever see."

Pussy shut them out. Fishing, she thought angrily. I want to hear about Sara.

"My love?"

Lew was looking at her, smiling, his eyes flat.

"The dessert," he said.

A server pulled back her chair, freeing her from the table. Pussy went to the kitchen. The chef had the copper serving dish ready for her, rows of crêpes perfectly overlapped from end to end. Lew had told her this was to be her contribution to the evening. Once, in New York, he had admired a hostess who carried a blazing dessert to the table like a proud queen bearing a sacred flame. "You'll do that," he had said to Pussy, who had quailed, and prayed that he would forget.

But Lew did not forget anything. And so Pussy stood beside the chef, ladling warmed cognac over the crêpes. "Madame is too generous," the chef said sternly, but she was afraid of walking in flamelessly, and added one more portion. She hoisted the heavy dish and went to the swinging door. "Light it," she ordered. The chef shook his head, but held a long, lighted match to the crêpes, and Pussy entered the dining room.

Flames shot up, singeing her hair. Flames cascaded over the edges of the dish in a molten cataract, engulfing her hands and wrists. With a cry, she dropped the dish, and flames spread over the carpet to the seven pairs of patent leather shoes beneath the table. The men leaped up and began stamping on the carpet, crushing crêpes and kicking aside the copper dish like a flaming football.

Pussy floated away, and, from her safe distance, watched wonderingly. The scene was frenzied and seething, like a performance video in an art museum: six sleek, dark-suited figures vaulting up and down, rising like specters from a bed of flames, making strange cries of gleeful abandon. Only Lew was unmoving, standing rigidly at the head of the table. Pussy saw him peripherally, but, raptly absorbed in the spectacle before her, did not look his way. This was her doing. The leaping, the high-pitched cries, the sudden life that awakened the stark, cavernous dining room . . . her doing, all hers. She was smiling: powerful, buoyant, alive.

But soon the flames subsided to scattered flickers of blue, and then died away. A ragged oval of charred carpet remained when the men, their gleeful faces turning sheepish, returned to their chairs. As one, they replaced sheepishness with concern. "Not serious, you know." "Shouldn't have dessert anyway; bad for my belt size." "Too bad about the carpet." "There's a guy can fix that, little Armenian can do anything. I'll give you his name . . ."

At last Pussy glanced at Lew's stony face. He'll kill me, she thought, and fled.

She could not go to the bedroom; it was the first place he would look for her. She ducked into the library, opened one of the pair of mahogany doors into Lew's study, and pulled it shut behind her. He would never look for her here; it was forbidden territory.

She circled the room, the only human-size one in the apartment, staying close to the walls, trying to imagine the future. Her steps were short and desperate and it occurred to her that observers would say she looked like a mouse on a wheel, or a laboratory monkey frantically searching for an escape from a pen. *And they'd be right.*

She sat on the leather couch. She hated leather; it was slippery and cold, resistant to curling up in a protective ball. In a minute she was pattering about the room again. I'll run away. I won't take anything of Lew's, I'll just go to Sara and she'll take care of me.

She stood at the desk and picked up the telephone. She knew the number by heart. "Sara!" she cried. "Thank heavens you're there. Can I come to live with you?"

"*Live* with me? You're leaving your husband?"

"Yes, yes, yes. I have to, have to get out, I've made him so angry, furious, *furious,* I can't stay, he'll kill me."

"You don't mean that, Mrs. Corcoran. Of course he won't kill you—"

"He will! He will! He's so—"

"But you've told me he's been angry at you before, and every time he's calmed down. Was that the truth . . . that he calmed down and everything was all right again?"

"It's like"—Pussy dropped into Lew's swivel chair. Leather again, but she had no choice, her legs crumpled—"you tell yourself everything's all right, but you can't forget what somebody said, and he can't forget, either, so it stays underneath everything, and it keeps hurting, so, no, I guess nothing is all right, not really, not ever." She was drawing circles, smaller circles inside them, circles trapped within circles, the pen gouging the sheet of paper as the circles became more desperate. "And this time I did something terrible, stupid, I ruined his dinner party and he'll never forgive me, business is the only thing he really truly cares about and I made a mess of it . . ."

"The whole evening or just some of it?"

Sara's practical voice cut through Pussy's wailing. "Dessert."

"So something went wrong with dessert. Surely that's forgivable."

"That was my only part, all I had to do. Except keep quiet and smile a lot." Her pen slashed through the circles. "Sara, I can't stay here, I don't have anyplace to go, I don't know anybody but you, please, Sara, please let me live with you! I won't be any trouble, I'll clean house—I know how—I'll do whatever you want, please, please . . ." She clamped her palm over her mouth to stifle her sobs, feeling ashamed. Sara wouldn't cry; she was too strong for that.

"I'll try to find a place for you tonight," Sara said at last. "I'm afraid it isn't a good idea for you to come here. Believe me, Mrs. Corcoran, I'll—"

"Call me Pussy! You never call me that! I've asked you before, and you ignore me! It's like you don't like me!"

"I do like you. And I want to help you. I promise I'll find you a safe place to stay while you think about what you'll do next. You can't make decisions when you're so upset; you need quiet and time. Everything will be all right, really it will. You're a strong person; you can make a good life; I'll do what I can to help you decide what to do next. I'll call you in an hour and tell you—"

"No! Don't call here! I'll call you. But half an hour, is that all right? He'll still be at dinner."

"I'll see what I can do. And . . . try to keep

calm. Whatever is going on, you won't do yourself any good by losing control."

Slowly, Pussy hung up the telephone. *Whatever is going on.* Didn't Sara believe her? If she couldn't count on Sara, she had no hope at all.

And she didn't call me Pussy.

But she said I'm strong. A strong person, she said. A good life. She wouldn't say that if she didn't mean it.

Pussy crooned the words to herself. A strong person. A good life. She put her head in her hands and sobbed.

Her tears fell on the papers spread on the desk, and she gasped, terrified again. She wiped the tears away with the side of her hand, pulled a tissue from a box behind her, and swiped it across the pages, wrinkling the top one. Oh, God, she thought, and, in a panic, crumpled the page completely and thrust it into the wastebasket, all the way to the bottom. Everything else looked fine. As good as new.

The pages were covered with long columns of numbers interspersed with close text; they jumped about in front of her, black on white, white on black, dizzying gibberish, and she thought of Lew, working with them, manipulating them as he manipulated people, moving through worlds and worlds of which she knew nothing. Just as she knew nothing of him. She had slept with him, married him, traveled with him, made two homes with him (if anyone could call them that), and if she were asked to write a brief description of who and what was Lew Corcoran, she could not do it.

Incredibly, she dozed a few seconds—minutes?—her head resting on her interlaced fingers, her elbows amid Lew's papers. She jerked upright and tried to focus on the clock, embedded in a world globe. Forty minutes since she had called Sara. Oh, God, she's probably gone out; she has other things to do than worry about me . . .

She snatched up the telephone and punched in the number. "Sara! I thought you'd gone out."

"How could I, when I promised I'd take care of you?"

A warm flood of gratitude lifted Pussy; her back straightened. Sara was taking care of her. "Thank you," she whispered. "Thank you—" And then the double doors of the office split apart and Lew was there.

"—Gardner," Sara was saying. "Nancy has

an empty caretaker's apartment; you can stay there as long as you like. Her address is . . . do you have a pencil?"

Staring at Lew, Pussy whispered, "Yes," but her hands were frozen and helpless.

"One thirty-four Elm; gray stone, a few stone statues in front. It's ten minutes by taxi from your apartment. You'll go there tonight?"

"Yes," Pussy whispered.

"What's wrong?" Sara said sharply. "What's happened?"

"Nothing. I . . . I'll do that. What you said." Her hands were shaking, and the telephone rattled as she hung up.

"How much have you read?" His voice was gravelly. He was still in the doorway.

"Nothing." Her eyes widened. What about the crêpes?

"Nothing," he snorted. "Spread out in front of you."

"But I don't under— I saw a lot of numbers but I don't understand them. What they mean. They're just . . . numbers. Words. They jumped around."

"I've told you to keep out of here."

"I know, Lew, but you were so angry—" *Don't remind him! Don't bring it up!* "I just needed a place to be quiet."

"So you chose my office. To spy on me. You fucking bitch, it wasn't enough to make a spectacle of yourself in there, to make a fool of me by being the class clown—"

The telephone rang. Pussy stared at it. Sara calling her back, wondering why she had hung up, why she had been whispering. Her hand went out to it.

"Leave it." He moved a step into the room. Without raising his voice over the endless ringing, he said, "And on top of everything, you spy on me . . . for what? Did you think you could blackmail me into forgetting that farce in the dining room? Isn't bed your place for blackmail? Stupid little cunt, trying to—"

Pussy screamed. Sweat ran between her breasts and down her spine; her black satin dress slithered on the leather chair (she imagined sweat patches on the dress, but she had no time to be embarrassed). She was sinking, and grabbed the edge of the desk, clinging to it, pressing her heels against the floor. Cold and wet, trembling, sure she was going to die, she felt a surge of pure hatred, so sharp she almost could taste it. "I didn't read your fucking papers!" she shrieked, astonishing herself as much as Lew, whose mouth—literally, she saw—

dropped open. "I don't give a shit for your papers, I don't give a shit for your friends, I don't give a shit for you!"

Her trembling had intensified so that her teeth were actually chattering as she scurried around the desk and rushed at Lew, so fiercely he instinctively moved aside. Crablike, she scuttled past him and kept going, not toward the front door, as she realized a moment later she should have done, but to her bedroom—only it was their bedroom—and slammed the door behind her.

He stormed in, almost on her heels, and watched her cower beside her dressing table. "Who the fuck do you think you are? Talking to me like a whore, like the whore you were when I dug you up—"

"Talking like you!" Pussy cried. "I learned from you!"

"Not a fucking thing. You didn't learn a fucking goddamn thing. You were a stupid cunt when I found you and you'll never change, you're no help to me, you make a mess of every fucking thing you touch, you're a useless piece of shit."

"You married me!" she screamed. "You loved me!"

He gave a snort of laughter. "Loved you!

For Christ's sake, I married you because I could own you." He snorted again. "Fucking bargain I got."

With a strangled cry, Pussy yanked open the drawer of her dressing table and grabbed the small pistol she had been keeping close for weeks. It was black with a silver slide across the top; she had chosen it for its sleek compactness and lightness, and having it made her feel better, but she had never thought about actually using it. Now it felt heavy, and slipped inside her wet palm, and she held it up with both hands.

"You bitch," Lew growled, and lunged for it.

Pussy closed her eyes and squeezed the trigger. But she had forgotten the safety lock on the silver slide. In the instant before Lew grabbed the gun she remembered the shop owner showing her how to release it. And then there was only the dark.

NINE

Mack set a vase of roses in the center of the table and stood back to admire his handiwork. "Dinner," he said, and held out his arm, bent at the elbow, to Abby, who slipped her arm through his, to be escorted to the table. At the same time, his arm bent at exactly the same angle, Doug escorted Carrie, who had long since stopped giggling about it and now liked it very much.

They sat in their usual places, Abby on Mack's right at the round table, Carrie on his left, and Doug between his sisters.

"Pretty fancy," said Doug, looking at the

centerpiece. "Are we supposed to do something special?"

"Are we celebrating something?" Carrie asked.

"We are," Mack said. "But first . . ." The four of them clasped hands and bowed their heads. "For what we are about to receive," he intoned, "we thank the Lord and ask His blessing on all our endeavors, and on poor Pussy Corcoran's soul, and help her enter heaven even though she committed suicide."

"Sara didn't say that," Doug protested. "She just said she died."

"How do you know she killed herself?" Carrie asked.

"Do you *know* her?" Abby asked.

Mack threw up his hands. "Besieged on all sides," he said dramatically, and pushed away from the table. He brought to the table the casserole Sara had made the evening before, and set a bowl of couscous beside it. "Dig in; all questioning questioners and their questing questions will be answered in good time."

Doug sniffed the casserole suspiciously. "What is it? We never had anything like this before."

"Moroccan chicken." Mack ladled some

onto a mound of couscous and passed the plate to Abby. "Evidently your courageous sis tried out a Moroccan restaurant one night when she was gallivanting with her mysterious beau, instead of staying home and being part of her family, and was so amorously enamored of the food she has dedicated herself to mastering preserved lemons, turmeric, and the like."

Doug reared back. "*Preserved* lemons? Like, petrified?"

"Oh, come on," Carrie said, heaping her plate. "Sara wouldn't make anything we couldn't eat. What did you mean, gallivanting instead of staying home—"

"Sorry, sorry," Mack said. "I forgot, we never criticize Sara."

"—and being part of her family," Carrie said. "You don't think she's part of our family anymore?"

"Of *course* she's—" Abby began.

"Of course she is," Mack said lightly. "I just was thinking it would be really nice if she acted like it some of the time." He looked at their confused faces. "For instance, Abby won't talk to me about Sean—and after all, why *would* she talk to me about such intimate things?—but I'll bet she'd like to talk to *some*body and that somebody could be Sara if she just thought about her family once in a while instead of how much fun she can have with her knight in shining armor."

"That isn't fair," Carrie said in a small voice. "I mean, she does think about us, a lot. And she's not having fun tonight; she's at a funeral."

"Memorial service," Mack corrected. "For an idiotic woman who shot herself to death. Everybody have enough food? Come on, then, eat while it's hot. It is so delicious I can't believe it came from a strange country off the coast of India."

"That's Madagascar!" Carrie said, giggling, her mood switching at once.

"No kidding! Then where—?"

"Africa!" Doug cried.

Mack looked astonished. "Morocco's in Africa? You mean, near Lake Victoria?"

"No!" Doug was grinning. "Golly, didn't you ever go to school? It's at—"

"He's teasing us," Carrie said.

"—the top of Africa, across the Mediterranean from Spain. They even *speak* Spanish there."

"They do not," Carrie said, "they speak Arabic."

"Abby, did you know all that?" Mack asked, but Abby was silent, her face tight and pale.

"So what's a memorial service?" Doug asked. "I mean, I thought tonight was supposed to be what's-her-name's funeral."

"She was cremated," Carrie said matter-of-factly.

"Well, can't you still have a—"

"It's a service to remember somebody," Mack said, helping himself to more chicken. "Usually a while after they've died. A funeral is right away; mourners mournfully mourning. A memorial service is later, sometimes a lot later, like Pussy's, three weeks after she shot herself, to give people time to gather from far and near, and by then everybody's usually more cheerful. No tears, just speeches and sighs. Hey, Abby, listen, I'm sorry I hurt your feelings." He put his hand on her shoulder. "I was just saying I'm here if you want me. Don't be mad at—"

"I'm not mad at you. I'm mad at Sara!" The last words came out in a rush of tears. Mack pulled his chair close and put his arm around her, and as she clung to him, crying into his shirt, he put his other arm around her and pulled her against him.

Doug and Carrie eyed Abby lying against

Mack's chest and became uncomfortable, without knowing why. After a moment, Doug said loudly, "So where's my gallery show?"

Over Abby's head, Mack grinned. "Too much attention on Abby? Not enough lime-light for Doug?"

"That's really mean," Carrie cried. "Doug was just—"

"You're right, you're right, I'm a mean son of a bitch, and I ought to wear a hair shirt and be shot at dawn and strung up from a lamppost and drawn and quartered and tarred and feathered and put in stocks in the village square for everyone to ogle."

Doug and Carrie were giggling and Abby had stopped crying.

Mack loosened his hold on Abby, and held out one arm. "Come on, guys, you know for me the limelight has room for everybody."

"You're upset about that woman killing herself," Carrie said wisely. "We understand. It must be awful to know somebody who does that. I mean, why did she, anyway?"

Mack sighed. "Hard to know. She was a nut, actually; didn't fit in anywhere. Sort of a pest, a pestilential, pestiferous, pestering pest. Didn't have any interests, didn't do a damn thing that I could see. Not like Carrie the story writer and Doug the artist and Abby the actress. She was a lousy wife, too. Maybe she finally decided there wasn't anything worth keeping alive for."

"What an awful thought," Carrie said.

Abby sat up. "I feel sorry for her. She sounds lonely."

"*Was* lonely," said Carrie.

"Yes, isn't that terrible? To think of her dead? I mean, all of a sudden, she's *not.* How can somebody who *was,* suddenly just *not be*?"

"It's like you erased a drawing," said Doug. "Like, maybe one of these days we could all get erased."

"Who'll do it?" Mack asked.

"I don't know. Ask Carrie. She's the one who writes things."

Mack shook his head. "You kids. You're not even close to dying; why think about it?"

"Because what's-her-name—"

"Pussy," said Abby. "She killed herself."

"Right, but why not?" Mack asked. "There's nothing so great about staying alive unless there's a reason to. If you're stupid and a nuisance, and you know it, what the hell, why fool around with getting up each morning and having another lousy day? Just get it over with, and do everybody a favor."

Carrie was staring at him. "Don't *you* want to stay alive?"

"Damn right, sweetheart; I have lots of reasons. But if they go away . . ." He drew his finger across his throat.

"But you could find *other* reasons."

"Maybe, maybe not. Hey, don't look so serious. Life shouldn't be serious; it's mostly a game. Like Monopoly, you know? If you get the right properties and hotels, you're a big shot and you can make things go your way and you're a happy camper. Things turn sour, what the fuck, the game's over. Has to end sometime, and I'll be damned if I'll let somebody else decide when mine ends."

Abruptly, Carrie turned to Abby. "Why are you mad at Sara?"

"What?" Abby asked, jolted from her thoughts of Pussy.

"Why are you mad?"

Abby shifted uncomfortably. "I didn't mean to say that. It slipped out."

"Which means it was right at the surface, waiting," Mack pointed out.

"Well, I'm not really mad at her, you know, I'm just . . . I mean, she used to come to my room all the time and ask me how I was and what I was doing and if I wanted to talk about anything and, you know, just about *me.* And then she stopped."

"But you wouldn't tell her anything," Carrie said. "I heard you, sometimes you wouldn't even let her come in your room."

"I know, but she'd keep trying. Or she'd go away and come back a few minutes later, and try again. And even if I didn't tell her everything, I mean when I'd just sort of clam up, and it wasn't nice of me, I know it wasn't, but she never got mad, she'd just talk about other things, and when we'd talk like that, about, oh, whatever, it was nice. Knowing she was there, and knowing she worried about me." Her voice rose. "But she *stopped.*"

"When?" Carrie asked.

"Oh, I don't know. A while ago. It's like she . . . gave up or something."

"She's busy," Mack said. "Reuben, you know. But what difference does it make? You don't need her; you've got us. Me. You can tell me anything; I'm the soul of discretion. Better than Sara, even, because I'm more objective and I've been more places. Sara's a stay-at-home, you know; whereas yours truly's been all over the world and knows how to get the better of everybody."

Abby frowned. "I don't want to get the better of anybody. I just want to be happy."

"COULD WE TALK ABOUT SOMETHING ELSE?" Doug shouted. "I'm tired of all this."

"All this what?" Carrie asked.

"People killing themselves and Abby not being happy and . . . *everything.* Can't we talk about happy things?"

"There aren't any happy things," said Abby, and tears filled her eyes.

"How about I tell a story?" Mack asked. "And doesn't anybody want dessert?"

"A story about what?" Doug asked, diverted, as they cleared the table and Carrie brought out ice-cream dishes.

"You tell me."

"What about that island you told us about? The one that's a whole country? Something about that."

"Nauru. Good memory, Doug. Well. Dessert first."

Sniffling, Abby spooned ice cream, and Carrie brought the cookie jar to the table. Mack refilled his wineglass and Abby's. "Okay, so it's a very poor island; I told you about that. No more mining—they ran out of the stuff a few years ago—"

"What stuff?" Doug asked.

"Phosphate," said Carrie. "I looked it up on the Internet. They speak English there."

Mack nodded. "They do indeed. Plus their own language, which is sort of South Pacific–ish. And they have computers. They're pretty modern, only they don't have any money. *But* there are whispers on the island about a hidden treasure. It seems that, a long time ago, when Nauru became independent, the new prime minister accepted gifts, gold and silver and whatnot, from governments who wanted rights to run Nauru's mines. The prime minister took the gifts and kept the mining rights, and then died. He told his son he'd hidden the treasure to keep it safe, but he never told him where. So one day a ten-year-old named Lagumot decided to find it."

"Is this a true story?" Doug demanded.

"Yes and no. So, Lagumot set out to find the treasure, with his friend Derog, who was thirteen."

"Our ages," Carrie whispered to Doug.

"Well, those two treasure hunters just about tore the island apart. They lifted stones and dug around trees, they snorkeled in the coral reefs and poked holes in the walls of houses. Then one night they broke into one of the country's main banks."

"Broke in?" demanded Carrie. "Where were the police?"

"They were swigging from a bottle and didn't hear a thing. Now this bank did a lot of business with American companies, so there were rows and rows of filing cabinets with American names on them. Lagumot read the American names and remembered his father telling him stories (he always thought they were myths) about gold and silver growing like breadfruit on the trees in America, huge houses with only one small family inside, long shiny cars, skies filled with airplanes, and supermarkets heaped high with food that rolled all over the place if you pulled an orange or something out from the bottom . . . anyway, he thought maybe the treasure, like all treasures, was in America, or the part of America that was in the National Bank of Nauru, and he'd be the one to find it and then his father would be so proud of him he'd never stop loving him. So he and Derog began opening the drawers of the file cabinets, and they were so *intent* on what they were doing they didn't know that someone was watching them from a peep-hole that had been drilled through the wall near the spot where they were. Neither did they hear, when it was almost dawn, the police coming down the stairs to see what was making all that noise in the basement."

"Well?" demanded Doug when Mack stopped.

"So that's all for tonight. You don't expect everything in one evening, do you? Have to spread out the pleasure, then it means more."

"You can't stop!" Carrie cried. "I mean, *I* don't stop when I'm in the middle of a story."

"They did in the old days. One chapter each week in the newspaper. And everybody had to wait seven whole days—one fifty-second of a year!—to find out what came next. Besides, it's good for you to learn you can't have everything at once. Be a little patient and wait your turn like the rest of the world, instead of being coddled and codlified codliferously and coswolloply."

Abby felt a shiver and saw confusion on Carrie and Doug's faces. They felt it, too, she thought. Mack made it sound like a joke, but his face looked as if he meant it, as if he hated them because they were spoiled.

But then he grinned and held out his arms. "More soon, and that's a promise." He stood up and pulled them all to him so they stood within the circle of his arms. Carrie's confusion faded. She felt cozy, being held in an embrace, being with her family, eating dinner around the table and telling stories and talking, even about death, in their warm kitchen with soft humming noises coming from the refrigerator and freezer, and the comforting ticking of the tall grandfather clock that had belonged to great-grandparents they never knew, and the corners of the room all shadowy while the hanging lamp over the table wrapped them in a little golden tent, just big enough for the four of them.

"We don't need Sara," Mack said, his humming voice blending in with the hum of the kitchen. "We're just fine, just us, together."

Abby tensed, and Carrie and Doug began to squirm. They pulled back against the tight band of Mack's arms. *I don't know!* Carrie wailed silently. *I don't know what to think!* She ran out of the room and up the stairs, to her room.

"Hey, Carrie!" Mack shouted. "What's going on?"

"Abby?" Doug asked tentatively, looking at his sister.

"Why can't you be nice?" Abby demanded, her voice quavering. "Why do you have to ruin things by being mean?" She closed her eyes. *I want Sara.*

And the telephone rang. And it was Sara.

"Where are you?" Abby cried as soon as she heard Sara's voice.

"At the funeral home, on my cell phone. I should go back inside in a minute. What's wrong, Abby?"

"Oh . . . nothing. Nothing! Everything's fine. We're fine, we're great, we're just sitting in the kitchen and talking and . . . laughing. You know. Having fun. We had your Moroccan chicken; it was good. Are people crying about Pussy?"

"No, it's really awful; there aren't many people and I don't think anyone knew her except me. And her husband; he's in the front row and I haven't talked to him. Abby, are you sure you're all right?"

"Yes! I mean, of course; why wouldn't I be?" Abby felt a flash of resentment. *Of course I'm all right! Does she think I need her?* "So, all those people . . . they never knew her?"

"I don't think so; I can't imagine who they are. The minister never knew her, either; he talks about life and death as if we're at a service for some generic person, not an individual. Abby, I don't really have to be here; I'll come home."

"No! You wanted to be there, you told me you owed it to Pussy."

"But you come first. I'm on my way."

Oh, thank you, thank you, Abby said silently.

"Abby?"

"Yes. Okay."

"I'll be there in half an hour."

Sara stood still for a moment, then called Reuben. "I'm sorry, I can't see you tonight. Something's wrong with Abby, or maybe all of them; I don't know what's going on, but I have to be there."

There was a brief pause. "I'm sorry. I was prepared to give you food and wine and music to cheer you up after the service."

"Exactly what I need. Where are you?"

"At my desk."

"I like to be able to picture you, where you are, what you're doing. Were you at River Bend all day?"

"I was. Tell me where *you* are."

"In the very dreary reception room of the funeral home, with the unpleasantly cheerful voice of the minister oozing through the closed door, talking about a woman he never knew. And now I'm walking out, toward my car. Did you talk to the people you wanted to see in River Bend?"

"Most of them. Nice people, concerned about their communities, confused about the conflicting information they're getting. Not confused enough to wait, however; they've scheduled demonstrations for Sunday, and the Sunday after that, and somehow they've convinced the county board not to approve annexation until we make concessions."

"What concessions?"

"We don't know yet, but my guess is they'll be ones we can't agree to. Whoever is behind this wants to force us to sell the land."

"So they can buy it and build . . . what?"

"No idea, except that I'd guess it won't be parks for the people. Isaiah's staff is looking into anyone who's shown interest in the property in the past year. No one tonight could tell us who it is; they genuinely didn't seem to know."

"But you're not selling!"

"Not yet, but there's a limit to how long we can carry the costs of the land without knowing when or if we can start building. Look, you have enough on your mind tonight; can you stay with me tomorrow night?"

"Yes."

"You haven't looked at your calendar."

"It doesn't matter. I'll cancel anything on it. Can we have a late dinner? I'd like to stay with the children until they've eaten."

"Any time you want. I miss you."

Standing beside her car in the parking lot, Sara closed her eyes, picturing Reuben at his desk in his book-lined study, idly moving chess pieces on the inlaid board beside his chair. "Yes," she said, and drove home thinking she could have said much more. *I miss you whenever I'm not with you, I store up things to tell you, I think about you no matter what I'm doing or where I am.* But neither of them was ready to make declarations. Both were too cautious, wary of what could go wrong.

Sara knew what it was to make plans, to invest herself in imagined scenarios only to have everything come crashing down. She supposed something like that had happened to Reuben to make him wary; it was more palatable to suppose that than to contemplate the possibility that he was a man incapable of commitment.

And I can hardly ask him. She smiled a little wistfully. They could talk about almost anything in the world, but she could not ask him that.

What she could do, what she had to do, she thought as she approached her house, was help Abby. The truth was, she hadn't been as much a part of their lives as she had been before . . .

Before Mack arrived.

And—*be honest*—Reuben.

The lights were on in all the rooms of the house, and at the game table in the library a spirited session of Monopoly was under way. "Sara, look what I just bought!" Doug cried as she walked into the room. "New York! You always win with New York! And the other orange ones . . . right?"

"The reds!" Carrie cried. "And I have all three of them and I'm about to build houses on all of them!"

Chilled, Sara stood in the doorway. All the

energy in the room was in the warm, close circle at the table; the rest of the house, for all its lighted windows, seemed somehow in shadow.

"Abby," Sara said, and Abby raised her head from concentrating on her property cards. "Hi," she said, her voice colorless. Sara saw resentment in her eyes, but also confusion. Abby was not happy, but she did not like it that Sara had come home, as if in response to a cry for help.

"Great game, sis," Mack cried gaily, without looking up from counting his money. "You want to sit in? Be somebody's silent partner?"

Sara kept her voice light. "You all look pretty well set. I'll be in my office." *If anyone wants me,* she started to say, but bit back the words, and turned blindly to the stairs, stunned by the fact that there were tears in her eyes.

Her office was quiet, with only an occasional boisterous shout of glee or despair from the library cutting across her thoughts. They did not need her anymore. Mack had taken over, and they were all happy with him. How had it happened? Stories from far-off places? A few gifts? A car, a writing journal, a promise (vague and so far unfulfilled) of a gallery show. Was that really enough? Or was it her absences? But it's only been two or three nights a week, she thought; wasn't that allowed?

Or was he a better parent?

She put her head in her hands. She did not really believe that, but the thought nagged: maybe he knew something she did not. This was absurd, she thought; once she had wanted nothing more than to shed the responsibility of a family and concentrate on her own goals, and now that Mack seemed to be helping her do just that, she felt discarded and depressed. Never satisfied, she thought, annoyed with herself, and then quickly raised her head as she heard footsteps on the stairs.

"Totally bankrupt," Carrie said, and dropped onto the couch. "They wiped me out. Maybe Doug was right about the orange ones."

"Was it a fun game?" Sara asked.

"Oh, sure. Well—" Carrie frowned. "Well . . . sure. But, you know, Mack is pretty mean about Monopoly. And things are really mixed up now."

Sara felt a surge of hope. "Mixed up?"

"It's, you know, hard to tell what's happening? I mean, one minute everything's really fun and *happy,* and then it's all . . . oh, I don't know . . . sort of . . . well, *not* fun . . . like you can't tell what's going on."

"Is it something about Abby or Doug?"

"No." Carrie sighed. "It's Mack. I can't figure him out. I mean, you ought to be able to figure out your own family, right? I mean, a *writer* ought to be doing that all the time, figuring out why people are odd or weird or mean or whatever. I should be able to *do* that, right? If I'm going to be a great writer?"

Sara waited a moment, feeling as if she were picking her way through a minefield. She sat beside Carrie and put her arm around her. "You're terrific at understanding people. All your stories show that. And, the truth is, I find Mack a puzzle a lot of the time."

Carrie looked up in wonder. "*You* do? But you know everything."

Sara smiled. "Not quite. I hope I know more than you do; otherwise, what good is it to get older? But I know for sure that I'll never know everything. The world is so big and complicated, and puzzling, that one person can't ever know everything, much less understand it all, and sometimes that even includes the mysteries in families."

"Like ours."

"Like ours." Sara paused again, her thoughts snagged on Pussy Corcoran's death. "The best we can do," she said at last, "is to store up information, and be able to pull out pieces of it when we need them, and relate them to other things we've learned, and put them all together to come to conclusions and make decisions. The most important thing is to be alert to what's going on around you. The more you see—really *see,* not just note in passing—the more you'll store up and understand and have available when you need it."

"That's observation. You're always telling me that."

"Because it's important for all of us, but for a writer it's essential."

"My English teacher said that, too. She said we should be observant and not let things slide by without paying attention."

"Good advice." They were silent. Sara thought of asking more about Mack—what did he do, what did he say?—but she thought she ought to let it come from Carrie, without prodding.

And then she could not stop herself. "Do Doug and Abby feel the way you do about Mack? Puzzled?"

"I don't know. Well . . . I guess so. We don't talk about it." She squirmed within Sara's arm—*as if she can't bear the thought of criticizing Mack*—and said abruptly, "I have an idea for a story. I guess I should go write it."

"Absolutely." Sara hugged Carrie and kissed the top of her head. "I love you. And I think you are wonderfully observant."

Carrie nodded soberly. "Thanks." She sprang up and started for the door, then turned back. "I forgot . . . Susie wants me to spend the night tomorrow. Can I?"

"Of course. Starting when?"

"Oh, afternoon I guess. We'll probably go to a movie. Thanks, Sara, I love you."

Sara smiled. *Just so I know they still love me.*

When the telephone rang, she went to her desk and answered it absently, thinking of the game downstairs, and heard Donna Soldana's voice, tense and breathless. "Sara, can I come to your house? I've got to come, I haven't anyplace . . . I mean, I don't know who to . . . Sara? Can I come? *Now?*"

Sara tried to switch to another set of problems. Donna had been so quiet lately, an efficient secretary with no talk of the father she had fled after he raped her, no tales of his stalking her or attempting to lure her somewhere.

"What's wrong, Donna? Where are you?"

"On Clark Street, a few blocks from your— Sara, you've got to let me come, I need somebody, I need you, I've been walking for hours, I'm so *tired.* I won't be a bother, I'll sleep on the floor, anywhere . . . Sara? Are you still there?"

Sara's thoughts were in turmoil, replaying the last time she had heard such a plea— *Sara, can I come live with you?*—when she had spent half an hour finding Pussy a place to stay instead of telling her, of course she could come, at least for that night, for two nights, for as long as it took to discover what had happened and what Pussy, with her help, could do about it.

Pussy, earlier than that, who had stood at the foot of the stairs, smiling desperately, saying "I need you," and now was dead.

"All right," she said to Donna. "You don't have to sleep on the floor; there's a sofa in the basement recreation room, if you don't mind that. Are you all right? Are you hurt?"

"Oh, you know . . ."

"What?"

"Anyway, the basement's fine. Anywhere's fine. I'll be right there."

And don't bother to thank me, Sara thought, and then was ashamed of herself.

"Sara, Mack's got a gallery for me!" Doug flung himself onto the couch. "A gallery! For a show! My *own* show! Just me, nobody else! Isn't that cool? He did it! Just like he said he would!"

"It's wonderful," Sara said cautiously. "He really has a gallery? I mean, a real gallery?"

"Right, he says it's in Franklin Park."

"I didn't know there were galleries in Franklin Park. And when is your show?"

"Mack says they're negotiating. 'Soon to be definitively datively determined,' he said. You know how he talks. And, you know, he was being sort of awful, before; you know, kind of mean, like he didn't like us at all, but he does, he does, and I'm going to have a show and be a real artist!"

"He was mean?" Sara asked.

"Oh, you know . . ."

Why do people keep saying "you know," when I don't? "What do I know?" she asked, not as sympathetically as she might have done.

"Oh, you know—" Doug bit it off. "He's just weird, sometimes, like he says things or makes fun of us, well, he doesn't really make fun of us, but . . . you know. But he's really cool, Sara, he really is. I mean, he's about the best brother I could ever have, right?" He jumped up. "I have to get going on my carvings, so I have enough; Mack says I need like thirty pieces at least."

"How many do you have now?"

"I don't know, a hundred, maybe. But I have to choose the best. This is my big chance! I have to be really good!"

Suddenly alarmed, Sara sat beside Doug, and put her arm around him, as she had with Carrie. "Doug, sweetheart, don't pin all your hopes on this; if it really happens, it's not a make-or-break event."

"It *is* going to happen!"

"It may. But you can't be sure until it's a done deal. You know that. All I'm saying is, whatever happens, nothing will be forever. You'll have lots of shows in the future; you really have a fine talent, and once it has a chance to mature—"

"You're always saying that." Doug fidgeted,

jumped up, nervously bounced on his toes. "Mack says I'm ready, and he *knows.* He's been all over the world and he knows a lot about everything. He told us this story about an island called Nauru, really tiny, but it's a whole country, you know, its own govern- ment and everything, and they're really poor, but there's a treasure, only it's hidden and some guys—they're as old as Carrie and me—are going to find it. Cool story."

"I think I'll talk to him," Sara said. "Where is he?"

"He went out. Can I stay over at Jeff's to- morrow night? He asked me at camp today; it's okay with his mom."

"Of course. Starting when?"

"I guess lunchtime. His mom might drive us to a movie. Okay?"

"Okay."

"Great. Night, Sara." His kissed her cheek. "Love you," he said, and was gone.

Sara stared unseeing out the window until she heard the doorbell. On her way to an- swer it, she met Abby at the foot of the stairs. "Someone named Donna. You said she could stay here? You're not giving her my room!"

"Of course not; she'll sleep in the recreation room. I wouldn't give anyone your room, Abby, you know that. Donna is my secretary and she's in trouble, and she needs a quiet place for a night or two, until we find her an apartment. She's nice; you'll like her."

Abby shrugged. "I don't like strangers in our house."

You've never objected to Mack.

Shocked, Sara thought, What is wrong with me? I don't usually have nasty thoughts, especially about my family.

"I'm sorry," she said to Abby, apologizing for words Abby had not heard, and gave her a quick hug just as Donna appeared.

"Sara, it's so awful, the worst—" The last word slid up the scale into a shriek, and she burst into loud tears and wrapped Sara in clinging arms. "Awful, awful. You don't know . . . the worst night of my life; I thought he'd kill me!"

Sara pulled away. "*Kill* you? But how—?"

"He was knocking me around and he— oh, God!" she wailed, the word screeching up and down the scale and through the house like the tribal cry of mourning women.

Doug and Carrie had rushed from their

rooms and were about to run downstairs, when Sara saw them and shook her head. "It's okay," she said, her voice calm beneath Donna's wails. "Everything's under control."

"But she's *screaming,*" Doug said.

"I know." Sara contemplated her quiet, efficient secretary, suddenly transformed into a banshee. "There's nothing to watch," she said a little sharply to Doug and Carrie.

"I guess we're not wanted," Carrie said, and in a moment the two of them, in lockstep, backed up to their rooms.

"He picked up a knife!" Donna cried. "And I couldn't—"

"What? Donna, listen to me. He was *inside* your apartment?"

"Oh . . . well, you know."

"No," Sara snapped. "I don't."

Donna wept more noisily. Sara waited.

"He started crying." The words gulped out between sobs. "Like a baby, he got on his knees and said I couldn't leave him, he'd *die*—"

"Leave him? What are you talking about?"

"Leave him! You know, like, never see him again."

"But he's your father; you left him when you left home."

"Sara, I'm so tired I don't know what I'm saying. Could I sit down?"

"I'm sorry, of course you can. I shouldn't have kept you standing here." She turned Donna with her, and met Abby's eyes, skeptical, even scornful. Sara had forgotten she was there. Jealous? she wondered. "Abby, please make up the sofa bed, and would you check the downstairs bathroom, too? Soap and a clean glass . . . you know what to do."

Abby nodded, and mouthed the words, "She's lying."

Sara's eyes narrowed. "I'll talk to you in your room." She led Donna to the kitchen. "I'll make a pot of tea for you to take downstairs. You need some time to yourself; we'll talk in the morning."

"Have you got anything to eat? I never got dinner."

Damn it, Sara thought, becoming more cranky by the moment, I really would like just a little gratitude. In silence (and thank heavens Donna did not start wailing again), she heated a plate of leftover chicken and couscous, and made a pot of tea. "This way," she said, and the two of them carried trays downstairs to the recreation room. Abby had made the sofa bed, folding back one corner of the sheet and blanket, and had turned on a floor lamp beside it. The light shone on the bed and a small table with a glass of water and two books. Sara looked at the titles: short stories by Balzac and O. Henry, favorites of Abby's, though not, perhaps, of Donna's, but how sweet of Abby to think of it.

"I'm so beat." Donna sighed. "And starved." She sat down at the small table and began to eat. "I guess I'll go to work with you in the morning, right?"

Sara stared at her. Was Donna so used to being catered to that she took it for granted? "Tomorrow is Saturday," she said shortly. "Good night."

"Thanks, Sara," Donna said, her mouth full. "Saved my life, you know?"

Sara went upstairs, closing the basement door behind her.

The house was quiet, the rooms settled back into their comfortable serenity. Even bustling with the activities of the four of them (no, five, including Mack . . . and where was Mack?) the house was always a center of comfort and warmth, the furnishings and rugs familiar and well-worn, the paintings luminous with the patina of age. The house stood, firm and unchanging, even when everything else seemed in turmoil. Even when Donna's wails had echoed through the rooms, the embrace of the house had not been shaken. Our sanctuary, Sara thought wryly, echoing the word her mother had used so often.

Upstairs, Abby's door was closed. Sara knocked. "Sure," Abby said, and Sara found her sitting in her new rocking chair, watching a DVD of *Victor/Victoria.* "See, it's just like this movie," Abby said as Sara sat in the armchair. "You can always tell when someone's pretending."

"Are you worried that I'll pay so much attention to Donna I won't have time for the three of you?" Sara asked.

Abby flipped off the film. "You mean, am I jealous? Good heavens, Sara, what a stupid thing to say. Sorry," she said quickly. "I didn't mean that. I'm really sorry."

"If it's not jealousy, what is it?"

"She's lying. I hate people who lie. I mean, if you can't count on people telling the truth, what good is anything?"

"You don't know that she's lying; it didn't sound like it to me."

"You're so trusting, Sara. You always believe the best of people. Even when you don't like them, you never believe they're bad."

"Not true," Sara said, thinking of Lew Corcoran, and, in fact, a small subset of her clients who fit the same arrogant, crude profile. "Tell me why you think Donna is lying."

"For one thing, she cries too much."

"Oh, Abby."

"Well, okay, I cried a lot when Sean . . . when I stopped seeing Sean. But I was brokenhearted. She was trying to impress you, to make you feel sorry for her. And then she tried to cover up things that didn't make sense to you. Like, she said something about leaving him, and you thought there was something wrong with that. And when she said the thing about the knife, and him being in the apartment . . . well, all that stuff."

Sara marveled at Abby, who most often seemed fifteen-years-old-self-absorbed, but could be as observant as Carrie hoped to be. And, maybe, more clear-eyed than Sara.

"I'll find out tomorrow," she said to Abby. "You could be right; I just don't know." She kissed Abby on both cheeks. "You're wonderful, Abby, and I appreciate your thoughts, even when they move too fast for the rest of us. Good night, sweetheart."

"Night," Abby said absently. "Oh, don't forget I'm sleeping over at Laurie's tomorrow night. Eight of us, it's her pre-sixteenth-birthday party. She says sixteen is so important you have to have lots of parties, before and after. Can I do that?"

"Sure. Tell me how many parties you want, and where and when, and we'll work it out."

"Really? You'll make time for it?" She jumped up and hugged Sara. "Thank you, thank you, I've already got so many ideas . . ." There was a brief pause. "Can I drive to Laurie's?"

"Abby, you know you can't drive alone; you don't have a license. When you're sixteen—"

"Well, could you go with me, and let me drive? You've done that a few times. How else can I practice?"

Sara nodded. "You're right. What time do you want to be there?"

"Four or four-thirty? She's rented a bunch of movies, and we'll send out for pizza."

Again, Sara nodded, but her thoughts had already moved ahead. *All three accounted for, happy with their friends. A whole night for Reuben and me.*

Abby, wildly emotional, kissed her again and again. "You are so good. I love you, I love you. You never make me wonder if you really like me or hate me, or if you're making fun of me, or if you think I'm just a baby or something. I love you, Sara."

"Who does that to you?" Sara asked quickly.

"Oh . . ." Abby shrugged. "I was just think-ing, it's nice that you don't."

None of them will say anything against Mack.

And Sara could not force them. All she could do—she had to keep reminding her-self—was be available when they needed to talk.

Which meant she had to be around a lot of the time.

How do I do that, and work, and see Reuben as much as I want?

The trouble was, she had to work eight or nine hours a day; there seemed to be no limit to the amount of time she wanted to be with Reuben, or that he wanted to be with her; and the various needs of Doug and Carrie and Abby took up chunks of time and energy that could crop up any time of day or night. *There aren't enough hours in the day. Not enough in the night. I have to figure out—*

But no one really figured it out, she thought. We just keep juggling all the things we want and need to do. How frustrating.

She stopped thinking about it. Instead she retreated to the privacy of her bedroom and called Reuben. They talked until midnight. Later, Sara reflected that each of their conversations seemed to flow from the one before, as if they never really stopped talking, but only took breaks to manage the other parts of their lives and get back to each other as quickly as possible. So she did not always remember which subjects came up in which conversations (though she always remembered that Reuben never failed to say, "I miss you," and she never failed to say, "I've been saving this up to tell you . . ."). But from the conversation this tumultuous evening, one of Reuben's observations nagged at her. "I'd put some trust in Abby's feelings about Donna. You're so focused on what people need, and how you might provide it, you can't let yourself step back and have doubts. Donna may be absolutely honest, but from what you've told me, I'd pay attention to Abby. She's a pretty sharp young lady."

"I'll think about it," said Sara, and did, through a restless night.

"Hi," Donna said, coming upstairs to the kitchen the next morning. "Great bed; I slept like a baby; I feel a million times better. God, it's a good thing you were here last night; I might have killed myself if you weren't. You know what, I should stop at the apartment and get some clothes and stuff. I won't look like much of a secretary if I keep wearing the same things every day."

"We'll find you a place to live," Sara said evenly. "We'll start today."

"But this is fine! I mean, I'm not in your way, am I? I'm really as quiet as a mouse, and I don't eat much, and we can drive to work together and everything. Not forever, Sara, but maybe a few weeks? Until I figure things out? I really like it here; you make me feel like I'm welcome, and until now"—tears filled her eyes and she reached out a hand to Sara—"nobody's ever made me feel at home. You're so—"

"Your mother didn't make you feel at home?"

"Oh, sure, of course she did! I meant, since then. Nobody's been like you, Sara, you've been understanding and generous . . . you're so *good.*"

Just like Mack, Sara thought abruptly. Sudden charm, smooth words, an appeal for the things she could not resist giving when they were asked for: attention, comfort, support, warmth. *Except with Pussy.* The thought cut into her, as it did every time she relived her failure. And she could not take a chance on something like that happening again.

That's irrational. Donna wouldn't kill herself.

But she just said she might have, if I hadn't been here.

And did I ever think Pussy would?

"You can stay for a while," she said at last. "But you need your own place where you can get settled and stay put. Not those short-term places you've lived in, or a borrowed bed in our recreation room; you need your own home." She waited until Donna nodded. "And we're going to the police about your father; you can't be harassed like this, and threatened; you need protection."

"No! You can't! Don't do that, Sara! Stay out of it!"

"*Out of it?* You brought me into it. You asked for my help; I'm trying to give it to you. What's wrong with you? Do you want to keep running from him for the rest of your life?"

"It's . . . it's my mother. You can't go to the police; it would kill her. Or"—her voice grew wild again—"*he'll* kill her. It would be like *I* killed her. Or *you* killed her! Something really awful—"

"Stop it! What are you talking about? Your father has raped you, he's harassing you, he threatened you with a knife. Why should you be afraid of him any longer? I know what I'm doing, Donna. We'll talk to a lawyer on Monday, and figure out how to protect your mother, and we'll go to the police. It's about time you took control of your life."

Donna's lips tightened, and Sara thought, She doesn't like being told what to do. Well, how many people would? She wants sympathy and refuge where her father can't find her; she's found them and that's enough for now. She thinks she already is in control of her life. Even if she lives from moment to moment, she feels in charge. Why would she be happy about my telling her what to do?

"Can I go back and get some clothes?" Donna asked sullenly.

Sara sighed. "You don't need my permission to go anywhere. This isn't a jail. You should have some breakfast before you go."

"I never eat breakfast. I need a key to the house, though."

Sara bristled. "We don't lock the door during the day. You can come and go."

"But at night."

"Will you be going out?"

"Well, sure. I have friends."

"We'll talk about it later."

There was a pause. "Okay. Bye. See you later."

Maybe it's because this isn't the office, Sara thought, watching Donna leave. If she were like this at work, I wouldn't keep her around for five minutes. And I won't keep her in my house very long, either.

"Sara, I wrote a story." Carrie thrust a sheaf of papers at her. "I did it last night. Would you read it?"

"How about some breakfast?"

"Sure, but will you read it *now*?"

"If you'll get breakfast for you and Doug. Abby will get her own whenever she gets up."

Carrie sprinkled raspberries over two bowls of cereal, poured milk into one, and sat opposite Sara, watching intently as she read.

Sara was the fastest reader in the family; everyone knew it. But this time she was slow. She had started out in her usual rapid way, but soon was pausing, turning back one or more of the four pages, rereading paragraphs or whole sections, studying sentences.

"What's wrong?" Carrie cried.

Sara looked up. "It's very different."

The story was set, like many Carrie wrote, in a house identical to theirs. But its tone was unlike anything she had ever written. Titled "Aurelia Rose," this story began late at night, in winter, when the trees were bare, the small, front garden empty of flowers, the raked soil barely covered with a thin layer of snow. The house was dark, but in the living room someone was moving about with a flashlight. In the next paragraphs, a thirteen-year-old girl named Aurelia Rose is awakened by a sound of shuffling. When she tiptoes down the stairs, she sees the robber. He is as handsome as a prince, and wears a dark cloak that swirls romantically as he whirls from room to room, lifting paintings from walls and rare vases from shelves, and stowing them in a large black bag. When the bag is full, he scoops up Aurelia Rose's small dog, named Monte Cristo, who has been sniffing his pants leg.

"How did the robber get in?" Sara asked.

"Picked the lock on the front door. I guess I should say that somewhere."

"Why didn't Monte Cristo bark?"

"Oh. Well . . . the robber sprinkled his pants with something dogs like. Meat juice, or . . . gravy or . . . dog-biscuit crumbs. Something like that. I'll have to put that in, too."

Sara nodded, and turned back to the story.

The robber was turning to leave when he saw Aurelia Rose at the foot of the stairs, every muscle in her terror-stricken body frozen. Cursing, his handsome face pinched by a deep frown, the robber dropped Monte Cristo and whipped a huge, black, vicious-looking gun from his pocket.

"Don't shoot!" exclaimed Aurelia Rose, desperately trying to keep her voice low to protect her innocently sleeping family. She knew if they heard her, they would leap from their beds in alarm, and startle the handsome robber, thus dangerously menacing all of their precarious lives. Aurelia Rose had always wanted to be a heroine, and even though she was frightened out

of her wits, she knew this was the time. She knew she was smarter than the robber, too, because why would he be a robber if he was smart enough to do something like be a doctor or a writer or a welcomer for the city? "Please," Aurelia Rose said very seriously, "I won't tell on you if you just leave and don't rob us of our beloved Monte Cristo. You can keep the paintings and vases and things . . . they'll make you obscenely rich! But leave us our darling Monte Cristo."

His hard heart was unmoved by the plea in her beautiful blue eyes. He held the gun firmly pointed at her heart. "You're just a kid. Kids can't be trusted. You'll tell on me the minute I'm out the door."

"I'm not a kid; I'm a teenager. And you have my word of honor."

The robber thought for a long time, flipping the gun from hand to hand in the careless way professional criminals do with their weapons, sending terror into the hearts of the helpless victims standing before them. "No," he said at last. "You are very beautiful, but I have a stone heart beneath this handsome face, and I cannot take the chance of your turning me in."

He held the gun steady and shot Aurelia Rose through the heart. Then he ruthlessly grabbed Monte Cristo and picked up the heavy bag. As he heard cries of fear emanating from the bedrooms upstairs, he calmly walked out the front door and disappeared forever.

The end.

Sara kept her eyes on the last page for a long time.

"Well?" Carrie demanded.

"It's . . . very different," Sara said.

"What's wrong with that? Writers are always writing different things, aren't they?"

Sara looked up. "Why did she have to die?"

"Because . . . *I* don't know why! That's just the story! I mean, he was bad, and he really didn't like kids, you know, even though sometimes he pretended to, and he . . . he was just a mean person!"

"Why did you choose him to write about?"

Carrie's eyes filled with tears. "You don't like it."

"Wait a minute, sweetheart, I was just asking why you chose to write about this man."

"Because . . . because I *did.* Because I'm a *writer.* Writers write about everything. They can't always write nice stories that are happy."

"Why not?"

"Because that isn't the way things are. *You* know that! You get mad at people, and you come home really frustrated with work, and Abby is all gloomy about Sean, and Mack gets really . . . I mean other things happen, like that Pussy person who killed herself—"

"What?"

"Mack said she shot herself to death. And bad things *happen,* and everybody knows it, so I *have* to write about those things if I'm going to be a great writer."

"Why were you and Mack talking about Pussy Corcoran?"

"He asked God to let her into heaven even though she was idiotic and committed suicide. We were praying, you know, before dinner."

There was a silence. "Carrie," Sara said at last. "Do you think . . . Would you say you're a happy person?"

Carrie shrugged. "Sure."

"No, think about it. Tell me, really. You usually write happy stories that are like *you* . . . all bubbly, full of excitement about being alive, and discovering new things about the world, and having friends, and loving your family. This story doesn't sound like any of that. Do you know where the idea came from?"

Carrie shook her head. "They don't come from anywhere. They're just . . . inside me. I mean, it sounds funny, but I think about writing like . . . you know, you think about making dinner? I mean, you all of a sudden know what you'll cook so you go and cook it. And I just all of a sudden have a story, you know, it just kind of *appears.* So I write it." She paused and Sara waited. "And sometimes they're happy stories, when I'm feeling happy, but sometimes I'm feeling, you know, sort of mad or worried or . . . oh, just confused, and then the stories are dark like that, but I don't *try* to do it that way. You know?"

Sara kissed the top of Carrie's head. "That's exactly what writers say when they talk about their work."

"Real writers? Who write books?"

"Real writers. But you're a real writer, too. You haven't been published, yet, and you may not be for a long time, but just from the way you talk about writing, and the way you feel it inside you, I can tell you're a real writer, a serious one, and someday you'll be a great one."

Carrie's face was shining. "Really? *Great?* Well, then . . . couldn't I start now? I mean, you know, Mack said he'd get my stories published in a magazine, and he got Doug a gallery, so he could get me published, and then you'd be really proud of me, and I'd *know* I'm a real writer."

"You mean you won't believe me until Mack confirms it?" The bitter words were out of Sara's mouth before she could stop them.

She saw confusion dim the brightness on Carrie's face. "I'm sorry, sweetheart," she said quickly, and kissed her again. "Silly thing for me to say. But, you know, I really doubt that Mack will find a publisher for your work. Your writing is very good for someone your age—" Carrie stiffened and her face closed. "Carrie, you may not like it that you're thirteen years old, but you are, and you've just begun to scratch the surface of what the world is all about, and why people behave the way they do. Did I ever tell you I wanted to be a writer once?"

"You want to be a doctor! You've always wanted that!"

"Almost always. When I was in high school I wanted more than anything to write long books filled with people who were beautiful and rich and smart and romantic—all the things I didn't feel I was—and with villains who were exactly like the people who didn't like me. Later I discovered I loved medicine even more."

"But I don't love anything more! And I do know about the world! I understand things!"

"Yes, you do. Just not enough. Sweetheart, even if you understood the whole world perfectly, you aren't ready to be published because you haven't learned the craft of writing. You can have terrific ideas and be a real artist inside yourself, but you have to know the mechanics of writing."

"You mean like grammar," Carrie said in disgust.

Sara smiled. "Partly, but mostly a kind of magic that turns your ideas and feelings into words and sentences that bring your readers into the worlds you create, move them to feel the emotions of your characters and understand their predicaments and decisions."

Carrie frowned. "Don't I do that now?"

"You try. You don't succeed yet because you haven't written enough. You have to write thousands of pages of stories and character sketches to learn to transform what's inside you into stories and books your readers will treasure."

"How do you know all that? You're not a writer."

"I tried to be, but I found out I was better studying the human body than I was writing about human beings. I think you'll find out you're better at writing than anything else. Then you'll get help from teachers and other writers and from reading books, but mainly, the more you write, the sooner you'll find your own style, your own special skills. And then you'll find a publisher. Lots of them, probably."

There was a long silence. Sara knew she was overloading Carrie with too much information, but she could not stop. "Please, sweetheart, don't build your hopes on fantasies. Enjoy these years of learning and soaking up experience and skills; be open to everything, and then you'll be ready to be what great writers are: people who help readers understand the world better, and deal with it, and get the most out of it. You'll do all that, but it takes time and maturity. Observation and understanding. We've talked about this."

"Endlessly." Carrie sighed dramatically. "You say the same things to Doug."

"They're just as true for him."

"But Mack got him a gallery."

"Have you seen a Douglas Hayden show?"

"No, but . . . they're working out details. Mack said."

"When it happens I'll believe it."

Carrie snatched the story from Sara's hand. "You don't like it."

"I didn't say that. I said it was different."

"You didn't say you like it. You always say you like it. You say it's wonderful or funny or . . . whatever. You always say you like it."

Because, Sara thought ruefully, it seemed like a good idea to be encouraging. Look where it's gotten me.

She searched for the right words. "It's hard to like something so sad. You made me care about Aurelia Rose, and that's essential in a story, but it didn't make me feel happy."

"You could be *impressed*," Carrie said angrily.

"I am," Sara said swiftly, grateful for the word. "I'm impressed with the writing, and the mood you created. You made me tense and worried and unhappy." She studied Carrie's face. "Is that how you felt when you wrote it?"

"I don't know! I told you, it was inside me and it just came out!" Carrie sprang up and was out the door before Sara could stop her.

She sat still for a long time. *I need a break from all this. There's too much emotional turmoil in this house.*

And, as if in response, by afternoon the house was empty. Sara walked through the rooms as if newly discovering them. Nothing had changed, but everything was different: hushed and still, in abeyance, as if waiting for the next burst of people and emotion. The rooms were cool, protected from the blistering heat of the first day of August by thick stone walls, and windows shaded by towering trees. My house, Sara thought. She loved it, loved being rooted in it, loved sharing it with her family. She had never felt so certain of that, walking through its strangely still rooms, knowing that, as precious as was the silence, the house was truly alive only when filled with the voices and emotional tremors of their intersecting lives. Savoring her solitariness, she still anticipated the time when Abby and Carrie and Doug would return and take their places in these rooms.

And Mack? Where did he fit in?

I wish he would leave, she thought. Everything seems to be changing, moving faster, spinning past . . .

But how do you tell a member of your family to get out of the house?

At her desk upstairs, she worked on papers she had brought home from her City Hall office, and, at five o'clock, called Reuben. "Everyone is safely ensconced with friends. I have no responsibilities until tomorrow afternoon."

"You have one. To spend those hours with me. I thought we'd have dinner here, instead of going out. Would that please you?"

"Yes, if we can cook together."

"A fine idea. When can you be here?"

"What time would you like?"

"An hour ago. A day ago. Now."

"Half an hour?"

"I'll be waiting."

He had never been inside her house. Neither of them mentioned it; they seemed to shun the idea, as if aware that the moment Reuben walked among the rooms she had made her own, with the family she had made her own, he would be more than friend and companion and lover. He would be . . .

what? Having no idea of the answer, they were not ready to confront the question. But Sara thought about it (and wondered if he did), imagining the time when he would walk through the front door and fit himself into their space, sitting on their couches and chairs, eating at the kitchen table or in the dining room, sleeping in the . . . well, no, she never got that far. But even without that, she could imagine that he would look as if he belonged. And by then perhaps he would.

He opened the side door as she drove up his driveway and into the double garage, beside his car. Two dark blue sedans, almost identical. Paired, she thought, at the same time telling herself she was thinking that way far too often.

"Welcome," said Reuben as she walked through the glaring heat, and they kissed in his doorway, the ease and rightness of it making them smile as they walked into the house.

But they had been apart for almost a week, and the ease of their greeting was swept away by the urgency freed with touching, and so they did not stop but kept walking, up the stairs and into Reuben's bedroom. In the shadowy coolness, Sara's sundress slipped off as easily as his khakis and shirt, and then they were on his bed, the long line of Sara's body like an ivory crescent on the blue-and-black madras spread.

"So beautiful," Reuben murmured, his hands moving over her, remembering the curves and hollows and textures he knew but still, each time they were together, learned anew. Sara pulled him to her, and involuntarily sighed as he fit himself to her, separate bodies transformed, like the final two pieces in a puzzle, each in its perfect place, clarifying, in a burst of illumination, an entire image. Away from the turmoil of recent days, she felt a deep letting go, only then realizing how tense she had been through the news of Pussy's death, the memorial service, Donna's encampment in her house, Abby's distress, Carrie's strange story . . .

But in Reuben's bedroom, beneath his solid weight, his hand on her breast, his lips moving over hers, teasing her, teasing himself, she opened to feeling, to desire, to the two of them. In that hushed space, there was room for no one else, no problems or questions or demands. Just Reuben and Sara, hands moving over and around each other in arousal and possession, bodies meeting and merging in a language theirs alone, discovering a oneness and a wonder they had never known, and, not knowing, could not have guessed they had been missing.

"You are an extraordinary woman," Reuben said when they were quiet again. He lay beside her, leaning on an elbow, his left hand lightly caressing her face. "When you're not here the silence in this house can be smothering, and when you're here, it sings."

Sara smiled. "Thank you. What a lovely thing to say. You give me so many reasons to be grateful."

"For what, exactly?"

She laughed. "There speaks a man who builds whole towns to scale and needs exactitude. Well, then, *exactly* for companionship, friendship, generous praise, good conversation, good advice—"

"Do I give advice? I try not to, unless asked."

"You advised me to listen to Abby about Donna. I think Abby was right, and so were you. But I don't want to talk about that tonight. Or even think about it."

"No, tonight is just for us. Let's go back to gratitude."

"You want more?"

"If there is more."

His eyes were serious—this was not a game to him—and so, seriously, she said, "For gentleness and understanding, for really listening without using half your attention to think of clever responses, for having so much to say and talking without ever talking down, for being interested in the world, for liking people, for loving books and music and art and theater, for knowing good food and taking it seriously, for being adventurous."

"And?"

"Oh, what a greedy man."

"Or perhaps anxious."

She brought his face to hers and kissed him. "For being patient and sensitive with my family. For wonderful sex, more wonderful than I ever imagined."

Reuben smiled. "Last but not least. Thank you for all that. If it had been my turn, I would have listed the same things, plus your courage and commitment to your family. And one more. I hope you would be as grateful for it as I am. For love."

Sara let the word settle within her. It had not been used hastily or cheaply; there was nothing about Reuben Lister that was hasty or cheap. Nor was there pretense in it, to gain some kind of prize. There was no place in Reuben Lister for pretense.

"Yes," she said. "I am most grateful for that, given and received."

As if the weather had shifted slightly, announced only by a breeze picking up, or the faint smell of ozone in the air, Sara and Reuben felt their private climate change, a subtle difference in the way they looked at each other and to each other, the way they spoke, the way they thought. Something had been settled, though not settled at all, only established as the foundation for a new step, new decisions, a new direction.

Dinner was late, but time, too, had shifted, at least for this night, freed from the schedules of work, the needs of family, the demands of acquaintances. Beyond the tree-shaded windows of Reuben's bedroom, the street was silent, a short distance away (but in fact a world away) from the Saturday-night sprees of Rush Street, where young people lined up outside bars and nightclubs; open convertibles crawled by, radios beating with basses and drums; couples and singles looking to be couples packed outdoor cafés and bars nursing one or two drinks and escalating to feverish excitement from the contagion of the crowds. Later they would pair off in various combinations of sex, age, race, height, and religion, and go to the Saturday beds where they would awaken around noon the next day, regretting or happy in their choice of partners. But now it was not quite ten o'clock at night, and Rush Street was jumping, and, in a quiet neighborhood, Sara and Reuben were preparing dinner, and everyone was convinced they were in exactly the right place.

Sara had slipped on her sundress, Reuben his khakis and shirt, and they had taken from the refrigerator the foods he had prepared earlier. Reuben poured two glasses of Meursault and handed Sara a salad bowl. "You didn't leave much for me to do," she said, emptying greens into the bowl.

"I thought you might be too exhausted to do more than a few simple things."

"From the past few days or the past few hours?"

"Exhausted from the past few days; energized for simple things by the past few hours."

Sara smiled. "What good planning."

She sliced avocado and hearts of palm

into the salad, watching Reuben slide a plat-
ter of salmon into the oven and stir-fry as-
paragus tips and snow peas. His movements
were smooth and practiced; he was accustomed to cooking alone, and clearly enjoyed
it. She liked watching his economical movements, his absorption in his tasks, his ease
with implements and ingredients. She recognized herself in the small creative steps he
took, deciding which spice to add, and how
much, and at what point. He was having a
good time, as she did in her own kitchen,
however rushed she was at the end of a day.
The kitchen was an oasis for both of them.

Reuben looked up and met her smile, and
took a few steps to kiss her. "It's a much better kitchen with you in it."

"It's a fine kitchen." Sara chose from a
basket of tomatoes, one red, one yellow. "I
like kitchens."

"And you have a good one at home?"

"It's quite wonderful. You'd enjoy it."

"Will you give me a tour sometime?"

"As soon as you'd like."

Another step; they both knew it. Now it
seemed perfectly natural for Reuben to fit
himself into her house, into her life.

A little flustered by the speed at which

they were being confronted with change, she changed the subject. "Tell me how you're roasting the salmon."

"At two-fifty for fifteen minutes." They talked about roasting and grilling, fish and salads and spices, until the vegetables were crisply stir-fried, the salmon perfectly roasted with warm sorrel sauce ladled on top, and the salad set on the sideboard, with olive oil and sherry vinegar beside it. And they ate, casually, in the small sunroom off the kitchen, where Reuben had set a small fig tree and bougainvillea in decorative Mexican pots beside a café table and two chairs in a corner overlooking the fenced backyard. Against the darkness outside, they saw their reflections against the lighted windows of the houses and apartments beyond the backyard and the alley.

They carried espresso and cookies to his study, and sat on the corduroy couch. "I have a great deal to tell you," Reuben said, setting down his empty cup. "I've put it off, ridiculously, as if by not talking about it I could make it vanish from my life. But what we have now is too important for make-believe; I want you to know what's real in my life, and what I have to deal with."

Another step, Sara thought, perhaps the biggest of all. The one she had been waiting for. She put down her cup. "Yes," she said.

But it was too late for unforced honesty. Because, in the next moment, the doorbell rang, and when Reuben answered it, Ardis was there, with her luggage.

TEN

It was like being conductor of a huge orchestra, Mack thought, pointing here, waving there, bringing everyone to heel. Each time he organized the increasingly boisterous demonstrations by NoMoGaRB (No Monstrous Growth at River Bend, coined by Mack and picked up in a *Chicago Tribune* headline), he reveled in the sound that rolled across masses of demonstrators to engulf him with confirmation of his power. It did not matter (not much, anyway) that Lew had ordered him to remain invisible, and therefore it was always some surrogate who started the march or stopped it, began the shouting or cut it off, increased or diminished it or sent it roaring to the skies. It did not matter (not really), because Mack Hayden was the mastermind behind every move, and he knew it, and Lew Corcoran knew it. *Master masterfully mastering,* he exulted from his post in a clump of trees a discreet distance away, looking out over two or three thousand pairs of eyes turned toward the leader he had chosen, waiting for orders. *My people.*

No sarcasm there. He was dead serious.

He'd attended most of the citizens' meetings, listening from an adjacent room when outsiders were present. At no point, decreed Lew Corcoran, could the demonstrations be seen as planned or directed by anyone but the neighbors. So Mack had not met the Carrano Village honchos, but he'd seen them: Isaiah Carrano, the deep pockets, burly and flamboyant, with a deep laugh that made everyone (except Mack) smile, and his partner, Reuben Lister. Sara's big flame. (Though maybe not; she hadn't gone out at night for almost two weeks, and there hadn't been any long phone calls; maybe they'd broken up, which Mack didn't appreciate, since he liked having the kids to himself.) He didn't know what she'd ever seen in the guy, anyway. He wasn't impressive: thin face, beard, glasses, narrow shoulders, tall and lanky, no bulk, no brawn, needed a haircut. His eyes were hard, but the rest of him was nothing you'd ever notice, walking down the street. Looked like a professor, not an opponent you'd take seriously. Except . . . one thing that was fucking annoying: no matter what anybody was talking about, Lister didn't change his expression or raise his voice. Fucking hard to deal with; you never knew what the guy was thinking. But he was manageable; Mack knew that for sure. Listen, he told an imaginary doubter: if I can manage Lew Corcoran, I can manage a wimp like Lister.

It was time to start the march. One last time, he surveyed the scene. TV cameras ready to roll, network helicopters hovering overhead, police lined up along the sides of the route, newspaper reporters strung out, with a few posted at the speakers' platform. Mack nodded to Ted Waszenski, his right-hand man, who stepped forward in view of the lead marchers, raised his arm, and dropped it sharply. Placards shot up, a forest of signs slashed with exclamation marks; banners were strung across the road between marchers; and the line began to move, sluggishly at first, those at the rear waiting for the forward movement to reach them, then more briskly as handpicked demonstrators began to chant, and marchers picked up their feet to the rhythm.

It was a wonderful moment. Everything was going according to plan; Lew would be proud of him. Mack closed his eyes in a brief moment of pure satisfaction. But, when he opened them, he got a jolt: Reuben Lister walking the line, talking to marchers, and a woman with him, half a step behind, small, thin, dressed in an expensive suit and high heels, heavy makeup, her eyes hidden behind huge sunglasses. Lister wasn't paying much attention to her, but she was with him, step for step, never taking her eyes off him, like her life depended on it.

The noise of the demonstrators was too loud for Mack to hear anything, and he could not move closer without being seen. Frustrated, he pounded his fist into his palm, and shifted his feet back and forth, hating the huge sound he had reveled in a few minutes before, hating Lister for trying to turn people against him, hating Lew Corcoran for forcing him to stay invisible, hating Sara for being secretive about Lister so Mack couldn't figure out how to deal with him; hating his mother for refusing to set a date to see him even after she'd said she would; hating his father for leaving him in the lurch, doing a disappearing act when Mack was strung out on drugs and owed money to everybody and needed help getting the fuck away from the mess he was in; hating Doug and Carrie and Abby because they were so fucking happy they'd never understand the problems he had; hating the marchers for making so much goddamn noise, for talking to Lister, for having a good time.

Mack was always amazed at how much there was in the world to hate.

He saw Lister look his way, and sprang farther back into the trees. Lister didn't see him; he couldn't have seen him. And anyway, what difference would it make if he did? He didn't know who Mack was . . . unless Sara had shown him a picture? Those pics Carrie had taken a few weeks ago . . . they could be all over the place by now. Lew would hate him for letting anybody take his picture; Christ, why had he done that? But why would Sara want to talk about him to her lover-boy? Didn't they have better things to do? But even if he'd seen a photo, he wouldn't be able to see into the trees . . . except that it was a sunny day . . . and he'd been looking straight at him . . .

Entangled in too many scenarios, Mack could not stand it; he turned and stumbled through the trees, doubling back to find his car. Let Ted handle the march and the TV cameras and the rest of it; he'd been a pain in the ass lately, pushing to do things his way without being held back; well, let him find out how hard it was; Mack Hayden was getting the hell out of there, and fuck Reuben Lister and whoever was with him.

Reuben saw the shadowy figure move deeper into the woods, and disappear. Curious, he thought, with all the activity out here, and attention from newspapers and television, why would anyone skulk in the shadows?

To avoid being seen.

To keep tabs on the action.

To watch for . . . what?

Maybe the kid, the one they talk about when I ask who's doing the organizing. "The kid. He and Ted; they do everything."

But for what? There was real organization here. Someone sent the kid to do the dirty work, told him to stay out of the limelight and deal with only a few key people. And report back.

To someone who was even more invisible. Someone who wanted to kill Carrano Village West.

Because . . . ?

Because he wanted the land for himself.

For . . . ?

It was not clear that anyone here knew the real answer. When Reuben talked to Ted, he heard well-memorized, well-polished phrases about traffic congestion, too many kids, sky-high taxes for new schools, trash pickup, roads, the wrong kind of people moving in, seeing the prairie filled up with concrete and stores and houses, when the people around here wanted lots of open space.

But Reuben knew it would be a safe bet that open space would not be what the people got if Isaiah dropped Carrano Village. What they would get was some unknown developer with a hugely profitable development in the works. There would be no other reason to go to the trouble of organizing weekly demonstrations and paying whoever had been hired to run them.

"What is it?" Ardis asked. She raised her voice to be heard above the crowd and the throb of the helicopters overhead. "Is someone spying on us?"

"I don't know." He turned back, once again facing the line of marchers. "Someone was hiding in the trees; I have no idea if he was watching us."

"I hope not. I'm not ready. I mean not quite. I mean, to face the public like a wife you're proud of."

Reuben kept silent. Later, he told himself. Not here, not on the street. Wait until tonight, at dinner. Tell her then.

Two weeks without Sara. Two weeks without any kind of conversation with her. But, in fact, infinitely more than two weeks. A span of time without measurement, a bleak vista empty of everything her presence had come to mean to him: the timbre of her voice; her quiet smile and rich laughter; the sharing of thoughts and ideas and the smallest details of their days; her body stretching along his, welcoming him, their eyes meeting in recognition; the languor of their breakfasts, bridging the night that had been theirs and the days they gave to the rest of the world.

He had not done much work in those two weeks; he had not slept much. Ardis moved about the guest room and bath at all hours of the night, noisily, so that he would hear her, be conscious, always, that she was in his home. When he had flatly, rudely, refused to let her share his bed, she had taken it with surprising grace, but then embedded herself everywhere else that she could: in his study, in the hallways of his house, in the sunroom and kitchen, where, improbably, she was up and waiting for him each morning, hair combed, makeup on, wearing a shimmering silk robe that softened her gauntness, offering him toast and coffee (more than she ever had done before in a kitchen). He had not been able to sit and eat under her bright gaze; each day he had claimed an early meeting and left, but she had beat him there, too, standing at the door on tiptoe, kissing him good-bye (aiming for his lips but each time meeting his cheek instead).

To his amazement, as far as he could tell, she was not drinking. She consumed great quantities of ginger ale, diet colas, black Italian coffee, and chocolate, putting enough caffeine in her diet to knock out the most dedicated caffeine addict. She did not look healthy, but neither did she look on the verge of collapse. She was almost pretty again, in spite of her still-drawn face; her hair was expertly cut and styled, her clothes beautiful and well chosen to make the most of her petite body, and disguise the sharpness of her bones. Her skin was still sallow, but she was clever with makeup. She had developed a subtly pathetic look that, with her pretty face, caused men in the march to look twice, and throw envious glances at Reuben, and, for a moment, it seemed to him that the intervening years had vanished and once again he walked with her, newly married, manly and protective of his rare and precious creature whom every male predator would grab if given the chance.

His pride and protectiveness had not lasted long into their marriage, but now, as he looked down on Ardis's bowed, blond head, her neck's frail downward curve, and the sad tremor at the corners of her mouth, and thought of what she was going through to avoid drinking, the urge to protect rushed through him once again, and he put his arm around her in a generous gesture that he would regret from the moment he did it.

Ardis spun around, reached up to encircle

his neck with her thin arms, and kissed him on the mouth. "Oh, Ben, I knew this would work. Didn't I tell you? I knew it, I knew it. We're so right together. Whoever she was, I forgive you, it doesn't matter; you were alone and lonely and I know how that is, God knows I know *that,* and I should have come to you a long time ago, but I had . . . work to do." She gave a small laugh that was almost a giggle. "On myself."

Reuben took an abrupt step backward, appalled that he had let himself be sucked in once again. It was no one's fault but his own; he knew better; he had had more than enough time to review his years with her, to see his weaknesses as well as hers, and to work out ways in which they could amicably bring their marriage to an end. Instead, like a child putting off an unpleasant task, he had avoided it, losing that perfect, ruthless moment when he could have forced it through: the moment he moved out and began his own life.

Which now included Sara. Had to include Sara. If she would have him again. He had called once, just once, in the past two weeks, and Abby had answered, but Sara had come to the telephone. "I won't ask you to talk about this now," he said. "I'm ashamed of what I let you in for, and of what I did to us, and no apology can make up for that. I've been wanting to tell you where I was in my life, but it was not an attractive story, and I delayed . . . well, you know that. I've wanted to end this marriage for years, which doesn't speak well of me, but there never seemed to be a compelling reason. Now there is, but I had no right to wait until . . . until I did a terrible thing to you. I'll try to make it up to you, if you'll let me, but I have to finish this first. I promise you, I'm doing that. And I'd like to call you again, if I may."

There was a long silence. "When you've . . . finished it," Sara said.

He let out his breath; he had not been aware how rigidly he had been holding himself. "Thank you. I miss you. I love you."

"Benny, let's get out of here." Ardis smiled gaily at him, the same curving smile that had first captivated him. "We'll go somewhere and have fun. Maybe"—her eyes were bright, wide, giving way to little flashes of desperation—"we'll go home and have some special time together. Love in the afternoon. It's been a long time, Benny."

Reuben fought with contradictions: disgust at her offering herself, throwing herself against him even as he distanced himself from her; and then a rush of memories of a warm, tantalizing Ardis, adventurous and exciting to the very young husband he had been. He wanted nothing to do with her, but memories wrapped them in a kind of cocoon, bound to each other, or simply to the past.

"Benny?"

When you've finished it. He spun about, so clearly had he heard Sara's voice.

"Ben!" Ardis cried, her voice grating.

He gave a short, angry laugh. *Like a French farce. One man, two women. But no contest.* "I've told you," he said, so softly Ardis had to strain to hear him, "that is not my name." He handed her the car keys. "I'll be here awhile; you can wait in the car or drive somewhere. Please be back in an hour."

She stared at him. "How do you know I'll come back?"

He shrugged.

Her face contorted . . . and there before him was the woman she had become within a few months of their marriage, wiping out, exactly as before, everything else. Jangling the keys, she stalked off, not easy in stiletto heels, but Ardis always had known how to walk away.

Reuben sought out Ted, and found him near the speakers' platform. "Quite a turnout," he said. "You're as good as a professional organizer."

Fiddling with a microphone, Ted did not look up. "I work at it. You want something? I'm kinda busy here."

"Could you give me a minute? I have a couple of questions."

He looked up. "A minute."

"What's the name of the guy who's helping you organize these marches?"

"You ask me that every time. I told you: Matt."

"He has a last name."

"He never said. What difference does it make?"

"Is he paying you?"

"What?"

"For doing all this. For not asking questions about who he is. Is he paying you?"

"None of your goddamn business. I'm helping my neighbors, my neighborhood. We don't want traffic congestion, all those kids, sky-high taxes for new schools, people who aren't—"

"I've heard all that. I know what you don't want. What do you think you'll get if we walk away from here?"

"Damn it, I've told you a few thousand times. *Open space.* How many times I hafta say it? Now go on; I'm busy; just leave us the hell alone."

Reuben shook his head. "You won't end up with open space. You'll have something else."

"What the hell you talking about?"

"If we don't build here, someone else will. Why do you think someone is spending money to get your people out every week? Whoever he is, he doesn't live here; he doesn't give a damn about traffic congestion or higher taxes in River Bend; he wants the land for his own development."

"Bullshit."

"It's not, and you know it. It must have occurred to you to wonder why you're getting paid for—"

"I never said I—"

"You're getting paid and you're spreading some of that money around. And for what? For something you can't even predict. It could be apartment buildings, even a factory or—"

"SHUT UP! YOU'RE A GODDAMN TROU-
BLEMAKER!"

"I'm trying to build a terrific village here,
with playgrounds and a gym and swimming
pool and baseball fields you'll all use. I'm trying to protect acres of open space—"

"What'd you say? This guy's gonna
build . . . what?"

"I don't know. I told you, it could be a factory, anything. But I guarantee you, this will
not stay open space. You'll be stuck with—"

"*You don't know.* You haven't got a fucking
piece of information we haven't got. You got
a hell of a nerve, buddy, coming here and
trying to scare the shit out of decent people
fighting for their homes. We're *fighting* here,
buddy, so get the hell out and let us do our
thing." He swung around, concentrating on
the microphone.

"When will you see Matt again?" Reuben
asked.

Ted shook his head. "Don't know."

"Would you call me when you hear from
him? I'd like to meet him."

"Well, he don't want to meet you. You got a
nerve. Asking me to call you? Like I got
nothin' better to do?" He looked at his watch.

"Christ, ten minutes late." He waved to someone on the platform, a small woman who stepped smartly up to one of the microphones and began to speak.

"Hello! Hello? Hello! I'm Margie Partopulous . . . hello? Hello!" The crowd quieted. "Thanks, thanks, guys, I'm a little nervous, you know? I mean, I'm not a . . . I don't make speeches, I'm not real good at this, I just take care of my family, but, you know, that's what I'm worried about, like, MY HOME and MY KIDS and my HOME VALUES and what I'm here for, you know, marching and all, why I'm here today, is, I'm here to PROTECT THEM!"

As if on cue, the crowd roared, banners waved, newspaper photographers and marchers alike snapped their cameras, and that night, on the ten o'clock television news, Doug and Carrie saw Reuben, standing beside the speakers' platform, scowling.

"Sara!" Doug yelled, and jumped up. They were in a room they almost never used anymore, a playroom still filled with toys and games, a rocking horse, a few dozen LEGO kits, dominoes, Scrabble, jigsaw puzzles, and a deep couch and two shabby armchairs near a large television set. Long ago,

Doug and Carrie and Abby had painted each wall a different color—buttercup, pale green, rose, and deep blue—making the room at once kaleidoscopic and, unexpectedly, warm and comforting. "Like our house," Abby had said happily. "Nobody else could live here; it's just *ours.*"

"Sara!" Doug yelled again, back on the couch.

"Don't," Carrie said sharply. "I think they broke up."

But Sara was there, coming upstairs after making dinner for the next night. "What's going on?"

"Uh, nothing," Doug mumbled. "Sorry."

"Doug just got excited," said Carrie.

Sara came into the room, and saw the River Bend demonstrators on the television screen. On the speakers' stand, a small woman was shouting and shaking her fist, and, in the corner of the screen, Reuben stood alone, surveying the crowd. The perspective changed as a cameraman in a helicopter showed the view from above while the reporter talked about "thousands of angry neighbors." And then, without a pause, the picture switched to a murder in a North Shore suburb.

"That looked like Reuben," Sara said casually. "I guess those demonstrations haven't stopped. Don't stay up much later, you two; you have camp and summer school tomorrow."

Puzzled, Carrie was scrutinizing her. "You're staying home an awful lot, I mean at night."

Sara laughed, amused, as always, by Carrie's transparency. "You're right. Most of my friends are on vacation this month, and Reuben and I aren't seeing each other."

"Ever?" Carrie asked anxiously.

Doug spoke without looking up from the television screen. "We kind of liked him."

"So did I," said Sara, aching inside. "I don't know about 'ever.' He has some things to work out; so do I. So I can't make predictions."

"He never made us feel dumb," Doug said sadly.

"He talked to us like grown-ups," said Carrie. "And he was nice, you know, I mean he stayed nice, he didn't flop around, nice and then not-nice." She frowned at Sara. "Don't you love him anymore?"

When did I ever say—? Sara gazed at

Carrie. And then she simply told the truth. "Yes, I do."

And am I happy about that, or not? I don't know.

"Well, then," Carrie said with finality.

"It isn't always enough. When things get complicated between two people . . ."

"But what's so complicated? You love each other and you like to be together. What else matters?"

A wife. Months of secretiveness. An unwillingness to share. Loss of trust.

"All the things that make up two lives." Sara tried to smile, but she felt hollow and lost, and all she wanted was to curl up in her room, alone and silent, not having to explain anything, especially things she could not understand. "There are so many layers to our lives, Carrie, so many things going on at once—"

"Like plots in a book!" Carrie cried. "But if it's your own story, you can solve all the plots and have a happy ending."

At that, Sara did smile. "When I figure out how to do that, I'll let you know. I'm pretty sure it's not quite that simple."

Doug turned off the television set. "I don't feel like watching anymore."

"Me neither." Carrie stood up. "I guess I'll go to bed."

Doug tossed the television control onto the couch, then whirled and threw his arms around Sara. "Don't be sad, Sara. We love you."

Carrie leaped into the embrace. Sara's eyes filled with tears, and then her earlier anger returned, flared up so that she forgot her longing. What right did Reuben have to lie to her? (Well, he hadn't exactly lied, but he might as well have, conveniently leaving out one simple fact that would have interfered with her believing him a free candidate for her to stroll with, to sleep with, to love.) What right did he have to pursue her when he was entangled, to let her become entangled when he was not free to make her a part of his life, or to become part of hers? What right did he have, now, to say he was sorry, he'd acted badly (damned right he had), and wanted to call her again?

"Sara, don't cry," Carrie said, and began to cry herself.

In an instant, Sara's anger turned on herself. Speaking of rights, she thought, what right do I have to impose my unhappiness on two loving children? What right do I have to burden children totally dependent on me with a misery they can't do a single thing about? What right to complicate their lives at a time when they have no complications, but stand on the threshold of years and years filled with complications of their own?

Her eyes dried. "There's nothing to cry about," she said briskly. "I live in the best house in the world with the best people. There's enough love in our house to fill me up as much as a whole Thanksgiving dinner. In fact, I'm stuffed, no room right now for any more."

Carrie giggled and raised her head. "Really?"

"Really."

"But Reuben . . ."

"Reuben's a great guy and maybe someday we'll get together again, but right now I've got all I can handle dealing with the three of you."

"And Mack," said Doug, loosening his hold on Sara.

"And Donna," said Carrie.

"She's really weird," Doug declared. "Is she ever going to move out?"

"Sara wants her to," Carrie said.

"Can't you just tell her to?" Doug asked

Sara. "I mean, nobody likes her very much and she doesn't pay any attention to us, except once in a while she gives me this big awful kiss and says how handsome I am. Why does she do that?"

"I didn't know she did," Sara said. "Why didn't you tell me?"

"She said not to. She said she just loved me because she could pretend I'm her brother, but I shouldn't tell you 'cause you wouldn't understand. It's not *fatal,* you know, Sara, it's just kind of awful. And weird."

"She bought a chair," Carrie said. "It's downstairs, next to her bed."

"What?"

"She said she didn't have a comfortable place to sit, you know, to watch television, so she bought this chair and a friend took it downstairs for her. Yesterday."

"There is no television downstairs."

"Mack gave her one. He said as long as she had to be in the basement, she ought to have a view of the worldly worldwide world. Something like that, anyway."

"*Why didn't you tell me?* Oh, I'm sorry," Sara said quickly, seeing the dismay on their faces as she snapped at them. "It isn't your fault. It's just that I do like to know what's going on around here." She paused, juggling all the new information, to make room for it among thoughts that kept swerving back to Reuben. "It's okay. I'll talk to her, and find out what's going on."

Doug looked alarmed at the note in her voice. "Don't tell her we said anything, you know, about kissing or chairs or . . . anything."

"Don't worry about it. Go on, now, time for bed. It's getting late."

"You're okay?" Carrie asked.

"I'm fine." Sara smiled. "You two make me feel wonderful."

"Sara," said Doug from the doorway. "I'll be home late tomorrow; Mack's picking me up at camp and taking me to the gallery, to figure out where I'm going to put all my pieces."

Can't get away from him, Sara thought; he keeps popping up. And evidently the gallery was real, and Doug's show was real, and she did not know what to think about that. She did not want to think about any of it, especially Mack. Right now, poised, at long last, to disappear into her bedroom and nurse her aching for Reuben, her anger at Reuben, her longing for Reuben, her worries about Donna, she could not deal with Mack.

She wanted him gone. She wanted Donna gone. She longed to have the house wrap itself around her and her family and be the haven it had been just last April. Only five months ago.

But Doug was watching from the doorway, wary, prepared to argue, and Sara was not about to argue.

"Do you know what time you'll be home?"

"Mack said we'd like pick up Carrie and Abby and go to dinner."

"He thought you'd have a date," Carrie said, trying to cover up Mack's leaving Sara out of their plans.

"Does Abby want to go?" Sara asked.

"I guess so. Mack said he'd ask her."

Sara did not let herself hesitate. "As long as you're home by nine. I'll be waiting for you."

"Would you like to come?" Carrie asked.

"No, it's your party. You'll have a fine time. Go on, now; I'll come and say good night in a few minutes."

And where was Donna? she wondered as she turned out lights in the playroom. Donna had her own key—finally there had been no alternative to giving her one—and came and went at odd hours, sometimes saying she had been apartment hunting all evening, most often evasive.

And Mack was out, too. Sara's anger flared again. On top of everything, she couldn't even go to bed knowing that everyone in her house was accounted for. Her house was not the safe, solid enclosure it had always been; now it stood open to the world. Or part of it.

She was being irrational. She knew it. In fact, she nursed it, since she wanted to be angry. It was better to be angry at Reuben than to long for him. She did long for him, but why dwell on that? Anger could almost replace it, at least for as long as she could hold on to it.

The trouble was, though she angered easily, she was not able to hold on to anger, recovering almost as quickly as it expressed itself. A real flaw, she thought caustically the next morning as she walked into Donna's cubicle and saw that it was still empty, her desk still cluttered from the day before, though the rule of the office was that all documents, private or not, were to be put away at the end of each day.

In her own office, Sara opened her calendar. A full schedule with nothing she wanted to do, each hour filled until almost six that night. *I could suddenly be sick and go home, hide in bed for a day, veg out, as Doug would say.*

Except that's not me. I need to know I've accomplished something at the end of each day. A little compulsive, maybe. But me.

"YOU SARA?"

She looked up at a burly figure in the doorway, a great bear of a man, dark-bearded, dark hair to his shoulders, black curly hair at the base of his throat and covering muscled arms that strained at his tight T-shirt. "Sara Elliott," she said. "Do you have an appointment? My secretary is not—"

"Your secretary! Shit! Your *little toy!*" Slamming his hands on the edge of her desk, he leaned on his arms toward Sara, crowding her. "I wanna know what the fuck you're doing to my wife!"

Sara stared at him. "I don't know your wife."

"The fuck you don't! Donna's my wife! Your little plaything secretary!"

"*Donna?* Donna is married?"

"Don't play the fucking innocent with—"

"Mr.—whatever your name is, and you

haven't had the courtesy to introduce yourself—no one talks to me that way. If you
can't do better than that, you'll have to leave.
And if you won't, I will."

"Fuck it, all I—"

Sara stood up.

"Sorry, Jesus, that's the way I talk. I tell
you how to talk? I *care* how you talk? I care
how you talk to *my wife.* You turned her
against me, you helped her cheat on me—"

"Just a minute. What is your name?"

He threw out his hands in frustration.
"Ziggy."

"And—?"

"What difference does it makes? Zigmund
Brouner. I use Ziggy."

"Mr. Brouner, you'll have to tell me what
you're talking about. My secretary is Donna
Soldana. She is not married; she's been living alone to escape a difficult situation at
home, and right now she's staying at my
house until she can find a new apartment
where she can be safe."

"That's a load of shit."

"I told you—"

"Oh, for Christ's sake, I don't change the
way I talk just for you. That's me, and you'll
take it 'cause you've stolen my wife, turned

her against me, helped her have a lover, shit, maybe more than one, and I could sue you in every fucking court in Chicago, but all I want is she comes home and you keep away from her. She's *living in your house*? Jesus. Tell her she has to come home! I'm there, she knows it, she *damn well knows it,* she comes back on weekends and we have a great time, then she's gone all week, said she was going to a hospital every day after work and staying overnight for treatments for asthma, you know, shots and special diet and this humidity room, she said she couldn't explain it all—she's smarter than me, so I figured I couldn't understand it any-way—but her asthma was really better, she never wheezes on our weekends, but she says it's bad at work—your air bad here, or something? Maybe you need a new ventilat-ing system, air-conditioning, whatever. Any-way, she said she had to go to the hospital every night except weekends, and I said that was okay 'cause it wasn't costin' us any-thing, her insurance paid for it, and I could be alone for a while 'cause she was getting well so we could be together all the time, that's what she wanted, all the time with me . . . *she said.* And all this time she's sleeping around . . . how many guys who the hell knows, and *she never went to any hospital.* She lied and you put her up to it and now where am I? Fucked over is where I am."

Beneath the onslaught, Sara sat limp and disbelieving. "What about her father?"

"Father? What father? Her mother never got married, had three kids, different men, she died a few years ago, drugs, they said, but Donna said she was just too mean and miserable to live any longer."

Stunned, Sara stared at him. "Sit down," she said at last. "Please. I need to understand—she's been coming to you on weekends?"

"*Comin' home* on weekends. And the rest of the time fuckin' whoever. There's one I know for sure, she told him her brother was after her, tried to screw her once and she needed a safe place. They hung out in his apartment, but she had her own place—that what you said?—and I guess took guys there, too. She's so fuckin' gorgeous, you know, everybody wants her . . ." His voice trailed away, torn between pride in his gorgeous wife who always attracted men, and jealous rage for being made a fool of.

"Mr. Brouner," Sara said at last, "I knew none of this. Donna told me she was being pursued by her father, that he had sexually abused her, so she needed a safe place to live where her mother could visit her and her father could not find her. I believed everything she said."

"Bullshit. Donna don't lie unless somebody puts her up to it. She's a little bitty thing, she don't know much about the world, she needs taking care of, she don't know her way around."

Sara shook her head. "Evidently she is quite experienced, quite shrewd, a masterful liar, and a pretty good actress."

"Bullshit! Bullshit, bullshit! *You're* the liar! You're an evil person. You're like a, what's his name, Houdini, the guy who got women to do things, like, hypnotized them, whatever, that's you."

Svengali. But she did not say it aloud. In fact, there was nothing she could say. He would not believe her, and she was not sure whether to believe him, though she suspected he was telling the truth. *I'd put some trust in Abby's feelings about Donna.* Reuben had said that on the telephone the night Donna showed up. She had begun to

think he was right. And then Donna had refused to go to a lawyer, had made such an
outcry Sara had given in. Abby was right,
she thought now. *And Reuben told me to
trust her. But I kept believing—*

The outer door of the office opened and
she heard Donna's footsteps.

"Donna!" she called. "Could you come in,
please?"

Donna stopped short in the doorway.
"What are you doing here? I told you never
to . . . you can't come here—"

"I can come anywhere I fuckin' want to!"
He was on his feet and enfolding her in a
bear hug. "I come to take you home, sweetie.
Get you away from this Houdini. She's bad
for you, honeybunch, she gets her kicks
fuckin' with you, makin' you do things you
don't want to do. She's evil. You need protection from people like her; you're too good. So
you're getting the hell out of here and coming with me."

"Okay," Donna said.

*Just like that. Doesn't she believe in any-
thing? Well, of course she does: she believes in whatever works for Donna.*

Still disbelieving, Sara said, "Where did
the bruises come from?"

Ziggy ducked his head. "I guess that's me. I get mad. It's not Donna's fault; she's the best little wife anybody could want, she never did anything—"

"Sure I do, I get you mad. Poor baby, I give you a hard time, don't I? But you're my big, strong guy who knows what he wants." She looked at Sara, as if, woman to woman, they could understand the intricacies of female needs. "I just need a break now and then."

Shaking with anger, trying to understand how she could have been so wrong (and how many mistaken ideas might she have about other people?), Sara went to the door. "I'll be home at five-thirty; you can come by after that and get your things."

"Yeah, but—"

"And you'd better look for a new job. I'm sure you won't have any trouble; you present a most convincing picture. Now you'll both have to leave; I have work to do."

"Sara, don't," Donna said. "I mean, I'm sorry, I know I made things up, but it didn't *hurt* anybody, I mean, it wasn't *murder* or anything like that, and, you know, I really did need a break, I mean, Ziggy's a lot to take in big doses, and I really really appreciated your help; you were terrific and I'll never forget it, never, anything I can do for you—"

"You can leave."

"No, you don't mean that. I love this job. I need this job. I mean, I hate to get started at new places, you know, it's not easy, and I really do a good job here, Sara, you know I do, you *depend* on me, and there's no reason why anything should change, I mean, I'm still me, your secretary—"

"You are not my secretary. Now will you both leave or must I call a security guard?"

Ziggy looked alarmed. "Let's split, honey. We don't need any trouble."

"But she can't *fire* me!"

"*Honeybunch,* we're outta here."

He pulled her through the door. Sara heard their footsteps fading away, imagined other workers peering from doorways to see what the fuss was about, and then there was silence except for the soft clicking of computer keys and telephones ringing in offices throughout the floor.

They came that evening, exactly at five-thirty. Somehow Sara had gotten through the day, meeting with a new client, calling the City of Chicago Office of Human Resources to say she needed a new secretary, searching within Donna's arcane filing system to find documents she needed, skipping lunch to rearrange files and respond to phone messages left on her tape. At home, she barely spoke to Donna or Ziggy; she had no patience or energy for them. It occurred to her that it was a blessing that everyone was out of the house for dinner, giving her a chance to calm down after Donna and Ziggy hauled the last batch of clothes, the new chair, and the television set upstairs to his car, and Donna slammed the key onto the kitchen counter after Sara asked for it, though even then (blessings seldom being unqualified), she was aware that the others were laughing at dinner while she was in a house that was painfully empty.

And so, feeling uncertain about almost everything—*wrong about Donna; wrong about others?*—she called Reuben.

Just to hear his voice. Just to share a few words, perhaps some that would give them a reason to laugh together.

But his wife answered and Sara, quickly furious, slammed down the phone. *Still there. Answering the telephone. Living with him, eating with him. Sleeping with him. Belonging.*

What could she have been thinking? He was a married man; he had a wife *in residence* and a life that had no room for Sara Elliott.

The interloper. The other woman. The homewrecker.

She would never call him again. He had said it himself, when he called her: he should not have put her in this position. She would not *be* in this position; she would not be humiliated.

She would not see him again. Or think of him. She was through with him.

"Goodness," said Ardis gaily, hanging up the telephone, "that must have been your other love. Or one of many?"

Reuben had been in the living room, and Ardis had raced to the study when the phone rang. "I told you not to answer the telephone in this house."

"Oh, Ben, of course I can answer the phone. I live here!"

"You are a visitor here." He wanted a drink, but ignored it; he owed her at least that much. He was not interested in the caller; since it could not have been Sara, it did not matter, and whoever it was would call back. He glanced at Ardis. She looked very pretty and very lost, swallowed up in a dark blue wing-backed chair, looking at him beseechingly, as a wayfarer might look, seeking the way home, the way to peace. "I can't give you what you want," Reuben said quietly, even sadly. "Too much has happened that can't be undone or forgotten."

He sat in a matching chair opposite her. A thermos of coffee was on the table between them, and he poured a cup for both of them. "You're going back to New York. Tomorrow, if we can get a ticket. You and I have nothing together anymore; you know that as well as I. You don't really want me; what you want is stability and security. But the only one who can give you those is yourself."

"Ben, no, I *love*—"

"You do not. And I don't love you. Whatever love we had has been gone for years; it is a farce to pretend anything else. I'm sorry for you, I have great admiration for what you are doing now—I'm sure it's the hardest thing you've ever done—but no two people can build a life on that. You have to build your own life; I am not going to do it for you."

"You're my husband! You have a responsibility to me!"

"I did. Not anymore. You killed all possibilities of it in a dozen ways. I am divorcing you, as I should have done years ago, and if you refuse to cooperate, it will be messy and end up hurting you much more than it does me. If we do it together, I'll be as generous as I can, and help you as much as I can, but if you fight me I will not do one damn thing more than I absolutely have to."

"It's that other woman—"

"I'm talking about us, about the end of our marriage. It has nothing to do with anyone else. It has to do with your life and my life, separate lives and how we shape them. I will no longer be part of your life and I will not have you in mine. I will not have you take part in anything I plan or arrange or think about, or regret. I want nothing to do with you."

"That's mean. You're a cruel man, Benny." She had shrunk back into the chair as if beaten down by hammer blows. "I tried so hard for you. I haven't had a drink—and it *hurts,* damn it. I've gone to hundreds of people for facials and hairstyling and massages and nutrition classes and exercises . . . even *yoga,* for God's sake. I've *worked hard,* to please you. And you haven't even noticed. I wanted this to work, and you don't care."

"No." He stood up. "I don't care. I agree with you: that's cruel. But it's the truth."

"*I don't want the truth!* What good is the truth if I can't have what I want? What good is it if I lose?" She took a breath. "I do love you, Benny, whatever you say. I want to live with you and sleep with you and cook for you and polish your shoes . . . whatever a good wife does. I haven't been a good wife, I know it, I know it, I know it, I know it . . ." She broke down in shuddering sobs. "But I would be, if you'd let me."

Reuben shook his head. "It's too late."

"Please, Benny, please, please give me a chance! Please . . . I can prove it to you, I can be everything you want. You wouldn't want anybody else, you'd have me." She thrust up her chin, suddenly defiant. "I'll start drinking again if you kick me out. It'll be your fault, *on your conscience!*"

"I'll live with it. If you throw your life away, the only one you can blame is yourself. I told you: what you make of yourself is up to you. I can't help you. If you get professional help, I'll pay for it, but that decision is in your hands; all the decisions from now on are in your hands. Not mine. Not ever again." He turned away. "I'm calling the airline; you'd better pack."

"I won't."

"Then I'll pack for you or send your things to you later. You choose. You have to get used to that."

"You're a monster. I hate you."

He nodded. "That's a good start."

She let out a piercing scream as he went to his study. *"Come back here!"*

He picked up the telephone, searching for the number in his file.

"I'll kill myself!"

He dialed the number and swiveled his chair away from the living room, ashamed of her, ashamed of himself.

"Damn you, damn you!" Ardis rushed into the library and snatched a stiletto letter opener from its holder. *"Monster! I hate you! I hate you!"* She stabbed at Reuben, embedding the blade in the leather chair a few inches from his neck. *"Oh, God!"* Sobbing, she wrenched it out to try again, but Reuben grabbed her wrist, twisting it, and she dropped the knife and crumpled. *"Oh God, oh God, oh God . . ."*

Reuben picked up the letter opener from

the floor. It was a replica of an Italian Renaissance stiletto, its handle worked in small gold houses. And it was a gift from Sara. How small a world we live in, Reuben thought hopelessly; we keep bumping into people, and, too often, hurting them.

He helped Ardis to her feet. "I'm sorry; I went too far. I let the worst of me take over. I'm sorry, Ardis; I am sorry."

She ignored him. Unsteady on her high heels, she tottered from the room. "I'll go pack." She paused. Over her shoulder, she said, "Can I keep the bracelet I bought that day downtown? I mean, it was your credit card . . ."

"Of course."

She brushed away her tears. "Just tell me what time the plane is, so I can be ready. You know, be at my best."

Reuben contemplated her for a long moment. His hand hovered above the telephone. And then he picked it up and deliberately punched in the number.

ELEVEN

Abby saw Sean coming toward her, and held her breath. She had not seen him all summer, and even before summer vacation, he had never even come near her. But today, the first day of school, with everyone milling about on the sidewalk and the wide steps leading up to the main entrance, he was there, he was walking in her direction, *and he was looking straight at her.* Abby felt dizzy, her breathing rapid and shallow. She had dreamed of this moment for months, but as the weeks passed without a telephone call or even a sighting of Sean's dark, hand-some face, she had sunk deeper into the bleakness of knowing it would never happen, that she would die old and unmarried, without ever feeling his arms around her again.

"How was your summer?" he asked casually, relaxed and—maybe?—a little amused at the expression on her face.

"Oh. Fine." She tried to stop a sneeze, but could not, then sneezed twice. "Something in the air," she said apologetically. "You know, I get . . . well, maybe you don't remember, but I'm allergic to something that's worse in the fall. It wasn't too bad this summer, I mean I was outside most of the time, I was a counselor at Doug's day camp, and . . ." Her voice ran down. "It was fine."

"Great. And now you're a senior. Happy to be getting out of this place, right?"

"No! I mean . . ." She tried to undo the fact that she had disagreed with him. "It'll be fine going to college, I'm excited about it, but . . ." Then honesty took over. "I *like* it here. I mean, I can be glad about college, but not in a hurry . . . Don't you like it here?"

He shrugged. "It's for kids. Which movie shall we see tonight?"

"Movie?" Abby clenched her fists. She had forgotten how Sean always made her feel

slow and inadequate, trailing a few steps behind him. But his voice made her shiver, and
his closeness was overwhelming; she felt
jumpy inside, and had to force herself to stay
still. "I can't. It's a weeknight."

"Sara still keeping the clamps on? You're a
senior; you're all grown up, *chonai croi*."

"What?"

"Gaelic for sweetheart. It's time you
learned a little Gaelic. Good for the soul. So,
which movie?"

Abby was in turmoil. "Couldn't we just go
for a walk or . . . something?"

There was a pause, then Sean shrugged.
"We'll walk over to Armitage; there's a new
bar I want to check out."

"I'm not twenty-one," Abby said faintly.

"I know that, you're still in high school. You
look it though, you could pass. Anyway,
you're close, right? Nineteen?"

Abby shook her head. "Not for . . ." She hesitated. Sean liked older women. "Four years
from September 20," she said miserably.

"Four years? Jesus, you're only—? Okay,
okay, forget it. We'll find some other place
tonight. A chocolate soda? What will it be?"

Abby laughed, relieved and wonderfully
happy. "A latte. With chocolate almond."

He shuddered. "The lady has exotic tastes. But . . . you got it. I'll be in front of your house at seven. Will you all be done with dinner?"

"No, but I can leave."

He nodded. "See you."

And that was all. But it was everything. They were together. Forever. The sun was shining, the world was beautiful. Abby danced into school with her classmates, smiling benevolently at everyone, loving them all, even the ones she had always disliked.

"It was wonderful," she said to Sara that evening, standing beside her in the kitchen, absently whisking tarragon sauce for the salmon. "It was wonderful to be back, my teachers are wonderful . . . it was wonderful."

"And what else happened?" asked Sara, smiling.

"What else?"

"To make it all so wonderful."

"Oh. Nothing special. Just being back." She whisked more vigorously. "Oh, I almost forgot. I'm going for a walk after dinner, with Sean."

Sara put the pan of potatoes into the bottom oven for browning, and stood still for a moment, her back to Abby. When she turned, she said, casually, "That's quite a change."

"I know. We started talking . . . oh, Sara, he's so wonderful." She whirled about the kitchen, once, twice, then threw her arms around Sara. "He is, you know, he's just . . . wonderful. And when he smiles . . . well, *you* know, you feel that way about Reuben. Oh, I'm sorry . . . I forgot you broke up. That must be awful; you were so happy with him. But anyway you know how I feel about Sean, you understand, you do, don't you? He's so . . . wonderful. When you know him better, you'll love him, too."

Briefly, Sara was amused by the self-absorption of almost-sixteen, but then Abby's words cut into her—*you feel that way about Reuben . . . you were so happy with him*—and she turned away until the pain receded. "Are you sure he's so wonderful, Abby? He hurt you so badly before."

Not wanting to be reminded, Abby turned back to the stove. "That was a long time ago. He's had a whole summer to think about it."

"Is that what he said?"

"Sure." Abby hated lying to Sara, but

sometimes Sara just forced her into it. "It was all so . . . natural. You know, like nothing had ever happened. He wanted to go to a movie, but I said I couldn't on a school night, so we decided to go for a walk, and he called me sweetheart. In Gaelic."

Sara was silent, worried but reluctant to push, held back by Abby's shining face.

"It's all right, isn't it?" Abby asked. "It's only a walk, you know, and ice cream or coffee or something; I won't be late."

"Yes, it's all right." Sara slid the pan of salmon into the upper oven. "But, Abby, please be cautious. Don't leap into a great romance; let it build slowly. If it's really good, it will last. If it's not, you'll know it before you get hurt, not after."

Look who's talking. What right have I to give advice about caution in a love affair?

The right of someone who was too trusting. Foolish. Even careless.

But learned her lesson.

Abby's face had tightened, the brightness was gone from her eyes. She doesn't believe a word I'm saying, Sara thought despairingly. I didn't handle it well. I didn't use the best words or the best timing or whatever would have convinced her, at least made her listen and maybe remember later on. But I don't know how to do that.

She looked at Abby's averted head, and suddenly felt drained and exhausted. *What could I have said to convince her? What would have been the right words? Oh, I am so tired of trying to be a real mother, and not knowing any tricks or secrets that would help. How do people ever learn them?*

But perhaps there was nothing she could have said that would make an impression on Abby. Would she have believed anyone who warned her to go slow with Reuben, not to be in such a hurry to go out with him, to think of him when they weren't together, to sleep with him?

I wouldn't have listened. I was sure of myself, and so is Abby.

And Abby could well be as wrong as I was.

She bent down to take the potatoes from the oven. "Just don't be too late."

"I *told* Sean I couldn't be late. I *know* that without being told. I *know* what time I have to get up for school."

Sara nodded. "Yes, you do. You're very good about that. Would you get Doug and Carrie? We're ready."

Unmollified, Abby stamped out, and, for

the first time that she could remember, Sara found herself dreading the time spent around the dinner table. But Doug carried them along on the ebullience of his chatter about the first day of school and his show, opening in three nights. "They're always on Friday, the artists' openings, and they have wine and stuff and everybody comes and lots of people buy, it's like a party, well, it *is* a party, you know, with everybody telling the artist how good he is and all that." He stuffed salmon in his mouth, the green tarragon sauce dribbling down his chin.

"Ugh," Carrie said, "you look like a demented creature from outer space."

Doug made a pass at his face with his napkin and lunged with his fork to spear potatoes. "Frank, that's the owner of the gallery, he says I'm the youngest artist he's ever had and he probably won't have another one like me for a long time if ever, but he's really cool, you know, he knows how to fix the lights so they show everything just right, and then he moves these little platform things around, you know, like pillars? And my pieces sit on them and the lights shine on them and it is so cool. They never looked that good in my room or at school."

"You'll be famous," Carrie said. She looked at her plate. "I guess I won't be, ever."

"You will," Doug said loyally. "You'll get your stories published. Mack *said.*"

"But he hasn't *done* anything. He was probably lying, just so I'd like him."

"You already like him."

"I know, but maybe not enough to satisfy him."

Sara gazed at Carrie, amazed, as often before, at the insights she dispensed so easily, probably unaware of how perceptive they were. But there was nothing she could say. She had been wrong about Mack's finding a gallery for Doug (how had he done that?); she could be wrong about his getting Carrie's stories published.

And then, once again, she would be on the outside, watching the two of them hang on Mack, as if he were not only big brother but father and friend . . .

Oh, stop it. You're just feeling sorry for yourself these days.

And that was what she reminded herself as she smiled and smiled during the opening of *Douglas Hayden Sculptures: New Works,* at the Franklin Stoaner Gallery on Friday evening, from 6:00 to 8:00 P.M.

Doug, wearing a new navy suit with a light blue shirt and red tie, grinned happily from his post beside the buffet of wine, cheese, and fruit, and drank one root beer after another. He sat on a painter's high stool, to look taller, and shook hands with everyone Frank Stoaner brought forward. They all seemed taken aback by his age, which Doug translated as amazement that anyone as young as he could do such brilliant work (that was what Frank and Mack said). Mack was wandering around the room—"circulating," he called it—and Doug kept looking his way, wishing he would stand next to him and help him talk to people. Lots of people stopped to talk, mostly the old ones, asking him how he worked and where he had studied.

"They talk to him like he's their kid," Carrie whispered to Sara, who nodded, amused but beginning to be worried, as she saw Doug looking more downcast each time the door opened and shut on people who left without buying anything.

Thirty pieces were arrayed about the large square room on white display stands: the terrified rabbit from their hike in Galena; the bear Doug had given his mother and retrieved just for his show; a group of dogs eating or leaping up to catch a thrown stick or curled up beside a pair of shoes; various other vaguely unidentifiable animals; and a dozen figures of children sitting at school desks, flying kites, eating ice-cream cones, making a bridge of LEGOs, racing with friends.

"Quite remarkable for a ten-year-old," Doug heard someone say. He scowled at him, a tall man with wavy hair standing a few feet away.

"Very nice," said the woman with him.

"He's got a future," the man went on. "Maybe we should buy one, while prices are low."

"Oh, Kurt, don't be silly. These are amateur."

"Harbingers of things to come," Kurt said stubbornly. "I want one."

"Fine. Buy it. But keep it in your office."

In the end, he did not buy anything. Doug watched them eagerly as they circled the gallery, then drooped in disappointment when they left.

Sara stood beside him. "What a good crowd. It's hard to get people to come out the last week in August; they're still doing summer things. But you brought them out, Doug; this is a real success."

"Nobody's buying anything."

"Maybe people don't buy on the first night. Maybe they look at everything and then go home and see where they might put pieces they liked."

Doug brightened. "Really?"

"That's what I'd do."

"Sara's right," Carrie said, having refilled her own root beer in the small kitchen. "Nobody spends money without thinking about it first."

"Everything okay here?" Mack appeared and surveyed Doug. "You look good, buddy, suit and tie, terrific. Manly, mannish, and mannified." He and Doug gave each other a high five. He kissed Sara on both cheeks. "Happy, sis? Great night for Doug; we're all happy, right? Right, Carrie?" He bent down and whispered in her ear, "You're next. Almost there. Prepare yourself for a starring role." He straightened and gave a mock salute to Doug. "Gotta go, my man. Couldn't miss this, though; great opening." He waved and cut a straight line to the door, stopping for a few words with Frank. And then he was gone.

But for all his grins and rapid talk, it seemed to Sara that he had been distracted: something else on his mind, nagging at him.

His words had seemed automatic, as if he had plugged himself in, given his little speech, then escaped. They had seen less of him at home lately, and she wondered if he was in trouble.

"Do you know what he said?" Carrie breathed to Sara. "He said I should prepare myself for a starring role." She giggled nervously. "It's my stories! He's getting them published!"

"Carrie, I really don't believe he—" Sara bit her lip. She had to stop this; she couldn't always be the one to throw cold water on their dreams. But then what? If she thought they were going to be hurt, wasn't it her responsibility at the very least to warn them, and at the most to try to prevent the pain?

How often? They're not with me all the time, in a few years they'll go to college, make their own lives; I can't possibly prevent every hurt they're going to have.

But I'd be an awful mother if I didn't try.

"We don't know what he meant," she said a little lamely, seeing Carrie's look harden.

"He said he was working on my career. I know what he meant."

An elderly man came up to Doug and shook his hand. "You're okay, young man.

Nice work. You have a long way to go: concentrate on proportion and scale, and developing your own style; most of what you're doing now is obviously derivative. You stick with it, though, and in a few years we could be hearing much more from you."

Doug was staring at him.

"Are you an expert?" Carrie demanded.

"Sort of," he said, smiling. "I'm a professor of art at Truman College."

Everyone fell silent. "Stick with it," the man said again, and smiled at them all before walking away.

"He didn't know what he was talking about," said Carrie.

"Proportion?" Doug asked. "Scale? Derivative? Mr. Albert never talked about those in class."

"I think those come a little later," Sara said gently. "But it doesn't change what you've accomplished here. Just enjoy tonight, Doug; don't let anyone take it away from you."

"Yeah." Doug sat up straight, then after a moment, slumped. "Abby didn't come."

"She wanted to," Carrie said. "But she's sick."

"She wasn't sick at dinner."

"She said she started feeling sick at dinner."

"Did she throw up?"

"How do I know?"

"If she didn't throw up, she's not sick."

"She could be! She could have . . . migraine or . . . sore throat or . . . gout."

"GOUT?"

"It's okay, Doug," said Sara, smiling. "Abby won't miss your show; she said she'd be here tomorrow or the next day."

"I know, but . . ." Doug's earlier glee in his starring role was gone. That professor was probably right; he didn't know anything about proportion and scale. He didn't even know what *derivative* meant. But Mack and Frank said his pieces were terrific. Then why didn't anybody buy anything? Nobody'd bought even one of his carvings. And, look, there weren't many people left in the gallery. They were supposed to stay from six to eight, but it wasn't even seven o'clock and most everybody had gone. And nobody was coming in. It was like everybody came, took a look, and that was that. Didn't they want to look some more? People in museums stood for hours in front of sculptures and paintings, and talked about them, and made notes, and listened to experts explaining things, and sometimes art students came and made copies of them. Why didn't anybody do that tonight? Didn't anybody *care*?

He hated them all. Especially that professor. They didn't know anything. They were really boring and dumb.

And this lousy tie made him feel like he was choking, and he just wanted to go home.

"I'm *glad* Abby didn't come," he muttered. "It's no fun here."

Sara kissed his forehead. "It's a very fine show, Doug; we're proud of you."

"She's probably somewhere where it's more fun."

"She's *sick*," said Carrie impatiently as Abby, miles away, thought, I feel sick. I feel awful.

She'd lied to Sara, and to Doug and Carrie. (And it was Doug's *show* tonight, and he *wanted* her there.) She had driven her car—against the law until next month, when she'd be sixteen, and certainly against Sara's rules—and now sat in it, parked a block from a small neighborhood bar, waiting for Sean and his friends.

"We'll just be a few minutes," he had said to her when they took their walk three nights before. They were eating chocolate sundaes and drinking lattes, and Sean was holding her hand, and Abby had not felt so happy as long as she could remember. "See, my little *chonai,* we've got to have money to send back home. The bastards are pounding the hell out of us—"

"Bastards? Us?"

"The wankers—Brit bastards—they're knocking us around. *Us,* our friends, our guys, *our side.* It's like a crisis; we've got to get them money, lots of it, they're out of it until we do. And that's what we promised when we came here, that they could count on us."

"Why do they need money?" Abby asked. "If they don't have enough to eat, we could collect food and send it—"

He gave a snort of contemptuous laughter, and her heart sank, knowing how stupid she must sound. He didn't mean food; he meant guns. She knew that, she just didn't want to think that Sean was sending money for guns to kill people.

"What are you going to do?" she asked.

Sean played with her fingers. "It's not such a big deal. There's a bar we know, does a big business on Friday afternoons, people come in early, like getting a head start on the weekend. They come in around four, by seven the place clears out, doesn't get busy again until nine or ten. *And they all pay cash.* No credit cards. Isn't that beautiful?"

Abby pulled her hand back. "You're going to rob them."

"Not the people, *chonai,* just the bar, after everyone's gone."

"But it isn't a *bar.* It's a person. Somebody owns it. Somebody tries to earn a living in it."

"What is this, a sermon? Look, this isn't hurting anybody. Whoever it is, he's got insurance, he'll get his money back, he'll be fine; we'll all be fine. Anyway, it's nobody you know; why are you worried about him?"

"Because . . ." Helplessly, Abby shook her head. "Because he's a *person.*"

"Abby," he said, and she looked up at the uncommon note of pleading in his voice. "The guys over there, they're desperate. Do you know how brutal the police are in this thing? They're not like the police here, you know, *they're* the murderers: they torture people and starve them, they threaten their families, their *kids.* They're the real enemy; they're tearing Ireland apart, and all we want is a peaceful country, one country, everybody happy. Wouldn't you want that, too, if it was your country?"

"Yes, of course, but . . ."

He waited. When she said nothing more, he said, "Some of the guys are my family, Abby. You know, cousins. I can't let them down. They're fighting for a grand cause, to get rid of an invader and take back their own country for their children, for the future. It's *our* country, Abby, shouldn't we decide how it's run? Isn't that the American way?"

"Yes, but you're talking about *robbing* somebody."

"In a greater cause. The cause of freedom. And saving the lives of millions of young people who are trying to throw off the yoke of the invader. Abby, look." He leaned forward and took her hand in both of his. "You won't have to do much. I just need you to drive us near the place and then wait for us. When we come back, you drive us home. That's it. You wouldn't be doing anything wrong, just driving some friends home. Nobody knows you; you'll be absolutely safe. *You won't be doing anything wrong.* You'll just be helping us. Me. And"—he kissed her hand—"I'll be forever grateful."

So Abby had agreed. She could have told him it was wrong to be the driver for people who committed a robbery, but she did not.

He kissed her hand and looked at her with his smile that melted her, and she thought of the awful months just past when there was no Sean, and she melted.

But now, sitting in her car on a quiet street, pale gray and sad looking beneath low clouds, she felt sick and lonely. She should be with Doug and her family right now, helping them, showing Doug she loved him. She did love him. But she loved Sean, and she was here, and there was no one she could talk to about how awful she felt. Only Sean, and he didn't want to know she felt awful and, anyway, she was helping him be a criminal.

Which made her a criminal. We won't like each other after this, she thought. And then, in a moment of clarity, she added, At least *I* won't like either of us.

She looked at her watch. Five minutes past seven. They said they'd be back by seven. Nearby, a man came out of a garage, pulled by a dog on a leash. Abby shrank back, trying to be invisible. The man lurched toward her as the impatient dog strained forward. Then, at last, the dog pulled him across the street and they moved slowly away, so slowly—did the dog have to stop at *every* tree?—until they turned a corner and were gone. Abby looked at her watch. Eight past seven. Lights were going on in the houses on each side of the street; instead of getting darker, it seemed to Abby the street grew brighter by the minute. She looked at her watch. Ten past seven.

The wail of an alarm cut through the silence, and shouts, and the clatter of running feet as the shouts grew louder. Frozen, Abby stared ahead, and so did not see Sean until he had opened the front door and flung himself inside. "Drive!" he shouted. "Get the fuck out of here!"

Panicked, she said, "But the others—"

"DRIVE!"

She pulled from the curb, pausing to look back to see if any cars were coming (she saw Sean's friends running, flinging their arms high, screaming at her to stop), and Sean, enraged, snarled, "Fucking cunt, *move.*"

Abby gasped in shock. Her foot slammed the accelerator to the floor and the car leaped forward, crossing the street. It rode over the curb onto the grass and careened toward a neat stucco house with green awnings. Abby saw a child in the window, his mouth opened in fear, and that roused her: she wrenched the steering wheel to the right and jerked her foot from the accelerator to stand on the brake pedal. The car skidded across someone's front lawn and through a flower bed, crossed a sidewalk, and was bouncing off the curb when the left fender crashed into a towering maple tree, sending its leaves spinning down onto the rattling hood and window.

The air bag exploded from its compartment, ramming Abby backward, crushing the air from her chest. She heard bones snap and then her own wheezing as she gasped for breath. The air bag was already deflating, and as the pressure eased, pain shot through her arm, up into her shoulder and neck, down to her fingertips, and her whole body began to shake. She saw the falling leaves and knew she was not dead, but she hurt everywhere, and her breathing scraped loudly through her chest and throat. She felt cold and hollow, fading in and out of consciousness, knowing that everything was over; nothing would ever be the same. She turned her head to Sean, but he was not there. His door was open; the seat where he

had sat, snarling at her, just a few minutes
before was empty.

People came from everywhere. They ran
to the car, slipping in the mud of the tire
tracks, and tried to open the door to reach
Abby. But the edge of the door was
smashed, and several men went to the open
door on the other side and one of them
reached in to grasp her arm. She screamed
at the pain, and she and the man looked at
the odd angle of her arm and elbow. "Broke,"
he said. "You'll have to scooch over, sweetie,
can you do that?"

She stared at him. He was fading, like a
scene in a movie, and then everything was
black.

The house was dark when Sara and Carrie and Doug returned, and Carrie ran upstairs to tell Abby about Doug's show. In a
minute she was back. "She's not upstairs.
Where could she—"

"Wait," Sara said. She was listening to the
taped telephone messages, and a woman's
voice asking her to call the emergency room
at Northwestern Memorial Hospital.

"She's not in her room?" Sara asked tightly,
dialing the number the woman had given.

"No." Carrie looked frightened. "What happened?"

"I don't know."

A nurse answered. "Mrs. Elliott, Abby's been in an automobile accident; she's all right, but she's in shock and has a broken arm, and is asking for you. How soon can you be here?"

"Right away." Picking up her purse and keys, she said to Carrie, "Abby's been in a car accident. I want you and Doug to stay here; I'll call as soon as I know anything."

"Is she going to *die*?"

"The nurse said she's all right. I'll call—"

"Why can't we go? Sara, we have to be with Abby!"

Sara nodded. Of course they did. "Okay, get Doug, we're going now."

"Doug!" Carrie yelled, and Doug dragged himself to the stairs, gloomy over the failure of his show, until Carrie told him what had happened, and then he raced with her and Sara to the car.

Carrie looked back at the house as they drove away—their solid, steady house looking the way it always did. Please don't let anything change, she prayed. Please keep everything the same, our family, our house, where we belong. I love Abby. Please don't let anything happen to Abby.

Abby began to cry when she saw Sara. "I'm sorry," she sobbed. "Sara, it was terrible, it's the end of everything, I'm sorry, I'm sorry, I'm—"

"Hush," Sara said softly. She closed the curtains encircling the bed and pulled up a straight-backed chair. Abby's arm was in a cast—"multiple fractures of the bones in her upper arm," the doctor had said—her other hand lay on the coverlet and Sara held it. "Carrie and Doug are here; we just want you to be all right. The doctor told me you'll be fine; it's just your arm and some nasty bruises, and they'll heal quickly. We can talk about what happened later."

"No! You don't understand! The police are looking for me. They're going to arrest me and I'll go to jail and it's the end of everything." Her sobs rose in a crescendo of wailing, her shaking made the bed creak, and Sara (thinking, Jail? What is she talking about?) flung the curtains apart, looking for help.

"Just a little shot," said a nurse, appearing around the edge of the curtain. "Can't have her thrashing about, you know. She'll be fine; your daughter is a brave girl, Mrs. Elliott, didn't cry at all until you got here and she just couldn't hold it in anymore. She certainly relies on you. Thanks for coming so soon."

But I had no choice. There never was a choice when it came to the children. For hours she had not thought of Reuben or anything else; she wondered now if he ever could have had a place in her life. *It's better that it ended. I don't have any room for him.*

But . . . jail? Was Abby delirious? No. Upset and frightened, but not delirious. Police. Jail. What had she—

And then it struck her and her thoughts switched to a new danger. Abby had been driving. In her car.

She had assumed it had been a friend's car. But obviously not. Abby had been the driver. Without a license. And not sixteen.

But police don't put youngsters in jail for driving before their sixteenth birthday. There are punishments, but not jail.

Unless she wasn't alone.

Of course she wasn't alone. That was the point. She was with someone, and they were doing . . . what? Something that meant jail if they were caught.

But the doctor had said Abby was alone in the car. Which meant whoever had been with

her had fled before anyone arrived. Someone who didn't care about her, didn't mind
hurting her (or if she was hurt), and ran off.
Someone who cared only about . . . himself.

Sean.

Abby was lying still now, turned away,
staring at the wall.

Sara took a chance. "Abby, why was Sean
with you in your car?"

Abby's head jerked around on the pillow,
her shocked eyes meeting Sara's. "How did
you know that? Did you see him? Did he tell
you? Or did the others tell you? Or did they
tell the police? Are they all talking about me?"

"As far as I know, no one is talking about
you." Sara's fear was growing and she tried
to keep her voice steady. "I haven't heard
anything about the others. All I care about is
you. If you're worried about being arrested,
I need to know why." Abby turned back to
the wall. "Abby, look at me. *Look at me!*"
She waited until their eyes met again. "This
isn't a game; you're smart enough to know
that. If you're worried about jail, then what
Sean and his friends did was a crime, and
you provided a car, I assume to get there
and to get away. In other words, you're an
accomplice, and you need help, and I want

to help you but I can't do anything unless I know what they were doing. Abby," she said urgently into the silence. "What were they doing?"

Abby rolled her head back and forth on the pillow. "I can't tell you. I can't be the one to get them caught."

"Why not?"

"Because I . . . Everybody would know about it. They know Sean and I got together again and . . . Sara, *we don't tell on each other!*"

"Even for serious crimes? Even when you've been betrayed?" Abby flinched, but Sara was angry now. "He abandoned you. He didn't care whether or not you were hurt, or dead; he didn't care if the police arrested you; all he cared about was himself. Why would you care about him? Is he worth protecting?" She waited. "Abby, do you still love him?"

The silence stretched out. "No." Abby looked at Sara wonderingly. "I guess I don't even like him anymore."

Sara sighed. "Then tell me what he was doing."

Abby told her, from the time Sean had first talked about the robbery to his lighthearted wave as he and his friends got out of her car,

"See you in a few minutes, *chonai*. Seven o'clock. Keep the car running." She could not tell Sara what he said when she did not move quickly enough, words so crude she was shocked into ramming down the accelerator. She would never repeat those words to anyone.

When she finished, Sara said, "Did they rob the bar?"

"I don't know. I heard sirens, and lots of shouting, and then Sean was jumping into the car and yelling at me . . ."

"Empty-handed?"

"What? Oh. I don't remember. Maybe . . ." She closed her eyes; she didn't really want to think about it, ever again, but Sara was trying to help. "It happened so fast . . . I don't think he was carrying anything."

"Did any of them have guns?"

Abby's eyes widened. "I don't know."

"But you didn't hear any shots."

Once again Abby squeezed her eyes shut. "No." She shook her head firmly. "Everything was so quiet, a man was walking his dog but he turned the corner and it was quiet, and then there were the sirens, and shouting. But . . . I don't really know what a shot sounds like, Sara."

"Popping, firecrackers, maybe. Anything like that?"

"No. Definitely not."

"Of course, you might have been too far away." Sara sighed again. "We don't know if they shot anyone. Killed anyone. If they did . . ." *Abby would be in very great trouble, and how much could I do to help her?*

A nurse parted the curtains around the bed. "Mrs. Elliott, Abby's brother and sister are very anxious to see her. It's fine with us if you and Abby agree."

"Abby?" Sara asked. "They're very worried about you."

Abby nodded, and started crying again. "They'll hate me for lying, and not coming to Doug's show, and . . . everything."

"They'll love you the same way they always do."

And they did love her; they were all over her, kissing and hugging her, and sitting on the edge of her bed until she winced with the pain from her arm and her bruises, and they moved to the chairs Sara had pulled up. Sara stood watching them. The nurse said Abby could be home that night, if she continued to improve, and then they would all be together again, in their house, feeling protected and safe. But until they knew what Sean had done, they were not safe. So far, the hospital officials had kept the police from Abby, but as soon as she was home, they would come to question her, and then Sara would find out what happened. A robbery, or a murder.

The police were on the doorstep early the next morning. Abby, with a sleeping pill, had slept all night, but Sara had been tense and wakeful, and met the police at the front door feeling groggy. So it was that when Abby came downstairs in a workout suit, her arm in a sling, and the police seemed gentle, almost sympathetic, Sara felt dazed, even disoriented. Wake up, she told herself; if this is a trick, I have to be prepared.

"How old are you, Abby?"

"Fifteen," Abby said after a moment's hesitation. "Sixteen next month."

He nodded. *Officer Pinder,* Sara read on his badge. Midforties, short and plump, balding. If he had not been in uniform, he would have looked like a salesman in suits or ties at Saks. "Been driving long?"

"Just . . . just this year."

"Enjoy it?"

"What?"

"You like to drive?"

"Oh. I guess. I mean . . . yes."

"And your friends ask you to take them places?"

"No! I mean, sometimes but not usually, because . . ." She took a deep breath. "They know I don't have a license."

"Right. But this was special, last night?"

Abby's eyes, red and swollen, filled with tears.

Officer Ryan, gray-haired, stooping, said, "I have a daughter your age, Megan, her name is. Junior in high school, pretty and smart and popular, but you know she's got a guy she's nuts about and sometimes she just forgets everything else. Me and her mother, her family, her friends, school, doesn't matter what, this guy is all she thinks about, and she's afraid to say anything or do anything that might make him mad."

No one said anything. "What *I* think," Officer Ryan went on conversationally, "is that Megan's a lot smarter than this creep and she knows what's right and wrong, and if she disagrees with him and he gets mad it's because he wants to do what he wants to do and the hell with Megan and what *she knows* is right, but she's got this thing about romance and she's afraid to lose it 'cause she might never get it again. Silly, isn't it? Pretty girl, smart, young, lots of good guys out there waiting to meet her. She'll figure that out one of these days; I just hope she dumps the guy before she gets in trouble because of him. Such a shame if she did; her whole life in front of her and all."

There was a long, exhausted silence. Officer Pinder wrote something in his notebook, then looked at Abby expectantly, waiting for an answer to his question.

Sara stretched her hand toward Abby, then took it back. This was not a time when she could do anything. Abby was on her own.

"So," Officer Pinder said at last, "let's say last night was special. For you and your friends. And how many friends were in the car with you? Like, maybe—"

"SARA!" Carrie shouted, and came dashing down the stairs into the living room. "Sara, look!" She shoved a thin magazine in Sara's face. "My stories! *Three* stories! They've been *published*!"

Mack and Doug were behind her; Mack was grinning widely. "Great writers always get pub—" He saw the police and stopped cold.

"Sara, say something!" Carrie cried.

Mack took a step backward, then another, looking everywhere but at the officers, who had glanced at him briefly, but now looked at him again, noting his reverse course with interest.

Sara stood and put her arm around Carrie. "It's wonderful and I want to hear all about it, but—"

"Why are the police here?" asked Carrie in alarm as she became aware of them.

"To talk about Abby's accident. This is Carrie and Doug Hayden," she said to the police, "Abby's sister and brother. And her older brother, Mack Hayden," she added, gesturing toward Mack, suddenly furiously angry with him . . . *for what? What has he done?* But she was too angry to sort out reasons; she could barely contain herself. "We'll talk about this later, but right now I want you all upstairs, Carrie, Doug, Mack . . . all of you. *Upstairs.*"

But Mack already had backed his way to the entrance hall. "Gotta get to work, guys," he called. "I'm late. Back for dinner." They heard the front door open and close.

"Didn't like the company," observed Officer Pinder mildly. He looked at Sara. "Any reason for that?"

"Not that I know of," she said shortly. "Carrie, Doug, I told you, I want you upstairs. We'll talk later."

"Why is Mack going to work on Saturday?" asked Doug.

"I don't know and I don't care!" exclaimed Sara in exasperation. "How many times—"

"Come on, Doug, they don't want us here," Carrie said gravely. The excitement, even the alarm over the police, had drained from her face. Her body slumped. Quietly, she laid the magazine on the table beside Sara, and put her hand on Doug's shoulder to turn him to the entrance hall and the stairs.

Sara, ashamed, said, "Carrie, I'll read your stories as soon as I can. I'll come upstairs when we're finished here. I'm very excited for you."

"Okay," Carrie said, and she and Doug went up the stairs.

"So, Abby," said Officer Pinder after a brief pause, "we were talking about how many friends were in the car with you. Four, maybe?"

Abby had been looking at her lap the whole time. Now she looked up, her eyes wide in surprise. "Yes," she whispered.

"And maybe there was somebody special, a guy maybe, in front with you?"

She looked at him as if he were a magician. Slowly, she nodded.

"And where were they going?"

"To a bar." Her voice was dull, without volition.

"To a bar."

Abby gave up. She looked at Sara, sitting near her, and said, "There's too much . . ." Finally, as the silence became unbearable, she said, "They were going to rob it and send the money to their friends in Ireland because they're having trouble and need help."

"Help in killing the Brits," said Officer Ryan.

"Occupiers . . ." Abby said weakly.

"Sure. Only murder doesn't get you very far, does it?"

Abby began to tremble. "Did they . . . did . . . any of them . . . ?"

"Kill anybody? No. Lucky."

"Sara asked me if they . . . if they carried . . . you know."

"A gun. One of 'em did. Sean didn't. Lucky again. For him."

"How did you know his name?" Sara asked.

"We picked him up," said Officer Pinder. "Got all four of 'em. Couldn't get far without a car and driver. That's why they wanted Abby."

"Didn't care about her, though," said Officer Ryan, shaking his head. "Didn't give a damn—sorry, Abby—what happened to her. Bad scene."

"When did you get them?" Sara asked.

"Right after Abby crashed the car. Three of 'em were runnin' down the street hollerin' like a tribe of Indians, and we found Sean a couple blocks away tryin' to flag down a cab. Amateurs."

Sara, angry again, said, "So you knew all this. You put a fifteen-year-old child through a grilling after she's had a terrible accident, and been injured and frightened, and still may be in shock, but you put her through—"

"We had to, you know," said Officer Ryan, not unkindly. "Make sure all the stories match."

Sara stopped and thought for a minute. Through her grogginess, she knew he was right. Her anger faded, and she was able to think about what was even more important. She looked at Abby and smiled, telling her silently that no one would think she gave Sean away; he had been arrested before she even got to the hospital. As dangerous as Sara felt Abby's code of loyalty to be, at least as an unconditional principle, she knew it was bedrock serious to those in high school, and since Abby had not betrayed anyone, it would be easier for her to get past this, get over Sean, return to her circle of friends, regain confidence in herself.

"What *did* they do?" Abby asked, her voice steadier now.

Officer Ryan snorted. "Not much. Scared the hell—sorry, Abby—out of the bartender; he ducked behind the bar, and when three of the kids jumped the bar and started beating him up he managed to get to the alarm switch. The kid with the gun never used it, lucky for him, they got the hell—sorry, Abby—out of there and took off for your car. Sean hadn't been behind the bar, so he was ahead of the others. Stupid, you know. There was a lot of money but it was all in the safe and it was armed; as soon as he opened it without disarming it, the alarm would have gone off. Amateurs." He snorted again.

"Attempted robbery, though," Officer Pinder said. "It'd be worse if they'd used guns, but still there'll be a price to pay."

In a small voice, Abby said, "For me, too?"

"Well, sure," Officer Ryan said. "Driving without a license, that's a violation punishable by a fine. You shoulda learned that in driver's ed, right?"

Abby, as if mesmerized, nodded without taking her eyes off him.

"Not a misdemeanor, though," he went on, "so it's a fine, not jail. Unless you skip showing up in court. Not a good idea. My advice, get a lawyer. Somebody to come with you to court. See, this ticket"—he produced a book of tickets from his pocket—"has a *you must appear.* Got that? And we'll write in a date. You show up for that, Abby, you'll probably get a lecture, a fine, I don't know how much, and then you're okay. Just don't do it again."

"But," Abby said haltingly, her voice low. "I drove . . . I mean, they were committing a *crime.*"

"Right. But maybe you didn't know what they were going to do. Why would they tell you? Guys don't trust girls to keep their mouths shut. Right?"

"But Sean did—" Abby caught Sara's sharp look and the quick shake of her head. "Oh." She was silent. She hated to say that anyone didn't trust her to keep a secret; everybody did trust her. But this time was different; she could see that. "I just gave them a ride?" She had meant to say it straight out, but it came out as a question.

"Sounds like it to me," Officer Ryan said. "Sounds like they went off and left you alone, and you didn't see them anymore, so you didn't know what they were doing. Worst I can see, driving without a license, damage to private property, nobody killed."

Sara held out her hand to the officers. "I'm sorry I was angry."

They all shook hands gravely. "Tough time all around," said Officer Ryan.

"Be okay now," said Officer Pinder to Abby. "Long as you're a little more choosy picking your boyfriends," said Officer Ryan with a wink.

"And it'd be smart not to drive again, even with your permit, until you get that driver's license," said Officer Pinder, picking up his hat.

When they were gone, Sara dropped back into her chair, drained and exhausted. Abby sat on a hassock beside her. "Sara, I'm sorry, Sara, I'm so sorry, I'm always saying that, I do so many things wrong. You're so wonderful to me, but I mess everything up. I'm ruining your life, I'm a cross you have to bear, like the albatross in 'The Ancient

Mariner,' I don't know how you can ever forgive me but I'll make it up to you, I promise, I'll figure out a way . . . *Sara!*"

Sara was laughing, a kind of wild laughter that shocked both of them. "It's okay, sweetheart," she said, calming down. "I'm not laughing at you."

I'm not laughing at anyone, she thought, it was hearing Abby exaggerate her apology, sounding exactly like Reuben. He always smiled when I told him he was doing that. Oh, damn, damn, Reuben, I miss you.

She laid her hand on Abby's bowed head and stroked her hair. "The one you've really let down is yourself, sweetheart. You have a good mind and you know how to use it, but you decided to ignore all that; you thought you were in love, so everything else seemed irrelevant. Abby, look at me." She waited until Abby looked up. "When you're sure something is right or wrong, and love tells you the opposite, something is wrong with the love, not with what you believe. It's a poor kind of love that demands that you diminish yourself by giving up what you believe. If you remember that, you'll have learned the most important lesson from all this."

She kissed Abby on both cheeks, and

stood up. "I'm going out for a while. Please tell Carrie and Doug they can come out of their rooms now; they probably feel as if I banished them. Come to think of it, that's exactly what I did. You can tell them everything is all right now."

"Where are you going?"

"Just for a drive. No place special, just . . ."

"Away. From all the problems I caused."

"Abby, don't start that again. Think about what I said. Take care of Carrie and Doug. Take a hot bath. Make pizza for lunch. My cell phone is on if you need me."

"We won't call you. You need lots of time to yourself."

Sara gave a small laugh, and kissed her. "I love you and I'm sure you'll be fine."

In the car, she drove without planning, winding through neighborhoods, content to be slowed down by stoplights and stop signs, rather than turning onto a highway. *If you don't know where you're going, it doesn't matter how long it takes to get there.*

Her thoughts drifted over everything that had happened since Doug's show, not even twenty-four hours, but seeming infinitely longer. Now, retrospectively, she wondered how she had gotten through it all with that stony determination that almost eliminated emotion. Did all parents somehow manage to switch to a kind of autopilot in dealing with crises, and then, when quiet returned, suddenly feel flooded by exhaustion and anxiety, unshed tears and a silent scream that too much was going on and there was absolutely no room or energy for one more problem?

But there had been room, and energy; she had handled it. And pretty well, she thought, with pride as well as wonder. Better than one might have expected from—to use Officer Ryan's word—an amateur.

Maybe I'm getting used to turmoil, she thought wryly, seeing a kaleidoscope of images of all that had happened over the spring and summer: Mack, Donna, Pussy Corcoran, Donna's husband, Ziggy, Abby's car, Carrie's leather journal, Doug's show, Abby's accident. And Reuben. All through spring and summer: Reuben. And of course, Reuben's wife.

Suddenly, she remembered Carrie. She had left without congratulating her, without reading her stories, without paying any attention to her at all. *I'll read your stories as soon as I can. I'll come upstairs when we're finished here. I'm very excited for you.*

She was at a stoplight. Carrie, I'm sorry, she thought. I really am sorry. I just had to get away and I totally forgot . . . What a rotten excuse. But it's the only one I have. I'll make it up to you when I get back.

"There's too much . . ." Abby had whispered to her. Too much, too much, Sara echoed in her thoughts: too much, and it was all running away from her. She couldn't understand it. They had had such an ordinary life; now it seemed to be spinning out of control, too complicated, too swiftly moving for her to feel she could connect with it, much less somehow have control over any of it. Did this happen to other people? Could any ordinary life become tumultuous and bewildering? Or had she done something wrong, leaving her family open to miscalculations and events piling on each other until they became problems, even crises, that seemed almost too much to comprehend or manage?

Foolish, she thought, but foolish or not it was real. *Mother would say I need a vacation.* She smiled to herself. *Probably. It's been a long time. Well, for today, this drive is my vacation: away from everything for a while.*

But not entirely. At some point she had taken an entrance ramp to an expressway, and now she realized she was in an area faintly familiar. Her gasoline gauge was low and she left the expressway, stopping at the first station, looking for the name of a town as she filled the tank. There was none that she could see, which did not bother her since she had no destination, and, driving on, she turned corners through neighborhoods, piqued by their familiarity, until she came to a chain-link fence and knew exactly where she was even before she saw the construction sign and a road sign pointing to the nearby town of River Bend.

She had not been here since the weekend they had driven to Galena and witnessed the first demonstration. The land inside the fence had not changed; no work had been done on Carrano Village West. *But how could it? Someone is preventing it.*

She found the opening in the fence where she and Reuben had walked onto the property, and, leaving her car, followed the same unmarked path into the fields. The grasses had lost the fresh green of May and were turning September sere and brittle, but flowers still bloomed among them, autumn flowers now, spikes of intense reds and yellows and purple luminous in the long rays of the early-afternoon sun.

Sara found the tree where they had picnicked, and sat against it in speckled sun and shade, her eyes closed. There were no sounds but birdsongs and the buzzing of flies and bees industrious in the foliage. After her sleepless night, she dozed and woke and dozed, her thoughts untethered but lighting here and there like the birds calling to each other above her. Things to do: help Abby recover from betrayal and loss of friends, and her own mistakes; bolster Doug in his disappointments over his show and help him focus on schoolwork and enjoying his art in each of its stages; support Carrie in her ambitions whether or not the magazine she had been carrying that morning was genuine; talk to Mack and somehow resolve the questions she had about him, and her growing discomfort with him. And go to work Monday morning and deal coolly and efficiently with demanding clients about whom she didn't give a damn.

And then her thoughts swung back to the center, as always, back to Reuben. *I miss you. I want to talk to you about everything that's happening; I want to know what you're doing, what you're thinking, if you think of me, if you miss me.*

If she's still there. If she always will be. If you're trying to be free.

I want to help you; I want you to help me. I want to love you. I want you to love me. I want your arms around me, mine around you, our bodies . . .

I don't want to do everything alone.

She dozed, and when she woke again she knew from the angle of the sun that it was getting late and she had to leave. Besides, she was hungry: she had not eaten since nibbling cheese and crackers the night before, at Doug's show.

In her car, she started the engine, then sat for a moment, looking back at the pristine fields. A shame to dig them up for houses and shops, but it was Reuben's dream, and she believed him when he said he would preserve as much of it as he could: broad, untouched spaces where people could sit against a tree with birdsongs above them, and dream and find a calm center, a sense

of balance, before returning to whatever turmoil awaited them beyond this place.

She drove to the corner and was waiting
to turn when a car drove past her and
stopped at the opening in the fence where
she had parked. Curious, she watched in her
rearview mirror as a group of men emerged.
Three of the men unrolled large blue sheets
of paper and flattened them on the hood of
the car, holding down the corners. The fourth
man was Lew Corcoran.

The men bent over the sheets of paper.
Now and then one would turn and gesture
toward the fields behind them, sketching in
the air. One man took pictures. Another
made notes on the papers before them as
they went through them. When one of the
men held the sheets vertically, Sara saw
blue lines, cross-hatching, and long lines of
type, with a logo, unidentifiable from this distance, in the lower right-hand corner.

Blueprints, she thought.

Lew Corcoran and blueprints. Lew Corcoran in real estate.

Mack.

*Corcoran Enterprises. Not exactly origi-
nal, but nobody asked me . . .*

. . . a big operator with lots of opportuni-

ties for a go-getter . . . There's big money in real estate . . .

The man next to Corcoran was looking at her car. Corcoran could recognize it, Sara thought (but didn't all Swedish cars look alike?), and drove away, turning the corner. She drove slowly, trying to remember the last time they had driven away from River Bend, with Abby, Doug, and Carrie in the backseat. Reuben had been talking about the demonstration they had left behind, about his interview with a woman, Charlotte something. *". . . There was a phrase she said she liked—meaning she'd heard it from someone else—about too many different kinds of people coming in. She said they'd destructively destroy a decent town . . . an odd phrase."*

And Carrie had said, *"That's the way Mack talks."*

What had the people in River Bend said to Reuben when he asked who was organizing the marches?

The kid.

Sara felt sick. She had never been able to trust him as, ideally, a sister would trust a brother, but she had let herself be lulled by his smooth words and smiles, the earnestness in his voice each time he said he wanted to be part of their family, and the affection he showed Abby and Carrie and Doug. (And how much easier to be lulled when she had wanted to be with Reuben; she could not let herself forget that.)

But her instincts had been right. He was not trustworthy. He had come to them not out of loneliness or love or a desire to belong; he had come because he needed a comfortable (and safe?) place to stay. Or, perhaps, to hide.

She had to talk to him and somehow he had to leave. She could not trust him in her house. She could not trust him with three young people who looked up to him (except when they didn't: *He can be really mean, Sara; I mean, we love him, but sometimes . . .*) and whom he had co-opted with gifts and storytelling and the air of a visiting uncle who offers play times and presents but none of the hassle of discipline or limits.

I'll talk to him when I get home, she thought. We are not going on like this, not one more day. He'll have to find another place to stay; I don't care where he goes, as long as he leaves.

But first she had to tell Reuben. He had

been fighting shadows since the demonstrations began, over two months ago; now she could give him information he could use to find out what was happening.

How can I call him? What if she answers?

She drove another mile, then another, until she was almost at the expressway.

It did not matter. She had to tell him. He had to know.

She turned into a side street and pulled over, to call him. His taped voice answered. At that familiar resonance, Sara flushed, her whole body responding as if he had touched her. Not now, not now, she told herself; just get this over with.

"Reuben, it's Sara," she said, her voice calm, neutral. "I've found out that Lew Corcoran has visited the Carrano Village site with blueprints. I don't know anything more, but I thought he might be behind the demonstrations and, maybe, the vote in the River Bend City Council." She hesitated. "I hope this helps," she added.

She could not tell him about Mack. *My brother has been organizing marches against you, trying to sabotage your project . . .* She was not sure of it (she felt quite sure but had no proof) and she owed it to Mack to confront him first (she felt she owed him nothing, but, still, she had no proof). More crucial, she felt, irrationally, that it was a weakness in her that her brother was a person she could neither admire nor trust, that it seemed he was working to undermine everything Reuben was trying to achieve. *My brother has been organizing marches against you . . .*

Someday Reuben would learn this. Most likely he would learn it when he investigated Corcoran. But Sara could not tell him.

As if she were still on the telephone, she could hear his voice, mundane words asking a caller to leave a message, a warm, intense voice that had settled deep within her. She started the car and drove onto the expressway, staying in the slower right lane, thinking how oddly like a mirage the road looked when seen through a film of tears.

TWELVE

Mack went to see his mother.

He went unannounced, and stood in the doorway, observing her as she read. He was shocked and confused by how much she had aged, her lined face accentuated in the bright sunlight. She felt his presence and looked up, and even Mack, who was not fanciful or poetic, felt the air freeze.

Abruptly, Tess reached toward a button on the wall. "Don't, please don't," Mack said. "I just want to talk for a while." He flashed a warm smile. "It's been a long time since I've been able to talk to my mother." He walked into the room, vaguely aware of its bright colors and luxurious fabrics, and sat in an armchair close to Tess. His smile thinned when she flinched, her finger still hovering near the wall button, and he pushed the chair a few inches back. "Is that better? I know you don't want me too close, but is this okay? I just want to talk, you know, talk to my mother, can't we do that?"

Slowly, Tess withdrew her hand. She closed her book, but kept her swivel table across her lap, like a barrier, and looked at him steadily. It was always difficult to read Tess's face, with one side paralyzed and the other often trembling or slack, but Mack did not know that; he saw only immobility, which he interpreted as stubborn anger.

He shook his head sadly. "You can't let go, can you? Still mad at me. God, that's so hard to take. My mother still mad at me. Still, yet, and always. From the fucking day I was born." Tess's good hand clenched, and because Mack had no understanding of her, and therefore could not know how desperately she was working to control her muscles and frantic heartbeat, he saw only further proof of anger. But the moments dragged on and she did not speak, and he began to realize that Sara and the kids had been right. His mother was locked in silence: she could not talk, and writing was so difficult she seldom resorted to it. Surrounded by a world of sound, she was condemned to do nothing but listen.

"Wordless in the midst of wordy wordiness," Mack muttered, not realizing how broadly he had begun to smile. He let out his breath and settled back. "You look very pretty, very *élégante* as Sara used to say when she was showing off her French. But then, you always did. My friends always said I had the prettiest mother of all. They envied me, did you know that? Told me how lucky I was. And I never said a word about the hell of my life at home. Why would I? I liked being envied. I guess they'd still envy me, since you're still so pretty. And you have a pretty room. Great colors. Did Sara do it for you?" He waited until Tess gave a small nod. "Good for Sara. Sara the good. Sara the perfect. Always doing the right thing. I grew up jealous of her, you know. My big sister, the anointed favorite."

A shadow that might have been a frown appeared on one side of Tess's face. "Sure she was. The perfect daughter, the firstborn, and for seven adorable years the only child.

Until I came along. You'd think you would have hailed me, you know, a son, the first kid with the new husband, beginning of a new life . . . and you know what?" He leaned forward, his voice dropping slightly to confidentiality. "I kept waiting for it. I kept waiting to be hailed, the prince of the household, the hope of the future, but it never happened. Because I wasn't anything like Sara, perfect Sara. *Sara* never got into trouble with the cops, *Sara* never flunked a course in school—shit, she never even got a B—*Sara* never came home drunk, Sara never borrowed money from her mother's purse, *Sara* never swore at her parents, not even once. What *did* Sara do, you might ask?" He shrugged. "Truth to tell, not much. That is, not much worth noticing. Which meant, to her parents, she took first prize."

He sat back, slowly shaking his head as if in wonderment. "Did it ever occur to you and my father that maybe I couldn't be like Sara, even if I wanted to? That I was made of different stuff? You know, I don't think it did. I think you two really thought you could turn me into Sara Number Two. You didn't love me the way I was; you'd only love me if I changed. That hurt, you know; it made me feel like shit. Which is what you thought about me anyway. I wasn't worth shit. I guess you still feel that way."

Restlessly, he stood up, saw Tess's hand reach for the button on the wall, and said quickly, "Sorry, truly, Ma, I'm sorry. I get carried away sometimes." Once again he flashed his warm smile, his blue eyes bright and crinkly, his face alive with humor and affection, suddenly handsome and boyish. He came back to the chair, shifting to find a way to relax. "Ma, listen, I came to talk, to be happy, not to have an argument. I just want to sit here and kind of figure out where we are. A lot's happened, you know, so much . . ."

His voice trailed away and for a moment he contemplated Tess's expressionless face. "All I ever wanted," he said at last, his voice low and intimate, "was to be first. I *was* your first kid with the name Hayden—let's not forget that Sara's an *Elliott*—and also the first son. *The first son,* Ma, you remember what the Bible says about first sons? They're first in everything. But how could I be first when Sara was around? I was always second, always going to be second. I cannot begin to tell you how I hated that."

He paused, then his smile burst forth. "But it's okay, you know, I've gotten over it, I don't even think about it anymore. Except, I come home after three years, ready to forgive and forget, because I'm lonely—you know?— wanting a family, wanting a home, *and my own mother won't let me see her.* The kids see my mother; *Sara* sees my mother. But not me. Now I'm in *fifth* place, behind everybody else. So there I was, in my house, in my old room, but still lonely. And nobody cared."

He scowled, as if sensing there was something wrong with that. "Well, what I mean is, of course I wasn't really *lonely.* I mean, I had the kids, and sweet Sara, a family, you know, but not my mother. Not my ma. The one I came home for. And I was so happy when Sara finally said you wanted to see me; I was almost crying, I was so happy. But whenever I tried to set a time, you'd say not yet. *Not yet.* Like a knife, every time you said that. *Not yet.* Like, what were you afraid of? That I'd come charging in and attack you because I was still mad at you? I'm not, Christ, I don't have time for that, I'm too busy. Busy," he repeated, and nodded at his mother, his smile flashing again, like a neon sign on a dark street. "A busy fellow."

He crossed and recrossed his legs, thinking for the first time that maybe it wasn't so
wonderful talking to someone who was
locked in silence. It was beginning to get on
his nerves. He needed some feedback. "The
thing is," he said at last, a small tremor in his
voice, "I never could figure you out, you
know? The two of you. I always thought parents are supposed to forgive their kids when
things go wrong: you know, endless love and
forgiveness. No judging. Parents don't judge,
right? But that wasn't you two. I used to sit
up there in my room and wait for you to
come up, for my father to come up, and give
me some sympathy. But you know what he'd
do? Knock on the door and ask me if he
could come in, that we had lots of things to
talk about. We didn't have anything to talk
about! I didn't need a lecture, I needed a father who would understand me, understand
that I was *not happy.* Did you think I *liked* being hauled around by the cops? Sitting in
those fucking police stations until you or my
father came and bailed me out, and hearing
the cops talk about me the whole time? One
of 'em called me a walking train wreck—I
never forgot that—and I told him he was an
asshole for mixing his metaphors and he

knocked me around. Nobody cared, so *he knocked me around.*"

He glared at Tess, willing her to answer him, enraged at her silence, enraged that, even capable of speech, she might have chosen silence anyway, because that was what she used to do: refuse to answer him when he swore at her or demanded to know why she said he could not do whatever he wanted to do. He bared his teeth and enjoyed seeing her wince. "I always wanted to tell you about the fucking cops knocking me around every time they hauled me in. You know why I didn't? Because one day you wrote me a letter. I don't suppose you remember, but it burned a hole in me. Christ, you could have come upstairs to my room— I said you could, remember? Anytime you wanted anything, you knew where to find me. I didn't hold it against you that we fought all the time—I didn't like it, but I didn't hold grudges—you and my father were the champions at that—anytime you wanted to talk to me you knew where to find me."

He stared at her, waiting for some sign, some signal that she wanted to defend herself. "Don't throw it up to me that I wouldn't let my father in—I did once, but he didn't have a clue what I needed; why would I do it more than once?—don't throw that up to me. I would have let you in anytime. Anytime you wanted to make me feel better, feel taken care of. That's what mothers are for, for Christ's sake! I didn't want you to tell me what I was doing wrong, I knew things weren't right, I just needed somebody to make me feel safe."

He flexed his fingers. "So you wrote me a stinking letter. Remember what you said? *Love ends.* You wrote that to your own son. Shit, I hadn't done one fucking thing to you or my father; everything I did was to other people. And then the last time the police hauled me in, for knocking off that 7-Eleven, you said you'd hire me a lawyer and then decide what you'd do with me. *Hire me a lawyer.* Criminals need lawyers; not high school kids who have parents to take care of them! I was *sixteen years old* and you said I was incorrigible. You know what incorrigible means? Incurable! Hopeless! So . . . what? It was the trash heap for me, right? That's where shit goes: to the trash heap. That's where I went: a month in that hellhole. Juvenile detention center. That was supposed to make me feel good?"

Tears squeezed into his eyes. "You were supposed to forgive me. Keep the front door open, give me a safe place. I called my father when I was in that hellhole—he ever tell you this?—and told him it was his fault I had to knock places off—he never gave me enough money—and if some people got hurt along the way, it wasn't my fault, things just got out of control sometimes. I explained it all, so he'd understand and get me out of there. You know what he said? You'd tried to understand me, and couldn't. Who's fault was that? He was blaming me because you couldn't understand. I did my best; you failed. But I was the one in jail."

He looked past Tess, through the window, and his voice turned ruminative, talking to himself as much as to Tess. "I was so mad all the time. I was never *not* mad. I never once woke up thinking I had a great day ahead of me; I always woke up feeling like shit and remembering everything I was mad at. Head of the list, you and my father for ruining my life. You were so *primitive:* all you could think of was punishing me. Did you think you'd change me by grounding me, for Christ's sake? And taking things away from me—driving privileges, allowance, what the fuck, everything you could think of. Did you ever think that if you'd been *giving* me things I wouldn't have been mad and I wouldn't have had to find other ways to get money? Shit, I just wanted to live a normal life and be in control of it, but you kept a leash on me and you'd yank on it whenever my idea of normal didn't match yours. You didn't do drugs, you never drank anything harder than wine, you drove at the speed limit, or near it, you never lied or cheated or committed a crime, at least you never admitted it. So *you* were good and I was bad, which meant incorrigible. So finally you wrote me a letter. Saying *love dies.* Or was it *love ends*? One or the other. Was that supposed to make me turn over a new leaf, a Sara-leaf? Sara gets mad at people, too, you know, she has a hell of a temper, she's just better at hiding it than I am."

He was so wound up that he leaped from his chair, not even noticing whether Tess reached for the button again, and strode to the window, then the doorway, then back to his chair, plunging his clenched hands in his pockets. "I cornered my father one day, he was coming home from job hunting, at least that's where he said he was—he ever tell you this?—I jumped in his car when he pulled into the garage, and we sat there and I told him he was a fucking failure as a father, as a *man,* couldn't get a job and support his family—Christ, first he was fired, then he went looking, *he said,* for a year, probably spent his time in bars or whorehouses. I told him he couldn't face the world, couldn't take care of his kids, probably couldn't even fuck his wife anymore. A total fucked-up failure at everything. So what did he do, the fucker? Ran away. Just up and left, walked out on all of us, no note, no phone call, no nothing. All I wanted was a father who'd be proud of me and help me when I needed it, and he ran off. Fucking coward."

There was a long silence. Tess's eyes, had Mack paid enough attention to notice, were icy. She had not collapsed, as she had when Doug let slip the news of Mack's return; this time she kept a visible grip on herself, muscles rigid, eyes locked on Mack, the good half of her mouth a tight line.

Mack's face lit in a smile and he came back to the armchair. "But, hey, look, we shouldn't be talking about this. You're so pretty, you know, and it's great that you're fine, sitting up and all, we shouldn't be arguing, or even talking about unpleasant stuff. I don't know how we got on the subject. Truth is, I don't think about all that anymore. I'm too busy conquering the world. I'll bet you don't believe I can do that. Not a lot of faith in Mack the Knife, right? Sara called me that once, she tell you that? That was after what's-his-name, the pharmacist I accidentally stabbed. I mean, it was an accident, and she knew it, and she said she was sorry, but it's like telling a jury to ignore something; shit, the words are out there, you can't just pretend you never heard them."

He shook his head in wonder. "She didn't understand me, either. You know how easy it is to hurt people? It doesn't take hardly anything, I mean, it doesn't feel like you're doing anything, you've barely moved, but you've . . ." He glanced at Tess, then away. "What I mean is, it's too easy; it ought to be harder. If people knew how easy it is, they'd be a lot nicer."

There was a long silence as Mack pondered it. Then he looked up brightly. "So, shall I tell you how I'm conquering the world? I know you'd like to hear it; parents like to be proud of their kids. You told me lots of times you wanted to be proud of me. Then you had to say you couldn't be. Just had to get that in, didn't you? Well, anyway, so here's where I am. I've hooked up with this guy, better than my father, 'cause he likes me and knows how good I am, and he's got a lot of irons cooking, plenty of room for me to move higher. No limit, that's what he says."

Tess thrust her finger at Mack, once, then twice.

"What? How the hell am I supposed to know what that means? You think I'm a god-damn mind reader?"

She pushed her finger toward him again and again.

"You mean me? What about me? Oh, you mean what do I do for him?"

Tess lowered her hand, nodded slightly.

"How about that? I figured it out. Pretty good, huh? You wanna know what I *do* for him." He grinned his infectious grin, wide, eager, open, his blue eyes crinkling. "Maybe you're wondering if I'm his hit man." He laughed loudly. "He's in *real estate,* Ma. He buys and sells buildings. And builds build-ings. All over the world. I've seen more of the world working for Lew than you or my father ever did. Places you never even heard of, like you want to know what my favorite is? I even tell the kids stories about it, it's so weird. It's a goddamned rock in the middle of the ocean called Nauru, wide open, no regulations, everybody there happy to help you clean up your money." He cocked his head, looking at Tess. "You don't know what that means? Laundering? Well, leave it alone. It's not your kind of thing. I'll tell you what I'm doing now: you'll like this. Lew's been granted the license for a casino on the Fox River— you know where that is? Way the hell out in the boondocks west of here—that is, he'll have the license as soon as he shows them he has the land. It's the only license the legislature's gonna okay for the next five years, and it's just about in Lew's pocket. I'm working on getting the land; some other guys want it, but they'll drop out so we can build."

He grinned again, thinking his mother's immobility this time was amazement at his success. It was okay now that she couldn't talk; she was an audience that didn't ask questions or criticize. Maybe this was what people paid psychiatrists for. Mack sat back, voluble and expansive. "You wanna know how come the other guys are going to drop out? Lew fixed it. You gotta admire him, Ma, he knows how things work. How people

work. See, the county decided they'd approve a new development on that land if the
town next door annexed it. The town politicians have to vote on it, and Lew's helping
'em decide. How, you ask. There's ways of
convincing politicians: same way all over the
world. They always need money, and they
like to play in the big leagues. You live in a
rinky-dink town in the boondocks, how often
you get a chance to work with a guy like Lew
Corcoran? He helps 'em out with a little extra cash here and there—they don't pay
taxes on it, that helps, too— and they're
happy, so they vote against annexing the
land next door as long as the other guys
want to build on it. The other guys pick up
their marbles and go home and—voilà!—the
local politicos vote to annex as soon as Lew
has his license in his hot little hand. And we
build our casino, and guess who'll be running it? You got it: yours truly, Lew's right-
hand man."

He sat back, beaming. "You'll see it; I'll
take you there. It's a riverboat, you know,
that's what the license is for, only it'll be per-
manently docked, connected to a second
casino, offices, what all, onshore. You'll be
blown away, Ma, you won't believe it: these

huge gambling rooms, you can't see from one end to the other, and five or six restaurants, high-class, not hot-dog joints, and marble bathrooms, the works. Lew's a man of vision, and nobody gets in his way. You wanna be on his side."

Leaning forward again, elbows on his knees, he stared earnestly at his mother. "And you know what? When the money starts rolling in, I'm gonna take care of you. Better than Sara, better than anybody. You don't like the way you're treated here, I'll buy the whole fucking place and run it the way you want it. You want new clothes, I'll get all your favorite designers here so they can show what they can do for you, in your chair and all. You want to see the world, I'll buy a plane and a crew to take you wherever you want to go. All that money, Ma, I'll have everything I want, and whatever you want, I'll give it to you, everything your little heart desires. How about that? My father couldn't take care of you, but I can. How's that for a good son?"

He leaned back, stretching out his legs and crossing them at the ankles. "I can take care of everybody, my whole family. I'm already doing it, you know: you should see the kids; happy as clams. I got Doug a gallery show; he tell you about that? His cute little carvings all over the Franklin Stoaner Gallery, that's a legit place, you know, none of your amateur hole-in-the-wall galleries. He was—" Tess was pointing her finger again, stabbing it at him. "*Now* what?" He thought for a minute, then grinned. "You want to know how I did it? Pulled it off for a kid who couldn't carve his way out of a paper bag?" Tess slapped her hand on her table, the unexpected sound like a shot in the quiet room. "Hey, okay, okay. He's not terrible, matter of fact, he's pretty good, but he's a *kid,* we're not arguing that, right? Well, anyway, how did I get him a show. I called some people. You know, you get people who owe you things, you can do a lot. Frank and his partner, they own the gallery, they were a little behind in their payments, not so far, but a little bit, enough for me to remind them that deliveries could dry up anytime."

Tess's face was contorted as she tried to frown.

Mack grinned. "Anybody listening?" He made a show of looking under his chair. He was feeling happy and chatty. "Drugs, Ma, the lifeblood of suburban America. They come to the city for their weekly supply, or nice guys like me make deliveries. They get all kinds of deliveries out there, you know, groceries, newspapers, vitamins, medicines, UPS, FedEx, whatever they want. So I make deliveries; I'm part of the American way of life. It's like when I helped Lew with his mess with Pussy . . . oh, you don't know all that, do you? Not important, Ma, just one of the ways I make myself useful." He grinned. "Indispensable. Lew shoots his wife; I make it look like suicide. Frank and his friends are crawling up the walls for their delivery; I deliver. And I let 'em get behind in their payments, just enough so when I need 'em, they're there. That's just good business. So I needed a gallery for one night and Frank and his partner helped me out. Boy, was the kid happy; it made him love me. See? Good son, good brother; what more could any mother want to make her proud?"

"Mom!" Carrie cried, rushing in. Her face was flushed. She looked challengingly at Mack. "Were you supposed to be here?"

"And hello to you, too," Mack said gaily.

"What are you *doing* here?"

"Hey, can't a guy visit his ma? You're here; why not me?"

"Because . . ." She frowned deeply. "I thought Mom said she didn't want to see you."

"Mom can't *say* anything," Mack pointed out.

"She can, too! You shouldn't talk that way! She says lots of things; we understand her! And she writes things, too, don't you, Mom?" She went to Tess and kissed her on both cheeks. "How are you?"

Tess laid her hand along Carrie's face, then pointed to the magazine in her hand.

"That's what I came to tell you." She hesitated, unsure of what Mack's presence meant, and uncomfortable with the odd way he was looking at her. In fact, the whole room felt uncomfortable right now. But her mother didn't seem to be sick or fainting or anything like she was when Doug made that awful mistake. So maybe everything was okay. "I got published!" she said, perching on the arm of Tess's chair. She laid the magazine on Tess's table and opened it. Then, through her discomfort, honesty made her say, "Mack did it. Remember I told you he promised? Well . . . he did. See, look. This one's mine, and this one, and the next one. Three in a row!" Her excitement returned as she talked. "And my name! In print! Carrie Hayden, three times!"

Tess put her good hand on Carrie's, then slowly turned pages in the magazine. They were thin, almost transparent, and the type seemed to fade in and out, making the letters look as if they were different sizes. The cover was blue paper, a little heavier than the inside pages, and on it was printed in large black letters, NEW STORIES. Tess opened the first page, and then the second; there was no masthead, no listing of publisher or editor or staff, and no copyright information. At the bottom of the second page was a name, MH Publishers, and a post office box in Chicago. On the next page, a table of contents listed six names in alphabetical order; Carrie's was the first. Tess flipped pages to the back of the magazine to find biographical information on the authors, but found only two more blank pages. There were just eight stories between two paper covers— three for Carrie, one for everyone else.

Tess turned the pages slowly, reading some of each, while Carrie beamed at the close attention her mother was giving them. "Isn't it wonderful?" she cried, jumping up. "Isn't it amazing? I mean, Mrs. Norton at school said I was too young to be published; Sara didn't believe I could, either. But Mack can do anything!"

Tess looked up and met Mack's eyes. His look had turned wary, his face closed. "I haven't had a chance to read it," he said flatly. "Carrie grabbed it. But she should," he added with a bright grin. "She's the author."

Tess was gazing at him steadily, and, abruptly, he stood. "Time to go, friends and neighbors. Duty calls." He turned to Carrie, as if a thought had just occurred to him. "I hope you weren't worried about interrupting us when you got here."

"What?"

"You might have worried about interrupting us and hung around out there, waiting to come in."

"Yes, but not very—" Caught off guard, Carrie stopped herself, knowing exactly what he was talking about. "No, I . . . came right in."

"Right in."

"Right. I mean, right in, right away." She giggled uncomfortably, wishing she didn't feel inadequate or guilty so often with Mack. "I mean, I wanted to talk to Mom, you know, that's all I wanted."

"No peeking through keyholes?" he pressed teasingly. "No listening at doorways?"

"No!" Desperate to feel better, to be happy with Mack again, Carrie turned and threw her arms around him. "Thank you for the magazine, thank you, thank you. I'll never forget it as long as I live. I'll make you proud of me, I promise. I'll write and write and someday I'll be famous and I'll tell people it was all because of you."

Taken aback, half turned from Tess's unwavering gaze, Mack dragged a hand across his face, wiping away the expression that had crossed it, like a shadow. Tess would never be sure whether it had been chagrin, as she first thought, or a trick of the light, but something had been there, and Carrie had seen it, too. Puzzled, unable to sort out everything that was going on, Carrie went back to perch on the arm of her mother's chair, frowning slightly at Mack, putting her arm protectively around Tess's shoulders. She felt strangely grown up, her mother small and vulnerable inside the curve of her arm.

Mack faced the two of them. "Two Harpies," he murmured.

"Two what?" Carrie asked.

"Beautiful women in Greek mythology. Loved by everybody as long as they behaved themselves." With a faint thread of his earlier grin, he waved over his shoulder as he left.

"He's strange, isn't he," Carrie observed. It was not a question.

Tess picked up her pencil and scrawled on her pad of paper, *Sara*.

"Hey, that was easier for you!" Carrie exclaimed. Her mother's hand seemed steadier than it had been in years. "You're getting better! I knew you would, I knew if we waited long enough—"

Almost impatiently, Tess tapped the word she had written.

"Oh, right. What about Sara? You want her now? Are you feeling sick again?" She jumped up. "I'll call her right away."

Tess put up her hand.

"You're not sick? You're okay? So, when do you want Sara? Tonight? Tomorrow?" She waited for a reply. "Well, I'll just tell her to come as soon as she can. Is that all right? I have to go home for dinner, and Sara can call and leave a message at the desk about when she'll be here. Is that all right? I mean, are you sure you're all right? I mean, every-thing's *okay,* isn't it?"

When Tess gave a small nod, Carrie kissed her again and again. "Love you, *love you,*" she said, and ran outside to the bus stop.

"She wasn't *sick,*" she told Sara in the kitchen, helping make the salad. "But she wasn't *right,* either. She was writing better, but, you know, she was so *quiet.* I mean, she always is, but . . . oh, you know. And she wrote your name. I was kind of worried."

Sara turned off the stove. "This is done; I'm going over there. You take care of dinner for you and Doug; I'll eat when I get back."

"What about Abby?"

"She's taking a nap. I'll check on her later."

"She's always taking naps! What's *wrong* that she can't even be awake and part of our family? It's like she doesn't like us anymore. I mean, she didn't crack her *head* or any-thing in the accident, just her arm, so why is she acting crazy? I mean, it wasn't a *tragedy,* it was just an *accident* and nobody was killed or—"

"That's enough," Sara snapped. "I'm ashamed of you. It was more than just an ac-cident, it was everything with Sean, her own judgment, how she can face her friends, how she can face herself. And there's the fact that she doesn't have a car anymore, a small matter, really, but it's part of everything. Abby went through a lot, and it will take awhile for her to deal with it and understand it. What you can do is be nice to her when she's awake and let her work things out in her own way, and not decide whether she's being crazy or not."

"I'm *sorry,*" Carrie flung out. Then, more quietly: "I guess her arm hurts."

"Probably everything hurts, especially her thoughts. It's pretty painful, being ashamed of something you've done."

"But it wasn't *her* fault Sean wanted to rob a place and the man got hurt! And he wasn't killed; Sean's friends just hit him a few times. Abby wasn't even there!"

"She drove them there; she waited for them; she knew they'd be committing a robbery and had to get away in a hurry. She knew it was wrong even if she wasn't part of it, and she knew she shouldn't be there. She knew all that and just . . . went along."

"Because she was in love."

"Because she wasn't thinking clearly. I'm going, sweetheart, you take care of you and Doug; I'll be back as soon as I can. Oh, one more thing. Was Mother upset by anything that Mack said?"

"I don't know. Is Abby ever going back to school?"

"Of course she is. It's only been a few days; please, Carrie, don't worry so much. She's a strong person; she'll work this out. And if she wants our help, we're here. Did you hear anything Mack said to Mother?"

"No! I don't know anything! I couldn't hear anything!"

Sara studied her flushed face. "You heard something and you don't want to talk about it, right? Well, I don't want you to betray Mack, but I do need to know what might have upset Mother. Do you understand that?"

Carrie nodded.

"Nothing to tell me?"

She shook her head.

"I can find out from Mother, you know; it will just take longer and be a lot harder than if you tell me now."

"There wasn't anything," Carrie said loudly. "I mean, he said something about being a good son and a good brother and wouldn't Mom be proud of him, and he was smiling, like he was really happy. Except . . . later he wasn't, so much."

"Wasn't . . . ?"

"So happy."

"When was that?"

"Just before he left."

"And what happened just before he left?"

"Nothing, he just changed."

"But what was he doing? What was Mother doing?"

"She was reading my stories, turning the pages, reading a little bit, and she looked in the front and the back for kind of a long time, and then she looked at Mack for kind of a long time, and he looked at her."

"That's all?"

Carrie shrugged.

"And then he left?"

"He said he hadn't read the magazine 'cause I grabbed it first. And then he said he had to go; he called us friends and neighbors, which was pretty weird. And he left, and I stayed for a while, and . . . that's all."

"Okay. I'll be back soon." Sara kissed her, but she was furious. Damn him, damn him for upsetting everything he touched. How dare he visit their mother? Tess didn't want to see him; she wasn't ready to see him; who the hell did he think he was, barging in on her? And what was Carrie worried about? Or afraid of? She acted almost afraid. Damn him, couldn't he leave them alone? Couldn't he just leave?

"Are you all right?" she asked Tess as she walked into her room. "Carrie said Mack had been here; did he upset you?"

Tess pointed to the clock on the wall.

"I know it's dinnertime, but I wanted to see you first. *Are* you all right?"

Tess gave her half smile, and Sara sat down, holding her hand. "He upset you."

Tess shook her head slightly. She pointed to her pencil and Sara placed it in her fingers. Tess hesitated, then wrote, *frst.*

"First. You were upset at first? I don't blame you; he just showed up, without calling? Well, he does what he wants, doesn't he? But did he say what he wanted?"

Her mother wrote, and Sara, watching her, realized Carrie had been right: Tess's hand was steady, almost firm. Something had happened to give her the strength or the will to control her hand instead of giving in to weakness. And boredom, Sara thought, and frustration, helplessness, so many fears. But now it's as if she's more sure of herself, at least sure enough to try.

Mack, she thought. He was here and she's

fine. She endured. That might be it. Maybe, somehow, she even got the better of him.

Amazed, she watched Tess write *proud.*

"Proud? Of something he'd done? Or he wanted *you* to be proud. Is that right?" She waited for Tess's small nod. "So he told you how busy he is, and how successful, and all the things he's done for Doug and Carrie, and how much they love him. And he smiled and was charming. And if he talked about me it wasn't flattering."

Tess wrote again, *d, u, g.* She stopped, and then, forcing herself, wrote the whole word. *Drugs.*

Sara nodded. "I know." After smelling marijuana in his room his first day back, she had told Mack not to use drugs in the house, and he had said he would not. It was odd that Tess knew about it, but she could imagine Mack wanting to shock his mother, or prove to her that he could do whatever he wanted, with her out of the way.

"He's not a very nice person," she said, voicing it aloud for the first time. "At least, not all the time. Or maybe I just don't like him, or trust him, or both. He might be unhappy, inside, and I'm sure I should be nicer to him, but it's hard, for me at least. Maybe I'm not a nice enough person. Carrie and Doug like him, I think, at least most of the time. I don't know about Abby. Are you tired?"

In an instant Tess had changed: she had shrunk into her chair, drifting away, as if the effort of communicating, or thinking about Mack, left her exhausted and uninterested. As if she's gone back to giving up, Sara thought, angry because if Tess did give up, they would truly lose her. "You have to keep trying," she said, and let her anger show. "That's what keeps you alive. If you think I'm going to let you just decide to die, you're wrong. We can rethink that if things get a lot worse for you, but until then you're still our mother and we need you. And you need us, and we'll help you, but you have to keep trying."

Tess gazed at her. "We need you," Sara said again. "We need each other. Isn't that what a family is all about?" She waited until a slow smile lifted Tess's lips, and her eyes turned brighter.

Sara sighed. "Thank you. I love you, we all love you. And you're getting better; I can see it. Anybody who can take a visit from Mack without confusion is a true survivor. Now get some sleep; I'm going home. I'll stop by tomorrow, and we'll all come and take you someplace special for dinner." She kissed Tess on both cheeks. "I love you."

But perhaps I'm really not a nice person, she thought, driving home. I didn't help Pussy when she asked for it, and I never tried to understand why Donna lied so much, and I get angry at Mack for no obvious reason. Why in the world would I be angry at someone who does lovely things for Doug and Carrie and Abby? Maybe I'm jealous. Maybe I just don't want anyone interfering with me in bringing them up. Maybe I'm just being selfish.

And why was I in such a hurry to think of Reuben as some kind of villain? I never gave him a chance to explain anything.

Well, come on, how much room for explaining is there, when the wife you didn't know about shows up on the doorstep while you're in bed with her husband?

I can't answer that because I never tried to find out. I just walked out.

Well, but she was walking in.

And after that I never called.

He only called once, and didn't explain anything.

He said he was working on it, changing things.

Easy to say, isn't it? And you did call, after you'd seen Lew Corcoran at the Carrano Village site. And he never called to thank you. So you were right.

Or he was busy juggling complications in his life, trying to figure them out, but I was so angry (and hurt; I was hurt) I never even thought of that. From the minute his wife showed up, I stopped believing in him.

Narrow-minded. Judgmental. Mean.

Oh, cut it out, you're not that bad.

I hope I'm not, she thought, pulling into her garage and turning off the ignition. I really was hurt. I really did have reasons . . .

"How's Mom?" Carrie asked as Sara came into the kitchen.

"Fine. Tired, but I think okay. I told her we'd all visit her this weekend."

"Not Mack."

"No, not Mack."

"Hi, Sara," Abby said. She was sitting at the round breakfast-room table, a dinner plate before her, scraped clean.

Sara kissed her. "You look better."

"Carrie told me I should be, so I guess I am."

Sara swung on Carrie. "I thought I told you—"

"No, I *am,* Sara, really," Abby said. "It's okay. I'm not mad at Carrie. I mean, she said I was acting like a heroine in one of her stories, and if she wrote it that way, you'd say she was being overdramatic and she should tone it down. And she's sort of right, you know. I mean, I feel really awful, but . . . dinner was good," she finished lamely.

Sara broke into laughter. Either she was too protective of Abby or not protective enough of Reuben—

"Oh, by the way, Reuben called," said Carrie casually. "He said he'd call back about ten."

Sara caught her breath. After thrashing around about him in the car, she had no idea what she thought now—of him or herself—and how could she talk to him until she knew what she thought? Having doubts about herself and her behavior did not mean she suddenly trusted him again, or could dismiss or excuse what she still saw as dishonesty and fabrication. She was not even sure if she really wanted to.

If she wanted to? Of course she wanted to; she missed him every day with an intensity that did not fade with time, but only deepened. Why would she lie to herself?

She wanted to be with him. Now. Tomorrow. Next year. All the years.

But still she could not imagine how they would begin. Two hours to mull it over, she thought, but, in fact, snatching her own dinner, talking to Abby and helping Carrie and Doug with homework left her no time to mull anything, and she was folding laundry in her bedroom when he called, exactly at ten.

"Sara, I couldn't come to you until I'd closed some chapters of my life. I've wanted to call to thank you for—are you well?"

She gave a small laugh, almost overcome at the impact of his voice. "Yes, thank you."

"And your family?"

"Yes."

"I think about them. And you. There is so much to explain, to ask you to understand, and forgive—" He stopped, and they let the silence stretch out. "Thank you for your message about Corcoran," he said at last. "It helped us look in new directions. I want to tell you about it. There is so much for us to talk about."

"A world to talk about," Sara murmured.

"And time. If you'll believe that."

If I can believe it.

"Sara, you'll know everything; I promise

you that. But not on the telephone; I want us to be together. Will you give me that much?"

She closed her eyes. His voice wound around her; she felt its weight, its solidness like a great cape, and wondered if she had been cold all the weeks since she had left his house. "Yes," she said.

"Thank you." He turned almost formal, and Sara remembered he had done that on his first telephone call, months ago, when he invited her to dinner. There is a time for emotion, she thought. We are not there yet. "I have to be in New York next week," he said, "just for a day or two. Is there a way you could come with me?"

"I don't know." She wanted to. This, too, she understood, that if they were to find each other again, it would be best to make a beginning away from everything here: work, responsibilities, the reverberations from their last night together.

She could take a day or two from work; she had vacation time accrued, and nothing urgent was on her desk; early September was always a quiet time.

But she had never left the three of them when she traveled. (But—it suddenly struck her—she had not traveled. Since moving back home, she had not left Chicago. Three and a half years of work and family: her job, the four of them together, the house, and, increasingly as Abby could take charge, the attractions of the city.)

Now, nearly sixteen, Abby could take charge for more than an evening. The three of them would be in school all day, and alone for only one night. Yes, Abby could do it, but, in the throes of recovering from her own conflicts, she was not in the best shape right now for taking responsibility.

Mack, Sara thought, but immediately rejected it.

"I'll try," she said at last. "What day are you going?"

"Monday morning. We could be back Tuesday afternoon."

"I should know by tomorrow." She thought about saying *I want to,* and then, whether it was wise or not, she said, "I want to."

"Thank you for that." There was nothing else to say, and everything, and, caught between those two poles, they were silent.

"I'll call you," Sara said at last, and Reuben had to leave it at that. He sat still for a moment in the silence of his library, a hushed enclave cut off from the sounds of the city, cursing himself for the mistakes he had made: his willful blindness in marrying Ardis, his childish clinging to illusions about their marriage, his defensive determination to skate on the surface of relationships from then on, avoiding any chance of anguish, even anxiety.

I would not have done that in my work. He knew that absolutely: he would have identified his mistakes and figured out ways to avoid making them in the future, reorganized and forged ahead in a direction holding more promise than the last. *I would not have given up, crawled whimpering into a hole, denying even the possibility of commitment. I would not have put a person I valued—loved—into a position of humiliation and pain. Idiot. How long does it take a man to grow up?*

Oh, come on, he thought. I'm not that bad. He could see Sara smiling at him. *Exaggerating again.*

He paced from the library through the living room, dining room, kitchen, sunroom. When he reached his study, he put on a CD of a piano sonata he had, in his teens, tried to master. *I never told Sara I studied piano for fifteen years, played in a jazz trio in col-*

lege, still play now and then. I never told her so many things. And there is so much I don't know about her. If I hadn't been so stupid, we would have had all this time to get to know—

Give it a rest, he ordered himself. There's a luxury in self-abnegation and I don't deserve that.

He laughed aloud. It was hard to give up the wallowing pleasures of self-pity. Sara would understand that; they could laugh about it together.

He wrote an e-mail for his travel agent to read first thing the next morning, to book two plane tickets to New York on Monday, returning late afternoon Tuesday. He could cancel them, if necessary, but writing the instructions made it seem a fact that Sara would be with him. He had two meetings scheduled in Manhattan, but he would keep them short. The rest of the time would be theirs.

He gazed unseeing at his bookshelves, imagining Sara in his bedroom in the pale wash of light from a single lamp, her head on his shoulder, her warm body within the circle of his arm, her skin, like his, cooling after lovemaking, her hand on his heart, her breathing slowing, matching his.

He could not remember ever wanting anything as much as he wanted Sara Elliott in his life, interwoven with his life, inseparable from his life. More than anything he wanted to know that they would begin and end their days together, their separate lives merging seamlessly into their shared life, their voices entwined as, together, they managed their worlds, the small, immediate one, the larger, more complex one.

He went to work: an antidote to dreaming, to flailing oneself for mistakes, even to reciting a litany of resolutions for improvement.

At his desk he reviewed what he and Isaiah had learned so far: Corcoran Enterprises, owned by a company in New York City in which Lew Corcoran was a minority shareholder, had obtained a provisional license from the Illinois State Legislature for a riverboat gambling casino on the Fox River, subject to obtaining an appropriate site. Sara's message had made it clear that Corcoran had chosen the Carrano Village site in River Bend: on the river, plenty of land for related businesses, perhaps even a shopping mall, and parking.

Everything else was a guess, though two conclusions seemed obvious: Corcoran was fomenting the demonstrations and letters to the newspapers that were preventing any progress on the village; and somehow he had influenced the River Bend City Council to delay action on annexation.

Somehow, Reuben thought sardonically. *Somehow,* in these cases, meant money: under-the-table gifts, contributions to political campaigns.

The problem was, he and Isaiah had no proof of any of this. There was no evidence that Corcoran had been in River Bend at the time of the demonstrations, or at any other time, except once, when Sara had seen him there. No one Reuben had interviewed in the town, or in neighboring towns, had mentioned Corcoran; they spoke only of "the kid," a mysterious manipulator whom, perhaps, Reuben had seen hovering in a grove of trees, vanishing when he saw Reuben looking his way. But even that was not clear.

Still, with what they had, they were moving ahead. Reuben was working on a brochure, a sheet of paper folded so that he had four sides. The front was complete: a photo of the property as it was now, wildflowers and grasses, the trees still green but a little faded in the shorter days of September, the stream that cut through the land a narrow ribbon of silver, and, in the distance, the sunlit gleam of the Fox River. Below the photo was one sentence, in bold letters: HOW DO YOU WANT THIS LAND TO LOOK TOMORROW?

Inside, on the left, the photo of the land had been altered with a computer-generated montage. The flowers and trees had vanished; in their place, a five-story riverboat casino was jammed against the banks of the Fox River, connected by an enclosed bridge to a sprawling casino and office building on-shore. The silver ribbon of stream was still there, alongside one of the asphalt parking lots surrounding the land-based casino on three sides. One of the lots stretched all the way to a long strip mall of shops near the highway. Reuben had taken the photo soon after he received Sara's message. It was a development called Casino Village, built ten years earlier on the Mississippi River, and it was busy twenty-four hours a day with gamblers from Iowa and Wisconsin, as well as Illinois.

A new definition of *village,* Reuben thought contemptuously as he sat at his computer placing Casino Village on what would be the village green of Carrano Village West.

On the right side of the brochure was a picture of Carrano Village as Isaiah's artist had drawn it for architects, engineers, and early investors: groups of houses separated by wide swaths of green space, with trees and bushes, flowers, ponds, a clubhouse and indoor sports center, a golf course, tennis courts, a swimming pool, playgrounds, and softball fields. In the distance, near the highway, were shops designed to look like gabled houses.

Beneath the picture of the casino, bold letters read: A LICENSE FOR A NEW ILLINOIS CASINO IS PENDING. COULD IT BE IN RIVER BEND?

Beneath the picture of Carrano Village, was the question: OR COULD RIVER BEND HAVE GREEN SPACE, LIGHT, AND AIR . . . AND *GOOD* NEIGHBORS?

Reuben was working on the text for the back page, a brief description of Carrano Village West, a very brief description of Casino Village on the Mississippi, and a paragraph comparing them, particularly how they fit in with their communities. He was checking to make sure he had made no accusations nor named any names, when the telephone rang. He looked at his watch—11:00 P.M.—and snatched it up, thinking it might be Sara, with an answer about their trip.

"Reuben, you're awake, right?" asked his lawyer in New York. "Not in the middle of a deliciously illicit moment?"

Reuben laughed. "Awake and working. Nothing illicit, delicious or otherwise. What's going on, Gus?"

"I just got off the phone with Ardis. I have been on the phone with Ardis since seven o'clock. In case your math is slow, let me tell you that this adds up to *five hours.* Unbearable in almost any circumstance; with this very angry lady it was torture. I am quadrupling my fee every hour I interact with your Ardis."

Not mine. Never mine, even when I thought I wanted her.

"Reuben? Have I stunned you into silence?"

"What does she want? She's accepted our offer."

"That was this morning. Since then, she's thought about it, agonized over it, she told me at length, and is now refusing it."

"She can't do that. We're signing the papers tomorrow."

"Not anymore. Not any-fucking-more, to use her exact words."

Reuben switched on the speakerphone

and was out of his chair, striding the length of the room and back, his anger building. "What does she want?"

"In a nutshell, more money. No, not a nutshell, a basket. No, a goddamn freight car. She wants a freight car full of money."

"She won't get it."

"How badly do you want this divorce?"

"I intend to get this divorce—haven't I made that clear?—but I don't intend to impoverish myself."

"Bravo. So how will you do that?"

Reuben picked up his letter opener. Sara had given it to him; Ardis had used it on him as a weapon. Our lives are filled with mixed messages, he thought wryly. "Gus, we made her an offer, a hell of a lot more generous than she deserves."

"What she deserves, according to her, is compensation for twenty-two years of love, devotion, homemaking, cherishing, support, encouragement, and . . . hold on, let me check my notes; I want to make sure I get this right. Yep, here it is: being forced to accede to sexual demands that verged on the bestial."

There was a long silence.

"Now, of course," Gus went on, "she can't

prove it. But neither can you prove it's a lie. In one day the lady found herself a new lawyer, and a clever one. I know him; he's good. A shark, but good."

Reuben's anger exploded. "How long can she drag this out?"

"Hey, don't yell at *me, I'm* not—"

"She keeps inventing new lies and ups the ante each time, is that it? For how long? Until—"

"Reuben! Hey, Reuben? Hold on, we know she's greedy, but we have to think of a—"

"—she's wiped me out, is that it? That's what's going on?"

"Don't kill the messenger," Gus said wearily. "I had five hours of Ardis yelling at me; I'm not up to another five hours with you."

"She agreed to our offer!" *And I called Sara to say I'd closed those chapters.*

"I know that. She knows that. Her lawyer knows that. She's got new ideas about those twenty-two years of devotion."

"She threw those years away." His fury was so great he flattened his voice to a monotone, to control it, even as he kept circling the room with seething energy. "She did what she wanted; she got what she wanted, from the time I married her, and she threw it away. She was a leech, sucking everything she could out of me, and it was all I could do to make a life with her hanging—"

"Okay, okay, I hear you. I don't need a litany of Ardis's bitchiness or the shambles of your marriage; I've known you for a long time, and I've seen it. It's not relevant now, Reuben, we've got to—"

"Relevant. Are you out of your mind? God-damn it, everything that happened between us is relevant." His hands were shaking. "She had three abortions without telling me. She knew I wanted children, we'd talked about—"

"Hold on, *hold on a minute*. Listen to me, damn it, is that true?"

"True? What the hell are you talking about? Why would I make up something like that?"

"You never told me."

"No." He stopped pacing. "The third one ended our marriage—well, in fact, the first one did, but I didn't leave until the third. I've never been able to talk about it. I thought . . ." He gestured helplessly. "I thought I wouldn't have to."

"Tied my hands, Reuben. It would have helped if I'd had this earlier tonight."

"You have it now."

"Okay, give me a minute to digest it."

His turbulent energy suddenly drained, Reuben sat in an armchair near his desk, hands clasped between his knees. He had called Sara because of the agreement this morning. He thought he had gone some distance, in a sane and accommodating way, to making up to Ardis for his harshness in the past, including the last time they had been together in this house. He had believed, with some self-satisfaction, that he had severed the bonds that had tethered him to his past. So much for self-satisfaction, he thought. It never goes unpunished.

On his feet again, at the bar in a corner of the room, he poured gin on ice and walked about the room, drinking. "Gus," he said at last to the speakerphone.

"Right. Okay, options. I always start with the one that requires the least work and the least expenditure for my client. Which means, the status quo. You support her but you don't have anything to do with her. She goes her way, you go yours. Married but not married."

"No."

"I didn't think so. Another lady?"

"I will not be married to Ardis. Under any circumstances."

"I understand that. But . . . another lady? Reuben, give me a break. I can't juggle blind; I need to have all the facts if you expect me to keep them up in the air. You just gave me something I can use after years of keeping it from me; give me another one."

"Yes."

"Yes there is another lady?"

"Yes."

"So that brings us to option two: How high do I go? Right now we're giving her the apartment she's living in, with the furnishings and art, seventy-five thousand a month, that's nine hundred thousand a year, for the rest of her life unless she remarries, in which case it's reduced in half to thirty-seven five a month. Generous but not lavish. She wants lavish. So how much higher do I go?"

It's only money; I can always make money. I want Sara; nothing else is important.

There is a limit to the money I can realistically expect to make. I don't build projects that maximize profits. I can't change everything I believe in to satisfy Ardis.

And I will not ask Sara to come to me if I cannot take care of her and her family in the way I want to take care of them. Three kids in college, for one thing . . .

He almost laughed. *Thinking like a parent already.*

"I have to know what she's asking," he said at last. "There's a limit."

"You want to tell me what the limit is?"

"Not now."

"That's supposed to be our negotiating position?"

"It's where I am right now. Gus, what the hell—"

"Okay. So, let's finish the options. Number three: I use the abortions. To a judge they might nullify the so-called bestial sexual demands, then we'd be back to our offer. And if she still balks, she could end up with a lot less. But, realistically, another judge might say she had no choice but to abort because she was impregnated in such unspeakable ways that she was sure the child would be deformed. Something like that; that's how her lawyer would play it, I think. But either way, my friend, it'd be about as ugly as you can imagine, and believe me you don't want that mess."

"What are the chances she'd turn it down if you threaten to make the abortions public?"

"Hard to tell. Lots of people get abortions these days; she might think it's a badge of honor, especially if she plays up her sexual victimhood. You know: 'I'd rather go through the pain and sorrow of an abortion than have the child of a bestial husband.'"

"You just said it would nullify so-called bestial—"

"I said it *might* nullify. Anyway, I have to think like her lawyer, that's one of the things you're paying me for. Okay, hold on." There was a pause. "Look, there's an option four, a Hail Mary, but in fact it works more often than you'd think. A testament to how nutty people can be. I call it the personal touch. It would cost you a little more money."

"Well?"

"Well, how about a charge account at Bergdorf's for five thousand a month, in perpetuity?"

"You're not serious."

"Actually, I am. True, it's peanuts when she's already got almost a million a year, but this is different. This is *personal*. The million doesn't say anything except that you're willing to pay it to get rid of her. Cold, legal, not exactly flattering. The sixty thousand at Bergdorf's says—and if she doesn't get it, I'll tell her—you know she's a beautiful woman, and even if you're not with her anymore you want her to look her best: sharp, glamorous, a head turner, on the cutting edge of fashion . . . *where she belongs.* You want that for her because you always admired the way she dressed and you know she deserves that. I know it doesn't make sense, but in a few cases it's been enough to tip the balance." He waited. "You following this, Reuben?"

"I'm depressed by this."

"Not surprising. You want to go with it?"

"That's it? Nothing bigger than that?"

"Not right now; let's give it a try. Look, she's not completely rational, therefore give her an irrational offer that's focused on her. It worked with my ex, with both of them, in fact. What the hell, it even worked with a guy I know; his wife, ex-wife, was my client and we offered him a practically unlimited supply of Armani suits for the rest of his life, and he bit. This is something that crosses all lines: gender, age, income. The personal touch. It could be the key to your future happiness. I hope she's terrific, your new lady."

"When will you offer this?"

"Tonight. Right now. I'm willing to bet she's

sitting by the phone, figuring I'm talking to you, waiting for some kind of miracle. Not drinking, though; did you know that? You have to hand it to her; the only thing she's done that I admire, and it's a big one. Maybe I'll get her together with the guy in the Armani suits, and they'll live happily well dressed ever after. *Is* she terrific, your new lady? You deserve it."

"Thanks. She is. Call me back."

"Right."

Reuben tried to work on the last paragraph of the text he had been writing—SHALL RIVER BEND HAVE OPEN SPACE, OR THE POSSIBILITY OF AN OPEN DOOR TO GAMBLING? SHALL THIS LAND BRING BENEFITS FOR THE COMMUNITY, OR POSSIBLE CAVALCADES OF POLLUTING BUSES BRINGING GAMBLERS WHOSE MONEY BENEFITS DISTANT OWNERS?—but he could not concentrate. He tried to picture Ardis sitting beside one of the telephones in her apartment—fifteen of them, because, she said, someone important might call her at any time—but he could not focus on her, either.

His thoughts swung, like the needle on a compass, to Sara, sitting beside him on the porch of the lodge in Galena; walking with him through the quiet, Victorian neighborhoods of Chicago; lingering over coffee in his kitchen on the rare occasions when she had been able to stay overnight; their first picnic; the last time they had made dinner together.

"You give me so many reasons to be grateful . . . companionship, friendship, understanding, being patient and sensitive with my family . . . wonderful sex, more wonderful than I ever imagined."

He shoved back his chair, fixed another drink, wandered from room to room, never far from a telephone.

If Gus's crazy idea did not work, he would have to call Sara and tell her he could not, in conscience, ask her to accompany him to New York. Nothing would be finished, and he could not predict when he would be able, finally, to say the chapters were closed. He had told her he would wait until then to come to her and he was not about to fudge that with caveats and excuses. He wondered if the past ever could be shed, or if it always hovered in the wings, butting in randomly on the present. *What was my hurry, that I called tonight, without waiting for signed papers, for the fact of divorce instead of the dream?*

He knew the answer. He was too impatient

to wait for certainty. Like a teenager, he thought, and remembered asking himself, earlier that evening, how long it takes a man to grow up.

Always longer than we'd like ... if we manage it at all.

(Of course, there might be another reason he could not see Sara on Monday, though he did not like to face it: the possibility that she could not get away. *One night,* he had thought impatiently when they were talking on the telephone, but he knew that childless Reuben Lister had no right to judge what Sara Elliott, responsible for three youngsters, could or could not manage.)

The telephone rang and he lunged for it. "Well?"

"She's turned cagey. Will you go to fifteen thousand a month?"

"That's more clothes than any one person can wear."

"Agreed. This has nothing to do with how often she changes her dress. She doesn't want you to like any of this. Be glad you don't have kids in the mix."

Reuben thought of the irony of that, and let it drop. "All right."

"All right for fifteen K?"

"Yes."

"Call you back."

This time it was only a few minutes. "Damn, Reuben, she's pretty tough. It must be being on the wagon; she's gotten stronger. She said she'd let me know tomorrow. The best I could do was tell her it had to be morning; the Bergdorf application in her name gets shredded at high noon. I still think she'll take it, but she keeps fooling me."

"It's not encouraging, hearing that from a lawyer."

Gus sighed. "I hope you don't use that tone of voice with anybody but me, and then only at midnight. Listen, she has a right to think about it; she may know it's as imbecilic as we do, but give her a chance to keep her dignity. I said I think she'll take it; it's only a few more hours. Reuben, go for a long walk by the lake; it's good for the soul. I'll call you tomorrow, as soon as I hear from her."

He went for a walk. A mist drifted over the park and the lakeshore, blurring the orange streetlights, turning the running path where he walked to a damp strip unrolling arrow straight through glistening grass. He could hear the lake, invisible in the mist, and he pictured waves washing over the rocks with long hisses and the sigh of retreat, punctuated with the cries of gulls. Zipping his leather jacket against the fog, he cut across the grass and climbed onto the square-cut boulders that lined the shore in stepped-down tiers to the water.

Once, Abby had told him she liked to sit on the rocks. "When I have a lot to think about, especially sad things, I like it there." He had wanted to ask her what sad things she thought about, but they were not yet close enough. And now might never be, he thought, frustrated and bitter. Ardis had had twenty-two years to stop drinking, to be strong, to keep her dignity; she chose now, when he finally had other plans. Consistent, he thought caustically; she never compromised anything to make room for me.

(How easy it would be to feel sorry for himself . . . and he did. Like a teenager, he thought again, and smiled ruefully. A lot of growing up still to do.)

He stood on the highest row of boulders and looked out at black water, whitecaps, long lines of waves breaking and curling over themselves. Fog drifted in long tendrils that muted the city lights around him and swallowed up the horizon. His life work was to transform space into livable communities while retaining a sense of space. Here in front of him was space that would be transformed by no one: self-defined, primitive, unconquerable. It was good to rediscover that: *there are only so many places we can conquer.*

But events were something else. Looking at the lake and the fuzzy outlines of Navy Pier to his right, its enormous Ferris wheel a ghostly circle in the haze, he made a mental list for tomorrow: finish the brochure, messenger it to a printer, and fax a copy to Isaiah in New York; set up an appointment with the mayors of River Bend and neighboring towns in the hope that community feeling soon would support them (breaking ground this fall instead of last spring, if they did get approval, which translated to more time and money, but at least it would be this year, not next), meet with the engineers and architects to revise the construction schedule; confirm a dinner reservation with friends for that night. And call Sara. It would be Saturday; she'd probably be home. He could walk from his house to hers; he'd never been inside it.

No. He stepped down from the boulders

and turned toward home. Of course he wouldn't walk to her house; they were not ready for that. A simple telephone call. To find out if she had arranged to go with him on Monday. Or to tell her . . .

Or to tell her the whole story with no neat conclusion. One way or another, whatever he heard from Gus in the morning, he would tell Sara everything that afternoon. He remembered the look on her face—dismay, humiliation, anger—when Ardis had appeared. If, tomorrow afternoon, he was still married and uncertain when Ardis would accept a settlement he could handle, why would Sara not think—correctly—that he had lied, or stretched the truth, when he called her to say he had closed those chapters in his life? Why would she not feel the same humiliation and anger as before? Or would her anger have faded, as it did so quickly the night the Corcorans came to their table at Spiaggia? Might she understand his struggle, and agree that two people who love each other could wait for some kind of settlement at some vague time in the future?

He knew Sara, but not well enough to answer with certainty.

But it did not matter; he would tell her the

story, in New York if possible, while Gus was writing the final divorce agreement, or in Chicago, where everything would be unknown.

Inside his front door, he hung his damp jacket on a coat tree to dry. He did not accept the second possibility. He focused on believing that he would call her tomorrow, midafternoon, when she would likely be home, to tell her he had their tickets for New York and would pick her up at nine o'clock Monday morning. Because of course by then she would have figured out how to leave her family, and Gus would have taken care of everything.

THIRTEEN

I'm thinking of going out of town," Sara said casually at breakfast. "Monday, just overnight. The problem is, Beth and Meg are both traveling, and Linda has her whole family visiting, so she can't stay with you. I thought I'd call—"

"No, no, no," Carrie said vehemently. "We don't need your friends, we can take care of ourselves. Anyway, we've got Abby."

"Abby is pretty wound up in herself these days; I don't think we can expect—"

"But we can take care of ourselves," Carrie broke in again, stubbornly. "We're very independent. And resourceful. *You* said that: you said we're amazingly resourceful. It's because of you," she added cagily, "the way you brought us up, so we're very"—she grinned proudly—"self-reliant. So we'll be fine because you taught us to be. And Abby's okay; you said yourself she's a strong person. What's so funny?"

Sara was smiling. "It isn't funny; it's wonderful. You're wonderful. But it's not really fair, you know, to throw someone's statements back in her face."

"Why isn't it fair, if you said them?"

Sara laughed. It was a relief to talk to Carrie after a sleepless night of thinking about Reuben and constructing various scenarios of where they could go from here, her thoughts riding on an undercurrent of worry that she would not be able to go with him at all. For the moment, it was a relief not to think of him. "You're right," she said to Carrie.

"Carrie's always right," said Abby, coming into the kitchen. "She's the smartest of all of us. Except for you, Sara. I just want a piece of toast."

"That's all anybody's having," Carrie pointed out.

"Fruit," Abby said, pointing at the bowl on the table, and shuddered.

"But you love blueberries!"

"I don't love anything."

"Not even us?"

"Anything else."

"You love us and not anything else?"

"Yes!" She jumped up and put bread in the toaster. "Can't you just stop talking about it?"

"Where is Doug?" Sara asked quickly.

"Dawdling," Abby said absently. "Making something with LEGOs, I think."

"Before breakfast?" Sara went to the stairway. "Doug!"

"Right, right, right." He came leaping down the stairs and threw himself into a chair at the table. "Can I have some bagels?"

"If you think you have time, go ahead."

"You mean I have to fix them myself?"

"Don't you always?"

"Well, yeah, but I may not have time. You're faster than I am."

Sara sighed and stood up.

"Sara's going away for Monday night," Carrie said. "You'll have to get your own bagels then."

Abby looked up from her glum slouch. "You're going away?"

"It isn't definite. I'm still—"

"She's worried about us," Carrie said, "but

I said we were independent and resourceful and self-reliant, and we'd be fine, and she should definitely go."

"Go where?" Doug asked.

"New York," said Sara. "Just overnight."

"Why?"

"A friend invited me and I thought it would be fun."

"Which friend?"

"Reuben, I'll bet," Abby muttered. "He's from New York."

"I thought you broke up," said Carrie.

"So, could I have a friend for a sleepover?" Doug asked.

"No!" Carrie cried. "It'll just be us."

"Well, Sara's gonna have fun, why can't I have fun, too?"

"Will Mack be here?" Abby asked.

No one spoke. Sara spread the halves of a bagel with cream cheese and set the plate in front of Doug. "I don't know. He's been gone most nights, sometimes all night, I think. Would you like him to be here?"

Abby and Doug and Carrie looked at each other. "It's okay if he is," Doug said. "I mean, we all like him, you know, even if he makes us feel . . . you know."

"Uncomfortable," Abby said distantly.

"He's strange," Carrie said, as she had to Tess.

"He's mostly cool," said Doug, "but then he gets sort of . . . weird. Anyway, he probably won't be here. I don't think he likes our house anymore."

"Well, I like it," Carrie said, "and I can take care of it, help take care of it anyway. I mean, I'm almost fourteen, and Abby'll be sixteen next week, so we're fine. So you should go, Sara, to New York, I mean."

"*Is* it Reuben?" Abby asked.

"Yes," Sara said.

Carrie said, "But I thought you broke—"

"*Some* people can be in love," said Abby gloomily. "*Some* people are lucky. *Some* people have happy lives while the rest of us sink into loneliness and despair."

"Oh, poor Abby," said Carrie, and looked at Sara to make sure her good behavior was being registered.

Sara let all of it go by. "What are you all going to do today?"

Abby shrugged. "It's Saturday."

"I'm going to Jeff's house," said Doug. "His mother's taking us to the museum, to see the mummies."

"I'm going to Barb's," said Carrie. "A bunch

of us are going to a movie. Can Barb spend the night, Sara?"

Across Abby's downcast head, they discussed their schedules, and then, still talking, Carrie and Doug cleaned the kitchen and went upstairs. At length, Abby rose languidly and, without looking in Sara's direction, drifted toward the stairway.

Sara stopped her. "Abby, please sit with me for a minute." After a pause, Abby drifted back and drooped into her chair. Sara gazed at her lovely face, barely visible through the screen of ash-blond hair. A pout pulled down the corners of her mouth; her eyelids were puffy. For the first time, Sara felt a spark of irritation. (Later she would admit that it was because of her chance with Reuben, of finally feeling, after so many things had gone wrong, that something might go right.)

"I know you feel very alone," she said, "as if no one ever felt this awful, no one ever could understand how you feel. The truth is—and you know this as well as I do—most people feel truly awful at times, and they'd all sympathize with you. I sympathize with you; this is a painful time. You're growing and changing, and sometimes it's hard to make sense of who you are and where you are now, and where you go from here."

Abby had parted the strands of her hair and was looking at her. Sara hesitated. Would a mother criticize a daughter who was in the midst of what seemed like a tragedy? I don't know, she thought angrily; how am I supposed to know? What am I supposed to feel? What she did feel was irritation, frustration, and anxiety about Reuben. She was sure those were not motherly feelings, but, like Abby, she felt alone and she had to make sense of where she was going from here.

Be positive. Start with the good things. "I'm very happy that you came downstairs this morning; I know you're trying. But we're trying, too, Abby, and you don't give us credit for that, or any help, either. We all want to do what's best for you. But we have to think about what's best for us, too."

She contemplated Abby's dejection. *She really is suffering; what an awful age this can be. I wouldn't be sixteen again for anything in the world.* But as unsure as she felt, she was being propelled by her own needs and desires, and finally she thought, The hell with it, and went on. "Abby, I want this trip on

Monday, it's important to me, and I don't want to spend it worrying about the three of you. That means I have to be sure you're in charge. Carrie and Doug are wonderful, but they're very young. I can't rely on Mack. You're the one I need to rely on, and I want to hear you say you'll do this for me, and do it like a grown-up instead of a self-indulgent child."

Abby's eyes widened. She had been coddled so much in the past days she had forgotten what it was like to have demands made on her. But then she remembered how awful she felt, and Sean was gone and he'd never really loved her, and she'd done a stupid thing and everyone would hate her, and everything was totally tragic, and she didn't want to be in charge, she didn't want to be responsible for anybody, she just wanted to curl up in bed and be taken care of, and she closed her eyes so she wouldn't have to look at Sara and think about Sara wanting something, too, and maybe feeling really bad if she couldn't have it.

The kitchen was very quiet. All Abby could hear was the hum of the refrigerator and freezer and, through the open windows, a bird singing up and down the scale as if everything in the world were fine and happy. Abby kept her eyes shut, and waited. Maybe Sara had left. It was Saturday; she always went grocery shopping on Saturday. She was probably gone, and the kitchen was empty, with nothing to stop Abby from going back upstairs to her room.

Slowly, Abby opened her eyes. Sara was sitting across from her, just where she had been. She hadn't moved; she still was looking straight at her. What do I do now? Abby thought, and closed her eyes again.

"You tried that and it didn't work," Sara said evenly. "I'm waiting for you to answer me. I'm not talking to myself, I'm talking to you, and I expect the courtesy of an answer." She waited. "I'm not asking for all that much, you know. I'm asking that you crawl out of this shell of misery you've created and stay out of it for Monday and Tuesday so you can take care of your brother and sister. That's all. If you want to crawl in again Tuesday afternoon when I get home, that's up to you. No one will stop you. We'd be sorry, because our family is only complete when you're part of it, but we won't stop you." She waited again, her fists clenched in deepening frustration. "Okay, one last time. I am telling you,

you're taking charge here for two days and one night, so that I can have something I want." *No real mother would do this; what am I saying?* "I'm tired of spending a lot of my time trying to figure out what you want and how to give it to you, instead of aiming for what I want." *What would a real mother do? Keep talking? Or shut up and apologize for sounding like a tyrant?* "It's my turn now, and I expect help from my family. I expect you to tell me you'll do this for me, and you'll do it like the adult you often tell me you are. Answer me, Abby."

Stunned, Abby was gaping at Sara; her mouth was open but no words came. Sara never ever talked about what she wanted (well, she used to talk about medical school but she'd stopped that a long time ago); Sara was the one they all went to when they wanted something. None of them ever said, on a Saturday morning, "And what would *you* like to do today, Sara?" None of them ever said, at breakfast, "We'll make dinner tonight, Sara; why don't you go out with your friends, or something?" It never occurred to them to say anything like that. Sara was just . . . *there.* Like one of the paintings on the wall, Abby thought, and felt ashamed.

She became aware of the stretched-out silence, and the lingering echo of Sara's command that she answer her. "Fine," she said, and cleared her throat. "I mean . . . fine. I'll take care of them." She felt miserable and she hated everybody, but she had to do this because Sara said so, and because something had happened to Sara, she was different in a way Abby couldn't understand, and that was scary, because they all depended on Sara being there for them, the Sara they knew, so she had to make Sara happy so she'd be the old Sara again.

If that makes sense, Abby thought despairingly.

But Sara wasn't leaving until Monday. What was she supposed to do until Sara left? All day today, all day tomorrow . . . She could go back to her room, but somehow that seemed crazy now that she'd agreed to take charge on Monday. So what could she do?

"Thank you," Sara said, and it sounded like a sigh to Abby, a long, long sigh. She came to Abby and hugged her. "I'm going to the farmers' market, would you like to come? I see a lot of your friends there every week." Abby cringed, and Sara kissed her on the forehead. "You don't want to hide from them forever, sweetheart. They're an important part of your life, and you're an important part of theirs. You know that's true; why else would they keep calling you, even though you won't talk to them?"

Slowly, Abby said, "They'll make fun of me for being stupid and . . . being fooled by . . . Sean."

Sara nodded thoughtfully. "It sounds just like them. They're cruel and thoughtless and make fun of you all the time, right? They'd never give you credit for being their wonderful friend who might make a mistake."

Abby smiled, then realized she was smiling and tried to frown.

"Well, think about it," Sara said casually. "I'm leaving in fifteen minutes and I certainly could use your help carrying things; I can never find a parking place close by."

Left alone, Abby imagined hiding in her bedroom, sinking into her new rocking chair that curved around her, shutting out the world. But she had to admit she missed her friends. And she missed school, and she had tons of homework to do that Sara brought home for her, every day after work going to school and picking up her work, and Abby hated knowing Sara had to do that on top of everything else, and she hated getting behind in her work, and everything was really a mess. Shit, she thought, and was disgusted with herself because she sounded like Mack. *I won't sound like Mack; I'd rather sound like Sara. I'd rather be Sara.*

"Okay," she said with a sigh to the empty kitchen. "So I'll go to the farmers' market. I guess I owe that to Sara. At least I'm good for carrying shopping bags."

And somehow Sara kept Abby busy through the weekend. The reunion with two of her friends at the farmers' market had been surprisingly (to Abby) natural, and as Sara moved away she heard the friends chattering away, and Abby beginning to respond. She let them rediscover each other as she walked from stand to stand, selecting fruits and vegetables and planning Monday night's dinner for her family, while she was away. (*While I'm away, while I'm in New York, while I'm with Reuben, with Reuben, with Reuben . . .*) She wanted to dance her way across the market, from potatoes to onions, from arugula and portobellos to tomatoes and basil. *I'll make a lasagna for them to heat up, and they can fix an arugula-and-tomato salad, and there's bread in the freezer, and sliced turkey for sandwiches for lunch on Tuesday . . . because I'm going to be with Reuben.*

Oh, for heaven's sake, she thought, I'm beginning to sound like Abby. On impulse, she bought half a bushel of apples, so when she returned the four of them would make pies and applesauce for the freezer, as they did every fall. A whole day just with them, she thought, to make up for my going off with Reuben.

At home, she and Abby put away their purchases, and then Sara suggested they spend the afternoon going through Abby's closets, "to see what you'll need for all the senior parties and dances coming up."

Abby shook her head. "I'm not interested in parties. Or clothes."

"I thought you had a good time with your friends."

"They were nice, but, you know, it was only two of them."

"Okay." Sara sliced bread for sandwiches. "We don't have to think about clothes, if you don't want to. I brought a lot of work home; I'll do it this afternoon."

"Oh." Disconcerted, Abby paused in apportioning slices of turkey. "You're too busy to do it?"

"I could be busy. I thought for today it would be more fun to spend the afternoon with you."

"I guess," Abby said after a moment, "I guess we could do it, just for a while. I mean, I don't need any new clothes 'cause I won't be going to any parties, but my closets do sort of need cleaning out."

"Well, then, we'll start right after lunch. Oh, and tonight I thought we'd rent a movie; there are a couple I've really been wanting to see."

Abby burst into tears and threw her arms around Sara. "I love you, Sara. You're the most wonderful mother in the world. Oh, well, you know, *sister,* but you're just . . . you're just wonderful."

Sara held her, thinking, It's all right, she's not angry, she doesn't hate me for making demands where I have no right to make demands, she loves me. Thank you, thank you, dear Abby, I'm not sure if I could have left on Monday if you were upset and angry and resentful. And then she thought, Everything will be all right.

Together they made lunch, and Sara listed plans for Sunday, to make it easier for Abby. "Doug needs to pick up his sculptures," she said, "and I'd like you with us; we'll go tomorrow afternoon."

Abby shook her head. "I'd rather stay home."

"I'd rather you came with us. You can help carry the sculptures. There are a lot of them. All of them, in fact."

"Nobody bought anything?"

"No. I was thinking of buying one, secretly, but it would have been terrible if Doug found out."

"Nobody bought even one."

"No."

"But why not? They're so good."

"They are. For a ten-year-old."

"Then why did those people let him have a show?"

"I don't know. I don't understand it."

"Well, you can tell me all about it when you get home. I really don't feel like going, Sara."

Sara nodded. "Doug and I need your help carrying, and we'll be glad to have your company. It won't take long."

"We can't go; they won't be open on Sunday."

"I called. They're open."

Abby slammed down the peppermill, and stormed from the kitchen.

"Do you want to drive?" Sara called after her.

Slowly, she reappeared in the doorway. "I'm not ever going to drive again."

"Oh, what a shame, I thought it would be good practice, driving on the expressway. Well, okay. I'll drive."

After a moment, Abby inched her way back and picked up the peppermill, grinding onto the salad with great concentration. "You think I'm good enough to drive on the highway?"

"I guess I do or I wouldn't risk my life being in the car with you."

A smile broke through Abby's determined gloom. "I suppose I could . . . if you think it's okay after . . . after . . ."

"I think it's okay," Sara said quietly, and on Sunday afternoon she was quiet in the car as Abby drove to the gallery, giving no instructions other than telling her the right exit and which streets to take, hoping Abby did not see her dig her right foot into the floor mat as if she were stepping on the brake. She concentrated on Abby's driving, not letting herself think about Reuben's telephone call the night before. He had called while they were watching movies in the library, saying he had reserved airline tickets and asking if she could go with him. "Yes," she said, and Reuben said, simply, "I'm very glad," adding that he would pick her up on Monday morning, to drive to the airport. "No, I'd rather meet you there," she replied. And that was all, as if they had agreed in advance that if there was to be emotion, the time for it was not yet.

"That was excellent," she said as Abby parked in the small lot beside the gallery. "You're really good, Abby," said Doug, opening the back door. "I wasn't worried or scared or anything."

Abby put her arm around him without replying; she could not decide whether to be elated at doing well and pleasing Sara, or in despair, because she really was suffering.

"Well, if it isn't our little artist," said Frank Stoaner jovially as Doug led the way into the gallery.

Doug stopped uncertainly. *Little?*

Sara moved around him. "We're picking up Doug's sculptures. We don't need help; I'm sure you're busy."

"They're gone," Doug cried, looking around. "Where are they?"

"In back." Stoaner rumpled Doug's hair. "Can't keep 'em here forever, you know, the show came down. But we took care of 'em for you; they're all packed up in the back room."

"But—"

"It was a one-night show," Frank said impatiently. "Never planned for anything else."

"One night?" Abby repeated. She had been contemplating two full-size mattresses hanging from the ceiling with road maps painted on them, but she turned to glare at Frank. "Exhibits don't last just one night."

"Some do," he said dismissively.

"Why?"

"Because that's how it is."

"But why?"

He threw up his hands. "I'll get your boxes."

"Just a minute," Sara said. "I'd also like to know why."

"Because they're different," he said angrily. "I run my gallery the way I want to, and each show is different."

"I understand that. I don't understand why you wanted to give a ten-year-old boy a one-night exhibit."

"Look, I don't want to quarrel with you—"

"Quarrel? I'm asking a simple question. No one is quarreling."

"Ask your brother," he said after a moment.

"I'm asking you. I'm aware that Mack arranged it with you, but he never told us it would be for one night. What was the arrangement?"

"Look, I did him a favor. He'll tell you about it."

"But I'm asking you. What's the problem? If it was a simple business arrangement, it should be simple to explain." She pulled over the stool Doug had sat on when his show opened. "I'm willing to wait for an answer."

Stoaner looked from Sara to Abby and Doug, and back to Sara. He gazed at the mattresses behind Abby. "Fuck it," he muttered. "Do a guy a favor and it's like you have to go on trial. I owed him something," he flung at Sara. "My partner and I, we owed him. So we gave him one night. Shit, lady, I'm running a legitimate business here, you think I can keep the place cluttered up with crap from a fucking kid?"

Doug turned pale; his eyes widened and filled with tears. He stared at Frank as if he could not turn away.

"You bastard!" Abby cried, and putting her arm around Doug, dragged him out the door.

"Yes, I actually think that's the right word," Sara said. She walked past Stoaner to the back of the gallery, and into a brightly lit room stacked with paintings wrapped in bubble wrap and brown paper, and, in a corner, six boxes with Mack's name on them. Silently, Sara picked up the top box and walked back through the gallery, setting it beside the entrance. When she returned, Stoaner roused himself and followed her, and without speaking they carried the boxes to the car and stowed them in the trunk. Abby and Doug were not to be seen.

Sara slammed shut the trunk and turned, gazing steadily at Stoaner. "Sorry," he muttered. "Nice kid, you know." With a vague gesture, he went back inside the gallery.

"Abby," Sara said without raising her voice. Abby and Doug came around the corner of the building, Doug's face streaked with tears, Abby holding him close to her side.

Doug flung himself at Sara. "Mack said I was good, he said I deserved a show." The words were strangled. "He said they *wanted* me in the gallery. He *said* that. Why did he lie?"

Sara's arms were around him. "I suppose to make you happy."

"I'm not happy!"

"But you were, and I'm sure he never thought you'd find out."

"He shouldn't have lied to me."

"You're right. Lies backfire too often. But maybe Mack hasn't figured that out. I think he swings back and forth between lies and the truth all the time."

Doug stopped crying. "He does?"

"I think so."

"I do, too," Abby said. "I mean, he talks like everything is wonderful, and he's wonderful, but you know, maybe it's not true."

Doug was scowling. "He lies a lot?"

"I think so," Sara said, "but we don't know for sure. Come on, now, let's get home. Abby, why don't you sit in back with Doug? I'll drive."

"That guy, what's-his-name, was wrong about Doug," Abby said as Sara drove out of the parking lot.

Sara nodded. "He's wrong about a lot of things."

"Like what?"

"Well, I assume what he owes Mack is

payment for drugs." She remembered when Tess had written *drugs,* after Mack had been there, and she had thought it meant Mack's smoking marijuana. But that had not been what Tess meant: Mack must have hinted, or told her, that he was dealing. "Which means I'll have to tell Mack to leave; he can't live with us while he's dealing from our house."

"I've smelled it, in his room," Abby said.

"I did, when he first arrived. I didn't know he was still doing it. You didn't tell me."

"It didn't seem to matter. I mean, most of the time he was so nice . . ."

"He isn't nice, he's a liar," said Doug.

"That wasn't nice, but he bought me a car, and got Carrie's stories published . . . you know, lots of things."

"Well, he's out of our house as soon as I can talk to him," Sara said.

But that means I can't go to New York. I have to make sure he's gone, and it would have to be before tomorrow morning, and what chance is there of that?

Her mouth tightened; she drove grimly, trying not to think. Behind her, Abby was telling Doug it was stupid to do drugs, and Mack was stupid for doing drugs and lying, and Franklin Stoaner was a stupid idiot, as Doug grunted in agreement, or simply to keep Abby talking.

I'll call Reuben as soon as we get home. Maybe we can find another time. As long as some other crisis doesn't come along. How long will a man wait for a woman with three children to find a weekend for herself?

Carrie came home from her friend's house, and they had a quiet dinner; everyone seemed worn out. Sara had left a message on Reuben's answering machine asking him to call her, and until then she kept her mind on dinner. When the telephone rang, she let Carrie run to answer it, putting off until the last minute saying aloud the refrain running through her mind. *I can't go. I can't go. I can't—*

"Sara, it's Mack," Carrie said, bringing the telephone to the dining room. "He says he's going away."

Sara snatched the telephone. "Going away?"

"Not quite, sis." His voice was jaunty. "Just a business trip, a few days, back Wednesday, maybe Thursday. Is that a problem?"

"No! No, of course not. I appreciate your

telling me. When you get back, I want to talk to you."

"Do I detect a note of criticism? I haven't been home much, and haven't told you my schedule? Sorry about that; guilty, he said guiltily, as charged. I'll reform, I'll improve, I'll turn over a new—"

"I'm not talking about your schedule. I have other things to talk to you about."

"When I get back, sis, I promise we'll talk as long as you want, about shoes and ships and ceiling wax, and cabbages and kings. Bye, now, take care of the brood."

"You didn't tell him," Abby said as Sara hung up the telephone.

"Tell him what?" Carrie asked.

Sara let Abby and Doug describe their afternoon at the gallery. *Everything is fine. I'm going with Reuben on Monday. Tomorrow is Monday and I'm going to New York with Reuben.*

And on Monday morning, for the first time since the accident, Abby went to school.

"I'm proud of you," Sara said, hugging her. "You're very brave, and I'm absolutely sure everyone will help you."

"Sean won't. He'll be mean." Her shoulders tensed. "I'm afraid to see him."

"I can't believe he'll be there, Abby. He committed a crime; there's a price to pay for that. He can't just go back to his old life as if nothing happened."

"You mean he might be in jail?"

"We would have heard about it if he was. I don't know where he is, but I don't think you should worry about it."

"But what if he *is* in school?"

"He won't be," Sara said sharply. "You're working yourself up over nothing. Stop thinking about it. Let's finish these lunches or you'll all be late." Casually, she added, "You'll leave school with Doug and Carrie, so you all get home together?"

"No," Abby said sarcastically, "I'm going to hang out at school and let them wander around without anybody knowing where they are or what they're doing."

Sara let it pass. "I'll call around dinnertime."

"Well, we certainly couldn't eat without hearing your voice."

"So I can hear *your* cheerful voices," Sara said, "and tell you I love you."

Carrie was staring, not only at Abby's nastiness, but also at Sara's restraint. "Have lots and lots of fun," she said, kissing Sara good-bye.

"Bring us something," said Doug, between short, smacking kisses. "Something that's just New York, not Chicago."

"Bye," said Abby, and after a hesitation, "I'm sorry I was mean." She kissed Sara, then put her arms around her. "I truly hope you *and Reuben* have a good time."

With the click of the door shutting behind them, the stillness of the house settled around Sara. Usually by now she would be on her way to work, but nothing about today was usual. Her suitcase had been packed since dawn, when she had given up trying to sleep; she had her ticket, delivered by messenger on Sunday morning; she had chosen a book to take, hoping they would have too much to talk about to allow time for reading. A long note was on the kitchen island filled with instructions ("Don't forget to turn off the oven when the lasagna is baked." "Do not open the front door to anyone." "My cell phone is always on."). She could hear Abby groan and Carrie say, "But we *know* all that," but she had not been able to stop adding other instructions and reminders until the list filled the page. Now, at the bottom, she wrote Reuben's telephone number and added, "There's a surprise DVD in the library for tonight."

And then, checking again to make sure the front and back doors were locked, she took a taxi to the airport.

Reuben was waiting just inside the entrance to the airline's lounge. They had not seen each other for almost a month.

He took her hands in his. Conscious of the attendant seated at a desk nearby, he said simply, "Good morning; I'm glad to see you," showed his membership card to the attendant, and he and Sara took the escalator to the second floor. Walking with him through the lounge, Sara was swept by an odd feeling of relief, as if now everything was all right and in place. She knew the future was still filled with unknowns, but still, there it was, that lightness and slight disorientation of relief.

Reuben had left his roll-on and briefcase on a pair of armchairs in a corner of the lounge. He and Sara filled coffee cups at the sideboard and sat together, and he took her hand. "Thank you for making this happen; I imagine it wasn't easy."

"Everyone said good-bye in very good

spirits," Sara said, as if it had been just that simple. "I think they'll have a fine time and wonder why I don't go away more often."

"That's something we should think about."

Beyond the plate-glass window, planes pushed into and out from the gates and taxied across the tarmac, small cars scurried in between and among them, and trains of luggage carts zigzagged across the tarmac, teetering with suitcases, occasionally tossing off a few as they rounded corners, causing drivers to leap out and retrieve them, flinging them back on top as if they weighed no more than a volleyball. Reuben and Sara were only vaguely aware of the constant activity, but it kept them grounded rather than drifting into the misty landscape of romances where lovers dream and speak of a future they can hope for but never predict.

In fact, they were rather somber, moving cautiously, like returning refugees alert for changes in the landscape, but mostly looking for anything familiar and loved.

"I want you to know everything that's happened," Reuben said, "and how it happened, and where I am now." His voice was low, almost drowned out by the loud conversations of those around them trumpeting business and life secrets on cell phones, and he and Sara leaned closer. "Later, when it's quiet."

She nodded. "Yes."

"And I want to know about you, what you've been doing, about your work and your friends, what's happening with Abby and Carrie and Doug. How was Doug's gallery show? And Donna Soldana, did she ever show up again? And do you have a new secretary? And are Abby and Sean still together? From the little she told me, I thought she'd have problems there." He smiled. "It sounds like an inquisition."

"It sounds like interest." And involvement, she thought, surprised at how much he remembered, and how deeply he had let himself become a part of her in only a few months.

"Much more than interest." He glanced quickly at his watch. "We have time. There's something else I want you to know. I reserved a room for you at a hotel near my apartment. I would very much like you to stay with me, but I want you to do whatever makes you comfortable."

Sara gave a small smile. "Abby would say, 'How old-fashioned.'"

"And she'd be right. But it's good to be

able to choose between past and present and take what's best for you at the time."

"You do that in your work."

"Yes." He was pleased; he liked being understood without having to explain or describe anything more than once.

Sara looked through the window, remembering the long porch of a lodge in Galena, the silvery river in the hushed darkness, and Reuben's arm holding her as he told her about his work. She said aloud one of the things he had said that she liked best. "'I want people's lives to mesh with a living environment, not concrete rectangles filled edge to edge with brick and steel, and only photographs to show them the past, what had been there before they arrived.'"

"The way to a man's heart," Reuben murmured, "is to quote his words exactly. Thank you for that; it isn't often I'm listened to so closely." He finished his coffee, trying to concentrate on coffee, on dialogue, on the time (again looking at his watch), anything to keep him distracted from wanting her so urgently he could barely stay in his chair. "Would you like some more?"

"No, thank you."

"That night in Galena, when I talked about

my work, was the night Abby called us old-fashioned."

Sara smiled. "And the desk clerk looked at us as if we were crazy."

There was a pause. Reuben could not sit still any longer. He looked again at his watch. "We should go; they'll be boarding in a few minutes."

"Yes." But they did not move. "I'd like very much to stay with you tonight," she said.

Their eyes met and Reuben knew, with relief and also with wonder, that her desire was as great as his. He kissed her palm, holding it against his lips. And that's all we have to say right now, Sara thought. She was very happy. Neither of them would rush anything; they would move gradually, and everything would feel quite natural.

On the plane, as the steward served orange juice and champagne, Sara asked about River Bend.

Reuben opened his briefcase. "Thanks to you, we're finally able to move ahead, I think to change the direction of things." He told her what they had learned about Corcoran Enterprises, and gave her a copy of the brochure he had written. "I have an appointment on Friday with the mayors of River Bend and two neighboring towns, and I'm expecting to hear from the *Tribune* and the *Sun-Times* and, I hope, some of the people who've been demonstrating. If they've read the brochure, they'll have questions. I may even hear from the kid who's been organizing things out there, but probably not; he keeps out of sight."

Sara twisted her hands together. "I think it's Mack."

"Mack? Your brother? That can't be. He's involved in this?"

"I wish he weren't." She paused. "He works for Lew Corcoran."

"I didn't know that. Is it coincidence? He came from New York and just happened to get a job with Corcoran who just happened to be a client of yours?"

"None of that was coincidence. Mack had worked for Lew Corcoran in New York. He told Corcoran to call me when he and Pussy got to town, to help them get settled. He followed Corcoran to Chicago, working for Corcoran Enterprises. He told me that soon after he arrived; he said there was a great future in real estate. The only coincidence is that you and Corcoran want the same property, but even that is understandable, since there are so few large properties left."

"And that you and I met."

Sara nodded. "But even that isn't really a coincidence; in my job I meet so many people who come here on business and need to get organized quickly."

Reuben thought about it. "Mack might work for Corcoran, but he could be selling real estate, not organizing demonstrations at River Bend."

"You're such a nice person," Sara said, "defending my brother against my accusations. Thank you, but I don't think it will change anything." She paused, her hands still twisted together. "After I saw Corcoran at River Bend, and called you, I remembered your telling us about the woman you'd interviewed the day we saw the marchers, Charlotte, I think her name was. She told you some kid said he'd get signs and banners if they wanted to protest the village, and later you said she used a phrase that seemed out of character, as if she'd heard it from someone else. She said the village would bring in strangers who would *destructively destroy a decent town.*"

"Yes, I remember, and Carrie said that Mack talked like—" He stopped, remembering the other phrase Charlotte had used. "Not even a token grandparent," he murmured.

"I remember. Another one that sounds like Mack."

"We didn't spend a lot of time thinking about it, but we did say it was unlikely."

"I don't think that anymore."

The steward offered coffee and breakfast; they accepted the coffee, and while he filled their cups, Sara turned to look out the window. Lake Erie was below them, towns strung like a necklace along its shore throwing off small flashes from the sun's reflections. The last time she had looked down on that lake, she had been on her way to medical school in New York. For the first time, she recalled the excitement and sense of adventure of that day without the sharp regret she had come to expect. There are so many ways to live a life, she thought, amused at her unoriginality, but pleased and relieved to discover that she was able now to acknowledge all that was wonderful in the way she was living.

And it did not exclude school. She could

go back; it was just a question of timing. She'd been deflected, she thought, a bump in the road, but thinking of Abby and Carrie and Doug, she knew that was a poor way to describe these past years with her family.

And meeting Reuben. The wonder of meeting Reuben.

(As if she knew already—mostly hope, but somehow assurance—that this trip would settle things between them, that he would not have let it happen unless his path was clear.)

"What can we do about Mack?" Reuben asked.

"Perhaps," Sara said a little hesitantly (after all, River Bend was hugely important to him), "we could forget Mack for a while. Not let him intrude on these two days."

And Reuben, who had thought her family was foremost in Sara's mind, the one concern that took precedence over all others, took her hand. "An excellent idea," he said.

FOURTEEN

Mack was asleep in Rosa's apartment in Hyde Park when his cell phone rang at six-thirty in the morning. He tried to ignore it, but the crazy tune he'd chosen repeated itself insanely until he gave up. "Shit," he muttered, and reached to the floor, sweeping his hand back and forth until he found it. Rosa never moved; she could sleep through a war. "Yeah," he said into the phone.

"What the fuck you been up to," Corcoran barked.

"What?" He sat up. "Nothing. I mean, the usual. I'm going to St. Louis today; you told me to—"

"You're not going anywhere. Get your ass over here."

"Now?"

But Corcoran had hung up.

Why did he have to work for a guy who blew up every time he turned around? Spouting off over nothing until Mack would set him straight, and then he'd calm down and get back to work like nothing had happened and not one fucking word of thanks or an apology. I'd go somewhere else in a minute, Mack thought, half a minute if something came along. But he knew he wasn't going anywhere; he had things too good with Corcoran. The pay was good, the hours were good, the work was a piece of cake. And he knew how to handle Corcoran. Mack was into Lew Corcoran, had him down pat. Still, he thought as he slid out of bed, not a great idea to keep the boss waiting.

"What time is it?" Rosa asked.

"Six-thirty. I thought you were asleep; go back to sleep."

"Nobody could sleep with your crazy phone. Why don't you make it ring like a normal one?"

"And be like everybody else?" He pulled on his shorts and looked around for his pants.

"Where are you going?"

"To see my boss. My bossy boss with great bossiness has demanded that his worthy worker worshipfully present himself."

Rosa giggled. "Pretty good for early morning. Couldn't you put it off for a few more minutes in bed? Look, I'm ready for you." Lying on her back, she spread her legs wide and stretched her arms above her head, grasping the headboard as if she were tied there. She was seventeen years old, slim, and olive-skinned. Her parents were at home in Sicily; she lived with an aunt, but had rented her own studio apartment, and now and then told her aunt she was spending the night with a girlfriend. Her nose was large, her eyebrows thick, her chin square—Mack had thought all Italian women were beautiful, but Rosa proved him wrong—but her sexual energy seemed limitless and she was smart. Mack liked smart women, and hung out at university bars and coffee shops where he could meet and charm them. "You want something different this morning?" Rosa asked. She flipped over, and kneeling on all fours, her firm buttocks teasingly high, she winked at him from beneath her arm.

"Get your juices flowing before you meet the big bad boss."

Mack paused for an agonizing second, then zipped his pants against the bulge straining against them. "Is that how they teach you to talk at the University of Chicago?"

"I talked that way before I got here."

"And when you're in class?"

"I talk about Aristotle and Homer and I really like it. I like it with you, too." She sat up. "Mack, you're not going."

"I'll be back."

"I won't be here. I have class. Aristotle."

"Call me this afternoon."

"Where will you be?"

"St. Louis, there's a new project we might start there."

"You are no good to me in St. Louis."

"I'll be good when I get back." He waved from the doorway.

"Don't I at least get a kiss?"

"You know the answer to that." Of course she did, he thought as he left the building. He never kissed; he didn't like it.

Away from her, he could think about Corcoran, figure out ahead of time what might be eating him, but in the twenty minutes it took to get to Corcoran's building, and park and take the elevator to the penthouse, nothing had occurred to him. He liked Lew's apartment: enormous high-ceilinged rooms with oversize furniture (Pussy had complained she got lost in the chairs and sofas; she got lost, all right) and wide vistas of the lake and the city, so that at night it was like being in a plane, and in daytime, when the clouds were below you and there was only you and the sky, you owned it all.

"Hi, boss," he said, and followed Corcoran through the foyer, turning toward the kitchen, expecting breakfast. But Corcoran was going in the other direction, toward his office.

"You got any coffee?" Mack asked. "I had one of my busy nights." He leered; it always got a laugh from Lew.

But not today. Corcoran took a brochure from his desk and thrust it at Mack. On the cover was a photo of the land near River Bend with a line beneath it that read HOW DO YOU WANT THIS LAND TO LOOK TOMORROW?

Puzzled, Mack opened the brochure and was hit with the photo of a riverboat casino. "What the fuck—?" A LICENSE FOR A NEW ILLINOIS CASINO IS PENDING, the text read. COULD IT BE IN RIVER BEND?

"Shit." He looked up at Corcoran. "How did they get this?"

"You tell me."

"How the fuck would I know? Christ, Lew, you don't think I had anything to do with this! I've been keeping it to myself, shit, why would I let it out?"

"Don't play games with me, you asshole. Who's paying you?"

"Paying me?" A wave of dizziness hit Mack and he reached out to sit down.

"I didn't say you could sit. Stay where you are."

"Lew, I don't feel good, I have to—"

"You give me answers, you can go to a hospital or any fucking place you want. First you tell me who's behind this."

"I don't know! Listen, nobody's paying— Honest to God, Lew—" Mack heard his voice whining, and began to cough, to give himself time to regain control, but the cough suddenly sounded like a sob, and, frantically, he plunged ahead. "Honest to God, I don't know anything about it. You know I've been keeping it a secret, I've done a good job, you told me yourself—" *Stop babbling!* He tried to stand straight against the dizziness sweeping over him. "Hey, Lew, I'm your guy, remember?

Whatever you want, I do it. You said keep it a secret, I keep it a secret. I don't know anything about this. You think about it, you'll know I don't; you *trust* me! Somebody found out about it. I mean, it's public, you know, anybody can call the Illinois—"

"You don't call unless you've been tipped off." Corcoran grabbed a bottle of scotch from the bar behind him and took a swig as he stood looking down at slips of paper fanned out across the desk. The apartment was air-conditioned to near freezing but Mack saw with surprise and a surge of fear that Lew was perspiring. *Why? What's he scared of?* There was a buzzing in his ears; his head vibrated and his fingers began to tingle.

Corcoran looked up. "You're through with me, but if you want to stay healthy, you'll tell me who's paying you."

Through? Stay healthy? What's he talking about? "Nobody's paying me! I work for you! You trust me! Look, why don't we sit down and talk about—"

"There's nothing to talk about and you're not sitting down. The only people who sit down are people who work for me."

Through the buzzing in his head, Mack forced a chuckle. "You don't mean that. I'm your guy. Well, hey, if you're too busy to sit down and talk, I'll come some other time"—he took a step backward—"I know how busy you are, you're a busy man, I'll come—"

Corcoran yanked open the top drawer on the right side of his desk, where, Mack knew, he had two guns, both loaded. "You fucking bastard, tell me who you're working for."

Mack felt a warm wetness spread across his groin. Sick with fear and embarrassment, still dizzy, he clasped his hands in front of him. Corcoran was looking at him, knowing he had wet his pants, and Mack started shaking. Everything was out of control, racing past him, leaving him behind, and he couldn't stand it, he felt as if he were back in the police station waiting for somebody to come and rescue him.

He lunged toward Corcoran, gleeful at Lew's instinctive lurch backward. He saw that the slips of paper on the desk were telephone messages from Lew's answering service, and knew, with the swift clarity of terror, that Lew's partners in the casino—and maybe the newspapers?—had been calling, had seen the brochures and had been calling to find out what the hell was going on.

That was why Lew was perspiring. That was why he was afraid.

Well, make him more afraid. Take control here. Who the fuck does he think he is, threatening me? He needs me!

"You better watch it." His voice was thick. "Watch it, Lew, you shouldn't threaten me, I've got things, things you wouldn't want me to show around . . . photos of what's-her-name, Pussy, when you shot her—"

He saw Corcoran's face change, but by now he could not stop. "You wanted it cleaned up, fixed like she was alone, shot herself, so you called me. *Me,* you called *me!* And I did it, did what you wanted, and you took off, left me alone with her and the mess, how about that, big man Lew Corcoran ran away but Mack Hayden stayed, cleaned up his shit. But Mack Hayden is *smart,* Mack Hayden *takes pictures,* Mack Hayden covers his ass!"

He backed away from the desk, almost blind with fear, but at the same time crazily exhilarated. Corcoran's face, dark with fury, wavered before him. "Nobody catches Mack Hayden sleeping! I'm the smart one, you're just a bully, wouldn't be anywhere without me. No demonstrations, no TV and reporters, no nothing. No casino!" He began to laugh. "Maybe no casino anyway! You know what, *Mr.* Corcoran? One of your partners did it. To get rid of you. They've got a plan, they're smart, not like you, get rid of you and have it all for them. Ask 'em!" he cried. "You'll see!"

He had backed himself almost to the doorway. Corcoran, momentarily arrested by the idea that one of his partners—or all of them together?—had thought this up, decided in the next instant it could not be true, and he pulled a gun from the drawer. "Photos," he said tightly. "You son of a bitch. Where are they?"

Mack looked at the gun, such a little thing, like a toy in Lew's broad perspiring hand.

"Where are they?"

"Put away." The words were strangled. His excitement had shriveled, leaving behind only fear. "Told lots of people, though. Hundreds. Anything happen to me . . ." The lie was so absurd it died away. The buzzing was worse, filling his head until he thought it would burst. He could not stand the fear and the pressure behind his eyes. He felt a scream rise in his throat, he hurt all over as everything inside him pushed to get out, and without thinking, in one reflexive motion, his hand shot out to a nearby table and grasped a bronze statue of a naked Greek Olympian. Like an enraged pitcher, Mack hurled it at Corcoran's head.

It happened so quickly Corcoran had no time to dodge, and Mack saw him fall before he was fully aware of throwing the statue. He stood trancelike beside the door, unable to move, everything, even the buzzing, suddenly muffled. He waited, his mouth slack, and then the buzzing increased, pressing inside his ears, his eyeballs, his scalp, until at last the scream burst from his throat.

It broke his trance. He scurried across the room. Corcoran lay behind his desk, blood flowing from a gash in his head. *He's dead. Or he'll bleed to death.* The thought did not come from him; it was part of the buzzing in his head. *Well, either way, serves him right. What the hell. Fired me. Gotta get outta here, get the hell out—*

No, wait. He was shivering in the frigid air; his wet pants clung to his groin and thighs, his fingers were tingling, and buzzing filled the room, but somewhere inside his bursting head words wove themselves into commands. *Can't leave now, not like this. Think.*

Think. Fix up the place. Did it with Pussy bitch, do it again now.

As if still in that strange trance, he bent down to look for the statue. What he saw first was the gun. It lay on the rug beside Corcoran's outstretched hand. *Leave it alone. His prints on it.* He bent farther, looking for the statue, until he saw it where it had bounced to the side of the room. He walked around the outside of the desk to avoid walking in Corcoran's blood, retrieved the statue, and wiped it clean with a napkin from the bar before returning it to its place on the table. He soaked a corner of the napkin in Corcoran's blood and smeared it on a corner of the desk, calculating which corner to choose by estimating the angle at which Corcoran would have fallen after striking it. *Smart thinking, haven't lost my touch.* He began to put the napkin in his jacket pocket, but stopped himself. *Jacket can't be washed; pants can.* He shoved the napkin deep into his pants pocket and looked around the room, checking it out. He had not touched anything else; the bastard hadn't let him touch anything, even to sit down.

With a last look, he scurried to the front door and opened it with his hand inside his jacket pocket. No one had seen him arrive, no one was there to see him go; Lew hated strangers in the apartment, and only tolerated the cleaning service when he was at his office.

Nobody here, nobody to hear. Mack gave a laugh that came out as a whimper, and let the door close and lock behind him.

I need a drink, he thought. Should have taken the scotch from old Lew's desk. He tried to grin, but his mouth hurt when he stretched it. *Have to figure things out, get away from here.* He drove up the garage ramp and onto Pearson Street, his tires screeching. *Christ, slow down, some fucking cop give me a ticket and then—*

He slowed down, crawling at the speed limit when every nerve in his body pushed him to fly, to flee, to shove the accelerator to the floor and leave everything behind. "Son of a bitch," he said aloud through the buzzing in his head. "Son of a bitch, I was all set, I had him where I wanted him, I had a future. Now what the fuck am I supposed to do?"

And where was he going now? He didn't know, but it didn't matter; he just had to keep moving. He turned south onto Lake Shore Drive. "Shit, I have to figure the whole thing out by myself. Like I always do. Nobody ever helped me with anything, I had to grow up by myself and get away by myself, and now I have to figure this out by myself. Fucking Lew Corcoran was supposed to take care of me, acted like a daddy and then let me down like a fucking daddy, like everybody else in my whole fucking life."

He drove all day. The buzzing went on and on, his eyeballs ached, his fingers tingled. But he drove. He drove to the Indiana border, turned north and drove as far as Wisconsin, and turned south again to Chicago, through the Loop and on to the university. He found a parking place on the Midway a few blocks from Rosa's apartment. Rosa would take care of him, put him to bed, feed him . . . but Rosa was in class all day. "Fuck it!" he screamed in frustration, the scream swallowed up by the stifling air in his car. The scream had not helped; he wished for a new vocabulary that said what he felt. *Run down, run over, run out of words*. He slammed his fist against the steering wheel.

Well, then, just look around; that always made him feel good, being part of the campus. But today it was no fun being there. The fucking students all belonged and knew where they were going, and chattered away and laughed with the hand gestures he'd sneered at in the past, but now he felt so far out of it that in a few minutes he drove away, hating the place and everybody in it.

He drove north, along the lake, to the suburbs. He parked near the Baha'i Temple in Wilmette, but the sun was going down and in the darkening streets the house lights went on, one by one, little golden squares in solid brick houses with their front doors closed, and he knew no one would open a door to him or even wanted him on their street, so he drove away, hating Wilmette, hating the houses and everybody in them.

He had to leave Chicago, he knew that, but there was no place waiting for him, not a city or town where he could call somebody and ask for a place to crash for a few nights. There were a couple of girls in New York, but he'd walked out on them without a word when Corcoran dangled a bigger salary and easy work and Chicago. Not New York, Mack thought. Home. I'll go home.

"Home," he said aloud, sitting in his car, the car he hated now, because it smelled of urine and sweat and was beginning to feel like a prison. "That's where I belong. Anyway, it's dinnertime. Have to eat, keep up my strength."

Traffic was heavy in both directions when he drove south on Lake Shore Drive, and it took a long time to get to his neighborhood, and then to find a parking place. At one time he would have parked anywhere, taken his chances on cops checking the area, but tonight he could not risk a ticket and having them check his license plate. Someone could have seen him enter Corcoran's garage or leave it at the time the coroner would say Corcoran had died.

Unless it took him a long time to bleed to death, in which case there was no problem.

Or he was not dead. Mack began to shiver in the warm September evening. He put his hands in his pants pockets and felt the slime of the blood-soaked napkin. I can't! he howled silently. I don't—I'm not—I haven't—

Nothing made sense; there were no words for the ripping apart of his world.

"Hey!" Carrie exclaimed as he bolted past her bedroom on the way to the third-floor stairs. "Weren't you going away for a few days?"

Mack kept going, taking the stairs two at a time.

"Boy, are *you* friendly," Carrie shouted after him. "We had dinner, lasagna, do you want—" But he was gone; she heard him stomping around upstairs.

She went to Abby's room. "Weird," she said.

"What is?" Doug asked, coming from his room.

"Mack. He's upstairs, in an awful mood."

"Mack?" Abby cried. "He can't be."

"He's not supposed to be here," Doug said.

Carrie shrugged. "He didn't say anything, he was running."

"Probably had to pee," Doug said. "I don't want him here; I hate him. He lied to me about my show, he probably lies all the time, I hate him." He turned toward the stairs. "I'm gonna tell him, I'm gonna—"

"Don't do that!" Carrie cried. "He's really mad about something, you don't want him mad at you, too. Leave him alone."

"I won't. He *lied* to me. He acted like he liked me, and he told me how good I was, and it was all lies! He's a liar and I'm gonna tell him I hate him."

"No, you're not," Abby said angrily. She didn't want to deal with Doug's volatility right now, or Mack's anger—and why was he there, anyway?—it was all just too much.

"You're going back to your room and finish your homework."

"Why should I?"

"Because I said so and I'm in charge! Now go on!"

She turned her back and bent over her desk, not seeing anything on it. She was so angry she was shaking. She'd managed to act like Sara all through dinner, asking about their day at school, really listening to what they said, making sure they had plenty of lasagna, even cutting an extra piece of chocolate cake for Doug. She'd been so good when all she wanted was to shut herself in her room so she could think about herself and her feelings. She was very confused these days. Her misery wasn't as strong as it had been; it was like a mosquito bite that itches, and then stops, and starts and stops, off and on, for no reason. But how could it stop, when she knew what she'd done, and how awful Sean had been, and how nothing would be the same, ever again?

At school everyone had been really nice, greeting her as if she'd just been away on a trip, except for that kid in the seventh grade who asked if she was going to try out for the Indy 500 next, and she just ignored him. But

Sean wasn't there and she couldn't ignore that because, the truth was, as much as she'd feared seeing him, somehow she wanted to see him, so she could ignore him, or maybe let him explain things in a way that made sense so she could forgive him. But he wasn't in school, which is what Sara had thought would happen. But then, where was he? In jail? Or back in England? It was awful not knowing, and she couldn't telephone his house, or ask about him; she couldn't let anyone know she was even interested.

So now she was in her room, finally alone, finally peaceful and quiet, and then Mack all of a sudden came back, Carrie and Doug wanted to talk, Doug wanted to march up to the third floor . . . *and I'm supposed to take care of all that. It isn't fair. I'm not ready to be responsible.* She felt very sorry for herself, but also noble, because she was doing all this for Sara.

The telephone rang and Doug leaped for it.

"Hi, love, is everything fine at home?" Sara asked.

"Sure, where are you?"

"New York, you know that."

"Yeah, but you sound like you're right here."

"Let me." Carrie grabbed the telephone. "Sara, Mack's here."

"What? He said he'd be out of town."

"I know, but he came in a few minutes ago. He looked really mad at the world."

"What did he say? Is he bothering you?"

"He didn't say anything, he ran upstairs, didn't even say hello. He didn't want any dinner, either."

"Let me talk to Abby, please, Carrie."

"But I can tell you—"

"I know you can, sweetheart, I just want to talk to Abby."

Carrie turned and saw Abby standing in the doorway of her room. "Sara wants to talk to you. She always asks *you* if we're right about something."

Abby ignored her and forced herself to think of Sara. She deserved a good time without worrying about them. "Don't worry about Mack, Sara; Carrie shouldn't have told you. He's not a problem; we're fine." Make Sara proud of you, she ordered herself. "Are you having a good time?"

"Yes," Sara said.

"Where are you?"

"In a taxi, going to dinner. Abby, didn't Mack say anything at all about why he was there?"

"I didn't see him. Carrie said he ran right past her and up to his room without talking, and looked like he was in a horrible mood. Where are you going to dinner? Is it elegant?"

"I don't know. It's called Gramercy Tavern."

"He's taking you to a *tavern*?"

Sara laughed. "I'm told it's a fine one. We'll all go together someday. Are any of you worried about Mack?"

"*No,* I told you. We're fine. Is Reuben okay?"

Sara looked at him; they smiled and their hands touched. "He's fine," she said.

"You sound happy. Are you happy?"

"Yes."

"Oh. Really?" Abby took another breath. "Good," she said emphatically. "What are you wearing?"

"Black pantsuit, pink silk blouse, the one you've borrowed a couple of times. Abby, where is Mack now?"

"I told you: in his room, probably sulking about something, and he'll probably go out later, and we won't even see him. You know he does that; you know he gets these moods. Sara, we're fine; don't worry about us. Nothing's any different; everything's normal."

Sara nodded to herself. Why wouldn't it be? What was she worried about? "Okay, sweetheart, call me any time you want to talk. Let me talk to Doug and Carrie, please." She listened for signs of worry in their voices as they chattered about their day, but heard none. And when the taxi stopped at the restaurant, she finally said good-bye.

The inner room of Gramercy Tavern looked as old as New York, with roughly textured ceiling beams almost black with age, heavy draperies falling in deep folds, and tables and chairs that were dark, gleaming, solid. The lighting was low, the tables spaced apart, and flickering candles illuminated diners in small circles of privacy. Sara smiled at Reuben as they sat down. "Thank you. It's perfect."

It was half past ten, and the restaurant had settled into the languorous murmuring of leisurely diners who would order another bottle of wine and let pauses in their conversations lengthen rather than end a pleasant evening. The hard edges of the day had softened, and the waiters, no longer quite as brisk as earlier, seemed to glide from table to table. Sara and Reuben were aware of it all as background: a warm and inviting place to be private.

When their waiter brought the wine list,

Reuben asked, "What shall we choose to begin?"

"White Bordeaux."

"Excellent choice. And red with dinner." He ordered both, and they turned again to each other. "Is there anything you want to ask me? I haven't given you much chance; I've done almost all the talking."

In fact, he had talked for over three hours. But that had been in the late afternoon. Before that, he had been in a meeting that began soon after they arrived, leaving Sara free to wander through Greenwich Village. She knew little of New York; her one year of medical school had been so absorbing she rarely left the neighborhood around Columbia University, and even then had gone no farther south than Lincoln Center.

Now she explored the angled streets of the Village, a mix of scruffy and polished, harkening to the past and soaring with new ideas, self-satisfied, modest, and exuding a kind of wayward charm. There was an enchantment to the rows of houses crammed as tightly together as burghers gossiping about city scandals, and the enchantment was unexpectedly deepened as the day turned overcast. Clouds moved in, white and pale gray, hanging low and darkening the streets until the antique street lamps began to glow. The day was still warm, and Sara, daring the rain to start, would not be forced into hurrying. She turned up and down the streets, happily losing her way, discovering churches, art galleries, parks, a cemetery, whimsical boutiques and sleek outlets of national chains, the high-rise buildings of New York University. In a craft shop she found a carving set for Doug with templates of the Brooklyn Bridge and the Statue of Liberty, and in a bookstore around the corner, she bought a collection of stories about Ellis Island for Carrie and, for Abby, biographies of New York actresses. Later, she stopped for salad and espresso at a small café, and walked again, letting her thoughts drift.

She was keyed up but oddly light, with a spring to her step. Because I'm alone, she thought, a tourist in New York with no children waiting at home, no dinner to make or homework to check, no lunches to fix for tomorrow, no work from the office to finish.

But there was more to it than that. She felt suddenly untethered from all the expectations and acceptances that had defined her life until now. The old definitions no longer seemed immutable. *Today my life will change.*

(That it could remain the same, that she could go back to Chicago and settle into the same routine and expectations as before, with nothing on the horizon to hint at something new, she considered briefly and rejected; it did not bear contemplation.)

After today, nothing would be the same; this was a day of decisions. The thought buoyed her through the timeless neighborhoods and cast a glow on shop windows and the intently focused faces of New Yorkers hurtling through their streets. She felt she was one of them, expansive and hopeful, with the same thought she had had on the plane flying in: Reuben would not have brought her here unless it was a time for change. *Today my life will change.*

Reuben was waiting for her when she found her way back to his apartment in the late afternoon, just as rain began to fall. When she had left her luggage there earlier, before beginning her walk, she had only glanced at the rooms, startled by the differences between them and the home he had created in Chicago. On her return, once again she could not believe this was

Reuben's home. In Chicago, he had filled his stately rooms with deep furniture, a grand piano, antique rugs in muted shades of blue, rose, sage, and chestnut, paintings of Milton Glazer and lithographs of Picasso that bridged rather than lurched from one century to the next. But here, in a New York loft near Sheridan Square, with a spiral staircase leading to a second floor Sara had not yet seen, he had, with harsh finality, slammed the door on the past.

On the lower floor, high-ceilinged and spacious, he had defined separate rooms with fig and citrus trees and high bookshelves open to both sides. French doors and tall, narrow windows, kept bare, looked over a broad terrace; earlier she had seen the skyscrapers of lower Manhattan, but now all she saw was the rain, a downpour that blew across the windows and dimmed the rooms to a somber palette of white walls, pale ash bookshelves, polished hickory floors, an unused fireplace, and angular couches and armchairs in white, black, and brown. The only color came from a few Indian and Turkish rugs, and, along a gallery stretching to left and right of the front door, enormous, slashing paintings by Franz Kline, Antoni

Tàpies, and Willem de Kooning. At the far end of the gallery was a dartboard, the bull's-eye deeply pocked.

Except for the dartboard, it looked like a hotel, Sara thought. Clean, simple, sleek, and beautiful. Everything matched, everything was in proportion. It was a work of art. It was not a home. She could not imagine curling up with a book anywhere in that living room, or kicking off her shoes and making a cup of tea.

She remembered the many times Reuben had talked of bringing past and present together in the towns he built: treasuring the best of the past, searching for ways to preserve it. How painful must have been his own past, she thought, for him to so brutally turn his back on it in making a new place to live.

But then she came to his study. Completely different, it was a small room carved out of a corner of the living room with its two outer walls formed by double-sided bookshelves. Inside the study, the third wall also was lined with shelves, all three walls crammed with books, standing upright, others lying flat on top of them, some barely visible behind propped-up framed lithographs of Toulouse-Lautrec and cartoons signed by

Hirschfeld. A desk lamp reflected off a polished walnut desk and a coffee table of the same wood in an angle formed by a couch and chair upholstered in dark green tweed. Those few pieces filled the room.

Reuben had pushed aside the books on the coffee table to make room for wine bottles and glasses, a bowl of assorted nuts, and a tray of Gruyère crackers. Sara sat at one end of the couch, happy to sit after hours of walking, happy to be in this room.

In the darkening afternoon, Reuben turned on floor lamps, lit the logs in a small stove in the corner, and filled their wineglasses. He sat in the armchair and began to talk. And, since he knew he should have done it months before, he told Sara everything because he could not be sure what seemingly small detail might later turn out to have been crucial. He told the whole sad, convoluted story of his marriage to Ardis, his own failings as well as hers, beginning with college and ending with Gus's telephone call Saturday, a few minutes before noon, announcing Ardis's signature on the financial agreement. "So you can stroll into a happily-ever-after with your terrific lady," Gus had said, and Reuben told Sara that, too.

When he finished, it was almost eight o'clock. Rain lashed against the windows, a constant drumbeat that enhanced the warm enclosure of the room.

"What I want you to understand," Reuben said, "is that no one forced me to do anything. I was convinced I was in love with Ardis, I knew I wanted to protect her in a world that terrified her. She'd fled the slums where she grew up, and once she found me and needed me I brought her into my life. It wasn't long before I realized that I'd taken her on as a project and called it a marriage."

He paused, but Sara said nothing; she had listened in silence since he began speaking. She kept her eyes on his, loving the sound of his voice in the hushed room, the way he kept his hands still so as not to distract from his words, the small frown between his eyes as he strove for the right phrase. She loved, it seemed, everything about him, even his revelations, which seemed more a tale of the inconsistencies and yearnings of youth, and then of lonely middle age, than of sins of a cosmic nature.

"I suppose," he said ruminatively, "love can flourish in the worst circumstances if one feels like a hero. But I think I've always looked for projects: the kinds of assignments that are built around people's needs. I don't know if it's because it's the easiest way to feel positive about myself, or the quickest way to satisfy an inordinate need to be loved and admired; I do know that I have to be reined in sometimes from trying to solve all the world's problems, near and far." He smiled ruefully. "A hero."

He poured the last of the wine into their glasses. "I don't feel that way with you. You're not a project; you're a strong woman who's had to make difficult decisions, and live with them in an admirable way. I know you can make your way in the world, you can make a full and rewarding life without me. I would like to think it could be more rewarding with me, but I know I'm not essential for that." Once again he waited, but still Sara said nothing. "And you can care for your family without me; you're wonderful with them now. As much a real mother as anyone could be. I'd like to think that, together, we could give them a life they'd thrive in differently from the one you're giving them now, but I'm not essential to that, either; they'll do fine if your family stays as it is now."

He sat at the other end of the couch from

Sara. "All this is a rather clumsy way of telling you that I love you, deeply and gratefully, and I want to marry you and make a life with you and shield you as much as possible from unhappiness and need, as I hope you would shield me. I don't believe anymore in one-way streets. Perhaps I never did. What I do know is that I want to give you and your family a good life, and a joyous one."

The room was silent. The rain had eased and, faintly, through a small opening in a protected window, came neighborhood sounds that reminded Sara of her neighborhood at home: the whoosh of traffic, a child shouting good-byes to friends, a dog barking, a woman calling someone to dinner. It was all familiar but remote, twelve floors below the room where Sara sat beside Reuben in spheres of lamplight, and felt as if she were drenched in gold. She leaned toward him and laid her hand along his face. "But you are essential. For everything."

And then later, much later, they went to dinner. Because, in each other's arms on the couch in Reuben's study, the only urgency was to go upstairs, to go to his bed, to rediscover what they had known before. But now there was no cloud shadowing Reuben's thoughts when he lay with Sara, no uncertainties trailing his words. When they held each other, their clear horizons merged and they went toward them with equal freedom and certainty and hope.

"Today my life has changed," Sara murmured to Reuben, and he responded, "Today our lives have changed."

So how could it be, after such a pledge, that she gazed at him as they lingered over coffee and cognac long past midnight, and had the thought, as sudden and swift as a bird darting into a tree and scattering leaves, that she was not sure?

But of course there was a reason: he came to her unencumbered, while she brought a family, the demands of growing children who needed an astonishing amount of attention and nurturing. She recalled thinking, after they had separated, that she had no time for Reuben, that it was a good thing they weren't together. Perhaps she had been right.

She watched as his gaze settled with mild interest on two couples at a nearby table lazily arguing over who would pay the check. Did she really want to attach her life to his? Alter in ways she could not foresee the life she had worked so hard to create? She had learned to balance a house, three children, a job, and her own friends; she could predict most of her days and know she could handle the crises that turned others upside down. How much unpredictability would she take on with Reuben? How much of what she had would she lose? (*Or gain, don't forget that.*) It had been years since anyone told her what to do or what not to do; years since anyone opposed her decisions or even suggested alternatives. She was used to making decisions alone and carrying them out alone. She had come to take that for granted.

Reuben turned back to her and met her gaze, and smiled.

She smiled and held out her hand on the table, and he took it, and she thought, Take it for granted? Why would I want to keep taking it for granted? The truth is, I get tired of being good and sensible and upright; I want the option of lying down on the job, knowing someone is there to keep things going until I'm back on my feet. Why would I want to make decisions alone for the rest of my life? Just to know that I can do it? I know it. I've proved it. It's time to prove that I can love someone enough to share my life.

That I love Reuben enough to share my life.

"Such a somber look in your eyes," Reuben said. "Can you share it?"

And, though instinct tugged at her not to tell him, not to leap into confidences quite so quickly, she told him. (*Because isn't that exactly what he did for so long? Kept his confidences to himself? Shut me out because he wasn't ready to be open with me?*) And it was all right, because he understood, and when they left the restaurant their arms were around each other, and when they walked through his front door they were a couple coming home together, climbing the stairway to the second floor together, and going to bed together, to awake to tomorrow, to all the tomorrows, together. Yes, Sara thought as she fell asleep, yes, we will.

And, "Yes," Reuben murmured early in the morning when Sara sat up beside him.

He was not awake: he had spoken that one word in a flicker of coming to the surface before sinking again into sleep. He slept neatly, on his back, arms at his sides, hands lightly clasped at his waist, and did not shift or turn all night. Sara, a restless sleeper, felt unruly beside him. She sat now, looking down at him as the sun rose in a translucent sky and light filled the room. Through the tall windows, she saw the vista of skyscrapers she had imagined the night before, sharply defined, washed clean by the rain. Everything was fresh and new, and she was happy and wanted the day to begin.

She leaned down and kissed Reuben and he opened his eyes, wide-awake. "Good morning. You're very lovely this morning."

"Only a lover could say that." She kissed him again. "You have a meeting at nine o'clock."

"I do, damn it. I just want to be with you."

"Breakfast? Lunch? Dinner?"

He laughed. "All of the above." He glanced out the window. "Would you like to walk this morning? My meeting is at City Hall and there's a little breakfast place close by, on Barclay Street. It's a long walk."

"I like long walks. And we have time; it's early." She kissed him again and slid from the bed, liking it that he was watching her as she walked, naked, across the bedroom to the bathroom on the left ("Yours," Reuben had said simply), where she had put her cosmetics bag the night before. She found his bedroom to be as anonymous as his living room, but the bed was wide and comfortable, which was all, for the moment, they wanted from that room.

The walk to Barclay Street was longer than Sara had anticipated, but she was exhilarated by the matched rhythm of their stride, unimpeded, at that early hour, by other pedestrians. They traversed quiet neighborhoods where an occasional early riser emerged to take in newspapers or walk a dog; shop owners revealed the merchandise in their windows as they clatteringly raised protective steel blinds; and other owners set out foods, furniture, books, and clothing in cunningly attractive arrangements for the day's trade. Hand in hand, Reuben and Sara walked briskly, and talked—there was so much to talk about—and breathed deeply of the sharp, almost spicy early-morning air, its grime and traffic fumes sluiced away by the night's downpour.

They walked for more than an hour, to Peg's Place, small, bright, bustling; loud with declamations on politics, the weather, Little League and taxes, fragrant with cinnamon and nutmeg, coffee and pancakes. They sat at the counter until a table became free and they moved to it, carrying their plates and mugs. "A do-it-yourself place," Reuben said.

"I like it," Sara replied, and they smiled at each other across the small Formica table because they were together and glowing from their brisk walk, the French toast and marmalade were delicious, the coffee perfect, and everything was wonderful.

"What would you like to do this afternoon?" Reuben asked. "I would have liked to take you to my parents, but they won't be back from Italy for a month. We'll come back then. Meanwhile, I have a listing of museum shows, or there are galleries I think you'd like, whatever you choose."

"Carrano Village," Sara said. "Do we have time?"

"Plenty of time. Thank you." He was grateful, and humbled, too, to discover, even now, when he had proven his success many times, how much he still needed someone (someone he cared about) to show interest in his work. *But who doesn't need that? All of us need propping up, to keep believing we're worthwhile not only on the public stage, but in our personal lives as well. And what better reason for marriage?* His thoughts lurched slightly. *As long as marriage works.* "We'll drive to New Jersey, as soon as I'm finished here," he said, "and go from Carrano to the airport. Our plane isn't until six-thirty; we'll even have time for a late lunch."

He finished his coffee. "Time to go. I'd rather stay with you and drink endless cups of coffee."

"I'll walk with you; I've never been to City Hall. And I'll explore the neighborhood."

"We'll get a map at City Hall. Do you have your cell phone? I'll call you when my meetings end."

He called twice, once "because I wanted to hear your voice," the second time to say he would be late. "Everything is taking longer than I expected; can you wait an hour or so?"

"Of course I can."

"Where are you?"

"On a bench in Battery Park."

"Looking at the Statue of Liberty."

"Yes, and it's so amazing. I've seen thousands of pictures of it, all my life, but now, suddenly, it's here, in front of me, larger than I expected, and far more powerful than I ever imagined. I have to bring Doug and Carrie and Abby here; I want them to experience this."

"We'll bring them here together, and give them the three-star tour of the city. I have to go; I'll call soon."

Sara sat quietly, gazing across the water at the gleaming statue, its torch held high against the dense blue sky, all the promise of this new land, whether fulfilled or pending, symbolized in that raised arm and pure white form leading ships into the harbor. The sun was warm on her face, the air soft, families and couples and school classes chattered all about her. She was happy to be alone. A tourist in New York, she thought, as she had the day before, exploring Greenwich Village. How pleasant to be a tourist, anywhere. *We'll bring them here together, and give them the three-star tour of the city.* A lovely thought, but, still, now and then, how satisfying to be alone, to think without having to speak, to absorb sights and sounds without having to verbalize them, and share.

Still, it was satisfying and wonderful to share the rest of the day with Reuben. (And thank goodness for that, she thought wryly.) They walked through Carrano Village East, and Sara was impressed (and thank goodness for that, too, she thought). It was far more attractive than she had feared (thinking of developments with rows of houses facing each other across rows of streets like faintly antagonistic teams of twins, scattered sterile play lots and dusty softball fields); in fact, it looked exactly as Reuben had described what Carrano Village West would be: clusters of individualized widely spaced ranch and two-story houses, expansive green space, dusty playing fields (but it *is* September, she thought, suddenly loyal), and a school, recreation building, and double row of shops designed in a generic Early American style. Firmly grounded in the rural New Jersey landscape, the village was warm and inviting, a place where one could imagine settling, raising children, making friends.

"Less than a family, more than a town," she murmured.

"Thank you," he said, grateful again. "That's always the goal."

"Is Isaiah here?" she asked as they walked back to the car. "I'd like to meet him."

"Not this week; he's fishing in Canada. His passion, after building towns for young families. He'll be in Chicago later this month; shall we take him to dinner?"

Sara glanced at him and saw his surprise at how quickly and easily *we* had become part of his vocabulary.

"Yes," she said simply. His vocabulary shifts were ahead of her, since *we* in her lexicon included three children and a mother, but leave it alone, she thought. One of these days they'd talk about her family, and it had to be soon, but not now, when they were talking about work he loved and places he was transforming. They would be transforming each other's life, she thought, so let them discuss it in Chicago, their home for a long time to come.

They stopped for coffee at a small restaurant near Princeton, and Sara called home. "Everything's *okay,*" Abby said. "You don't have to keep calling, you know. Everything's the same every time you call."

"I like to know that," Sara replied. "Did you have a good day at school?"

"It was fine. Well, Carrie's in some kind of state, maybe her day wasn't so great, she's upstairs in her room, but she'll be fine, she always recovers from these dramatic moments."

"Does she want to talk to me?"

"She doesn't want to talk to anybody. She's okay, just . . . you know, being Carrie."

"Is Mack there?"

"I don't know. We just got home, just before you called. It's pretty quiet; he's probably gone somewhere. You'll be here by nine, right?"

"Probably before that. There's food in the freezer; did you find it?"

"Of course we did; we're *fine,* Sara."

Sara laughed as she clicked off the phone. "The only thing I have to worry about is not being missed."

"I have a feeling they're not letting on—"

Reuben's phone rang. He listened for a long moment. "This is not good," he told Sara. "New York and New Jersey airports are shut down, the word is 'temporarily.' Evidently someone thinks there's a security problem. Possible security problem."

"But we haven't heard a word about it."

"We haven't been listening to the radio."

"But no one's mentioned it."

"Maybe rural New Jersey is the last to hear. Anyway, we don't know how long this will last; I'd better call Isaiah. We can use his plane."

"Isn't he in Canada, fishing?"

"Damn it, he is. And he took his plane."

"I'll call the children," Sara said after a moment. "I wish I could give them a time we'll get there."

"We'll keep checking the airports. Meanwhile, shall we go home?"

"Home—?"

He smiled ruefully. "This home. We seem to have three at the moment. Two of them we can't get to."

"Yes, why not? I can't imagine sitting in the airport for hours."

Reuben drove, and once again Sara made a phone call. "Closed!" Abby exclaimed. "How can they do that? Just shut them down? What about all the people who have tickets?"

"It seems they'll all have to wait, as we do."

"How long?"

"I have no idea. I'll let you know as soon as I know anything."

Reuben put his hand on hers. "We'll charter a plane if it doesn't get cleared up soon. Abby shouldn't worry."

"Did you hear that, Abby?" Sara asked.

"Sure. Does he hear everything we say?"

"If I have the speaker on. Do you mind?"

There was a pause. "I guess not." Another pause. "I guess a train is too slow, right?"

"A train wouldn't get us there tonight. But I told you, we'll charter a plane if we have to."

"What if you can't? What if there aren't any planes?"

"Then we'll fly back tomorrow. Would you mind that terribly?"

"*Of course not.* I keep telling you we're fine. But what if the airports aren't open tomorrow?"

"Then we'll drive." Sara looked at Reuben, who nodded.

"How long would that take?"

"I'm not sure; I've never done it. If we leave early in the morning, we should be there by dinnertime. But if you want us to drive now, we can do that."

"No, it's okay. Forget it; you can come later tonight. Or tomorrow. Whatever. We'll be fine. Can we go out to dinner?"

"Of course. You don't want to eat at home?" Of course they didn't, Sara thought. Much more fun to go out. "Use your credit card; I'll pay you back."

"Is it okay if we go to O'Fame? Doug likes the pizza."

"You all like the pizza. It's fine; have a good time. Ask Carrie to come to the phone."

Sara heard Abby call—"Sara wants to talk to you!"—heard her put down the phone and call again at the foot of the stairs, and come back. "She's sulking. We could call you later."

"Yes, call me anytime. And I'll let you know what's happening here."

Hanging up, Sara turned to Reuben. He

had turned down the volume on the radio, and she said, "Has anyone said anything about planes flying later tonight?"

"Not yet. It sounds as if everything's all right at home."

She nodded. "They're really wonderful; they don't cling, but I think you were right when you said they probably weren't letting on that they wanted me home." She thought for a moment. "I should be there. Can we charter a plane?"

"I'll try. It occurs to me that if the airports are closed, even private planes can't take off." He made the call while Sara listened to the radio. "No," he said at last. "Nothing's moving. We can drive; we can lease a car and leave anytime."

"But if the airports open sometime tonight, we'd be there sooner."

"Yes."

"Then let's wait awhile."

They were quiet, listening again to the radio. "Shall we go out for dinner?" Reuben asked.

"Oh, we've done so much today . . . and we're waiting to hear . . . could we make something at home?"

"A very good idea."

Stopping and starting in the gridlock that stretched for blocks at the entrance to the Holland Tunnel, it struck Reuben as surprising and anomalous that at this moment, when it seemed he had no control over any of his movements—planes grounded, Isaiah in Canada, traffic gridlocked, all his schedules knocked out the window—he felt more powerful than ever in his own life. An odd disconnect, he reflected, between a private life, where, most of the time, we manage to shape our days and years, and the larger world around us, where a governmental decision or something as seemingly innocuous as too many drivers in too many cars can exert enough power to disrupt our plans and force us into different channels. Neither the government nor any of these other drivers set out to stymie us; they don't give a damn about us. But, still, we're powerless to alter the situations they cause.

Except, he added, changing lanes, though he knew that, at best, it might gain him half a minute, we will get home at some point—this home, the homes in Chicago—and meanwhile, here is Sara, beside me: reason enough to feel powerful.

They made dinner together. Reuben

cooked trout and Sara made salad and wild rice, and they carried everything to Reuben's study, where he called the airline once again, reaching only a recording. *Another kind of loss of control; a small detail that turns out to be one of the most enraging in modern society.* He opened a Meursault, and they sat quietly, watching the sky turn translucent, metallic gray deepening to fiery orange and magenta, yellow and red streaks edged in pale green. But quickly, too quickly, the flaming colors faded to silver gray and then, as if reluctantly, to the attenuated black stretching to infinity above the orange-red nimbus that hovers over great cities at night. "If we have to stay another night," Reuben said, "would you be worried?"

"I think they'll be fine," Sara said. "It's just that this isn't the way I planned it, and I hate having to tell them I can't be there. I hate it that I feel so helpless," she added vehemently. "I know it's silly, it isn't earthshaking and I shouldn't be so upset, but, good heavens, New York to Chicago, such a simple trip; we just assume it will happen all day, every day."

They were quiet again, and then they began talking about the time they had been apart. Sara talked about Abby's accident;

her despair over Sean and, even worse, her giving in to him; Doug's gloom after his fake gallery show; Donna Soldana's lies and her besotted husband; and Carrie's published stories. "It doesn't look like a real magazine to me, but it could be one of those little, obscure ones, I can't be sure, and anyway I couldn't say anything; she is so excited."

"And Mack?" Reuben asked.

"I don't know. He's so much *there;* we're always aware of him, even when he's away from the house. I'm uncomfortable with him around, and I think the children are becoming uncomfortable, too, mostly because he's so unpredictable . . . I just don't know. I can't figure him out."

After a moment, she laughed slightly. "Such a catalog of dramatic events. I always thought we were so ordinary, but all this sounds like a heavy play, something Carrie might think up." After a minute, she said slowly, "I thought, each time, that I wasn't handling things well, I could have handled them better, but so much was happening, and it was all going by so fast, I couldn't reach out and stop it long enough to think about what was the best thing to do, or even what all my options might have been. I kept trying to feel in control, but I couldn't. That's the way I feel now; I can't even get home; such a simple thing, but I can't do anything about it." She shook her head. "There's just too much. As if we can't do anything about anything."

"I can't believe that," Reuben said quietly. "We do have ways we can feel in control; if we didn't, we couldn't get through—"

The telephone rang. Reuben looked at his watch—ten o'clock—as he answered it. "Reuben, where's Sara?" Abby demanded.

"Right here." He held out the telephone.

"What is it?" Sara asked.

"I don't know." Abby's voice was high and wavering. "Something's wrong with Mack, he's . . . he's *awful* and *scary* and I don't know what to do."

"What has he done? *Has he hurt you?*"

"No, he's mostly upstairs, but we saw him once and he looked . . . I don't know . . . awful. Like he smiles but it's just his teeth, you know, all tight together, that's all you *see*. And he says weird things, and says it's all our fault."

"What is your fault?"

"I don't know! He's so weird! He said we'd turned everybody against him, and . . . I can't explain it," she said, her voice rising higher, "but I don't know what to do! We've got a movie on in the library, but it's hard to watch when we keep thinking about . . . you know . . . everything. I called the Abbots and the Pierces, but nobody's home, and I don't know what I'd say, anyway. My brother's acting weird, could we come to your house? I mean, nothing's happened, it's just that . . . Sara, couldn't you come home? Couldn't you, like, rent a plane or something, and come home? Please, Sara, couldn't you find a way? We really want you to."

Sara looked at Reuben, but he had heard Abby's high, pleading voice, and was already calling, on another phone, the answering service for his car leasing company. "We can leave within an hour, and we'll drive straight through. I'm pretty sure we can be there by morning."

"We'll drive," Sara said to Abby. "We can be there by morning. Tonight I want you and Carrie and Doug to stay together. If Mack comes downstairs, don't argue with him; don't talk to him any more than you have to. You don't know what might make him angry, so just be friendly and don't get into big discussions. You can tell him we're on our way home, in fact, you should tell him that; you can say we left a few hours ago. If he bothers you again, keep calling the Pierces and the Abbots; they'll be home eventually. I'll keep calling, and you call me whenever you feel like it. Anytime, okay?"

"Okay, but how long will it take you?"

"I really don't know. I told you Reuben thinks we'll be there in the morning. I'll let you know where we are each time I call. We'll be there as soon as we can, I promise."

She stood up and looked at her watch. Ten-fifteen. "We're on our way," she said.

FIFTEEN

Carrie hated the house without Sara in it. Actually, she didn't really hate it, because she loved it, but it wasn't the same house with Sara gone. All the rooms were big and hollow as if some giant took a beautiful apple and cored out all its insides, so the shape was still the same, but everything else was different, and she and Doug and Abby couldn't fill up the rooms no matter how much they ran around or talked as loud as they could. Someday she'd write a story about it, she thought, it would have tension, and her teacher said she was good at that.

But it would be sad, too, and weird because that's how it was with Sara gone. It was weird from the minute they came home from school on Monday afternoon and started thinking about making dinner and doing homework and doing whatever they wanted. They'd had dinner without Sara lots of times, when she had to work at night, but this was different, because they knew she was in New York, and that was odd to think about all by itself, and then she wasn't there to say good night to them, and the next morning her bedroom was empty and she wasn't in the kitchen asking if they had everything for school, and then after breakfast they left and locked the front door and none of it was right.

In fact, Carrie realized, it was just like that when her mother went to the hospital and the nursing home, like she'd died, even though you knew she hadn't, and she and Doug and Abby sort of tiptoed around like they were afraid if they moved too fast or talked too loud something would break, and the whole house would collapse.

But the worst part was Tuesday afternoon when she ran home from school feeling miserable, wanting Sara to put her arms around her and tell her she wasn't a failure or a fake, she was a good writer and she'd have a wonderful career, and everybody loved her. But Sara wasn't there and all Carrie could do was run up to her bedroom and slam the door and curl up in her armchair that Sara had helped her choose, and cry.

Through her closed door she heard Abby downstairs, talking to Doug or maybe on the phone. A few minutes later Abby called her from the bottom of the stairs—"Sara wants to talk to you!"—then called her again, closer this time, but Carrie didn't want to talk to anybody, so she remained silent. But in a few minutes Abby was knocking on her door.

"Carrie, can I come in?"

"No."

Abby opened the door. "What was so terrible that happened today? You wouldn't even talk to Sara!"

"Nothing happened, I mean . . . nothing! Abby, could you just leave me alone?"

"Sara's coming home, but not—"

"I know she is! I'm waiting for her! Just leave me—what time's her plane?"

"They can't get one, that's what I'm trying to tell you. For some reason the airports are shut down, and none of the airplanes can fly, so maybe she won't be home tonight."

"She has to come back tonight! I need her."

"We all need her. She said they'd get here as soon as they could, they'll rent a plane or something."

"But *when will she get here?* What am I supposed to do till then?"

"Do you want to talk to me?"

"No. I'll figure it out."

"Damn it, Carrie, I'm just trying to help."

"Don't yell at me! Please."

"We all want her home, you know." Involuntarily, Abby looked toward the third-floor stairs, then back to Carrie. "We just have to wait, and take care of ourselves until then."

Carrie pointed upstairs. "Is he home?"

Abby nodded. "I heard him moving around. Maybe he's been here all the time."

"I don't like him anymore."

"Nobody likes him anymore. Just keep away from him. Sara says we should stay together and not . . . you know, annoy him, get him mad . . . madder than he is."

"What's he mad about?"

"How should I know?"

"He looked mad last night, when he ran past me. Maybe he's gone crazy, seeing demons and ghosts and enemies everywhere. It's pretty scary."

"Come downstairs, Carrie, let's do things together. We'll do our homework in the library, and then we're going to O'Fame to dinner."

"I'll come down in a while."

"Come down now!"

"I will in a little while! You can't tell me what to do; you're not Sara, you know!"

"I'm in charge of the house! And I'm *ordering* you—"

"Don't yell at me! And you can't order me around! I'm not a baby; I'm thirteen years old and I'll come down when I feel like it!"

Abby stood indecisively. Her shoulders slumped. "I'm glad I'm not Sara," she muttered. "Fifteen minutes," she threw out angrily, "you be downstairs in fifteen minutes," and slammed Carrie's door as she left.

Carrie dropped back into the armchair. She heard Abby telling Doug to come downstairs with her. "Just do what I say!" she snapped, and Carrie felt sorry for Doug. She felt sorry for herself, too. She knew she ought to go downstairs; Abby really was in charge when Sara was gone, Carrie knew that, too. But there was something she had to do first: after what happened in school today, she had to talk to Mack. She had to know the truth.

She opened her door and stood at the foot of the third-floor stairs, listening. There was not a sound, but she knew he was up there because she smelled him smoking pot even though he'd promised Sara he wouldn't do it in the house. He might be nicer if he was high. Or meaner. You never knew with Mack; he wasn't like other people. But it didn't matter, if he got mean, she'd run downstairs, and if he was nice, she'd find out the truth and then she'd go downstairs.

Taking a deep breath, she climbed the stairs, not letting herself think about what might happen, putting each foot down hard so he would hear her coming. At the top was a little square hallway with one door, and the door was closed. Carrie knocked on it, but she had begun to shake and her knuckles just brushed the door; even she didn't hear the knock. She opened the door an inch and found herself facing a burlap curtain he'd hung from the ceiling so even if you opened the door you couldn't see into his room. "Get the hell out," he barked from the other side of the curtain.

"Can I come in?" Carrie asked. It was a

silly thing to say, since he'd just told her to get out, but she didn't know what else to do.

There was no answer. Mack turned over in bed, burrowing his face into the pillow. He'd slept all day, waking up only to smoke a joint, then sink again. Now the kid was here; what the fuck did she want? What did any of them want? Why the hell couldn't they leave him alone?

"I have to ask you something," Carrie said. "It's very important. It'll just take a minute, and then I'll leave."

"Shit." He tried to wake up, forcing himself up on one elbow and shaking his head like a dog throwing off water. "Well, what the fuck are you waiting for?"

Carrie pushed aside the burlap curtain. He was sprawled on top of the quilt on his bed and his eyes were red and puffy (but Mack wouldn't cry, she thought). She had never been in his room, but it only took her a few seconds to decide it was awful. It was so bare it was like nobody was ever in it, no clothes or shoes lying around, a few magazines in a neat pile on the nightstand, bare walls, not one single photograph or decoration anywhere, just a small rug lined up with the bed, and the bed was lined up with the desk and dresser, and they were lined up perfectly with the long wall of the room. What a control freak, Carrie thought. (Sara had used that phrase once and now Carrie finally thought she knew what it meant.) The only sign of disarray was the ashtray on the night table, overflowing with crushed and crumpled stubs. The air was filled with a haze of blue smoke, and Carrie wrinkled her nose. "It stinks in here."

Mack narrowed his eyes, trying to get her in focus. "That's your important shit?"

She was standing just inside the burlap curtain and he did not ask her to come in or sit down, so she stayed where she was, the fabric brushing against her back as she shifted from foot to foot. "My teacher told me it's not a real magazine. It's a made-up magazine."

He shrugged. "So?"

"It's not real! You lied to me! You said it was a famous story magazine and they wanted to publish my stories because they were the best, but my teacher said the other stories were lifted from other magazines, she read one of them in *The New Yorker,* she said, and it looked like somebody just re-typed them and stapled the pages and pretended it was a real magazine, but it's not, it's a fake, and nobody cared about my stories at all, they didn't think they were the best, they didn't think anything, they just typed them. So why did you lie to me? Did you lie? I mean, my teacher could be wrong or . . . something. Was she wrong? Or something?"

He stretched his mouth into a humorless grin. "Something."

"What does that mean? Tell me! I have to know!"

"Why? You were happy. What else matters?"

Confused, Carrie stared at him. It was true: she was really happy when he gave her the magazine. And now she wasn't happy; she felt awful. But . . . "It was a lie," she said loudly.

He shrugged again. "So is everything else. Christ, you're so fucking literal. Believe what you want to."

"No, that's not right! I mean, I don't know what to think! I don't know if I'm any good or not. How will I ever know if people lie to me? How will I ever get help if people just keep lying to me?"

"It's not important. Nothing is. Christ, this

is so boring. Look, you idiot, I was trying to make you happy. And I did. Why the fuck can't you leave it that way? When things are good, leave them alone."

"I can't do that." Carrie was dismayed to feel tears running down her face. "I can't be happy if it isn't true."

"Nothing's true, for Christ's sake. Everything's a lie. You work it out; I'm not responsible. You're an idiot, you and your whole family, and you bore the hell out of me, so get the fuck out and tell your asshole brother and sister to stay out, too."

Carrie caught her breath as the enormity of Mack's words sank in. "You really think we're idiots? You don't love us? Or even like us? Did you ever? Were you lying the whole time?" She stared at him, and felt a wild surge of anger. "You're the idiot! We practically gave you a whole family, you just walked in on us and we said okay this is your family, and we loved you, and then you started making things up and saying they're not important, but they are, love is important and the truth is important and being good at something is important, and you're a mean person, and I hate you and Doug hates you 'cause you lied to him about his show in that gallery and I did hear what you were saying to Mom in the nursing home, about drugs, and delivering them, and Pussy being shot and you making it look like suicide, and you're not nice and you swear too much and nobody believes you or likes you—"

He had leaped from the bed, his face a grimace. "Shut up! Shut your fucking mouth! Who else knows what you heard?"

But Carrie was swept along by anger. "—and you should be the one to get out . . . *you* get out of our house; we don't want you here!"

"Shut up, you bitch. Shut up! Who knows what you heard?"

Carrie clutched the burlap curtain, suddenly terrified. "Nobody! I didn't tell anybody!"

Mack's face was all screwed up, as if he couldn't decide what to do, and Carrie, in a moment of awful clarity, knew she should not have said she was the only one who knew. She scurried behind the curtain, clutching it so hard its flimsy rod broke and it collapsed behind her. "I told Sara!" she cried, already out the door. "And Mom told the police!"

That was a lie but it just came out, and Carrie ran down the stairs, almost falling over her feet, all the way to the first floor and into the kitchen, flinging herself against Abby, who was standing at the open refrigerator. "I'm sorry, I'm sorry, I got him mad and I didn't mean to, but he said awful things, and now I'm scared!"

"You went up there?" Abby demanded. "Why? You weren't supposed to!"

"I had to ask him—" Carrie burst into tears and buried her face against Abby's arm, begging to be held the way Sara held her, and Abby put her arms around her, not with the same tight comfort Sara gave, but it was better than nothing.

"What did he do?" Doug asked. "Why are you scared?"

Carrie shook her head. Abby's sleeve was soaked with her tears, but she could not stop sobbing.

"Carrie, *what happened?*" Abby snapped, and that made Carrie cry even harder, so Abby took a long breath. "Sorry, I didn't mean that. Can you stop crying and tell us what happened? I'll tell you what. We're going out to dinner; you can tell us all about it then."

"I can't talk about it."

"Yes, you can. How do you expect us to

help you if we don't know what happened? Come on, now, talk to us."

Carrie's sobs diminished to sniffles, and she looked up. "I got your shirt all wet."

"It's okay. I'll change before we go to dinner."

"Let's go now," Doug said. "I'm hungry."

"You're always hungry. And it's only five-thirty."

"Lots of people eat early. Anyway, it'll be after six before we eat."

Why not? Abby thought. It's a distraction, and I guess we all want to get out of here for a while. "Okay. Wash your hands and we'll go."

They trooped upstairs quietly, obediently washing their hands while Abby changed her shirt for a sweater. When they were ready, Abby picked up her shoulder bag, and they went to the front door.

"I wish you still had your car," Doug said.

"I couldn't drive anyway," Abby said shortly. "I'm not sixteen." She hated being reminded that she'd wrecked her beautiful red car, and that she wasn't old enough to drive alone, anyway, and that Sara hadn't said a word about letting her take the car out by herself after her birthday next week. Just because she'd let her drive to the gallery to get Doug's carvings, it didn't mean she'd let her drive alone. But why would Sara trust me? she thought despairingly. I did everything wrong.

"What do you think he's doing?" Doug asked as Abby opened the front door.

Abby shook her head. "I don't know and I don't care. I don't want to deal with him right now. Or ever. Maybe he'll be gone by the time we come home."

Mack heard their voices, heard the front door close, could almost feel silence rise from the floor below and wrap around him, crushing him into a tiny space. He had started after Carrie when she fled, but he was not ready to face all three of them; he had to think. He could take them on; they were kids and he could get rid of them with no trouble, but first he had to have a plan. He always had a plan; that was why he was so good at whatever job he did; that was why he was indispensable to Lew.

The name clanged inside him and he shrank even more. Bastard. Fucked me up. Blamed me for some shit I never heard of, never saw before. Fired me, the fucker.

But I shouldn't have . . . shouldn't have . . .

He forced himself to say it aloud. "Shouldn't have killed him."

Shouldn't have killed him, shouldn't have killed him, shouldn't have— It messed everything up. As soon as they found the body the cops would call him because he worked for Lew; they'd ask trick questions, try to pin it on him. He had to have answers; he had to have a plan. He paced around the room, muttering to himself.

He had a clean record. They couldn't touch him. Except . . . how much had the little bitch really heard in the nursing home? Whatever she heard it was probably too much; goddamn Mother got me talking. But . . . hold on a minute. What difference does it make? Nobody had a fucking thing on him. Everybody knows kids make things up, nobody believes them, they're just trying to be important, the center of attention. But Tess . . . well, what the hell, nothing to worry about there, either. It didn't matter what he'd told her or what she thought she heard, or what she told the cops (*if* she told the cops; how the fuck would she tell the cops anything?). She'd tell them about a gallery show for the kid. Big deal, a joke, not a crime.

Drugs? Another joke; nobody could prove anything different. Something about suicide? Lew had that under control; it was finished. Would the cops believe a defective shut up in a nursing home, making up fantasies all day long? Nobody'd believe her any more than they'd believe the kid.

He'd overreacted. He should have ignored the little bitch.

But she'd said she told Sara. Well? So what? Her word against his. And who the hell was good sister Sara? A little cog in City Hall. While Mack Hayden was vice president of Corcoran Enterprises, and as soon as they built their casino he'd be running it, he'd be invited everywhere, his picture in the society pages—

But he wouldn't be running it. Lew had fired him. He wasn't a vice president, either. Lew had promised to make him one when the casino was built. And it probably wouldn't be built now. And it didn't matter, because he wouldn't be running it. All down the drain.

Shouldn't have killed him. Should have left and waited for him to cool down; I can talk my way out of anything.

He had a gun.

He shook his head. Wouldn't have used it. He's a coward.

He used it on Pussy.

This was different. This was me. Mack Hayden. He trusted me.

Shouldn't have killed him. Should have found another way.

So, now what? He had to get the hell out of there before the cops came. But it was easier not to move from his bed, and finally he thought, Why the fuck should I let them chase me out of my own house? I'm smarter than all of them put together. I can handle this.

But the kid, yelling about drugs and the gallery. The cops could put all that together and if Frank and the others talked . . .

Have to get rid of the kid. She was lying, probably hasn't told anybody. Unless she blabbed to the other two. Sure she did, the three of 'em, always blabbing together. So, get rid of all of 'em. Get them first, before they get me. Wait too long and they'd probably kill me in my sleep. *Nobody believes you or likes you.* So, do it. Tonight, before Sara gets home. What time was her plane? They hadn't told him. She'd said she'd be back tonight, that was all. So he had to move fast.

Figure out what to do, make a plan, make it look like an accident and be somewhere else, with somebody who can say I'd been there all afternoon, all night.

Rosa. She'd say anything for me.

The telephone rang, and Mack shrank from the sound. It was too quick; he wasn't ready for the cops. Just ignore it. He listened to it ring, heard the telephone tape click on, and then silence. No message. Somebody didn't want to leave a message. Somebody . . . who was after him.

Or, what the hell, one of those assholes selling something.

He clenched his fists. Why the fuck couldn't he leave a message, whoever he was? What right did he have to hang up, leave just silence?

He had to know . . . and he couldn't know. *Son of a bitch.*

He yanked his duffel from beneath the bed and flung clothes and shoes into it, shoving them down—*more than I came with; all the things I bought because I was in business, a vice president*—then swept his business cards and Swiss Army knife off the bureau and into the duffel. Last to topple in was a small wooden giraffe Doug had carved when

Mack told him there really would be a gallery show. "Because I love you," Doug had said, holding it out to Mack. And he had thrown his arms around him. "You're a great brother."

Mack rubbed the giraffe between his palms, and collapsed on the floor, weeping. "I didn't mean to," he said. He had no idea what he meant, but he could not stop. "I didn't mean to, I didn't mean to . . . I don't know what to do, tell me what to do. I don't know what to do!"

He yelled curses, but nothing was loud enough to banish the silence of the house. He was alone and he had no one to talk to. *Nobody believes you or likes you . . . get out of our house; we don't want—*

"Bitch!" he screamed at Carrie. "I won't get out! This my house, my family, I have a key, I belong here—"

He choked and coughed, huddling on the floor, gasping for breath, while everything inside him shrank from the truth: this was not his home, it was not his family. He had thrown them away.

But he could not face that. The bitch did it. Spying on me, telling lies about me, not loving me. And did he mean Carrie? Or Sara?

Or his mother? What difference does it make, he thought bitterly. They're all against me.

"Hey, Dad, come get me," he said aloud, as he had said in years past, slumped in police stations until his father came and took responsibility for him. "Take me home, sorry about all this . . . didn't mean to."

Crouching on the floor beside his duffel, he shook his head, trying to understand. Dad? What the hell was he talking about? His father had let him down, betrayed him. Lew let him down, too, betrayed him. They should have taken care of him, watched out for him, made sure he succeeded, that he had a smooth life; they should have acted like fathers. But the sons of bitches kicked him out of their way, like trash, didn't give a damn what happened to him. Dad? Why the hell would he be calling for Dad? What was wrong with him?

Going crazy, he thought; have to stop this, have to get my shit together.

But he could not move; he crouched on the floor, his face resting on his duffel. His sobs had stopped, but raspy breaths exploded in little bursts from his open mouth, and now and then he swore at someone, at everyone.

Faintly, he heard the front door open and the three kids talking as they came in. After a minute he heard the door close tightly and the upper lock being turned. *Didn't even check to see if I was here. How would I get back in, with the door double-locked?*

They didn't give a damn. Nobody gave a damn. He was alone like he'd always been alone, nobody to help him, nobody caring where he went or what he did. Then get out. Get out before they get the cops here; they'd do that just out of spite. And hate. Full of hate. Hateful kids. Hateful house.

He shoved the carved giraffe among his clothes and shoes and zipped the duffel shut. Figure out a plan, then I'm gone.

The telephone rang again. He dashed down the stairs, to listen. "Sara!" Abby cried. "Where are you? . . . We're fine, you just talked to us in the restaurant, you don't have to call every— No, we haven't seen him; I guess he's still upstairs, or maybe he's gone out— Of course it's locked! . . . We're in the library, we're going to finish our homework and then watch *The Return of the King.* Where are you? . . . Reuben's apartment? What's it like?"

Who the hell cares, Mack fumed as the silence downstairs stretched out. When's she coming back? What time's her plane?

"They're fine, they're doing homework, do you want to talk to them? . . . Okay, I'll tell them. I love you, too. Talk to you soon. Bye."

Mack shook his head, as if to clear it. Why hadn't Abby talked to Sara about her coming home? It was already . . . what time was it? He looked at his watch. Almost nine o'clock. She was supposed to be back tonight. And she was still in the boyfriend's apartment? Was that in New York or Chicago? He closed his eyes. He hated being confused.

". . . left my math book in my room." That was Carrie's voice.

"We'll go with you," Abby said, and in the next minute Mack heard them coming upstairs. He opened his eyes, and saw the three of them standing a few feet away—three witches, three evil spirits—staring at him.

"Boo!" he shouted, and grinned when they jumped. The grin stretched his mouth, and he showed the witches his teeth. "Whaddya want? More presents? Presents all gone. Happy days all gone. You fucked it all up, little bitches, little bastard, couldn't leave well enough alone, could you?"

"What are you talking about?" Abby demanded. She had stepped in front of Doug and Carrie and was glaring at him.

"It's the famous driver talking!" Mack cried. "The super-duper driver can't find her fucking way out of somebody's front yard, has to take a tree with her and her little red car. Don't tell me what to do, you bitch—"

"Don't you talk to Abby that way!" Carrie shouted. "You're crazy, why don't you get out of our house?"

Mack lunged forward, and as the three of them scurried backward, Doug stumbled on the top step. "Abby, come on," he said shakily. "Downstairs. I mean, let's—"

"The artist!" Mack cried gaily. "The artist and the writer! The famous pair! Let's give a big hand to the famous artist and writer!"

Doug ran downstairs.

"And that leaves the witches!" Mack said wildly. His grin was gone, his gaiety was gone. "Witches, bitches, snitches, it's all your fault; everything was fine, I was fine, I was getting around Sara, all of you thought I was God's gift to the whole fucking family, but you couldn't leave it alone, you had to tell lies and turn Sara against me, turn Lew against me, the whole world letting me down—"

"We don't know what you're talking about," Abby cried.

"Get out, get out, get out!" Carrie screamed. "Nobody wants you! We hate you!"

"Shut up! I'm not going anywhere! I live here. You shut up or you'll be gone, not me"—his voice rose—"all of you, I'll take care of that. Get out of my way!"

The girls stood still, staring at him. They were not in his way; they were nowhere near him. Mack thrust his head forward. "I'll take care of you," he shouted, and turned and ran up the stairs.

"What should we do?" Carrie whispered to Abby.

"I don't know." Abby knew Carrie was waiting for a firm directive that would make her feel better, but she could not think of anything. I don't want to be grown up, she suddenly thought. I don't want to take care of people, I don't want anybody leaning on me and asking me what to do . . . because I don't know.

But Carrie's eyes had filled with tears, and Abby had seen the fear in Doug's eyes, and she remembered Carrie saying *Abby'll be sixteen next week,* and she knew she had to be in charge because there was nobody else. Sara must have felt like this when she had to come back and take care of us, she thought. I'll never get mad at her for anything, ever again. She took a deep breath, and put her arm around Carrie, holding her close. "I'm sorry I yelled at you, sweetheart," sounding like Sara, and suddenly proud of herself. "Don't cry, don't worry, we'll figure things out. Come on, now, let's go downstairs and see what Doug is doing."

"What about . . ." Carrie gestured toward the third floor.

"He'll probably stay up there and sulk." She took Carrie's hand and led her downstairs.

Mack heard them go. He was sitting on his duffel, trying to make a plan, Carrie's voice bouncing around in his head. *Hate. Hate. Hate.* Why would she say that? Nobody hated Mack; he was everybody's friend, doing favors, making deliveries, giving presents. He was the one who had the people in River Bend following him like he was the Pied Piper. He was a king out there. The King of River Bend.

That was when things were the best; those were the best days. Everything was terrific then: he had a real home, the kids loved him, Sara liked having him help her with the kids and the house, he was spending nights with Rosa, there was his lucrative sideline of supplying Frank and all his classy suburban friends, a network that grew larger all the time, and, best of all, Lew had big plans for him, treated him like a son. He'd called Mack, nobody else, to fix up the mess he'd made when he shot Pussy, that was how much he relied on Mack; he'd appointed Mack, nobody else, to organize River Bend, get the folks all worked up without ever knowing who was really behind it, and why; he'd named Mack, nobody else, the manager of the casino when it was built. Good times, Mack thought. Great times. Most of those days he felt okay: everything in place.

Where had it all gone wrong? He liked having a home, where he had his own key and people always there for him. He liked buying things for the kids that made Sara's eyes pop. He liked working for Lew, better than any job he'd ever had. He liked Rosa and being near the university and wearing neat clothes. Everything had been fine, and now it wasn't.

If he could figure it out, maybe he could repair the damage and start again, get back to the good days.

But there wasn't time. Those crazy kids were getting ready to call the cops, he knew they were, they'd say they were scared— they *were* scared; he'd scared the shit out of them—and then they'd tell the cops about . . . all of it. Everything the little bitch had heard about the gallery and Frank and drugs. And Pussy. And then the cops would dig up other stuff from New York once they got started . . .

He stood in the doorway of his room, listening. Faint sounds from the library; they were watching a movie. He could go in there, shoot them all, and get the hell out.

His cell phone rang. *Don't answer it.* It rang three times. *Rosa.* He fumbled it out of his jacket pocket. "Rosa, I need to talk to—"

"You fucking bastard, we'll get you," growled Corcoran, his voice rasping. "We'll get—"

Mack screamed. He hurled the phone across the room, then pushed both fists into his mouth. *Can't let them hear . . .* But the screams went on inside him, burning in his throat, reverberating in his head. Raving, frenzied, he plunged onto his bed, pounding the mattress, screaming into his pillow, his head bursting.

Didn't kill him. Didn't kill him. He's there . . . He's there . . . Didn't kill him.

His world was ripping apart, the pieces flying everywhere, too wildly for him to grab them, to try to put them together again. He struck the mattress again and again. Should have killed him. Should have killed him.

SHOULD HAVE KILLED HIM!

Get out, get out, get out. Get away from here.

He leaped up. No wait, the kids . . . Can't just leave them here . . . *drugs . . . deliveries . . . Pussy shot . . . you making it look like suicide* . . . Little bitch, spying bitch. She knew too much. Told the others, too, no doubt about that. Can't leave until they're taken care of.

He stood, indecisive, agonizing.

Leave 'em alone; they can't do anything.

They get the cops after me, the cops'll say I killed Lew.

Didn't kill him.

What the fuck difference does it make? Almost killed him.

Who cares, if you're out of here?

I don't know! I can't take the chance.

Where will you go, anyway?

I don't know! Someplace safe. Nauru. I'll go to Nauru. Safe little island nobody ever goes to. I've got money there, in the bank; they know me there; they like me. They'll protect me. And nobody knows I've ever been there.

The kids knew; all those stories about that funny little island.

But they'll be gone.

Lew knew about the island. But Lew and his guys had laundered too much money through the Nauru banks; of all people they'd keep quiet about it.

Anyway, the people would protect him. He'd bought them gifts, played cards with them. They loved him. They'd take care of him.

First get rid of the kids. Then go to Nauru. Then I'll be happy.

He went to the stairs. Wait, it has to look like an accident. Mack Hayden far away. His legs suddenly weak, he sat down on the top step. He was trembling, unable to move, unable to decide anything. *Make a plan!* He lit a joint. *Think of something. Not much time.* Lew. The kids. An accident. He smoked the joint to a stub, and lit another, watching the smoke drift away. And then, suddenly, it was fine; he knew what he was going to do.

"I smell smoke," Carrie said beneath the music on the screen.

"He smokes joints," Doug said gloomily. "Sara told him not to, but he does anyway."

"How do you know that's what it is?"

"I've smelled it before."

"Why doesn't he just leave?" Carrie asked. "It's awful that he just . . . hangs around."

"You've said that about twenty times," Doug observed.

"Well, it is awful. Abby, can't we do something? I don't like him in the house."

"I called the Pierces and the Abbots," Abby said. "Nobody's home. It's like everybody we know cleared out of our neighborhood."

"I don't want us to go somewhere else; I want *him* to go somewhere."

"We could call the sheriff and have him evicted," said Doug.

"What are you talking about?" Carrie asked.

"I don't know. They do it in a lot of movies."

"You can't evict somebody who hasn't done anything wrong," said Abby. "Anyway, are you going to call the sheriff and say you don't want your brother in the house? That sounds pretty bad."

"Does Chicago have a sheriff?" Carrie

asked. "I thought they were only in the Wild West."

"Oh, forget it," Doug said glumly.

"He's quiet now," Abby said. "If we just ignore him, we'll be fine."

"I know," Carrie said. "But I wish Sara was here."

"Me, too," said Doug, and he looked at Abby as if she could make Sara appear.

Abby leaped up, turned down the volume, and savagely punched numbers into the telephone. "Reuben, where's Sara?" she demanded.

Carrie and Doug listened, holding hands, which they almost never did. When Abby hung up, they both said, "When will she be here?"

"They're getting a car." Abby stood uncertainly in the middle of the library, not knowing how she was going to get them all through the hours of waiting. "Sara says they're on their way."

"But when will they get here?"

Abby sighed. "Tomorrow morning."

"That's too long!" Carrie exclaimed. "They have to get here sooner!"

"They should drive faster," Doug said.

"I can't do anything about it," Abby said, losing her temper. "I have to wait just like you and I don't like it, either, but they can't get a plane and they're going to drive all night and probably not get any sleep and if you don't stop complaining I won't talk to you anymore." She waited but Carrie said nothing, shrinking back into the couch, still holding Doug's hand. Abby turned the volume up. "We're going to sit here all night and watch all our movies, every single one if we feel like it, and make popcorn, and then Sara will be home, and everything will be fine."

"Do we have to go to bed?" Doug asked.

"I said we'd stay here all night."

"I don't want to go upstairs."

"Fine. We're staying here."

"I don't want to go upstairs, either," said Carrie.

"We're staying right here!"

"Can we have ice cream *and* popcorn?" Doug asked.

"You can have anything you want."

"Anything?"

"Whatever you want."

"Starting now?"

"Anytime."

"We're going to the kitchen and get ice cream, and then after that we'll make popcorn."

"Fine."

"We can really have both?"

"Damn it—!"

They scurried out, and Abby sank into an armchair, letting the silence settle around her. She was exhausted. How did Sara manage everything? No wonder lots of times she shut herself up in her own room; she needed this lovely silence. Not to have to talk, to explain, to make others feel good when you didn't feel good yourself. The silence stretched out, and she let it settle around her, hearing clattering from the kitchen, and chatter, which meant they were happy and not worrying, at least for now. The telephone rang, and she grabbed it.

"Hi, love," said Sara, "I just wanted you to know we're in the car and leaving New York. Is everything quiet?"

"We're fine. We're watching movies and Doug and Carrie are getting ice cream and everything's quiet. Don't worry about us. Here, they want to talk to you."

Doug and Carrie were coming back and Abby held out the telephone. "So how come you're not flying home?" Doug asked.

"We can't get a plane. We'll be there as

soon as we can. Tell me what you did today. Do you have a lot of homework?"

"I did it. We all did, so we could watch movies. Abby says we can watch all of them, every one we have. And we're having ice cream and then popcorn. Abby said we could. Do you want to talk to Carrie?"

He held out the telephone and Carrie took it and said that everything was fine, they were okay, nothing was happening, but there was this boy at school . . . Listening, Abby thought it was as if the three of them were in an unspoken conspiracy to keep Sara from worrying. Carrie had not even mentioned whatever had sent her up to Mack's room that ˙afternoon, nor how upset she was about . . . whatever she was upset about. She still refused to tell Abby, and Abby had stopped asking her.

But right then, in the library, as Carrie talked about school, it seemed for a few minutes like an ordinary evening, with Sara calling from work to tell them when she'd be home and to make sure they had everything they needed for dinner. Just another night, Abby thought, and˛curled up in her chair with the dish of ice cream Doug had brought her, with two biscotti stuck in it like rabbit ears, and Doug took back the telephone and Carrie chose a movie while he said good-bye to Sara. "And we'll see you in a little while, right?"

"Right," Sara replied, and when she hung up, she said to Reuben, "I hope they know how elastic 'a little while' is."

"Isn't time supposed to be elastic when you're young?"

"If you mean it stretches out endlessly when you're anxious for something to happen, yes."

"So it will stretch out for all of us. Do you think you could get some sleep so you could take over driving in a couple of hours?"

"I can't sleep, but of course I'll drive."

"Try to sleep. There's a pillow on the backseat."

Sara smiled. "You thought of everything." She arranged the pillow and put her head back, closing her eyes. "Don't turn off the radio."

"It might keep you awake."

"It definitely will keep you awake."

Reuben took her hand and kissed the palm. In the close darkness of the car, he felt a deep tenderness for her, not sexual, but protective and nurturing. He wanted to give to her, just give, without specificity, anything she might ever need or dream of. And he knew she felt the same urgency: both of them wanting to give, openly, steadily, without expectation of reward: give freely to each other whatever each could give that would make their separate and joined lives full and fulfilled.

When had he ever felt this before? He had not; he had not known himself capable of it. He had not known he would find a woman capable of offering it to him.

They had not talked about this, but Reuben knew it with absolute clarity. He supposed he would have known it in any circumstances, once they had found each other, but it seemed to him now that sharing the frustrations and inchoate worries of the past hours, the feelings of helplessness and then a regaining of control, and now this race to get to the children, had bound them in new ways that transcended the attachment of two people who had decided they would share their lives, without, at the time, having any idea what that sharing might encompass.

He did not resent this; he welcomed it. Never before had he been responsible for someone who was not dependent. Now he knew how much he had missed that, especially now, when he knew Sara's strength, and knew that she, like he, needed not guidance, but support.

The highway was crowded, as others turned to driving for their travel. In the stream of cars, he tried to keep up his speed, hoping for a clear highway as they moved west across New Jersey and into Pennsylvania. He glanced at Sara. Her eyes were closed and she was breathing steadily, but her hands were clenched in her lap; she was not asleep, but willing her body to rest so that she could drive when it was her turn. He wanted to touch her, to warm her tense hands and relax them, to hold her so she would not feel worried or fearful, would not even imagine worrisome or fearful things.

I love you, Reuben said to Sara silently, and wondered at the simplicity of a phrase, that, at one time, with one person, contained a universe and a lifetime.

And yet . . . The thought sprang abruptly: You're driving to a house where there are problems, where there are three children who need help and advice, comfort, encouragement, love, parenting. Where there's a brother who's a wild card and may be involved in criminal activities. Where there are demands you have never faced. It was one thing, he mused, to marry and then have a baby—babies—to guide through the stages of childhood and adolescence; it was another to leap into a maelstrom of them without preparation. Even worse: to leap without knowing if these particular adolescents wanted him or gave a damn whether or how quickly he learned (or failed) to offer all that they required. It was almost a given, he thought, that they would prefer the familiar and predictable: Sara by herself, the four of them together with no interference from outside. Why would they want anyone else? A father to replace the one who had abandoned them? If they did, or thought they did, what would they expect of him? And how could a man who had never been a father even begin to meet those expectations?

Is that what I want with this woman? All the baggage she brings with her? To love her, to be with her, to share my life with her . . . these I want with all my heart. But all of it will be shaped by her obligations, responsibilities, distractions. Even today, when much is changing, most men and women who fall in love and marry, meet unencumbered: two people finding their own direction as a couple, eventually easing—yes, that is the only way to say it—into parenthood.

Sara and I can never have that.

After weeks of wrangling with Ardis to be free while longing for Sara, after the discoveries of their first hours together in New York, after the traumatic events of today, he never would have thought he would have doubts. But now, all toward which they were driving came into focus. At the center was Sara, surrounded by three young children, a brother who was unpredictable at best, a helpless mother, a life of complications, while, at the center of the life behind him, lay independence, a world of prestige, and the multiple attractions offered a successful, eligible male in the urban centers of the world.

Was ever a choice so starkly presented?

He looked at Sara again. She had not moved but she was watching him. Reuben wondered how clearly his thoughts had shown on his face. She smiled, and stretched out her hand, and he took it, and they were quiet, holding thoughts that may or may not have meshed. But for Reuben, that silence and the clasp of their hands were all that truly mattered. In the dark intimacy of the car flickeringly illuminated by the red taillights of cars in front of them, the glaring headlights of those behind, and streaks of lights as they sped past towns along the highway, with talk and music alternating on the radio as an undercurrent to his thoughts, he wanted her beside him, anywhere, everywhere, burdened or not.

Every couple starts out with obligations, responsibilities, distractions, he thought, realizing with faint amusement that he was stating the obvious. There are no magic couples who start free and clear as newborns. *We'll deal with what we have, and what we are. And I'm not the only one who has a lot to learn; five of us will be learning at the same time. We'll figure it out, and make it work, because Sara and I will not admit to an alternative.*

"I have to call home," Sara said. She sat up, and took the cell phone from the console between them.

Reuben lowered the radio volume, and his smile met hers. "Of course you do," he said.

SIXTEEN

I'm on my way over," Mack said on the telephone. "Just giving you a heads-up."

"Do you know what time it is?" Rosa demanded.

"No." He looked at his watch. "Son of a bitch. Time flies when you're having fun. I'll be right over."

"It's four-thirty in the morning, you woke me up, I have an eight-o'clock class tomorrow—today, actually—I've had exactly thirty minutes' sleep, and I'm not interested in you right now."

"But you're interested in sex, right? Like always."

"Come off it, Mack. Go to sleep. Call me tomorrow."

"I have to come over now. In fact, I've been with you most of the night."

"What?"

"I've been with you since, oh, ten or so tonight. Maybe eleven."

"What are you talking about? I've been with my friends until about an hour ago."

"Yeah, but I was there. Look, it's no big deal; all you have to say is I've been there since eleven tonight, in your room, you know, you were with your friends and I was reading. The thing is, you knew I was there. Right?"

"It sounds like an alibi."

"Hey, who said anything—look, you'd say I was there, that's all. What the fuck, Rosa, I'm with you a lot, how much could it hurt to say I was there tonight?"

"An alibi for what? What did you do? Never mind, I don't want to know. You're crazy, Mack. You want me to lie for you? Why would I do that?"

"For Christ's sake, I'm asking you—"

"To lie for you. Why should I? Because we've been together awhile? Come on, Mack, you're cute and not bad in bed but we're not exactly going out. Anyway, you're weird, you know, always trying to control everything, me included, but what you really want is for somebody to take care of you, me, I guess. How can you do both? It's a little creepy but not very interesting, and sometimes you're not interesting, and there's no way I'd risk anything for you. Lie for you? Get in trouble with the police or a lawyer or a jury or whatever? You're nuts. Go to sleep. And don't come around until you get yourself straightened out."

Mack held the telephone long after she had hung up. It was as if another corner of his world had broken off and shattered. He stood still, listening for something, anything, to break the smothering silence of his room. There was something, far off, television, maybe, but too faint to sound like he had company. He looked around, a full circuit of the room. Empty. It didn't even look like his, not really; it didn't even before he'd packed his things. Nothing in it had ever said "Mack Hayden." He hated photographs; he wasn't interested in paintings, sculpture, or whatever, anything decorative; he only read magazines, not books, and threw them away when he was finished; he always stowed his clothes and shoes so that nothing was exposed.

Still, it was his room. In his house. Where his family lived.

Get out! Nobody wants you! We hate you!
Who would take care of him?

He felt sick. Nobody. Just himself. In all the world, the only person he could count on was himself.

So think about me. And get moving. Any minute now Lew'll figure out I might leave and send one of his guys . . . He yanked open the zipper on his duffel, threw out sweaters, and piled in the T-shirts and shorts he would need in Nauru, where it was always hot. He couldn't go to Rosa, scratch that; he'd go to O'Hare, catch a plane, any plane, just get the hell out of Chicago, and then get to Nauru. He had a credit card and plenty of money in the bank; find a cash machine at the airport. He could live like a king in Nauru, never have to worry about anything again.

He zipped shut the duffel and dragged it to the window. Nothing breakable inside; if it could survive airports, it could survive this. He lifted it to the windowsill, and shoved it out. He had calculated that it would land in the soft flower bed in front of the house, but unexpectedly it plummeted at an angle, propelled by his shove, and struck the sidewalk just beyond the garden. In the light from the street lamp, Mack saw it hit, saw one corner split open, saw his clothes tumble out as it bounced once and again before coming to a rest on the curbing, one end in the gutter.

Rage and bile churned in Mack's throat; screams piled up inside him until he thought he would explode, jump out of his skin in a maelstrom of fury. His mouth worked as he glared at the jumble of clothes far below, but the curses racing through his mind were weak and flabby, used too carelessly in daily life to have any force in relieving the frustration churning within him. His body shook with hatred, of everyone, of everything. Blindly, he turned from the window. Forget the clothes, he'd buy new ones. He had a plan; he had to go through with it; it was set in his mind; he could do what he had to do without thinking.

He stopped thinking. Nothing mattered now except what he was doing. He was saving himself.

Not bad in bed.

Rosa's words rang out loud and clear, as if

she were next to him. *Not bad?* He was terrific; every woman he'd ever been with said
so. She was crazy. He was a sexual lion;
some girl had called him that and he liked it.
She'd miss him, Rosa. Serve her right when
she called tomorrow and found him gone.
He'd have another girl in a minute. Sexual li-
ons aren't alone for very long, ever.

So, forget the bitch. Get to work. Move!

Methodically, he arranged the room the
way he'd planned it: rumpled bedsheets,
indented pillow, open magazines strewn
about, overflowing ashtray on the nightstand
beside a half-empty pack of cigarettes. This
would all be ashes by the time the experts
arrived, but still, it had to look realistic; you
never knew what bits and pieces they could
put together to re-create a whole scene.

He lit a cigarette, took two or three drags,
and let it fall to the top sheet. He stared at it,
willing it to burn. Nothing happened. And
then his fury returned. Bitch, he thought.
Fire-retardant sheets. His fucking mother;
getting in the way of every goddamn thing he
wanted to do.

He lit another cigarette and placed its lit
end against the first, and blew on them. He
added another and then another until eight

glowing cigarettes radiated out like spokes in a wheel. And finally the sheet charred, and a small hole opened up. He lit another cigarette and smoked it as he stared, fascinated, at a thread of smoke curling upward and the charred hole spreading like a stain on the sheet. He grinned around the cigarette still clamped between his lips. With one last look at his room, shrugging because it didn't mean a damn thing to him that he was leaving it, he ran down the stairway, past the closed bedroom doors on the second floor, and down the wide staircase to the first floor. He still had two more fires to set.

A gay little song ran through his head. *Number two and number three, how exciting that will be! One at the front, one at the back, and an exit they will lack!*

He heard voices in the library. People here? At five in the morning? He peered around the doorjamb. The witches, all three of them, asleep. A movie playing to no audience. Three witches, alone in the house, and sound asleep.

Time to leave, not to cleave, a chance to fleeve, you better believe. Giggles bubbled in his throat. He was better than all of them, cleverer, funnier, smarter. Nobody stood a chance against him. The giggles tickled his tongue and spilled out. The sound of it shocked him. *Careful, careful, mustn't wake up the witches.*

In the kitchen, he piled newspapers, paper towels, kitchen towels, a couple of cookbooks haphazardly against the back door. *Fire, fire, never tire; they'll wake up to something dire.* He pulled a book of matches from his pocket.

Stop! Can't do that!

Who the hell—? No one. No one was there. But from somewhere inside him, a voice had ordered him to stop.

Why should I?

The voice cut through the cacophony of ditties and rhymes clanging in his head. *An accident. You forgot that. It has to look like an accident.*

That was the plan. Make it look like an accident. Kids dead; nobody telling the cops about his dealing or fixing up Pussy what's-her-name's suicide. House burned down, accident, nobody looking for Mack. But . . . nobody'd be looking anyway; kids dead, no reason to look for Mack.

So why make it look like an accident? What difference did it make? Who cared?

You care.

And he knew that he did. He knew that Mack Hayden could not stand it if everyone in the world believed he had deliberately burned down a house with three children in it. He'd be gone; who else would they blame?

But then, where was his plan? He had to have a plan; he always had a plan; it kept him ahead of everybody else. Where was his plan?

Set three fires. That was the plan.

Make it look like an accident. That was the plan.

Can't do both.

Frantically, his thoughts bounced around, trapped. Within the space of a few seconds, he knew that his infallible plan was actually a mess.

He thought he smelled smoke from the third floor. *An accident.* Nothing else was left of all his planning. In a frenzy, he shoved the newspapers back into the recycling box, tossed the paper towels onto the counter, returned the kitchen towels to the drawer. He pushed the drawer shut, and it slammed into place, echoing like a shot through the silent house.

"Who's there?" called Abby. "Sara? Are you home?"

Get out, get out, get out. The words hammered inside Mack's head.

But I'm not finished, have to fix the fucking—

You shouldn't talk like that. Sara doesn't like it.

Listen, you little cunt, you can't tell me how to—

It isn't nice, it's not the way nice people talk, people who aren't ignorant and crude.

Get away from me! Leave me alone! Have to get out, get to Nauru!

Briefly, he could feel the heat of the Nauru sun on his bare back, see the welcoming smiles of the protective people who loved him. No one would find him there, no one would ever touch him there, his memories would fade away, and he'd finally forget this house and everybody in it.

He looked around the kitchen to see if he had forgotten anything, his gaze catching on the armchairs where he and Sara had had espresso and she had welcomed him home. That was a good night, one of the best, that was a time when he'd been almost content.

Too late, too late, it was all gone. He reached for the back door.

No, wait. Almost forgot . . . go the other way—

He dashed through the house to the front door, thinking of only one thing, all other thoughts, all his plans, shut down. The giraffe. Doug had carved it, polished it, given it to him. *Because I love you.* Mack remembered putting it in the duffel; it had to be there, couldn't have fallen out, it was there, and he had to get it. He did not stop to ask why; he only knew he had to take it with him. Focused on that, he jerked open the front door and slipped out—*get going, get moving, sun's almost up, it's already light—*pulling it shut behind him.

The door slammed, and Abby said again, "Sara?" When there was no answer, she thought she must have dreamed it, or maybe it was part of the movie that was still on. She blinked at the screen, two people talking, cars in the background, no doors slamming. She looked at Doug and Carrie, sound asleep, curled up at each end of the couch. They hadn't heard anything, so maybe there hadn't been anything.

Abby had been fighting all night to stay

awake; three times she had made coffee, but all it did was make her jumpy and sleepy at the same time. Vaguely she remembered someone giggling, and then two loud noises, but she wasn't sure she'd really heard them.

Faintly, she smelled smoke. He was still awake up there in his room, awake and smoking. What had happened to him that he was so awful today? Worse than he'd ever been before. Almost out of his mind. Abby didn't really have any idea what people were like when they were out of their minds, but the phrase had popped into her slow, groggy thoughts, and it seemed to fit Mack, at least today. Every time Sara had called, just about every hour, and asked what Mack was doing, Abby always said he wasn't doing anything. "I guess he hasn't left the house; I would have heard him. So he's still up there. Probably sleeping. Or smoking. Where are you?"

And Sara said, at first, New Jersey, and then Pennsylvania. Whatever she said, it always seemed a long way from the library where Abby kept watch over Doug and Carrie, and one movie flowed into another on the television set.

She knew Sara and Reuben were taking turns driving, to get home faster, and a little while ago she called them, Reuben answered. "Here, you want to talk to Sara," he said, but, surprising herself, Abby said quickly, "No, it's okay. Where are you?"

"Indiana, near a town called Elkhart. Shall I tell you what it's like?"

"Yes, please." *How amazing; he knows I want to keep talking. Maybe he knows a lot of things, maybe that's why Sara loves him.* "I'm trying to stay awake. What time is it?"

"Almost four-thirty in the morning. You could sleep for a while."

"I'm taking care of Doug and Carrie. Tell me what it's like there."

Reuben settled the phone in its cradle, turned up the volume so Sara could hear both sides of the conversation.

He looked through the window. "It's still dark, so we have to do a considerable amount of imagining. We've just crossed the St. Joseph River, and we're driving due west, paralleling the border with Michigan. There are a few lights, insomniacs or very early risers in farmhouses and the small towns that flash by so quickly we barely glimpse them before they're behind us. Your sister Sara is an amazing driver; she likes speed and she has great concentration and reflexes."

A small gasp came from Abby, and Sara gave Reuben a quick glance.

"But it took lots of practice to get this good," he went on smoothly. "Practice, and thinking about what she was doing. She told me you're a good driver, by the way; you'll be as good as she is, as long as you make good decisions. Which is true of all of us, at any age, wouldn't you say?"

There was a pause. "Thanks," Abby breathed. "I mean . . . thanks."

"Anyway, this is fine countryside; flourishing fields, orchards, neat farmhouses, groves of trees along the rivers. It's like a tapestry, or a mosaic of shapes and colors. And there are sand dunes—"

"Oh, we've been there! Sara took us a couple of times, her friends have a weekend house in Lakeside, and our school had a field trip. But"—her words were slow and sleepy—"tell me what they're like anyway."

"Okay, and you tell me what you remember. First of all, they're enormous—people are dwarfed by them—huge rounded hills of sand all flowing into each other, stretching almost to the lake, wild grasses and trees and bushes growing up and down the slopes, with rippling sand between them sculpted by wind and rain. The area has bogs and wetlands, too, almost swamps, and forests . . ."

He described the area to Abby as if he could see it alongside the highway instead of as he remembered it from a visit long ago. "And farms, of course. The Amish are here—"

"We studied them. Sara bought an Amish quilt from Indiana once."

"They make wonderful quilts, some of the best. I have one . . . had one." He paused briefly, then took a chance. "I'd like another; maybe we'll drive out here one weekend and do some exploring. If you find one you like, we'll buy you one, too. You'll like the Amish farms; they're very beautiful, homey and or-derly, with trim buildings and picket fences, and the furniture in their houses is wonder-fully simple and perfectly proportioned."

He described Amish furniture and the life of the farms: buggies and tools in the yards, the first hay bales of fall, squash vines, and apple and cherry orchards. "Perfectly spaced rows of primitive-looking trees like abstract art, gnarled, almost grotesque but quite dignified."

"How can they be dignified if they're gnarled and grotesque?"

"Staunch, solid, striving up and outward, seemingly unshakable in a shaky and changing world. And the apples have won prizes, according to my atlas, which makes the orchards even more respectable." Reuben paused, then took another chance. "When we come back looking for quilts, if it's autumn we can pick our own apples, and try out the cider and apple butter, and you can decide how well I described it."

"You said you were imagining it."

"If I can't see beauty around me, I try to imagine it. Don't you?"

There was a silence. "I like that," Abby said. "Did you say—?" She stopped, and Reuben closed his eyes and waited. "You said we'd all go there. Quilts and apples. Are you and Sara getting married?"

Reuben looked at Sara. Had he ever asked her? Had she asked him? Their eyes met and they both remembered the quiet evening, a deluge outside, his study warm and sheltering, when they had known they would share their lives. Only two nights ago, he thought, but it had been so clear and obvious that it seemed, now, as if it always had been that way. Briefly taking her eyes from the highway, Sara smiled at Reuben and reached out to touch his hand before turning back as she said, "Yes, Abby, we are."

"Sara? I didn't know you were there. I mean, I knew you were there, but not listening."

"Sara is driving at a speed that does not allow conversation," said Reuben. "All she can do is eavesdrop while we do the talking."

"Oh." There was a pause. "When are you . . . ?"

"We haven't set a date. All of us have to sit down and find the best time for everyone."

"Oh. You mean . . . you want us to be part of it? The wedding?"

"You are part of it. How could we get married without you? And your mother; she has to be there, too."

"Oh."

"What do all those *ohs* mean, Abby?" Sara asked.

"I don't know. I mean, I thought you'd broken up and then all of a sudden . . . you're getting married."

"We've talked a lot," said Reuben, "and been through a lot in the past couple of days. Sometimes you just know what's right for you. No more doubts."

"I never had that."

"You will; give it time." Reuben winced, remembering his own irritation every time his father had said those words to him. I have to learn to be a different kind of father, he thought, and was instantly amused, knowing that, already, he was sounding like other parents, everywhere.

"That's what everybody says when you're fifteen." Abby was so sleepy it was hard to keep her head up, but she knew if she lay down she would really and truly fall asleep. "When will you be home?"

"Two hours, maybe. Three at the most. Is everything quiet?"

"Yes, I can smell him smoking; he hasn't come downstairs at all."

"Call us anytime," Sara said. "If something's bothering you, don't wait, just call. Anytime."

After that Abby had been unable to stay awake and had slept until she heard the noises and thought Sara was home. It was probably the movie, she thought, and then she smelled the smoke again, and realized, for the first time, that it was not marijuana. "Something's burning," she said aloud.

Carrie opened her eyes. "What?"

"Something's burning," Abby repeated. "Doug, wake up. There's a fire."

"He's smoking," Doug mumbled. "Leave me alone."

"Get up! We have to find out what it is, and I don't want to go up there alone."

"You're supposed to take care of us."

"Up! Now!" Abby snapped.

"I don't want to go up there," Carrie said.

"We're going. All of us. Doug, get up."

Prodding and pushing, she got them into the hall and up the stairs to the second floor. "I smell smoke," Doug said.

"No kidding." Holding their hands, Abby led the way to the third-floor stairs.

The smell was stronger, acrid, stinging their noses, and as they climbed the stairs they saw gray filaments of smoke crawling along the ceiling of Mack's room and into the stairway. "Mack!" Doug shouted. "He'll burn up!" Pulling his hand free, he dashed the rest of the way up the stairs.

"Doug!" Abby ran after him. "Get out of there!"

"The fire extinguisher!" Carrie cried, and ran back down to the second floor.

"No, call 911!" Abby called after her, but Carrie was already pulling the fire extinguisher from its clamp on the wall.

"Come on, Doug, Carrie's calling—" Abby stopped. She was standing in the doorway beside the tumbled burlap curtain Carrie had pulled down earlier. Across the room Doug was dancing around Mack's bed, coughing, kept back by flames shooting up beneath a cumulus of gray and black smoke. Some of the flames had traveled down a sheet that dragged on the floor, and were licking at a small throw rug and a crumpled cigarette pack lying on its fringe. On the other side of the bed, flames had consumed the burlap curtains at the windows and were clawing at the wood frames.

"He's in there!" Doug gasped between coughs. "Burning up! We have to get him out!"

Abby squinted at the bunched-up shape in the center of the bed. It could be Mack, or just a pile of blankets and sheets. She moved closer. Amid the flames she could see only rumpled shreds of a sheet and blanket.

Coughing in the smoke, she grabbed Doug's arm. "There's nobody there, it's just—"

"Here!" Carrie cried, running up with the fire extinguisher held in both arms. "You do it, Abby."

"Did you call 911?"

"No, I thought—" Carrie saw Abby's face and burst into tears and then began to cough. "I thought we'd just put it out!" She dropped the fire extinguisher and looked at the bed. "He's in there!"

Doug was coughing and jumping up and down, trying to pull away from Abby's grip, when the small throw rug burst into flames. They all leaped back as the rug was engulfed, smoke billowing through the room. There was a terrible smell, and burning bits of the rug's fringe floated in the smoke, landing in their hair.

Doug screeched and he and Carrie frantically slapped their heads where they felt burning in their hair. Abby grabbed their hands, and coughing, her eyes stinging, she pulled them to the stairs.

"No, no!" Carrie shrieked. She was afraid and excited at the same time. "The fire! Abby, put out the fire! Our house can't burn, it's—Abby, do something!"

"He'll die!" Doug said, and began to cry. "He's my brother!"

"We're not killing ourselves for Mack," Abby snapped. "Or a house," she muttered. She shoved the two of them ahead of her and down the stairs and pinned them to the wall as she punched in the numbers on the telephone. "Our house is on fire," she cried as soon as it was answered, trying not to cough as she rapidly went through their name and address. Slamming down the receiver, she said angrily to Carrie, "I told you to call them!"

"I'm sorry!" Carrie wailed. "I thought it was just a little—"

A loud ripping sound made them all look up, just as the ceiling gave way and pieces of plaster and burning wood fell around them, striking their faces. "My hair!" Doug yelled, and tried to cover his head with his arms. A splinter of burning wood caught on a silk chair beside the telephone, and then the fringe of the rug running down the center of the hall began to smolder. Carrie screamed and Abby grabbed their hands again and pulled them down the wide stairs to the first floor.

"No, wait," Carrie cried, "my journal! It's in

my—" She tried to pull away from Abby, but Abby, furious and afraid, tightened her grip, dragging her toward the front door. "Abby, my journal!"

"Damn it, you'll write a new one. Don't be stupid."

"But my drawings!" yelled Doug. "They'll burn up—" He yanked his hand from Abby's and started for the stairs.

"Stop, you're crazy!" Abby screamed. She shoved Carrie out the front door and went after Doug, hauling him back down the stairs. They could see flames in the hallway where they had just been standing. "They'll burn up!" Doug yelled.

"You can make more; you can't if you're dead!" He was too heavy to pull; Abby got behind him and shoved as hard as she could.

Doug tumbled over, howling, and while he was scrambling to his feet, Abby shoved him again, through the front door. She was crying and coughing and couldn't see where she was going, but she was so angry and afraid she just kept going. *Away, away, away.* Nothing else mattered. "You're an idiot, you're both idiots, how can you be so stupid? Get outside, move, damn it, *damn it, move!*"

They stared at her. Abby never shouted at

them, she never swore at them, she never looked at them that way.

Sirens cut through the air, and they ran to the curbing. "There's a duffel—" Doug began, but his attention was taken by two fire engines coming to a stop in front of their house, and two police cars that stopped across each end of the street, blocking any traffic that might come. Firemen leaped from the trucks, uncoiling hoses while others unhooked long ladders from the sides of the trucks.

After that, everything blurred together for Abby. She saw neighbors come out of their houses, but she and Carrie and Doug shrank into the shadows of the trees between their house and Mrs. Pierce's. More neighbors arrived, pulling coats over pajamas and nightgowns, calling out, but Abby shook her head.

"We don't need help; we're fine."

"But, honey—" a neighbor said, and Abby cried again, "We're fine!" her voice rising, and at her vehemence the neighbors backed up a little, still close enough to help if anyone asked. Numbly, Abby and Carrie watched flames fill the second-floor windows. "Our bedrooms," Carrie whispered, trembling, while Doug jumped around them, his fears about the house and worries about his carvings swept away by the thrill of being so close to the firemen and the excitement of the trucks, their lights flashing the whole time, the firemen shouting back and forth, heavy ladders screeching as they were set up against the house, hoses snaking across the sidewalk and their small front garden, and the loud hiss of water. Even the policemen were exciting, though they stayed beside their cars, out of the firemen's way.

Abby was transfixed by the flames: greedy, voracious, yellow, orange, red, green, magenta, shooting straight up, whipping back and forth as if to make sure they consumed everything, with strange noises, like high winds, like whistling. In the awful, flickering orange light that lit their street, she stared at the fire, terrified by the hugeness of it. This was nothing like the lovely fires they made in the fireplace in their library; it was more like the fireballs they saw sometimes in movies. And when the windows shattered in the heat of the flames, shards of glass falling to the flowers below, she shrank from the destructiveness, and tears came to her eyes. The world was a place of dangers she'd never comprehended. How did people live, knowing that? How did they get through each day if they knew danger was always waiting and even their house, which had always kept them safe, could be destroyed?

"Our house, our poor house," Carrie whispered over and over, "my beautiful chair and curtains, and my bed, and my journal, oh, my journal . . ." and Doug heard her and stopped jumping and stood beside her, watching the two upper floors almost hidden by flames, and when Carrie began sobbing, he did, too.

Abby put her arms around them and held them, thinking she shouldn't have yelled and sworn at them; terrible things were happening, and all of them were afraid. "But we're safe and we're together," she said, "and that's the most important thing. Nothing else really matters. We got out in time—"

"And called the firemen," Carrie gulped. "You called them. You're the heroine. I'm going to write about it, Abby the fantastic heroine, you woke us up and *forced* us out, *dragged* us out, and saved our lives, and rescued us from burning up into black, shriveled, stinking—"

"Carrie!" Abby said sharply, hearing the hysteria in Carrie's babbling.

"What?"

"Just . . . calm down."

"How can I? We almost burned to death."

"Mack did," said Doug. His eyes were scrunched and he bent over, coughing. "He's dead."

"We don't know that," Abby said. "I don't think he was there."

Carrie looked up, her face streaked with tears, speckled with bits of ash, her eyes red and puffy. "If he's not dead, where is he? I mean, he didn't come downstairs, we would've seen him. And he didn't jump out the window . . . did he?"

They looked up at the third-floor windows, and down to the ground. "The duffel!" Doug said. "I saw it, you know, when we came out, and then the fire engines came—"

"There's clothes all over the place," Carrie said.

"Mack's," said Doug. He rubbed his burning eyes. "It's his duffel, too."

"Are you sure?" Abby asked.

"Sure, he bought one, he said he was going on lots of trips, and it looked like that one."

"They all look alike," Carrie said. Like Doug, she was rubbing her eyes.

"Don't do that," said Abby. "It makes them worse."

"It's his clothes, too," Doug said, still rubbing.

"But we didn't see him leave," Carrie said again.

"We were asleep," Abby said. "I fell asleep after I talked to—" And suddenly she remembered Sara.

Sara would be calling and she wouldn't get any answer. She'd be so worried . . . I have to call her, Abby thought, but her cell phone was in the house. "Stay here," she said to Carrie and Doug. "I have to get the phone, to call Sara."

But firemen stopped her. "Nobody in the house, get back, sweetheart, you the one who called?" She nodded. "Good job, but just keep away now."

"But my phone . . . it's in the kitchen . . . my sister . . . I have to—"

"Keep out! Out of the way!"

She backed up. Firemen on the ladders were smashing whatever windows were not already broken, and climbing through, while two firemen stood on the ground, aiming gushing hoses at the windows, and two other firemen ran through the front door dragging hoses behind them. Heads back, Abby and Carrie and Doug stared through stinging eyes at the smoke pouring out, and with each passing moment they became more terrified as they imagined disasters that might have happened: the three of them trapped on the third floor, cut off from the stairs by fire and smoke, flames dancing all over them the way they had danced over Mack's bed, three charred corpses found by the firemen when they got up there. I didn't take good care of things, Abby thought; Sara won't ever trust me again.

Sara. I have to call . . .

"Abby!" Mrs. Pierce, who lived next door, was plowing through the crowd of neighbors, and the neighbors came forward with her, gathering around as Mrs. Pierce embraced Abby and Carrie and Doug. "You poor lambs," she cried. "Where is Sara? Is anybody still inside?"

"Mack," said Doug. "Mack's dead."

Mrs. Pierce squeezed them against the folds of her ample form. "Thank God you're all right, but, oh, dreadful about Mack, a terrible thing. But where is Sara?"

"Driving back from New York," said Abby,

her words muffled against Mrs. Pierce. "They'll be here pretty soon."

"They?"

"Sara and her . . . fiancé." She was convulsed by coughing, and Mrs. Pierce cried out to a neighbor to bring bottles of water. "They're getting married," Abby gasped out.

"Well, that's lovely, but they're not here now and you need help. We're going straight to our house, get you cleaned up, you're awfully grimy, all that smoke, and . . . oh, my goodness, Doug, your hair's burned! Carrie, you, too! Come on, we'll get you gallons of water, and put you to bed, you all look exhausted. Come on, come on, since Sara's gone off, you need someone to take care of you."

Abby heard the criticism at the same time as she felt her authority being snatched away. She pulled out of Mrs. Pierce's embrace. "No," she said. "I mean, thank you, it's nice of you, but"—she stopped to cough—"we're fine; we can take care of ourselves."

"Now look, young lady, obviously you can't, and with Sara off gallivanting—"

"She's not! She went to New York just for one night, and she calls all the time and worries about us, and it wasn't her fault the airports got closed! And we can take care of ourselves! We didn't start the fire, it started in Mack's room, he was smoking and he was probably in bed and everybody knows you're not supposed to smoke in bed, and Sara will be here in a little . . . any minute, and we're fine!"

"Well, my goodness, you don't have to shout, Abby, I was only trying to help. Your house is burning down, and here you all are, shivering and coughing and crying . . . would you rather I just ignored you?"

"I'm sorry." Abby shook her head helplessly; whatever she did seemed wrong. "I'm really sorry, but, you know, we're okay and we want to be here—"

"The fire's out!" Doug exclaimed, and they all looked at the house. The firemen were still pouring water through the windows, but the two who had run into the house were coming out, pulling the hoses with them. Acrid smoke still billowed, and the smell of wet ashes and burning wood and fabric filled the air.

"It stinks," Carrie said.

Abby was blinking, trying to see through the stinging in her eyes. "The downstairs looks okay. We could wait for Sara there." She backed away from Mrs. Pierce. "We have to be here when Sara gets home. If she came back and saw this, and we weren't here, she'd be really worried . . ."

"You can leave her a note."

"No! We don't want to go anywhere!"

The firemen had descended the ladders and were outside the house. "All out, kids," said one of them. "Good thing you called when you did. You're all heroes."

Carrie threw a triumphant look at Abby.

"You the lady of the house?" the fireman asked Mrs. Pierce.

"She's our neighbor," Abby said quickly, horrified that anyone would think Mrs. Pierce was their mother. "Our older sister takes care of us and she'll be here in a few minutes." They were frowning at her and, uncertainly, she said, "Thank you for coming." It sounded as if she were thanking them for coming to a party, and she berated herself again. Why can't I do things right?

"I can tell you anything you need to know—" Mrs. Pierce began.

"Where's Mack?" Doug demanded.

"Mack?" asked the fireman.

"He was on the top floor, his bedroom. His bed was on fire, and we saw him in it, so we knew he was dead. Where'd you take—"

"Nobody's dead. Nobody's up there. There was a sheet and a couple blankets piled up, that's probably what you saw. I'll bet he smoked, huh? That's how the fire started?"

"He's not there?" Carrie asked. "Really?"

"Piled up?" Abby echoed. "Why?"

"Probably pushed 'em there getting out of bed when the fire started. Dumb-ass thing to do, smoking in bed. Did he smoke?" They nodded. "Stupid ass. You don't know where he is, huh? Cut out without warning you? Sounds like a bad deal to me. Friend of yours?"

They looked at him without answering.

"Well, that's good news!" cried Mrs. Pierce. "Not dead!"

Two policemen had joined the firemen. One of them held a clipboard, and while the other one asked questions he wrote everything down. Abby felt uncomfortably guilty; it was exactly like the time the police were questioning her after she crashed her car. I didn't do anything, she thought; Mack did it. I got us out of the house. I did what I could.

The police asked Mrs. Pierce what she saw, and when she admitted that she had come outside when the fire already was burning, they dismissed her and turned to Abby.

"Well, if you don't need me—" Mrs. Pierce said. "Abby, you just come on in, all of you, when you're ready; the door is unlocked. You shouldn't go into your house, stay out of it."

"She's right about that," the policeman muttered. "Okay," he said to Abby, "your name?"

"Abby Hayden."

"Age?"

"Almost . . . I'm sixteen."

He turned to Doug and Carrie. "Doug Hayden, I'm ten, almost eleven." "Carrie Hayden, I'm thirteen."

"And you all live here?" the policeman asked.

They nodded.

"Your sister's taking care of you?" he asked Abby. "What's her name?"

"Sara Elliott, she's twenty-seven, almost twenty-eight."

"I thought your name's Hayden."

"It is. Sara's our . . . our half sister."

"Taking care of you."

"She is! She's wonderful."

"So if she's so wonderful, where is she?"

"She's coming home. Driving. I mean, the airports in New York were closed . . . she was in New York, just overnight, just for one night, and then the airports shut down. She'll be here any minute. She called and said she'd be here right away."

"Driving from New York," the other policeman said, writing on his clipboard. He looked up. "Where's your parents?"

"They're—" Abby started to cry; it was so complicated to explain, and it sounded awful—our father ran away and we've never seen him again and our mother is in a nursing home, she can't walk or talk—how could she say that? "We're fine, Sara takes care of us, she's as good as our mother, she's as good as any mother!"

"Doesn't sound as if she's taking care of you. Could be child abandonment, that's a felony."

"Sara isn't a criminal! What are you talking about? She's wonderful, she's our real mother! And she calls all the time, and she's always thinking of us! Anyway, I'm old enough, I earn money babysitting, if I can do that why can't I take care of my brother and sister? It's not our fault Mack set fire to the bed! Leave Sara alone; why can't you leave all of us alone?"

"Hey, take it easy," said the policeman with

the clipboard. He looked contemptuously at his partner. "Got a little excited there."

The other policeman shrugged. "Weird setup."

The policeman with the clipboard took over. "So, okay," he said, "she's coming back. Where is she now?"

"In Chicago! She called and told us she'll be here any minute! Almost right away!"

"Hope so," the policeman said ambiguously. He thought for a minute. "Okay, then." He turned to Abby. "You smelled the smoke and you went upstairs . . . and then what?"

Abby told them what had happened, cutting off Doug and Carrie when they tried to interrupt with their own versions. "It seemed like a little fire," she said, "but it spread a lot faster than we thought it would."

"Usually does." The policeman took a long look at the third-floor windows. "If he was smoking, he's responsible. Could've killed you all. You sure you don't know where he is?" They shook their heads. "You're not protecting him?" Again they shook their heads. "This all goes in our report, you understand that. We have to say that Mack . . . Mack what?"

"Hayden," Doug muttered.

"Hayden. A relative."

"Our brother," Doug said, scuffing the ground with his shoe.

"Brother? Older brother?" They nodded. "How old?"

"Twenty," Abby said.

"Twenty. And didn't warn you? Didn't tell you when he started the fire? Or when the fire started?"

Doug and Carrie were silent. "No," Abby said.

"Missing, probably started the fire, left you in the house. Mack Hayden's got a hell of a lot to answer for. You got a picture of him we can have?"

"No," Abby said.

"You mean they all burned up."

"He hated having pictures taken. He didn't have any in his room, of anybody."

"Weird setup," said the first policeman again.

"Huh." The other policeman shook his head. "We can put out an all-points, but without a picture . . . He have a car?" They nodded. "You know the license?" They shook their heads. He muttered to himself. "Well, you hear from him, let us know. Okay? Right away, okay?"

They nodded.

"Anybody else in the house we don't know about?"

"No."

"You sure?"

"Yes!"

After a moment, the policeman shrugged. "Need to talk to the sister," he said to his partner, so Abby knew they would be back. But that was okay; by then Sara would be home. Right now she just wanted everybody to go away and leave them alone.

The firemen had coiled their hoses and returned the ladders to the trucks. Doug watched them put everything tightly in place. He would have liked a ride on one of the fire engines, but he was pretty sure this wasn't the right time. He didn't even think he should ask them if he could have a ride another time. Everything was too mixed up and he felt bad about Abby. She took good care of them; why were the police giving her a hard time?

And they still hadn't gone away; what were they waiting for? "Well, okay," the policeman said to Abby, "you tell your sister to call us soon as she gets back. We need some information so we can find Mack." He looked at the three of them, standing tightly together. "Call us with any news. Anything, right?"

"Can we go in our house?" Abby asked.

"I doubt it." The policemen called out the question to the firemen.

"Absolutely not," said one, walking toward them. "Not structurally safe. Kitchen's the best, if you need something, but don't stay long. Everything's a mess anyway, you don't want to be there, water, you know, smoke, everything's pretty much ruined." He looked around. "Where's your parents?"

"We can go next door," Abby said quickly. She couldn't stand the questions anymore. *Where was Sara? Why didn't she come and rescue them?*

"Oughta do that," said one of the policemen. He gestured to the neighbors who were still hovering a little distance away. "Any of 'em probably be able to help. Don't forget," he said to Abby, "tell your sister to call us. The minute she gets back."

And at last they were gone, the men, the fire engines, the police cars. All that was left were sheets of rippling water on the street and sidewalk, a thick layer of broken glass, pieces of charred wood and paper obliterating the front garden, and smoke still coming from the upper windows of their house, an ugly, blackened hulk sitting atop the stones of the first floor, darkened by smoke and water, with gaping holes of broken windows.

"Our poor house," Carrie mourned.

The neighbors came up and offered food, clothing, whatever they needed, and asked about Sara. When Abby said she would be home any minute, and refused their offers to come home with them, practically screaming that they were okay and if they needed anything they'd ask, they drifted away. The sky had turned bright blue with puffy clouds; the sun was glaring. Exhausted, Abby thought of bed. *But I don't have one anymore.* Anyway, she had to call Sara and get Doug and Carrie somewhere. In our house, she thought; the fireman said we could go in the kitchen, at least for a while, we could wait for Sara there, even sleep in the armchairs until she gets home.

"Abby!" Mrs. Pierce was in her doorway. "Sara's on the phone. Says she's been trying to call for over an hour. Pretty worried by now."

Carrie beat Abby into Mrs. Pierce's kitchen. "Sara, we had a fire! Our house is all—"

"Mrs. Pierce told me. Are you all right? And Doug? Where is Abby? Is she hurt?"

Carrie launched into the story of the fire, her voice rising and falling as drama and hysteria reinforced each other, but Abby snatched the phone, sitting down because her legs were buckling. "Where are you? I told the policeman you're in Chicago."

"We are, just about; we'll be there in less than an hour. Abby, is anyone hurt?"

"No, really, we were scared and coughing a lot, and our eyes hurt from the smoke, but we're okay, only the house . . . the house is really awful, Sara, it's mostly gone."

"I know, and it's terrible, it must have been terrible to watch it burn, and sad and scary, but—"

"And what are we going to do, with no place to live? And no clothes and no . . . we don't have anything!"

"We'll figure it out, Abby, everything can be replaced. What's most important is that you and Doug and Carrie are all right. Nothing else matters. Are you really all right? Not hurt? Carrie started to say something about her hair burning."

"She and Doug got singed a little bit."
Abby felt so relieved, just talking to Sara,
and she was so sleepy that she felt a little
giddy. "They'll probably brag about it at
school," she said, almost cheerfully. "They'll
be the center of attention."

"But nothing else happened," Sara said.

"No, really, nothing else; we got out and
we're fine."

"Thank God," Sara breathed. And then:
"Mack, too?"

"We don't know where he is. We thought
he might be dead, the fire started in his bed
and Doug thought he was in it, but the firemen said nobody was there. And he's gone. I
mean, he was upstairs in his room, I smelled
him smoking, and then later the fire started,
and when we went to look, he wasn't there."

"Tell me what happened."

Abby repeated the story she had told the
policeman. "He was probably smoking in bed
and fell asleep. That's what the fireman said.
But the police said that Mack had a lot to answer for, if he started the fire, or even knew
about it, and ran away without warning us."

"I can't believe he would do that."

"He was pretty mad all day. Maybe he got
scared."

"But why didn't you see him leave?"

"We all fell asleep. Oh." Abby thought back. "Something made a noise, two noises. They woke me up and I thought you'd come home."

"What kind of noises?"

"I don't know. Kind of a bang. I can't remember. Maybe it was the door closing, though, because I thought you were back."

Sara covered the phone and looked at Reuben, listening while navigating through early-morning traffic. "I don't want to frighten them any more than they are, but I have no idea what's going on with Mack, and if he decides to come back, I don't want them there. It doesn't sound as if the house is safe anyway."

"Mrs. Pierce," Reuben said. "Can you think of a good reason, without frightening them?"

Sara uncovered the phone. "Abby, you need to get some sleep so we can talk about this when we get there. I want you to tell Mrs. Pierce you need some sleep and you can't sleep in all the smoke and water in our house."

"The fireman said the kitchen was mostly okay," said Abby. "We really want to go home, Sara; we don't want to be anywhere else."

"I know, but I don't want you in the house. We don't know if it's safe, and you need to get away from everything that's happened. Anyway, you're already there, and Mrs. Pierce has offered her guest rooms, and that's where you should be, just until we get there. Please, Abby, do this for me."

When, reluctantly, Abby agreed, Sara talked briefly to Carrie and Doug, giving them the same instructions. "They'll do it," she said to Reuben. She took a long breath; she was trembling. "They could have been . . . could have died."

Reuben pulled the car to the side of the road, and reached out to hold her. "They're all right. Don't blame yourself for this."

"I shouldn't have left them."

"How many times," he asked after a moment, "would you expect the airports to close and a fire to start in your house, all in the same night?"

Involuntarily, she smiled. "Not even once."

He kissed the top of her head. "You left a sixteen-year-old in charge of a ten-year-old and a thirteen-year-old for one night. No one could fault you for that."

Sara was silent, then she shook her head. "We shouldn't have stopped. Do you want me to drive?"

"Still my turn," he said, and pulled away from the curb.

"I'm sorry, I know you wanted to comfort me, I'm grateful for that. It's just that I have to see them."

"How much farther?"

"Without traffic, maybe forty minutes."

"We'll forge a path."

And he did. Sara began to relax as Reuben recognized streets and drove without needing directions. How amazing, she thought, that I can feel relaxed, even a little bit. But at the same time she knew it was because of many things: she was almost home, she had talked to the children and knew they were safe, and she had shared these hours with Reuben, shared the driving, the telephone conversations with the children, her worries, her relief, instead of managing everything herself.

And then Reuben, as if completing her thoughts, said, "We have to decide what to do about Mack."

Sara took a long breath. "Thank you," she said. "I know this is a lot more than you ex-

pected, than any man expects when . . ."
She opened her hand and it fell.

Reuben smiled. "You never pretended you
didn't have a family; you told me about them
the first night we had dinner. I knew this
would be more complicated than a fairy tale."
Stopped at a red light, he held out his hand,
and Sara fit hers into it. "I did think about it,"
he said. "I didn't ignore the complications or
pretend they might not be difficult. I just
knew they weren't difficult or complicated
enough to make me willing to lose you."

"Thank you," she said again, simply, thinking that perhaps the greatest gift two people
can give to each other is understanding, and
simple gratitude.

As the light turned green, Reuben said
musingly, "Did you mean it when you said
you thought he would come back?"

"I suppose he might, but I really can't believe it; how could he? He left the three of
them in the house with his room on fire;
made no attempt to warn them . . ." She began to tremble again. "I can't even think
about . . . They could have burned to death,
or jumped out . . . three stories . . . How
could he leave them? It's monstrous, what
he did."

"I'd guess he panicked. Woke up with a fire in his bed and ran."

"Is that an excuse?"

"Absolutely not. He might have run, instinctively, but he had time to come back for them. There was plenty of time, it seems; isn't it odd that they had time to get up there? From what Abby and Carrie said, it must have burned at a pretty low level for quite a while, the whole time Abby was smelling it but not realizing it wasn't marijuana."

"We can thank my mother for that." Sara smiled faintly. "Poor Tess, always on the alert for disasters, making our house a fortress, down to fire-retardant fabrics, but having no way to prevent the real disasters, or even anticipate them."

"She probably saved the children's lives today."

"Yes. But I can't tell her that. I don't know how we'll keep it from her, but I hope we can."

"And if she asks about Mack?"

"He left once; we'll tell her he left again. I think we all assumed he would, at some point."

"And no one would mourn him."

"No one, isn't that terrible? To have no one

care if you come or go? In fact, to have your own family want you gone." Sara paused. "He did try to make us love him. But he wasn't a giving person. He gave gifts but not himself. I think he never even liked us. He wanted to live in our house, but not because he liked us or loved us."

"A sanctuary?" Reuben asked.

"How odd. Yes, maybe. I'm sure he remembered Mother calling it that, a long time ago. A place to retreat and be protected. That was what she called it. I don't have any idea what he was worried about, or afraid of, to make him seek sanctuary, but he did seem to want that, at least sometimes. Maybe his job, working for Corcoran, but I never knew what he did there, unless he really was behind the demonstrations at River Bend, but even then I don't know why that would make him fearful. Oh," she said, remembering the brochure Reuben had showed her on the plane.

Reuben nodded. "That could be it. If Corcoran held him responsible for our finding out he's involved . . ." At a stoplight, he turned to her. "As far as I know, the Illinois secretary of state found Corcoran Enterprises listed as the licensee for the casino that was approved a few months ago. I'm assuming Corcoran wanted the River Bend property for a docked riverboat and one or more buildings on land. He couldn't buy the property—we owned it—but you saw him there with blueprints; what good were they, since he didn't own the land? This is mostly guesswork, but it makes sense to me: he had the license, he wanted the property, he had blueprints ready, and about that time it just so happened that the people of River Bend and their neighbors began to demonstrate against Carrano Village West. There is no way I can believe that was just coincidence, any more than I believe it was coincidence that at the same time the local governments just happened to back away from the approvals we'd gotten so far. I turn here, don't I?"

"Yes. Left. Do you remember the story Carrie was making up when we drove to Galena and saw that first march?"

"Something about a character who scares the neighbors and gets them to demonstrate— I'll be damned. And what was the rest of it? He wanted the land for some nefarious purpose or other."

"I think it was to make counterfeit money or package marijuana."

"Or hide stolen treasure. Maybe Carrie should be a detective."

Sara smiled. "Or a novelist. For now, I think we'll just let her believe it's all imaginary." She paused. "Why would the local governments change their minds about the approvals they'd given you? Corcoran bribed them?"

"I think he did, and so does the secretary of state. At least, he's looking into it. If that's what happened, Corcoran would be in serious trouble. I don't suppose it's a crime to stir up demonstrations, but bribery definitely qualifies. If all our guesses are correct, Corcoran would forfeit the casino license, and could be indicted for bribing public officials. If he sees that coming, he'll blame someone, and it could be Mack. In which case, I'd guess sanctuary is exactly what Mack would need."

"But we can't let him come back."

"No, we can't. We'll have to find him, find a way to keep him out of your life. Our life."

Sara smiled briefly, grateful once again, but then she made a helpless gesture. "How would we do that? He's part of my family—"

"That complicates it," said Reuben, "but I don't think it dictates a single way to do things."

They were on Lake Shore Drive now, and moving steadily, the steel blue of Lake Michigan on their right, the harbor still filled with summer's boats, the city on their left. After a moment, Sara said, "You'll be ready to start building soon."

"I think so. We have a lot of work to do with the neighbors. You were right from the beginning: we didn't do the door-to-door work we needed to make sure they understood what we wanted to do, and how they'd benefit from it. We took them for granted, as if they were just some of the local flora and fauna and we could bulldoze them if they got in our—" He sensed Sara's smile, and glanced at her. "I gather I'm exaggerating again."

They laughed quietly, the first simple laugh they had been able to share in what seemed like a long time. "Well, anyway," Reuben said, "we didn't do a good job before all this happened, so now that's the first step. We still need approvals from the local governments, but I hope they'll see this as a quick way out of a mess. They can say they were misled with incomplete or false information, and thought they were saving their communities by taking action to keep Carrano out. I suppose they could claim those

weren't payoffs; they were the first install-
ments in upgrading community facilities,
building new ones, that sort of thing. And
they might get away with it, especially if
they've given us approval and we've broken
ground, and we're all good friends. The
state's attorney probably would be just as
happy to have Corcoran; he's the bigger
fish."

"Or they'd be happy to get Mack."

"Could be. Even if he was just an errand
boy, Corcoran could offer him up as a sacrifi-
cial lamb. It won't be easy for him, whatever
happens. I think we're past the worst part of
the rush hour. We should be there soon."

From then on, with the Gold Coast high-
rises on their left, and then through Lincoln
Park, Sara thought only of getting home and
seeing for herself that the children were all
right. Nothing else was important. For now,
Mack could wait.

SEVENTEEN

What they saw first was water, the street glistening, streams running along the curbs carrying leaves and broken twigs. And then they saw the house, a blackened stone hulk open to the sky, with gaping holes where windows had been, and the enormity of it struck Sara for the first time. "Oh, no," she whispered. "No, no, no," overwhelmed by loss, and rootlessness.

Reuben drove past the house, looking for a parking space. He maneuvered between two cars and put his arms around Sara. The desolation struck him, too, and he tried to imagine the destruction of his new home, here in this city, already filled with Sara and with everything that spoke to him of belonging. "But you told Abby it can be replaced," he said. "And you're all alive."

"Yes." Tears were in her eyes as she turned within his arms to look at those stones they had thought impregnable, the sanctuary her mother had created, the place they had always known awaited them, wherever they were. But she forced herself to grasp that crucial fact: "Everyone is alive; everyone is all right. My God, when I think of what could have happened—" She stopped, and after a moment said, "We knew we loved it, but I don't think we realized how much a house could be like one of our family, always there, always welcoming us with an open door, and protection and shelter, keeping us together no matter what happened on the outside."

"Houses don't do that, people do," Reuben said quietly. "You made your house what it was, just as you made your family. You would do that in any house you made your own."

"History has a lot to do with it," she said, almost impatiently, thinking of photographs, mementos, collections now gone. She opened the car door.

"It does. We make our own, every day." He stepped out and they stood beside the car, gazing at the house and the devastation of the street: the sidewalk littered with splintered wood and glass, scraps of scorched fabric, fluttering pages of magazines, whole books, charred books, burned books, broken branches, twigs and leaves. "Where were your photos?" Reuben asked. "On the second floor?"

"The children's were. A few in my room. Most of them were in the library." Sara smiled for the first time. "What luck. Unless they were destroyed by water."

"But they must have been in cabinets."

"Yes."

"Then we'll find them, probably in good condition or at least salvageable."

"You were never inside the house," Sara said as they walked up the street. "I kept thinking how wonderful it would be, the first time you stepped into our house, into our family. It was so much a reflection of us, I did want you to see it."

"Do you think you might be exaggerating the importance of a house, when there are five of us about to make a life together?"

Sara felt a brief spurt of anger, but almost

immediately she laughed. "Tables turned," she said. "You're not the only one who exaggerates. Thank you, I guess I needed that. Okay, I think I'm ready to talk about all this to the children."

"Which house is Mrs. Pierce's?"

"Next to ours, on the left." They came to the ruined flower garden in front of her house, pausing at a duffel bag with clothes spewing from it, lying in the gutter. "Where did that come from?" Sara murmured. "From your house?" Reuben asked. She shook her head. "I never saw it. I wonder if it's Mack's; the children might know." She looked up and saw the front door of her house ajar, wide strips of yellow tape forming a large X across it. "It shouldn't be open," Sara murmured, and walked up the sidewalk and the front steps, kicking aside charred wood and paper and broken glass. Almost overwhelmed by the acrid smell of smoke and wet wood and fabrics, she pulled the door tight. "I don't want to look inside yet. Soon enough." She and Reuben crossed to the house next door. "I hate to wake them; maybe we'll just take a look—"

But Abby was running down the front steps. "Sara! Oh, Sara, I'm so glad you're—"

She threw herself at Sara, and burst into tears.

Sara held her tight and stroked her hair, crying with her because Abby was in her arms, she was alive and all right, she was fine, nothing had happened to her, none of them were hurt, and they had been so close to being . . . Once again her thoughts stumbled on the word; she could not formulate it. Gone, she thought. Close to being gone. What would I be without them? Nothing is more important than this. She held Abby, waiting for the sobs to subside, her own tears drying.

"It was so awful," Abby gasped between sobs. "We watched it, watched the fire, Carrie said it was eating up our house, the flames were huge and they got bigger, and moved so fast, it took forever for the firemen to put them out . . . And all our things," she wailed, "and our rooms and my new rocking chair and our whole lives, it was like watching *our lives* burn up, watching *us* burn up, it was so *awful* . . . And it was my fault!" Her voice rose again. "I was supposed to take care of everything! I was in charge and now you'll never trust me—"

"Hush," Sara said, more sharply than she

intended. She softened her voice. "Don't even think that, Abby, you were wonderful, you got out in time, you saved three lives. What could be more important than that? Some furniture, some possessions . . . how could they be as important as the three of you? You were smart, and alert, and you took charge. It could have been a tragedy but you gave it a happy ending. I'm so proud of you, and I love you, and I'd trust you with anything."

Abby looked up, her face shiny with tears. "Really? You mean that?"

"You know I do. You're my heroine."

"Oh. Thank you." She shook her head. "It was so terrible, you know, it felt like I was always doing things wrong instead of—oh." She saw Reuben standing a few feet away, and shrank back into Sara's arms. "I thought . . . I mean, I know he was with you, and we talked on the phone and everything, but . . . I thought it would just be . . . you know . . . us."

Not ever again, Sara thought, but this was not the moment to say it aloud. And then Reuben said quietly, "I'll try not to get in the way, Abby."

Abby met his eyes for a long moment,

struggling to adjust to a new order of things, a new definition of family, even in the grip of fatigue and shock from the fire. "It isn't *you*," she said at last. "I mean, not you particularly." She sighed; she wasn't doing this right, either. "I mean, I wasn't trying to insult you, Sara told me on the phone that you were going to get . . . that you were together. It was just . . ."

"You didn't insult me." He smiled. "You wanted Sara and you were waiting for her and I didn't fit the picture." He thought for a moment. "Maybe it will be easier for you if I tell you how I feel about Sara, and what I hope, for all of us. You have a right to demand that, so do Doug and Carrie. I love Sara, Abby; I cherish her and respect her and admire her, and I want to do all I can to make her life as complete and happy as she has ever dreamed. That means making you and Doug and Carrie happy, because Sara can't be happy if you're not. And I couldn't be, either, because I'm absolutely sure that, when we get to know each other, I'll love the three of you almost as much as I love Sara."

"You mean you hope you do," said Abby, with a spark of mischievousness.

Reuben laughed. "It definitely will be awkward if I don't."

A brief hesitation, and then, tentatively, Abby stretched out her hand. Reuben came up and took it between both of his. "We'll have a family and we'll all be very proud of us. And if ever there's another crisis like this one—" Abby looked instinctively toward their house. "We'll rebuild it," he said. "We can make it exactly the same as it was. We can even duplicate the furniture."

Her eyes wide, Abby searched his face. "Is that true? We can make it like it was?"

"Exactly. Do you have photos of the rooms?"

She nodded. "Sara said we should have them in case of . . . oh. Fire."

"Wise Sara. I don't suppose you have blueprints?"

Abby looked at Sara, who said, "If they existed, I have no idea where they would be. Maybe the basement. More likely the third floor."

"Which is gone. But we can get blueprints made; some of my best friends are architects. And, Abby, you and Carrie and Doug should give this a lot of thought. We can make changes, too. Any changes you'd like.

Maybe you'd like your rooms bigger, or smaller, or maybe round or triangular. Who knows?"

Abby broke into laughter. "You can't make them round."

"We can do almost anything, within Chicago's building codes. We have to be a little practical, but we'll have a lot of fun—"

"Sara!" Carrie and Doug were running from the house. "Why didn't you wake us up?" Doug yelled. They threw themselves at Sara as Abby had, and once again Reuben stepped back. And then Mrs. Pierce was on her front porch, inviting them in for breakfast.

Later, Sara thought of that breakfast, when Mrs. Pierce finally left them alone in the breakfast room, as their first family meal. It began with a squabble, even before they sat at the long, narrow breakfast-room table, when Doug and Carrie raced for the chair with its back to the window and the view of the burned ruin of their house. "I don't want to look at it!" Doug shouted as he pulled the chair away from Carrie. "Neither do I!" she cried, "and I was here first!"

"Cut it out," Abby said crossly. "Reuben'll think you're incorrigible."

"What?" Doug demanded, momentarily distracted.

"I know what it means," Carrie said. She yanked the chair from him and sat down.

Sara set another chair beside Carrie's. "You'll be crowded, but you're such good friends it won't matter."

Abby laughed and sat at the long side of the table, turning her chair so that she was almost sideways, her back toward the window.

"Sara and I get the view," Reuben said with a smile. "I think we can handle that. Carrie, may I cut you a piece of coffee cake?"

"I could handle it, too," Doug said angrily. "I just didn't want to. And we don't need a father, you know. We already have one."

"Doug!" Abby exclaimed. "That's really rude. Anyway, we don't have a father."

"We do, too," Doug declared.

"Then where is he?"

"How do I know? Somewhere."

"How do you know he's not dead? You don't know anything about him. He's gone. We haven't had a father for *years.* And you were really rude to Reuben and you ought to apologize because he wants to love us."

Doug looked at his lap. "People keep leaving," he said, so low they barely could hear him. "Dad left, and I hardly knew him, and Mom left, I mean, she doesn't live with us anymore, and Mack left, and now he's gone again, and he wasn't always nice but he was, like, a man in the house, and . . . *nobody stays with us.*"

Sara knelt beside his chair. "We stay. We stay with each other."

"It's not the same," Doug muttered.

Reuben leaned forward, folding his arms on the table, looking straight at Doug. "I'd like to stay, if you'll let me. I think it would be a lousy idea to leave."

Slowly, Doug looked up. "Why?"

"Because I love Sara." Faintly amused, Reuben wondered how often he would be repeating this. *It's a good thing I like to say it.* "And I want to be with her for my whole life, and make a home and a family with her. And because I haven't lived in a family since I left home for college and I've been hoping for one all that time. And because I don't believe in giving things up when they're really good; I'd have to begin again from the beginning, and that would be stupid and exhausting and maybe not even possible, so why in the world would I leave?"

Carrie was scowling at Reuben. "Are you

going to have a baby?" Reuben was so startled it made Carrie giggle. "I mean, Sara
doesn't have time, you know, she's really
busy taking care of us, so it would be too
much to have a baby in the house." Her face
fell. "Except, we don't even have a house
anymore."

Reuben grasped at that. "We're going to
build a new one."

"We are?" Doug cried. "Here? In the same
place?"

"The exact same place."

"And it'll look the same?"

"It will look any way you want it to look."

"But what about a baby?" pressed Carrie.

"We might," Sara said quietly. "We haven't
talked about it. There are lots of possibilities."

"Like medical school," Abby said. "You
could be a doctor after all. And quit your job.
I mean . . . Reuben could . . . uh . . ."

Reuben smiled. "Earn enough for all of us.
Yes, I could."

"Would we tear down our old house?"
Doug asked. "I mean, all of it?"

"I'm pretty sure we'd have to," said
Reuben. "It's the first thing we'd ask the engineers and architects."

"But do you want a baby?" Carrie demanded of Sara. She frowned. "I guess you do. Then you'd be a real mother."

"She's real now," Abby scolded. "She does everything a mother does, better than a lot of other mothers, and that's what *makes* a mother. How can you say that? Shame on you."

"I only meant . . ." Carrie's eyes filled with tears. "I didn't mean . . ."

"It's okay, sweetheart." Sara put her hand on Carrie's. "It's only a word, you know. It's what we do and feel that counts. As long as we feel like a family, that's all that matters."

"We are a family, but, you know . . ." Carrie shook her head helplessly. "It's so mixed up. Mom's in that nursing home, and Dad isn't anywhere that we know of, maybe dead like Abby said, and Mack . . . I can't figure him out even though he's my brother, and now he's somewhere, we don't know where, and . . ."

"But where would we live?" Doug asked. "I mean, while we build our house."

"What?" Carrie asked. "Are you still talking about that?"

"Where would we live?" Doug repeated anxiously.

"I have a house," said Reuben.

"Live with you?" Doug asked suspiciously. "So you'd be in charge of us?"

"Doug, that's enough," Sara snapped.

"What does that mean?" Reuben asked Doug. "If I'm in charge of you."

Doug scowled at him. "You know."

"I guess I don't. I'd appreciate it if you'd tell me."

"You'd boss us around. Make us do things your way, clean our rooms and help in the kitchen and . . . do our homework . . . you know, all those things."

"You do all those things now," Abby said pointedly. "Sara tells you to."

"She's in charge of us!"

"And I'm not," said Reuben, "so I wouldn't be giving orders. I might ask you to come to dinner; would that be all right?"

Doug was still scowling. "It's not a joke."

"I know it's not. I'll tell you what. If you decide to live in my house for a while, you and I will sit down and make a list of what you want to do there and what you won't do. We'll have to coordinate with Sara and Abby and Carrie, but I'm sure we can work it out so nobody feels bossed around. Does that make sense to you?"

"I don't know."

"Reuben," said Carrie solemnly, "I think it would be fine if you live with us. I mean, if you live with us in our house or your house, or wherever. I've been thinking about it, and I think it would be fine."

Reuben felt an amazing sense of triumph. A thirteen-year-old girl had said she approved of him, and it made him feel victorious. "Thank you," he said, just as solemnly.

"What's your house like?" Abby asked. "We've never lived anywhere but our own house. And we always had our own rooms."

"And you would in my house. Our house. It has bedrooms upstairs, the same as your house, only there are five of them, and a basement with a Ping-Pong table and a billiard table, and a small movie theater—"

"A what?" Doug cried.

"Why don't we go there now?" Sara asked. "It's very beautiful; you'll like everything about it."

"A movie theater," Doug whispered. "Cool."

"But what about school?" Abby asked.

"That won't change," Reuben replied. "My house is about a fifteen-minute drive from here, so you'd still go to Parker and see your friends as much as before. And I have an office at home with a drafting table, so we could be planning the new house while we're there, and we'd drive over whenever we want to supervise the construction. It would take about a year and a half, I'd guess, before we could move back here."

"What if we like yours better?" Doug asked.

"Better than our house?" Carrie demanded.

"It has a *movie theater*," Doug said.

"We can choose when we see both of them," said Reuben.

"But ours will be special," Abby put in. "Reuben said we could make it any way we want. We could make a movie theater! We could even make our rooms round."

"Round?"

Sara felt herself relax as the voices rose and fell around her, as if she were floating on the comforting waves of their chatter, so familiar but so new with the intertwining of Reuben's deep voice. All night long she had been tense with driving, and then with nightmarish images of the children trapped in the flaming house, overcome by smoke, unable to find the doors, screaming, clinging together then leaping from upstairs windows, running back to retrieve something precious from the blaze . . . Carrie's journal or Doug's carvings or whatever Abby most prized at the moment.

And a question had kept intruding: How would she bring Reuben into the tight little group the four of them had created, for protection as much as for love, when Tess was taken to the nursing home? In fact, she had done almost nothing: Reuben had managed it himself, by being himself. A kind of magic, she thought, and watched his face as he answered a question of Carrie's. He really likes them, she thought. More magic.

And then, finishing the last crumbs of the coffee cake, Doug asked, "What if Mack comes back?"

There was a pause. "He won't," Carrie said flatly. "He did a dumb thing, smoking in bed, he'd be too embarrassed to come back."

"He left his duffel," Doug pointed out.

"That is his duffel?" Reuben asked. "Sara and I wondered."

Doug nodded. "I saw it in his room"—he looked quickly at Carrie—"one like it, anyway, but it looked like his clothes."

Sara looked up. "He packed? He packed

and took his duffel outside and then fell asleep in bed, smoking?"

"Weird," Carrie said.

"But it's all ripped," Doug said. "It wasn't ripped when I saw it in his room."

"Maybe it fell out of his window," said Carrie.

Sara and Reuben exchanged a look.

"Anyway," Carrie insisted, "he can't come back, we don't want him."

"But what if he *does*?" Doug asked.

"We'll have to tell him he can't live with us," Sara said. "He could visit us, but he'd have to find his own place to live."

"But he's . . . I mean, he's, like, family."

Another silence fell, and stretched out. Sara sighed. With both parents gone, she had worked so hard to give them all a sense of family, and now they were faced with the dilemma of being forced to modify it. "Do you think," she asked carefully, "he behaved as if he wanted us to be his family?"

Doug mumbled something.

"I'm sorry; I didn't hear that," Sara said.

"I guess he didn't, not all the time anyway, but . . . *I* wanted to be *his* family."

Sara's heart sank. *Damn him for doing this, for making them love him and then dumping them as if they were toys he didn't need anymore.* She went to Doug and hugged him. "I know you did. You were the best kind of brother he could ever want, and he let you down. He let us all down, don't you think?"

"Maybe we didn't try hard enough."

She thought about it. "Maybe we didn't. You and Carrie seemed to be trying as hard as you could, as far as I could tell. I'm not sure what else we could have done."

"Maybe," Reuben said thoughtfully, "being part of a family has to be earned."

Doug looked puzzled. "Like money?"

"Like respect." He looked at Sara to make sure he was not intruding, and when she smiled at him, he went on. "I'm not an expert on families, but I always thought people had to work at being good family members to get respect and admiration, maybe even love."

"That's stupid. You like people in your family—respect and all that stuff—because they're there. I mean, a family isn't like, you know, people at school or somewhere."

"That's true. But it's hard to keep any group happy unless all the people in it feel responsible for each other."

"Sara said I should learn to be responsible for me."

"She's right. But at the same time shouldn't we feel responsible for helping our family, maybe people everywhere, feel good about themselves? That helps any group of people stay strong. Look, suppose one day you go up to Carrie and tell her she's not pretty, or her writing stinks, or something like that. Would that help your family or hurt it?"

"Why would I tell her those things? They're not true."

"Thanks," Carrie said.

"Maybe you stopped being nice that day. I don't know the reason, but for some reason, you were mean to her."

"She'd beat me up."

Reuben looked at Carrie with interest. "She would?"

"Sara doesn't let me do it anymore." Carrie sighed.

Reuben felt he was getting tangled in a discussion that might have no way out. Sara was watching him with rapt attention, waiting to see what he would say next. "Okay, look, if somebody in a family down the street was cruel to his sister or brother, or played tricks on them, or never thought of anybody but himself, the people in that family might begin to think he doesn't want to be part of them anymore, that he doesn't care about their feelings, that he doesn't feel any responsibility to help them have good lives. If you were in that family, what would you do?"

"I don't know. Tell him to shape up."

"Or what? Would you say, 'Shape up or else'?"

Doug saw where this was going, and shrugged.

"'Or else you can't live with us anymore.' You might say that. It's hard to talk that way to someone in your family, but maybe that person has forfeited the right to stay there. If he doesn't treasure you, or help make your family better or happier or more comfortable, in fact, if he does things to make your family unhappy and less comfortable, would it be fair to say he shouldn't live with you anymore?"

"Yeah, but—"

"We wanted him gone," Carrie pointed out.

"I *know* it! He was awful sometimes."

"All the time, lately," Carrie said.

Doug nodded dolefully. "I kept wanting it to be like it was. Like when he first got here." He looked at Reuben. "Did you have somebody like that in your family?"

"No, I was lucky."

"So who did you have in your family?"

Reuben told them about his parents and their bakeries, and his brothers, and the house they lived in and the games they played together.

"So you could go get a doughnut whenever you wanted?"

"Whenever my parents let us."

"Doug," Sara said, "did you get the point of anything Reuben said? Other than getting doughnuts any time of the day?"

"I got it," Doug said impatiently. "I'm not *dumb.* He says we have to try to be nice to each other. I knew that: you say it all the time." He looked at his hands. "So, what if he comes back and just, you know, moves in?"

Reuben refilled his coffee cup. "I'd ask him to tell us how the fire started."

"Smoking in bed," Carrie said, nodding wisely. She saw Sara and Reuben exchange another look. "What?"

"Nothing," said Sara. "That would be a good question to ask him."

Carrie's eyes narrowed in thought. "And we could ask him about delivering drugs."

Reuben looked at her quickly. "He said he delivered drugs?"

"He told Mom. And something about Pussy Corcoran, when she died."

Sara frowned. "You did tell me that, something about . . ." She shook her head. "What was it, Carrie? Do you remember?"

"We prayed for Pussy, you know, before dinner one night? Because she killed herself and she was a nut and a . . . a pest, something like that. He said she was a lousy wife, too. It wasn't nice, you know, because she was dead."

"But how could he know about her—" Sara bit off her words as she and Reuben exchanged a quick glance, sharing the same thought. *Don't let them think he could be involved in a death. Let them keep some illusions.*

"But could he, like, have dinner with us or something?" Doug asked. "I mean, if he asked nicely? And was nice to us?"

"If he wants to come to our house," Sara said, "of course he can come. But he'd have to answer our questions."

"But maybe we'll never see him again. Or even know where he is."

"I think people are looking for him," said Reuben.

"The police are," Carrie put in.

Reuben nodded. He glanced at Sara and knew she, too, was thinking the police definitely would be looking if he and Sara shared their suspicions that Mack had set the fire deliberately (which seemed bizarre, and he wondered if they ever would know what drove Mack to do the things he did). And he knew Sara was thinking, as he was, of Corcoran, a more fearful prospect for Mack: more dangerous and probably more persistent than the police, probably not giving up until he found Mack. He might even have a good idea of where he went. Wherever Mack might think he would find sanctuary.

"It's awfully hard knowing what to think," Carrie said. "I mean, did things used to be simpler? Or were they always so mixed up? It never seemed so complicated, before."

"Before what?" Abby asked.

"Before now. Like, I guess . . . when I was little."

"Life's always simple when you're little," Abby said gravely. "Wait till you're grown up, like me, then things really get complicated."

Once again, Sara met Reuben's glance (how wonderful to be able to share so much, so easily), and murmured, "Short childhoods."

"*What?*" Carrie asked again, frustrated at being left out of silent adult communications.

"Short childhoods," Sara said aloud. "You have so few years to think things are simple; I wish you could have more."

"Life moves faster with the Internet," Abby said.

"It moves faster period," Doug declared.

"Probably," said Sara. "Right now, though, for us, things really are complicated. Usually high drama gets spread out, so we have time to adjust, instead of having it all crammed into two or three days. I'd guess we'll have simpler times ahead."

Now there's a prayer: give me simple times.

"I'm going to write about all this," Carrie said, suddenly drowsy. "I mean, when I figure it out."

In a moment, all three of them were drooping, their spurt of energy depleted. Abby felt as if she were sliding away from the table, away from the room, into a soft sinking space. But, then, in the midst of that warm drifting, she had a swift moment, like a camera flash, of feeling perfectly, absolutely wonderful. *Life* was wonderful, she thought. Full of wonders. She was alive, and her body was strong and resilient, and she was with people who loved her and would watch over her, and ahead of her lay college and discoveries, new friends and . . . life. *Oh, earth, you're too wonderful for anybody to realize you.* Emily said that, in *Our Town,* and now, for the first time, Abby knew exactly what Emily meant. She took a deep breath, smelling the fresh coffee Reuben was pouring into Sara's cup, the pungent cinnamon of the coffee cake, and the spicy chrysanthemums on the kitchen counter; she saw through half-closed eyes tiny dust motes dancing in a beam of sunlight and heard the steady hum of the refrigerator; she was young and strong and loved. Her family was changing, but that was okay, because Reuben was nice and Sara was happy, and it was really depressing when Sara was unhappy, and now things would be more fun and exciting. In fact, the world was exciting again. She loved everyone, she loved school and—

"School," she said aloud. She sat straight. "We should be in school."

"Why? It's . . . oh, it's Wednesday." Carrie jumped up. "It feels like Saturday." But then she sat down. "We can't. We don't have any clothes. Or books. And . . . all my homework burned up! And I'm too sleepy anyway."

"We're going to get you to bed," Sara said.

"No, wait," Abby said. "We don't know what we're going to do. I mean, I don't even know what's happening tomorrow."

"Then let's make some plans. A quick list. Five minutes and then you're going to bed." Sara took a pencil and pad of paper from her shoulder bag and, sitting at Mrs. Pierce's table, determinedly not looking at the ruined house next door, they told her what to write.

"Call the principal's office and tell them why we can't come in today."

"Move into Reuben's house."

"Move what? We don't have anything."

"We have us."

"And we'll buy new clothes."

"And new shoes, new books, new everything."

"And draw our new house."

"And take a vacation. Like Galena, only bigger and more different."

"And Sara and Reuben getting married," Abby said, struggling to stay upright. "We're going to be part of it."

"Cool," said Doug. "Do I carry the ring or something?"

"Something." Reuben smiled.

"We have to tell Mom," Carrie said, rubbing her eyes. "She'd want to know."

"Not about the fire," Abby said. "That would be too much for her."

"We'll decide what to tell her and how to do it," said Sara. "I don't want all of us running over there with different stories."

"She has to meet Reuben," Carrie said. "And we can tell her you're getting married and maybe having a baby."

Sara and Reuben exchanged a swift glance, reminded yet again of how different their marriage would be from that of a young couple striding into the future with private, unedited plans. "Reuben and I will visit her," she said with a smile. "You stay out of this one."

"But we have to have *something* exciting to tell her," Doug objected. Like Carrie, he was slumping lower in his seat. "She likes exciting things."

"We have plenty to tell her. We'll just work out how we do it." Sara stood up. Without the tension and suspense of the past hours to buoy them up, she, too, was exhausted. "Reuben, we should—"

"Reuben," Abby said at the same time, "could we go to your house? I'm really sleepy."

"Right now." Reuben scooped up Doug, holding him upright. "I'll take you there and let you get settled and take naps and showers, and then you can do some shopping for tomorrow."

"But you'll be with us."

"For dinner. First I have to go to work. My bet is we'll be breaking ground very soon for Carrano Village West."

Doug fought to keep his eyes open. "Can I watch the bulldozer?"

"You can ride the bulldozer. As many times as you want."

"Wow."

Sara was caught between laughter and tears. A bulldozer for Doug: what more perfect beginning to their life together? Better than a gallery show for a ten-year-old, better and more understanding, at the moment, than anything else Reuben could have offered. "Thank you," she murmured. And he said, quietly, "I thank you," grateful to her for welcoming him into what he had not known for so long: family, sharing, belonging. And they both knew that that was the real wonder of it: that love was never the end of the story, only the beginning.

They stood together, Abby and Carrie

leaning against them, Doug heavy on Reuben's arm, almost asleep, and, over the heads of the children, they kissed. It was too soon to begin to absorb all that had happened and all that lay ahead; they still were shaken by the too-recent fears for the children, and then the destruction of Sara's house.

The loss of a house, Sara thought, and the discovery of a family. So much that impacted their lives, that would somehow become part of what lay ahead of them: discoveries and adjustments, triumphs and joys, troubles and sadness. But it will be all right, she thought, it will be wonderful. Because we'll all be together and we'll control what we can in our lives, and what we can't control we'll try to understand.

Swift images came and went of the past six months, of the people and events that had seemed overwhelming, from Donna Soldana's lies to the loss of their house. We do what we can, she thought again: control what we can, influence what we can, and try to incorporate the rest into our days and years in ways that make sense, or at least help us shape our lives.

She remembered that despairing moment

when she had said to Reuben, *There's just too much . . . we can't do anything about anything,* and he had responded, *I can't believe that.* Perhaps, together, as a family, they could help each other truly discover all they could do, all they could become, how to connect with what was best and right for them and be a part of the larger world, influencing it in their own ways.

Much easier to contemplate, she thought, and accomplish, if we aren't alone.

"We have a lot to do," Reuben said, echoing her thoughts. They kissed again, the children weighing on them. "But first," he said as they turned toward the door, "it's time to get our family home."